A Very Fake Fiancée

FIONA BRAND

First Published in Great Britain 2017
By Mills & Boon, an imprint of HarperCollins*Publishers*
1 London Bridge Street, London, SE1 9GF

ISBN: 978-0-263-92988-1

05-1117

THE FIANCÉE
CHARADE

BY
FIONA BRAND

Fiona Brand lives in the sunny bay of Islands, New Zealand. Now that both her sons are grown, she continues to love writing books and gardening. After a life-changing time in which she met Christ, she has undertaken study for a bachelor of theology and has become a member of The Order of St. Luke, Christ's healing ministry.

Once again huge thanks to my editor, Stacy Boyd.

To the Lord, who helps and supports me in all things—especially writing. Thank you.

Come to me all you that are weary and are carrying heavy burdens, and I will give you rest. Take my yoke upon you, and learn from me; for I am gentle and humble in heart, and you will find rest for your souls.
—Matthew 11: 28, 29

One

Zane Atraeus Dates Good-time Girl....

The tabloid headline halted billionaire banker and entrepreneur Gabriel Messena in his tracks.

A subtle tension gripped him as he paid the attendant at the Auckland International Airport newsstand and flipped the scandal sheet open to verify just which good-time girl, exactly, his wild cousin Zane Atraeus had been dating this time.

His gaze was drawn to the color photo that went with the story. Every muscle in his body tightened as he studied familiar Titian hair, creamy skin and dark eyes; a long, sensually curved body that possessed the engaging grace of a dancer.

Not just any woman, Gabriel thought with a bleak sense of inevitability as he studied the cheerful glint of Gemma O'Neill's gaze. Once again, Zane was dating *his* woman.

Emotion, sharp and clarifying, clenched his stomach

muscles and banded his chest. When he had first discovered that Zane was dating Gemma, he had checked out the situation and had been satisfied that the dating was on a strictly business level. Although, according to the tabloid, at some point *that* had changed.

The attraction Zane felt for Gemma was a no-brainer. She was gorgeous and smart, with an impulsive nature and a fascinating bluntness that had captivated Gabriel when she had worked on the Messena estate as a gardener. Although, he couldn't understand what drew Gemma, who had never seemed to be the A-list party-girl type, to his younger, wilder cousin.

Jaw taut, he examined the fierce sense of possession that gripped him, the powerful desire to claim Gemma as his own, despite the fact that he hadn't seen her in almost six years. His growing fury that Zane, who had women lining up—and, apparently, enough time in his schedule to date them all—just couldn't seem to leave his former personal assistant alone.

Damn, he thought mildly. He had no problem identifying the emotion that held him in thrall, destroying his normal clarity. He was jealous of Zane: searingly, primitively jealous.

It was an emotion that made no sense given the length of time that had passed and the fact that what he and Gemma had shared had been nothing more than a steamy encounter that had spanned a few incandescent hours.

Hours that were still etched in his memory because they were literally the last fling of his carefree youth. Two days later his father had been killed in a car accident along with his mistress, the beautiful Katherine Lyon, a woman who had also happened to be the family housekeeper.

Amidst the grief and the scandal, the responsibility of managing the family bank, his volatile family and the media had descended on Gabriel's shoulders like a lead weight. Any idea that he should echo his father's disastrous mistake by continuing a liaison with an employee, no matter how attractive, had been shelved.

Until now.

Frowning at the sudden sharp desire to pick up the threads of a relationship that had its basis in the same kind of obsessive fatal attraction that had brought his father to ruin, Gabriel refolded the paper.

Strolling to the first-class counter, he checked his luggage and handed his passport to the attendant. While he waited for his boarding pass, he glanced again at the sketchy article, which also chronicled a number of Zane's fiery liaisons. Affairs that Zane had apparently been conducting with other women while he had kept Gemma on the back burner.

Intense irritation gripped him at the idea that Gemma had clearly thrown away her pride and reputation in favor of pursuing Zane. That she would allow herself to be treated as some kind of standby date. It just didn't gel with the strong streak of independence that had always been such an attractive part of her personality.

His gaze snagged on a phrase that made every muscle lock tight. Suddenly, the anomaly in Gemma's behavior was crystal-clear.

She was no longer strictly single. At some point in the past couple of years, she'd had a child. Presumably, Zane's child.

Taking a measured breath, Gabriel forced the humming tension from his muscles, although there was nothing he could do about the slam of his heart, or the curious hollow feeling as he grappled with the information.

Too late to wish that he had listened to what the tabloids had been blaring for almost two years. That at some point,

Zane had decided that having Gemma as his PA had not been enough, that he had installed her in his bed, as well.

He jerked at his dark blue silk tie, needing air. He needed to refocus, to reassert the control he'd worked so hard to instill in himself in place of the hot-blooded, passionate streak that was the bane of all Messena men. But something about the sheer intimacy of Gemma bearing a child cut deep. The fact that the child belonged to Zane, his own cousin, rubbed salt in the wound.

It was an intimacy that Gabriel, at age thirty, hadn't had time for in his life, and which was not in his foreseeable future.

But Zane, with all the irresponsibility of youth, had experienced that intimacy. And now, evidently, he no longer wanted the woman whom he had bound to him with a child.

But Gabriel did.

The thought dropped through the turmoil of his emotions like a stone dropping through cool, clear water.

Six years had passed. But in that moment the stretch of time barely registered. He felt like a sleeper waking up, all of his senses—the emotions he'd walked away from the night his father had died—flaring to intense, heated life.

He studied the photograph again, this time noting the way Gemma clung to Zane's arm, the relaxed intimacy of the pose.

A hot jolt of fury cleared away any reservations he might have had about claiming the woman he had walked away from in order to preserve his family and business.

Gemma had had a child. A baby.

Logic didn't alter his sense of disorientation, the disbelief that the pressures of business and his high-maintenance family had somehow blinded him and he had missed something…important.

Although the fact that he hadn't registered changes in Gemma's life shouldn't surprise him. Running an empire encumbered by an aging trustee who Gabriel now believed to be suffering from the early stages of dementia, in theory he didn't have time to sleep.

And he almost never had time for personal relationships. When he dated it was invariably for business or charity functions. The fact that he went home to an empty apartment every night he wasn't traveling hadn't bothered him.

Until now.

Taking his boarding pass with automatic thanks, he strolled through the busy airport, barely noticing the travelers jostling around him. In the midst of a crowd, it was an odd time to feel alone. An even odder time to examine the stark truth, that despite the constant demands on his time, his own personal life was as sterile and empty as a desert.

But that was about to change. He was on his way to the Mediterranean island of Medinos, the ancestral home of the Messena family. And the place where Gemma just happened to presently reside.

If he had a mystical streak, he would be tempted to say that the coincidence that he and Gemma would finally be together at the same location was kismet. But mysticism had never figured in the Messena psyche. Aside from the passionate streak, Messena men had another well-defined trait that went clear back to the Crusades. Ruthless and tactical, fighting for the Couer de Lion, Richard the Lionheart, they had flourished in battle, winning lands and fortresses. The habit of winning had been passed down a family line rich in sons, culminating in large holdings of land and enormous wealth.

Plundering was no longer in vogue. These days, Messena men usually leveraged what they wanted across boardroom tables, but the basic principle was still the same. Identify the objective, execute a plan, obtain the prize.

In this case the plan was simple: remove Gemma from Zane's clutches and install her back in *his* bed.

"Gabriel Messena…engaged before the month was out…"

The snatch of conversation flowing in off the sun-washed terrace of one of the Atraeus Resort's most luxurious suites stopped Gemma O'Neill in her tracks.

Her grip tightened on the tea tray she was carrying as fragments of the past surfaced like pieces of flotsam, taking her places that for six years she had refused to go, making her feel emotions she was usually very successful at avoiding.

A still bay, a clear midnight sky, studded with stars and pierced by a sickle moon. Gabriel Messena, his long, muscular body entwined with hers; hair dark as night, the cut of his cheekbones spare and faintly exotic, reminding her of crowded souks and the inky shadowed alcoves of Moorish palaces…

With an effort of will Gemma blinked away the too-vivid image, which was probably a result of being on Medinos, the kind of romantic destination that attracted newlyweds in droves.

Now, rattled instead of being simply on edge as she'd been before, she brought the trolley to a halt beside the dining table. The clatter attracted the attention of the two guests she had been tasked with settling in. They were VIPs in the most important sense of the word on Medinos, because they were close connections of the Atraeus family.

Although, in terms of Gemma's past, one of the guests was much more than that, even if Luisa Messena, Gabriel's mother, didn't seem to have a clue that the person serving afternoon tea and petit-fours was one of her ex-gardeners.

And her son's ex-lover.

Pasting a professional smile on her mouth, Gemma apologized, all the while keeping her face averted in the hope that she could hang on to her anonymity.

With crisp movements, she snapped a damask cloth open, settled it on the glossy little table then began the precision task of aligning plates and napkins. As she off-loaded a carved silver teapot that was probably worth more than the car she needed to buy but as a single mother just couldn't afford, she fiercely wished she hadn't offered to give the hotel staff a hand with the influx of VIP guests.

"He's certainly waited for her long enough…she's perfect.… The family's wealthy, of course.…"

Despite the fact that she was doing her level best not to listen, because as far as she was concerned Gabriel Messena was old history, Gemma's jaw locked on a surge of annoyance. Clearly Gabriel was on the point of proposing to some perfect preselected creature, probably a beautiful debutante who had been groomed and educated within an inch of her life and who was now finally ready for the wedding nuptials.

She ripped the tab off a bottle of chilled sparkling mineral water and tossed it in the little trash can on the bottom shelf of her trolley. A tinkling sound indicated that the tab had bounced off the side of the trash can and rolled onto the floor. Retrieving the tab, she placed it in the trash can with careful precision and poured mineral water into two glasses. Her jaw tightened as some sloshed over the side and soaked into her trolley cloth.

The knowledge that Gabriel was finally getting around to marriage after years of bachelorhood in the hushed stratosphere of enormous wealth in which he moved shouldn't have impacted her. She was happy for Gabriel. Perfectly, sublimely happy. She would have to remember to send him a congratulatory card.

She could do that, because she had moved on.

The conversation out on the terrace had segued from Gabriel to the more innocuous topic of shopping, which was a relief. Gemma guessed she couldn't hope to feel a complete absence of emotion about Gabriel, because as a teenager, he had been her focus; the man of her dreams. She had fallen in puppy love with him, and had mooned after him for years. Unfortunately she had been wasting her time because she hadn't had either the wealth or the family connections to be a viable part of his world.

One night, Gabriel had quenched the flare of passion that had bound them together as systematically as she imagined he would have vetoed an investment that lacked the required substance. He'd been polite, but he had made it clear they didn't have a future. He hadn't elaborated in any detail; he hadn't needed to. After the scandal that had hit the papers shortly after the one night they had spent together, Gemma had understood exactly why he had dropped her like the proverbial hot potato.

His father's affair with the family housekeeper had shaken the very foundations of the family banking business, which was based on wealthy clientele who were old-school and conservative. Gabriel had been in damage control mode. He hadn't wanted to inflame the scandal and undermine confidence in the bank any further by risking having his liaison with the gardener exposed to tabloid scrutiny.

Despite her heartache, Gemma had tried to see things from his perspective, to understand the battle he had faced. But the rejection, the knowledge that she had not been good enough to have a real, public relationship with Gabriel, had hurt in a way that had struck deep.

As soon as Gabriel had left after the short, awkward interview in which she had managed to remain superficially upbeat, she resolved to never look back or to even remember. It had been the emotional equivalent of sticking her head in the sand, but over the past six years, the tactic had worked.

Gemma took extra care transferring the bone china from the trolley to the table. Even so, an exquisitely delicate cup overturned on its saucer and a silver teaspoon that had been balanced on the saucer skidded off and hit a pretty bread and butter plate with a sharp ping.

She could feel the subtle tension and displeasure at the noise she was making. Her jaw set a fraction tighter. She had worked for the Atraeus Group for some years and normally didn't mind in the least helping out with any task that needed doing. The Atraeus family had given her a job when she desperately needed one, and they had treated her very well, but suddenly she was acutely aware of her role as a servant.

She dumped a glistening silver milk jug and sugar bowl down next to the teapot and swiped at an errant droplet of milk that marred the once pristine tablecloth.

Not that she had an issue with doing a good job, but it was a fact that she wasn't waitstaff. Just like she was no longer the gardener's daughter on the Messena estate.

She was a highly organized and well-qualified PA with a degree in performing arts on the side, and she was still trying to come to grips with the fact that by some errant trick of fate, she had ended up once more in the role of employee to a Messena.

Serene and perfectly groomed, Luisa looked exactly as she had when Gemma had last seen her in Dolphin Bay,

New Zealand. The friend accompanying her, though casually dressed, looked just as wealthy and well-groomed; her dark hair smooth, nails perfect. Unlike Gemma's hair, which she'd been too tired after a near-sleepless night on the phone to New Zealand to do anything with except to coil the heavy waves into a knot.

As she placed the crowning glory of the afternoon tea setting, an exquisite three-tiered plate of tiny cakes, scones, pastries and mini sandwiches, in the center of the table, she caught a glimpse of herself in a wall mirror.

She wasn't surprised that Luisa hadn't recognized her. The housemaid's smock she was wearing was at least a size too large and an unflattering pale blue, which leached all the color from her skin. With her hair pulled back into a severe knot, she didn't look either pretty or stylish.

Definitely not the gorgeous hothouse flower who by all accounts had been reserved for marriage to Gabriel, despite the fact that Gemma had borne his child.

The thought was overdramatic and innapropriate, and she regretted it the moment it was out.

She had cut her losses years ago, and from the snatches of conversation, Gabriel was practically engaged. If that was the case, then she was certain the manner in which he had selected his future bride had been as considered and measured as the way he managed the multibillion-dollar family business.

What had happened between her and Gabriel had been crazy and completely wrong for them both, a combination of moonlight and champagne, and a moment of chivalry when Gabriel had saved her from the groping of a too-amorous date.

By the time she had realized three months later, despite a couple of skimpy periods, that she was in fact pregnant, the decision to not tell Gabriel had been a no-brainer.

From the brief conversation that had taken place when Gabriel had told her he wasn't interested in a relationship, she had known that while he had been prepared to look after her and a baby if she had gotten pregnant, all he would have been doing was fulfilling an obligation. On that basis alone, she had chosen to take full responsibility for Sanchia. But there had been another driving force to staying silent about the baby.

Bearing a Messena child would have entailed links from which she would never have been free. She would have remained a beneficiary of Gabriel's family for the rest of her life, forever aware that she was the employee Gabriel Messena had made the mistake of getting pregnant but who hadn't been good enough to marry.

In the quiet solitude of her pregnancy, with the hurt of Gabriel's defection fading, Gemma had made the decision that in order to avoid more heartache, Sanchia would be hers and hers alone. Keeping her daughter's existence a secret had just seemed easier and simpler.

She straightened a cake fork. She guessed the part that made her hot under the collar about Gabriel's pending engagement was the idea that he had been waiting for his bride to become available. If that was the case, it meant that Gemma had never been anything more than a diversion, a fill-in, while he waited for the kind of wife he really wanted.

More memories cascaded, distracting her completely from her final check of the table setting.

The pressure of Gabriel's mouth on hers, the way his fingers had threaded in her hair...

Another pang of annoyance that Gabriel had given up on them so easily, that he was shallow and superficial enough to select a wife rather than fall passionately in love, started a sharp little throb at her temples. She wheeled the trolley with a little more force than was necessary to the door, clipping the side of a sofa in the process.

Luisa Messena, who was just walking in off the terrace, threw her a puzzled look, a frown pleating her brow, as if she was trying to remember where she had seen her last.

Bleakly, Gemma parked the trolley by the door and hoped Luisa didn't recall that it was the summer six years ago when she had thrown caution and every rule she'd lived by for years to the winds, and slept with Luisa's extremely wealthy son.

Jaw taut, in a blatant disregard for etiquette, Gemma didn't offer to pour the tea. Smiling blankly in the general direction of Luisa, she opened the door and pushed the trolley out into the hall.

Closing the door behind her, she drew a deep breath and wheeled the trolley toward the service elevator at the other end of the corridor, stopping short when her cell chimed.

Worry at the recognizable ringtone clutched at Gemma.

Checking that she wouldn't be overheard, she lifted the phone to her ear. Instantly, the too-serious voice of her five-year-old daughter filled her ears.

The conversation was punctuated by a regular *squeak-squeak* sound, which instantly translated an image of Sanchia clutching an old bedtime toy, a fluffy puppy with a squeezy sound in its tummy.

Gemma frowned, hating the distance between them when all she wanted to do was hug her close. Sanchia had clung to the toy as a baby, but these days she only ever picked it up if she was overtired or stressed.

Always precocious and older than her years, Sanchia had a familiar list of demands. She wanted to know where Gemma was and what she was doing, when she was coming to get her, exactly, and if she was bringing her a present.

There was a brief pause, then Sanchia's voice firmed as if she had finally reached the whole point of the conversation.

"And when are you bringing home the dad?"

Two

Gemma's heart sank. She had suspected that her daughter had overheard the discussion she'd had with Gemma's younger sister, Lauren, which had been half frivolous, half desperate. Now she had her proof.

The reference to "the dad" was heart-rending enough, as if obtaining a husband, and father for Sanchia, was as straightforward as shopping for shoes or a handbag.

Needing privacy even more now, Gemma walked down a short side hall while she tried to figure out what to say next.

Normally, she was composed, focused and highly organized. As a working single mother she'd had to be.

Although, lately, ever since disaster had struck in the form of a nanny who had left her daughter locked in the car while she gambled at a Sydney casino, Gemma's focus had undergone a quantum shift. A passerby had seen Sanchia and had called the police. Gemma had managed to explain her way out of the situation, but it hadn't helped that in the same week Gemma had also gotten caught up in a media scandal, courtesy of her connection with her ex-boss, Zane Atraeus.

To add insult to injury, when Gemma had dismissed the nanny, the woman had then turned around and sold a story to the papers claiming that Gemma was an unfit mother. The story, a collection of twisted truths and outright lies, hadn't exactly been front-page news, but because she had once worked for Zane, the gutter press had locked on to the story and run with it until another more juicy scandal had grabbed their attention.

Thankfully, the media attention had died, but the pressure from both Australian and New Zealand child welfare agencies hadn't, despite a number of interviews.

When she had tried to leave Australia with Sanchia for Medinos and her new job, the situation had taken a frightening turn. She had been accused of trying to escape before the welfare case was concluded and both she and Sanchia had been detained. Her mother had flown to Sydney to provide a stopgap answer by taking temporary custody of Sanchia and taking her home to New Zealand. But, to complicate matters, shockingly, her mother, who did not enjoy good health, had then had a heart attack and now required a bypass operation.

In the interim Sanchia had been fostered out, which had utterly terrified Gemma. She had barely been able to sleep, let alone eat. She had been desperately afraid that once the authorities had Sanchia in their grasp, she would never get her back, that no matter how much evidence she supplied to prove that she was a good mother, she would lose her baby girl.

Luckily, Lauren, who had a houseful of kids, had managed to convince the welfare caseworker to release Sanchia into her care until Gemma could get back into the country. Although Lauren had stressed to Gemma that it was a one-off favor and the situation couldn't go on for too long. With four children of her own, she was ultrabusy and on a shoestring budget.

Gemma had broken into her savings and transferred a chunk of money to Lauren, but there was no getting past the fact that she was out of luck, and almost out of time.

After all of these years of struggling as a solo parent, she was on the verge of losing her baby. She now had one imperative, and one only: to convince the welfare agency that she *was* a suitable mother for Sanchia. After racking her brains for days, she kept coming back to a desperate but foolproof solution. If she could establish that she was in a relationship with a view to marriage, that would instantly provide the stability they wanted.

Her only believable hope for marriage was her ex-boss, who she had dated for the past couple of years. Despite being a bachelor with a wild reputation, Zane fulfilled a lot of the qualities on her personal wish list for a husband. He was gorgeous, honorable and likable, and most of all, he loved kids. She had often thought that when she was ready to fall in love again, it should be with Zane.

He also happened to be the man whom the tabloids had claimed she'd had a series of on-again, off-again affairs with. It wasn't true; so far they really were just friends, but it was also a fact that whenever Zane had needed a date for a business or charity function, he had consistently come back to her.

For a man who was as wary of intimacy as Zane, that was significant. Gemma had poked and prodded at the issue until she was tired of thinking about it. In the end she had decided that if Zane really did nurture a secret passion then he was obviously waiting for a *sign* from her, or a situation, that would allow him to declare his feelings.

If they got engaged, in one stroke the untrue claims of both the nanny and the tabloids would be discredited. The "notorious affair" would instantly morph into a relationship and the notoriety that had been attached to Gemma would be discredited because it was a well-known fact that the tabloids sensationalized everything. The fact that Zane was currently here, on Medinos, had set the plan in concrete.

The only aspect that worried Gemma was that Zane was Gabriel's cousin. If she married Zane, that would put Sanchia into Gabriel's orbit.

The silence on the other end of the phone line was punctuated by another *squeak, squeak.* "I heard you say to Aunty Lauren you've got *someone in mind.*"

The verbatim piece of conversation made Gemma frown. Smoothly ignoring Sanchia's insistence, she changed the subject and asked her about her cousins.

"The wallflower lady came to visit us today—"

The welfare lady. Gemma's heart pounded at the cut-off statement, the brief rustling sound as if someone else had taken the phone. A split second later, her sister came on the line.

"Gemma? It's okay, it was just a routine visit. She wanted to check your arrival date and luckily you had sent me your flight details, so I gave them to her."

Gemma could feel her anxiety level rising. "They didn't need to bother you. I emailed them my itinerary days ago. Plus they know the reason I'm not back in New Zealand yet is because I'm busy trying to fulfill *their* stipulation that I have a stable job."

Gemma's fingers tightened on the phone. Before everything had come to pieces she had accepted an appointment as a PA on Medinos to the Atraeus Resort's manager. She had hoped that by coming to Medinos, the Atraeus Group's head office, instead of resigning over the phone, she might be able to arrange a transfer to one of the Atraeus enterprises in New Zealand.

There was a small awkward silence. "Maybe whoever received the details didn't pass it on. You know what government departments can be like…."

Gemma took a long, deep breath and forced herself to sound light and breezy, as if it didn't matter that the welfare case worker was sneaking around, checking up on her. *Trying to take Sanchia.* "Sorry, you're absolutely right. I'm just a bit stressed."

"Don't worry." Lauren's voice was crisp. "No way will I let them take Sanchia again. Just get back soon."

"I will." No pressure.

Once she had gotten the dad.

Gemma hung up. Collecting the trolley, she made her way to the service elevator and stabbed the call button. The stainless-steel doors threw her image back at her as she waited, the shapeless smock that swamped her slim frame, cheeks now flushed, dark eyes overly bright.

She frowned. The emotion that kept clutching at her chest, her heart, was understandable. She missed Sanchia and she was ultrastressed about having to prove she was a good, stable parent. Plus it had been a shock to run into Luisa Messena and find herself plunged into the past. Into the other area in which she had been deemed not good enough.

Grimly, she switched her thoughts back to her small daughter. With her straight black hair and sparkling dark eyes, Sanchia was a touchstone she desperately needed right at that moment.

Gemma might have made mistakes, and as a single

mother she'd had to make a lot of sacrifices, but everything she had gone through had been worth it. Sanchia was the sweetest, most adorable thing in her life.

Although she was now far from being a baby. Like most of the O'Neills she had been born precocious, and she had grown up fast. The only difference was that unlike her red-haired cousins, Sanchia was dark and distinctly exotic. Just like her father.

The doors slid open. Blanking out that last thought, Gemma stepped inside and hit the ground-floor button.

Gabriel was going to marry.

She frowned, wishing she could stop her overtired brain from going in circles. The news shouldn't have meant anything to her. Years had passed; she was over the wild schoolgirl crush that had dominated her teens.

Drawing a deep breath, she tried to make an honest examination of her feelings. Dismay, old hurt and the one she didn't want to go near. The thought that somewhere, beneath all the layers of common sense and determined positive thinking, she might still harbor a few unresolved feelings for Gabriel.

Chest tight, she tried to distract herself from that possibility by watching floor numbers flash by. When that didn't work, she took a deep breath and squeezed her eyes closed for long seconds, trying to neutralize the emotion that had sneaked up on her.

Despite her efforts hot moisture leaked out from beneath her lids. It was stress and tiredness, nothing more. Using her fingers, she carefully wiped her cheeks, careful not to smear her mascara.

The doors slid open onto an empty corridor. Relieved, Gemma pushed the trolley into the service area and left it near the door to the kitchens. Head now throbbing with a definite headache, she walked to the sleek office that should have been officially hers as of next week, if the child welfare authorities hadn't changed her priorities.

Instead of settling in her new job on Medinos and bringing Sanchia over to live with her here, she was now flying home on the first available flight. This office, and the job she had been about to start, would now be someone else's.

Collecting the resignation she had written earlier, she walked briskly through to the manager's office. It was empty, which was a relief, and she just placed it on his blotter. He was probably personally conducting other VIP guests, all here to attend the launch party of Ambrosi Pearls the following evening, to their rooms.

With her resignation now official, Gemma felt, if not relieved, at least a sense of closure.

As she turned to leave, she noticed a typed guest list for the Ambrosi Pearls party. It was being held at the Castello Atraeus, but resort personnel and chefs were handling the catering.

She flipped the list around. Gabriel Messena's name leaped out at her.

She felt as if all the breath had just been knocked from her lungs. He would be here, on Medinos, tomorrow night.

An odd feeling of inevitability, a dizzying sense of déjà vu, hit her, which was crazy. With an effort of will, she dismissed the notion that fate was somehow throwing them back together.

Gabriel appearing on the scene right now, when she was trying to cope with a long-distance custody battle for Sanchia, was sheer coincidence. He was about to get engaged. There was no way on this earth she should ask for his assistance despite the fact that he was Sanchia's biological father.

She needed to stick to her plan.

If Zane truly did want her, and they could cement their

relationship in some public way, all of her problems would be solved. The welfare people could no longer claim she was an irresponsible "good-time girl," the nanny's lies would be discredited and her financial situation would no longer be a problem.

Although, scarily, to get them to that point, she was going to have to take the initiative and somehow jolt them off the platonic plateau they had been stranded on for the past two years.

It was possible that Zane felt constrained by the fact that she worked for his family company. But as of today, she was a free agent. The specter of an employer/employee relationship was no longer an issue.

Three

Gabriel checked his wristwatch as he walked off his flight to Medinos and into the first-class lounge, which was filled with a number of businessmen and groups of gaudily dressed tourists.

Impatiently, he skimmed the occupants. His younger brother, Nick, who was due in from a flight from Dubai, had requested an urgent meeting with him here.

Five minutes and half a cup of dark espresso later, Gabriel glanced up as Nick strolled in, looking broad-shouldered and relaxed in a dark polo and trousers. Dropping into the seat next to Gabriel, he flipped his briefcase open.

Gabriel took the thick document Nick handed him, a building contract for a high-rise in Sydney, a thick sheaf of plans and a set of costings. "Good flight?"

Nick grunted and gave him a "you've got to be kidding" look, then transferred his attention to the newspaper Gabriel had set down on the coffee table with its glaringly bright photograph. "Zane." Amused exasperation lightened his expression. "In the news again, with another woman."

For reasons he didn't want to examine, Gabriel folded the newspaper and placed it on the floor beside his briefcase.

He had read the article again on the flight. The journalist hadn't gone so far as to say the child was Zane's—the details supplied had been sketchy and inflammatory—but the inference was clear enough.

Turning his attention back to the document Nick wanted him to look over, he forced himself to concentrate on his family's most pressing problem. An archaic clause in his father's will, and his elderly uncle and trustee, Mario Atraeus, which together had the power to bankrupt them all if he didn't move swiftly.

The situation had been workable until Mario had started behaving erratically, refusing to sign crucial documents and "losing" others. Holdups and glitches were beginning to hamper the bank's ability to meet its financial obligations.

Lately, Mario's eccentricities had escalated another notch, when he had tried to use his power as trustee to leverage a marriage between Gabriel and Mario's adopted daughter, Eva Atraeus.

In that moment, Gabriel had understood what lay behind Mario's machinations. A widower, he was worried about dying and leaving his adoptive daughter alone and unmarried. In his mind, steeped in Medinian traditions, he would not have done his job as a father if he hadn't assured a good marriage for Eva.

Gabriel, as the unmarried head of the Messena family, had become Mario's prime matchmaking target.

Gabriel was clear on one point, however. When he fi

nally got around to choosing a wife, it would be a matter of his choice, not Mario's, or anyone else's.

He would not endure a marriage of convenience simply to honor family responsibilities.

Placing the document on the coffee table, he checked his watch. "I can't release the funds. I wish I could. I'll have to run it past Mario."

A muscle pulsed along the side of Nick's jaw. "It took him two months to approve the last payment. If I renege now, the building contractor will walk."

"Leave it with me. I'll be able to swing something. Or Mario might sign."

"There is one solution. You could get married." Nick's expression was open and ingenuous as he referred to the grace clause in their father's will, which had its base in Medinian tradition. Namely, that a formally engaged or a married man was more responsible and committed than a single one. It was the one loophole that would decisively end Mario's trusteeship of his father's will and place control of the company securely in Gabriel's hands.

Nick slipped his cell out of his briefcase. "Or you could get engaged. An engagement can be easily terminated."

Gabriel sent his younger brother a frowning glance, which was wasted as Nick was busy reactivating the phone and flicking through messages. No doubt organizing his own very busy, very crowded, private life.

Sometimes he wondered if any of his five brothers and sisters even registered the fact that he was male, single and possessed a private life of his own, even if it was echoingly empty. "There won't be a marriage, or an engagement. There's a simpler solution. A psychological report on Mario would provide the grounds we need to end his trusteeship."

Either that, or hope that he could work around the financial restraints Mario was applying for another tortuous six months until he turned thirty-one and could legally take full control of the family firm.

"Good luck with getting Uncle Mario to a doctor." Nick's gaze was glued to the screen of his cell as he thumbed in a text message. "I don't know how you stay so calm."

By never allowing himself to get emotionally involved with his own family.

The practice kept him isolated and a little lonely, but at least he stayed sane.

Nick gave up texting and sat back on the couch, the good-humored distraction replaced by a frown. "Mario could ruin us, you know. If you can get him to the doctor, how long will it take to get the report?"

Gabriel repressed his irritation that Nick didn't seem to get it that the last thing Mario wanted to do at this juncture was cooperate in the process of proving that he was past it, and wresting his power from him. "I'm seeing Mario as soon as I get back from Medinos."

Nick rolled his eyes. "Before or after his nap?"

Gabriel crumpled his empty foam cup and tossed it into a nearby trash can. "Probably during."

Nick said something short and flat. "If I can't get the family firm to finance me, I will go elsewhere."

Otherwise he would lose his shirt financially. Their younger brother, Damian, was in the same position, as were a number of key clients. If Gabriel couldn't streamline their process, they could lose a lot of business. Worst-case scenario, the bank's financial rating would be downgraded and they would lose a whole lot more.

Gabriel checked his wristwatch, placed the document in his briefcase, collected the newspaper and rose to his feet.

Nick followed suit, picking up his briefcase. "My finance deadline is one week. I don't want to take my business elsewhere."

"With any luck, you won't have to. Apparently Constantine wants a favor." His cousin Constantine Atraeus was the whole reason Gabriel was on Medinos in the first place. Constantine, who was the head of the Atraeus Group and enormously wealthy, was sympathetic about Gabriel's situation. He had faced a similar problem with his own father, Lorenzo, Mario's brother, who had behaved just as erratically in his old age.

Nick grinned. "Cool, that means you've got leverage."

But Gabriel didn't miss the flat note in Nick's voice. If he couldn't obtain Constantine's backing to have Mario removed as trustee, and at the same time extend Gabriel a personal line of credit that Mario couldn't interfere with, Nick would walk.

His brother kept pace with him as he strode toward his gate. He directed a frowning glance at the folded paper. "Isn't the girl with Zane the O'Neill girl from Dolphin Bay you dated once?"

Gabriel's jaw tightened. He hadn't expected Nick to remember Gemma. "It wasn't exactly a date."

Date was the last word he would use to describe the unscripted, passionate night they had spent together in a deserted beach house. "Gemma works for the Atraeus Group. She was Zane's PA."

Nick shrugged. "That explains it, then. You know what the tabloids are like. They were probably just out on some business date."

"Maybe." But if the child was Zane's, there was no question that Gemma had gotten herself entangled with Zane, to her detriment.

And if that was the case then he bore some of the responsibility for her predicament. If Gabriel hadn't been in

Sydney the day the Atraeus Group was interviewing for office staff and put in a glowing recommendation, Gemma would never have beaten off some of the applicants who had applied for the position.

Unwittingly, Gabriel's recommendation had eventually put Gemma directly in Zane's path.

He didn't know Zane as well as he knew his other two Atraeus cousins, Lucas and Constantine, but well enough to know that marriage had never been Zane's favorite topic. He was more interested in short flings.

Or, apparently, longer, convenient arrangements.

Something snapped in him at the thought that Gemma had allowed herself to be seduced into a liaison with his cousin when Zane's interest was self-serving and superficial. Despite the child, marriage obviously wasn't on his agenda.

As he approached the exit doors for the airport, he recalled one other piece of information the article had offered. Apparently Gemma had just made the move from Sydney to Medinos in order to be close to Zane.

The fact that Gemma had been left out on a limb with a child, but was still intent on maintaining some kind of relationship with Zane shouldn't matter to him, but it did.

The decision to reclaim Gemma settled in. If Zane had shown any hint that he wanted to commit, Gabriel would have backed off, but he hadn't. Zane seemed quite happy to allow Gemma to shoulder all of the responsibility for the child. Added to that, Gabriel had made some private inquiries during the stopover in Dubai and discovered that Zane had been seeing someone else.

As far as Gabriel was concerned that settled the matter. Gemma was vulnerable and in need of rescue and he planned on being her rescuer.

He didn't know how or when the opportunity would

arise; all he knew was that with Zane's cavalier attitude and a new girlfriend in the mix, it would be sooner rather than later.

Gemma mingled with the guests at the Ambrosi Pearls party, to which she had gained entry by using the invitation she had received a couple of days earlier.

Accepting a flute of champagne from a waiter, she skimmed the crowded reception room of the Castello Atraeus, which was lit by the soft shimmer of chandeliers. Elegant groupings of candles and bouquets of white roses and glossy dark greenery added a hothouse glamour to the room, which suddenly seemed to be filled with tall, dark lions of men. Wealthy and powerful members of both the Atraeus and Messena families.

Gemma's heart skipped a beat as she caught a glimpse of broad, sleek shoulders, a clean, masculine profile and tough jaw. Even though she had come prepared for a face-to-face meeting with Gabriel, for a split second her heart seemed to stop in her chest.

The glittering crowd of guests shifted, a kaleidoscopic array of expensive jewelry and designer gowns, affording her an even clearer view.

In the wash of light from a chandelier, Gabriel's features were tanned, as if he'd spent time outside under a hot sun, his jaw rock solid and darkened by the shadow of stubble. His hair, gleaming and coal-black, was longer than she remembered, now brushing the collar of his shirt.

Her fingers tightened on the lace clutch that matched her simple but elegant black dress.

Realizing just how tight her nerves were strung, Gemma reminded herself to breathe. She had hoped against hope that Gabriel wouldn't actually attend the party. He didn't normally show up at lavish promotional parties, even though he was often invited. On the few previous occasions that he had actually attended, she had usually found out ahead of time and found an excuse not to be there. Tonight she didn't have that option. In order to buttonhole Zane, it was an absolute imperative that she was here.

A group of beautifully dressed women obscured her view, then she caught sight of Gabriel again. In that moment, as if drawn by her intensity, his head turned and the dark gaze that had continued to haunt one too many of Gemma's dreams locked on hers.

Her heart slammed in her chest. Any idea that Gabriel hadn't known she was here dissolved. He had, and from the way his brows jerked together, he wasn't pleased to see her.

A sharp little pang of hurt shocked her into immobility.

Taking a steadying breath, Gemma did her best to shake off her oversensitive reaction. Unnerved by the direct eye contact, she placed her half-full champagne flute on a side table. Neatly changing direction, she almost walked into a waiter with a loaded tray.

Blushing and mumbling an apology, she sidestepped the waiter and threaded her way through the suddenly overheated, overperfumed room. A little desperately she noted that there was still no sign of Zane, who she was hoping would have been here early so she could get this whole situation resolved one way or another.

As she walked she was unbearably aware that, even though she could no longer see Gabriel, he was still watching her.

Her stomach clenched on an uncharacteristic burst of panic.

She had known Gabriel could attend, so it shouldn't have been such a shock to see him. She just wished that her perfect record of avoidance hadn't ended tonight of all nights.

A knot of guests parted and Zane finally appeared, striding directly toward her.

Nerves strung almost to breaking point, she noted the three studs in Zane's lobe, which she had always privately thought were a little over the top, unlike Gabriel's sleek tailored suit, which conferred a quiet, rock-solid power.

Calling on all of her acting skills, she tried to project her usual bright, outgoing persona.

The quick hug, which was punctuated by the intrusive flash of a camera, was not unusual between friends, but in that moment, hugging Zane felt horribly fake.

She was the problem, Gemma realized. Until she had seen Gabriel, her decision to try to shift her dating friendship with Zane into a regular relationship and enlist his help in getting Sanchia back had seemed viable. Now, in the space of just a couple of minutes, everything had changed.

Seeing Gabriel had unnerved her in ways she couldn't have imagined. One piercing look from him and she felt guilty about choosing Zane, as if in some subtle way she was betraying Gabriel, which was ridiculous. While it was true he was Sanchia's biological father, that was all he ever had been, or could be.

It was a relief when Zane, who appeared as distracted as she, didn't respond in a positive way to her labored attempt to catapult their friendship into more intimate territory or show any desire to linger.

When he turned down her suggestion that they should go out onto the terrace, so she could launch into the very private conversation she needed to have with him, unnerved, Gemma made for the nearest exit. As she hurried out, her spine tingled with the knowledge that Gabriel was in the room and that he had witnessed her hugging Zane.

In that moment she saw her actions from Gabriel's viewpoint and she didn't like the needy picture that formed.

Anger stiffened her spine. For the first time in her life she was attempting to lose the strong independent streak that had been ingrained from childhood and ask a man she liked if he would consider having a relationship with her.

Gabriel could disapprove all he liked, but it was a fact that he had stepped out of the picture six years ago.

Plan A had failed. Now, unfortunately, she would have to resort to Plan B.

Four

Gabriel refused the glass of champagne a waiter offered him. His dark gaze swept the crowded reception room. A knot of gray-suited Japanese businessmen shifted and he was rewarded with another clear view of creamy skin, flame hair and black lace.

Constantine Atraeus lifted a brow. "Gemma O'Neill. Girl's going places, or was. She's just had to resign, a personal commitment."

An instant replay of Gemma stepping into Zane's arms made his jaw tighten. Then Constantine's statement about Gemma resigning because of a personal commitment sank in.

His gaze sliced back to Constantine, with whom he'd been closeted earlier in the day, during which time he had agreed to oversee the start-up of a new Ambrosi Pearls venture in Auckland. However, he'd been unable to commit to a loan from the Atraeus Group because Mario was a significant shareholder and would instantly veto the deal. He could raise the amount Gabriel needed personally, but it would take time, which Gabriel currently didn't have. "She's finally gotten engaged to Zane?"

"Zane?" Constantine looked surprised. "As far as I know they're friends, and that's all. It's not public yet, but Zane is on the verge of getting engaged to Lilah Cole. Although, an engagement is probably exactly what Gemma needs at this point."

Gabriel frowned at Constantine's reference to another tabloid story he had found online, that Gemma was having custody difficulties with her small daughter.

Constantine's wife, Sienna, a gorgeous blonde, joined them, ending the conversation. The next time Gabriel searched out Gemma, she had disappeared from sight, and so had Zane. Jaw tight, he excused himself and went outside.

The large stone terrace, with its spectacular view across a deceptively smooth stretch of sea to the island of Ambrus and the clear, star-studded sky, was empty. The tension that hummed through him loosened off a notch. Walking to the parapet, he gripped the railing and stared at the line of luminescence on the far horizon, the last soft glimmer of the setting sun.

He didn't know what he would have done if he had found Gemma and Zane locked in an intimate clinch. His reaction to the situation so far had not been either considered or tactical, it had simply been knee-jerk.

Gaze still caught and held by the purity of sky and sea, he let the soft chill of the night settle around him. An image from the past, of dark red hair across his chest, Gemma soft and warm against him, filled his mind, blotting out the night sky.

In the midst of the grief and betrayal of his father's

death there had been no time for the passion that had hit him like a thunderbolt.

But that was six years ago. Since then the situation had changed. His family had recovered from the double blow of his father's death and the resulting scandal. The bank's financial performance had been brilliant, thanks to his careful management and his younger brother, Kyle's, flare for investment. The only fly in the ointment was Mario and his machinations, which had recently begun to stall business.

The raw relief he'd experienced when Constantine had said Zane was about to get engaged to Lilah Cole, a high-profile designer for Ambrosi Pearls, replayed itself.

His fingers tightened on the parapet as he recalled the earlier sight of Gemma with her arms around Zane's neck. It was clear that she didn't understand she had lost Zane to another woman.

The fact that Zane hadn't had the courage to inform Gemma he was going to marry someone else made his jaw tighten. If he wasn't mistaken, Gemma was about to be badly hurt.

It wasn't exactly a repeat of the situation that had thrown them together six years ago, but it was oddly close.

The thought that, after years of careful control, utter focus on his work and family life, he could step into the maelstrom of passion that had swept him away in Dolphin Bay tightened every muscle in his body, but the desire to do so was tempered with caution. He couldn't forget the power of the obsessive passion that had ensnared his father. There was no way he could abandon himself to desire, and suddenly he had his plan.

Gemma needed relationship stability in order to establish custody of her child. With Constantine unable to guarantee the loan he needed within a forty-eight-hour framework, he could use a believable fiancée, on a strictly temporary basis, to cut through the legal clauses preventing him from taking full control of his company.

A fake engagement would provide the solutions they both needed and in his case, a safe, controlled environment in which to explore the passion that coursed through his veins.

Satisfied, he left the terrace and strolled back into the Castello and the ornate reception room. Gemma was nowhere to be seen. Neither was Zane.

He would find Gemma, it was just a matter of time. Thanks to boyhood holidays spent running wild on Medinos, he knew every nook and cranny of the Castello. He only hoped he didn't find Zane with her. If that was the case, he decided coldly, he would deal with the situation in the time-honored way, down on the beach and without an audience.

Gemma walked quickly down a small corridor and stepped into an anteroom that was currently used to hold coats and wraps. Closing the door behind her, she leaned on it for long seconds, allowing her breathing and her heart rate to steady.

Pushing away from the cold, dark wood of the door, she searched amongst the jumble of bags to find the canvas bag she had stashed in the room earlier.

Relief flooded her as her fingers closed over the strap. Hauling it from out of the expensive collection of designer handbags, she placed it on an ornate carved table that had probably been in existence for centuries and was no doubt worth an obscene amount of money.

The fact that the Atraeus family could put an heirloom antique in a room that was little more than a storage room underlined the yawning abyss between their lives and hers. Zane was not a typical Atraeus, which was another reason why she had found him so easy to get on with. Even though he bore the name Atraeus, he hadn't come from wealth originally. He understood what it was like to be poor.

Fingers shaking with an overload of adrenaline, she checked the black lace negligee and a bottle of champagne that was rapidly losing its chill. At the bottom of the bag she had also stowed a glossy magazine she'd found with an article titled "How To Seduce Your Man in Ten Easy Ways."

After careful thought, she had chosen the birthday surprise scenario, with her as the surprise. Nervous terror clutched at her just at the thought of actually having to resort to that tactic. Even viewing it as a scene she was acting, she wasn't sure she could go through with it.

At the last minute, she had also slipped into her evening bag an envelope of melt-your-heart snapshots of Sanchia.

Plan C. Just in case she couldn't go through with the seduction plan.

Gemma hurried down a corridor lined with cold fortress stone and archaic-looking brass lamps that glowed a soft buttery gold in the dimness. Mouth dry, she opened the door to Zane's private quarters, using the spare key she had obtained from the cleaner's office downstairs, and stepped inside.

A large sitting room with French doors opened onto a stone terrace. An ultramodern kitchenette occupied an alcove. Opening the fridge, she placed the now warm bottle of French champagne on a shelf to chill.

Briskly, she set about completing her preparations. If Zane had only agreed to talk to her, she wouldn't have had to resort to these lengths, but as she stepped into Zane's bedroom and was confronted with what looked like a king-size bed, the risk she was taking suddenly loomed large.

A niggling doubt surfaced. Encountering Zane's coolness at the launch party had leached away her confidence. The fear that she had resolutely suppressed, that proposing a real relationship was a ludicrous solution, came back to haunt her.

The idea of proposing a fake engagement was seeming more and more viable.

The fact that she had an alternative solution cheered her up and brought her normal positivity and optimism bouncing back to the surface.

Heart beating even faster, she walked through to the bedroom, her gaze automatically flinching from the king-size bed.

Now that it had come to the crunch, her seduction plan seemed basically unworkable because of one chilly little fact. Sexually, so far, she hadn't really felt anything for Zane.

It was a glitch she had happily glossed over, but that now loomed large—a fatal flaw in her plan.

She didn't know why she couldn't quite whip up the enthusiasm to fall passionately in love with Zane, despite both working and socializing with him. According to magazines and tabloids, practically every other woman on the planet was desperate for her ex-boss.

Instead she was shaking like a leaf and suddenly the whole idea of touching Zane, of actually shifting out of the comfortable casual friendship they'd shared to actually kissing him, seemed absurd.

An image of Gabriel and his cool, assessing gaze flashed into her mind. She stopped dead in the middle of the high-ceilinged lounge decorated in the spare but dramatic Medinian way, with dark furniture and jewel-bright Kilims scattered on the floor, her already shaky resolve wavering further. In that instant an oil painting featuring a woman draped in vivid, hot pink silk caught her eye. Pink was Sanchia's favorite color.

The thought of her daughter and their predicament was a timely reminder.

Grabbing the bag with the negligee, she walked resolutely through to the bathroom. Keeping her gaze averted from a wall-length mirror in a heavily carved gold frame, another exotic museum piece, she quickly changed into the negligee.

As she straightened and shoved her dress into the bag she caught a full frontal view of herself and blushed. With her hair tousled, her eyes dark, her pale skin gleaming through the lace, she looked like a high-priced courtesan.

That was the whole idea, of course, so she could hopefully shock Zane into seeing her as a woman instead of just a friend. But crazily, she still felt as if what she was planning was some kind of betrayal of Gabriel.

Although why should she feel guilty that after two years of dating she was finally attempting to launch her relationship with Zane on to a proper, intimate footing?

Unless, in her heart of hearts, she did still carry a torch for Gabriel?

She blinked at the thought, which had been at the edge of her mind ever since she had overheard the conversation in Gabriel's mother's hotel suite.

It would explain her emotional reaction, then the tension that had zinged through her when she had caught sight of Gabriel tonight. Not just tension that he was in the room and could possibly find out about Sanchia, but an acute feminine reaction that had shivered along her nerve endings and heightened all of her senses.

The kind of reaction that had hit her six years ago, and that had ended in a pregnancy.

The kind of reaction she had failed to feel for Zane.

The stark realization that she had been incapable of falling for anyone since the passionate interlude with Gabriel hit her with enough force that she froze in place.

She drew a shaky breath, feeling faintly ill. It was time to take her head out of the sand. The utter lack of sex and passion in her life wasn't because she was too busy as a working mother, and simply too tired to date. Or that she was ultrapicky about a man's qualities because, first and foremost, she needed to choose someone who would be good for Sanchia.

It was because somehow Gabriel Messena did still matter to her in a deep, intimate, personal way.

Blankly, she walked out of the bathroom. Stomach tight, legs feeling like noodles, she came to a halt in the middle of the sitting room. Dazed, she stared at the cool white walls, the rich trappings of the room. She didn't know how it could have happened, just that it had.

On an intellectual level, she had convinced herself that she had cut ties with Gabriel and wasn't attracted to him in any way. But the problem was that she had been a virgin when they had made love. Gabriel was her first and only lover. She had never fallen for anyone else in her entire life, including her teenage years. All of her experiences of love, sex and passion were bound up with Gabriel.

It was no wonder her body had reacted. She had seen Gabriel and the emotions and sensations she had only ever experienced with him, and that she had never gotten closure for, had resurfaced.

A knock on the door sent adrenaline shooting through her veins.

Logic told her it couldn't be Zane; he wouldn't knock. The thought that it could be Gabriel made the breath catch in her throat, although the whole idea that, after glimpsing her at the party, he would come after her, or even know that she was in Zane's room, was ridiculous. He hadn't contacted her in years, so why would he now?

Clutching the lapels of her negligee together, she gripped the medieval iron door handle and opened the door a crack. It was Lilah. Knowledge and guilt seared her as she registered the hurt in the other woman's gaze.

She had known Lilah was attracted to Zane and seemed to be pursuing him with limited success. She had ignored the complication, because a great many women had chased after Zane.

Lilah's expression chilled as she took in what Gemma was wearing. "You should stop trying and go home. Sex won't make Zane, or any man, have a relationship with you."

A sharp pain stabbed at her heart. Six years ago, instead of bringing them closer together, sex had destroyed any chance of a relationship with Gabriel. He had probably thought that she always gave in on a first date.

Although why she was thinking about Gabriel again, when this situation was entirely different, she didn't know. The whole point of the seduction scenario was that Zane would see her as the woman she was and stop treating her like a younger sister.

She lifted her chin. "How can you know that?"

The same pain Gemma had experienced just seconds ago flashed in the other woman's gaze. With a jolt, Gemma realized that Lilah was in love with Zane.

"Logic. If you couldn't make him fall in love with you in two years, then it's probably not going to happen."

The fatal flaw in her plan.

Relief rolled through Gemma. Lilah had stated the one simple fact that she had somehow managed to talk herself around, but that happily undermined every one of her plans. Time had passed and nothing had happened between her and Zane, and there had been plenty of opportunities.

She had put it down to the fact that she was always so tired and stressed with juggling Sanchia, a never-ending stream of nannies and a job that often included travel. Sex had just not been a priority. But it should have been for a hot alpha male like Zane.

The grim fact was that they were more like brother and sister than possible lovers.

Sudden embarrassed heat washed through her as she realized how exposed she was to Lilah, dressed for seduction and obviously waiting for Zane. And now she couldn't wait to leave.

Zane. Panic jolted through her.

She had to get out of his suite before he found her.

With a brief apologetic look toward Lilah, she closed the door, found the bag with her dress and raced to the bathroom. Wrenching the negligee off, not caring when the fine silk and lace caught and tore, she fumbled into her dress, dragged the zipper up and jammed the negligee into the bag, out of sight.

She did a quick check of the bathroom and bedroom to make sure she left nothing behind. Walking through to the small kitchenette, she retrieved the bottle of champagne she had put in the fridge.

Embarrassed heat burned her cheeks as she found her shoes, jammed them on her feet and did a last hurried check of the sitting room before she left.

She must have been mad, certifiable, in thinking that she could have convinced Zane Atraeus that she could be more than just an employee and friend, that she could possibly be his lover or his wife. It was the same mad optimism she had clutched at when she had made the mistake of sleeping with Gabriel.

She could still remember the dull depression when she had realized that the few hours they had spent together hadn't meant a thing to him, and she'd heard the relief in his voice when she'd said she wasn't pregnant.

Lilah Cole's pale, blank expression minutes ago said it all. Gorgeous, hot billionaires did not marry small-town girls with no substance behind them. Slinging the strap of her evening bag over her shoulder, she headed for the door, now desperate to get out of the suite. But as she reached for the handle, Murphy's law—the one that states that what can go wrong, will go wrong—kicked in. The door popped open and Zane strode in.

An excruciating few moments later, after realizing a stunning truth, that Zane was in love with Lilah, Gemma made a hasty escape.

A giddy sense of relief clutched at her as she practically jogged down the corridor. High heels tapping on flagstones, she almost failed to recognize a reporter she had seen circulating at the party walking straight toward her.

She caught his sly grin as she spun on her heel and started back the way she had come. She had no intention of reentering Zane's suite. There were a number of other doors, and what looked like an exit onto a terrace ahead. She would find a door, any door that was unlocked, and hide out for a few minutes.

With dismay, she noticed Zane's door, which she had closed behind her, was now ajar. A flash of movement confirmed that Zane was near the door, zipping a bag closed, on the point of leaving.

Panic clutched at her. When Zane stepped out into the corridor, the reporter would get a picture of the two of them together. Now that there was no possibility of a relationship, that was something she absolutely did not want to happen.

She broke into a jog again, determined to get past Zane's

door before he stepped out. At that moment another door popped open right in front of her. It was one of two concealed doors, which she vaguely remembered reading about when she'd studied up on the Castello, that led to the old armory and the stables. A secret network built into the fortress in case of attack, and as such designed to be unobtrusive.

A dark, masculine head ducked under the low lintel.

Startled, Gemma almost ran full tilt into him. Lean hands closed around her arms, steadying her as she clutched at broad shoulders. Heat and a clean, male scent engulfed her.

Not a member of the staff using the convenient shortcut with fresh linen or a tray, but a bona fide member of the Atraeus family who, in centuries past, would have fitted the mold of fortress protector. Gabriel Messena.

Her heart slammed against her chest at the sheer shock of running into Gabriel. The pressure of his hands on her bare skin sent a raw shiver up her spine. Almost in the same moment she registered the flash of a camera, the shadowy shape of the reporter still lurking at one end of the corridor.

Gabriel's gaze dropped to the bag she was clutching, the incriminating trail of black lace and the foil top of the champagne bottle. Knowledge flared in his dark gaze.

Hot color washed across her skin, her stomach clenched on an acid burn of shame. She didn't know how, but Gabriel knew exactly what she had attempted.

Instead of loosening his hold, his fingers tightened, anchoring her in place, close enough that she could feel the heat radiating from his big body.

His head bent, his breath feathered her cheek, warm and damp. "Zane is about to get engaged." The sexy low timbre of his voice shivered all the way to her toes, making places inside her that should be frozen and immune instantly melt. "If you don't want the newspapers to report that you've moved from being Zane's girlfriend to his mistress, you should consider kissing me."

Five

Another flash from the reporter's camera lit up the dim corridor, making her stomach hollow out. Although not as much as the knowledge that Gabriel must have read the various tabloid stories and assumed that she was involved in an affair with Zane. "I know Zane wants Lilah. *Now.*"

Something like relief registered in his gaze. "Good."

Her jaw tightened against another heated rush of humiliation. In terms of the welfare case against her, she absolutely could not afford to be viewed as Zane Atraeus's mistress. "One kiss."

Lifting up on her toes, she braced her palms on the hard muscle of his shoulders. The firm touch of his hands at her waist, drawing her closer, sent a sensual shock through her as she took a shallow breath and touched her mouth to his.

The kiss, as brief as it was, sent sensation shivering through her, unexpectedly powerful and laced with memories that were still sharp-edged and bittersweet.

The humid warmth of a summer's night, the sibilant wash of waves on the beach, the weight of Gabriel's body pressing down on hers...

She inhaled and the faintly resinous scent of his cologne shivered through her. If she hadn't known before that she had made a mistake in kissing Gabriel, she knew it then.

It had taken her years to be able to view what they had shared as a casual encounter that had gotten out of hand, years to get over his easy defection.

The heated tension cut off as another camera flash temporarily blinded her, followed by the sound of retreating footsteps as the reporter made his escape.

The reporter. Her stomach churned at the new publicity, which she hated, even though she knew that in this case kissing Gabriel had been expedient. Doing so negated the earlier, potentially damning photo that had been taken of her hugging Zane.

Gabriel's head lifted, and in that instant she was aware of the creak of a door opening a few meters down the hall. It was Zane. Thankfully, his back was to her as he stepped out into the corridor, juggling bags and keys.

A split second later, darkness engulfed her as Gabriel pulled her through the opening into the narrow space behind the wall and even more tightly into his arms.

The door, which appeared to be spring-loaded, snicked shut behind her, the fit seamless, closing them into a dim, claustrophobic hallway that smelled of damp and ages-old dust. She had expected the ancient hide to be pitch-black, but surprisingly, the very modern glow of an electric lightbulb glowed at one end, illuminating a stone stairwell.

Heart still pounding with an overload of adrenaline and the curious humming excitement of being close to Gabriel, she released herself from his hold and stepped back in the narrow space. Her bare back brushed against smooth stone, cool enough to make her flinch.

Closeted in the narrow space, with the pressure of his kiss still tingling on her mouth, it felt, crazily enough, as if they were a couple. For a few dizzying seconds Gemma ceased to think about everything that had gone wrong and simply wallowed in the moment.

"This way." Gabriel indicated the set of stone steps ahead. "They go down to the armory and the stables, which have both been converted into garages and a guest suite. Not exactly as romantic as the old days, but a convenient shortcut if you've forgotten your car keys."

She caught the flash of his grin and out of nowhere her stomach turned a somersault.

The small warning jolt that went with that reaction was swamped by a surge of pure happiness as she found herself smiling back. She had just done a completely stupid thing: she had embarrassed and humiliated herself with the bungled seduction attempt and a reporter was brewing another scandal. But as she stood, crowded close to Gabriel in the secret hideaway, a dangerous thrill shot down her spine.

Lips still damp and tingling, on edge and acutely aware of the intimacy of being alone with the one man she thought she would never be alone with again, Gemma followed Gabriel.

Her stomach churned at how close she had come to disaster. She knew why she had kissed Gabriel. It had been the rescue she had needed, but she had no idea why he had kissed her.

With every second that passed the gratitude that had flooded her when he had stepped in to help dissipated, and Gabriel's presence in the exact moment when she had needed help became stranger and more confusing. Kindness? Definitely. Desire?

She drew a sharp breath at the question that had been hovering at the back of her mind. Not seriously.

As he paused at the top of the stairwell, the light from the bare bulb gleamed over taut cheekbones, a blade-straight nose and the lash of an old scar over one temple. As his gaze locked with hers, she remembered with a small jolt that he had gotten the scar during a knife attack on Medinos when he was a teenager.

Trained in self-defence, as were all the members of his family, he had taken the knife and ended the attempted mugging, but the scar invested Gabriel with a barbaric quality. New Zealand born he may be, but she couldn't let herself forget that he was the head of an ancient and wealthy family that could trace its lineage back centuries.

"Don't worry about the reporter, he can't follow unless he knows where the mechanism that opens the door is, which reminds me…"

He paused at the head of the steps, his expression shifting instantly back to neutral as he slid his cell out of his trouser pocket.

His conversation with the Castello's security—who should have checked the man's press credentials—was brief and to the point. His gaze touched on hers again as he hung up. "I didn't see a press card on his lapel. If he doesn't have an invitation, with any luck, they'll stop him before he gets out of the Castello and erase the pictures."

Her face burning uncomfortably hot again, Gemma glanced down at the incriminating gleam of black lace in the carry bag, the handle of which was still looped over rm. Surreptitiously, she tucked the negligee lower.

you."

h she didn't hold out much hope that erasing om the reporter's camera would be the end of the matter. Knowing her luck, the photos had already been emailed to the editor of some tabloid scandal sheet.

"When we reach ground level, we'll be close to where my car is parked. If you want I can give you a ride back to your hotel."

Gemma sent him another strained smile. "You don't have to do that." She already felt stressed and indebted to Gabriel. Now that she was finally back to thinking logically, rather than simply panicking and reacting, the last thing she wanted was to impose on him any further. "I've got my cell with me. I can call a taxi."

Pausing beneath the glare of the single bulb, he glanced at his wristwatch. "If you haven't prebooked a taxi, you'll probably have to wait. Medinos doesn't have that many, and when Constantine throws a party, they're mostly booked in advance by the guests." His gaze touched on hers. "You could always wait out front. Chances are you could find someone who will be willing to share one with you."

A shudder of pure horror went through Gemma. In that moment, she was also certain that Gabriel knew that standing on the front steps of the Castello, where journalists could easily find her, was the absolute last thing she wanted.

That meant he had probably read the press stories about her, which made sense of his timely appearance almost directly across from Zane's suite. She was grateful he had decided to intervene, although wary of his motives. Given that he had suggested the kiss, she would be naive to discount the fact that as crazy as it seemed, Gabriel still felt something for her. As seductive as that fact was, she was also overwhelmingly aware of the danger. Gabriel had the power to make things better, but if he ever discovered that he was the father of her child, he could also cause further complications.

Lifting her chin, she met his gaze. "I think you know that exposing myself to any further media attention is not exactly at the top of my 'to do' list."

"I know there's a child. I also know there's a problem with custody, in which case pressuring Zane was the last thing you should have tried."

Gabriel watched the warm color drain from Gemma's face, leaving her looking pale and a little shocked. He hadn't meant to be so blunt, but neither did he have much patience with subtler approaches.

He vowed to have a word with Zane before he left Medinos. He didn't care how irresistible his cousin found Gemma, if he was getting engaged—in Gabriel's book—that meant that he now left Gemma alone, permanently.

A heady sense of satisfaction wound through him as he led the way down the steep flight of worn steps. Sound and light receded as they descended a good three levels and ended up in a dank and chilly hallway. Flagged with stone, the narrow corridor ran alongside the kitchens and pantries, and was redolent of the smells of a spicy Medinian fish stew and fresh-baked bread. Opening a squat, heavy door, he ducked under another low lintel and stepped out onto the windy northern side of the Castello.

A cold breeze, laden with sea salt, funnelled through the narrow alleyway that ran between the Castello and a set of garages. As he held out his hand to Gemma, her hair fluttered in the breeze. Gleaming strands flowed across his shoulder, sliding gossamer-soft against his jaw, filling his nostrils with the warm, tantalizing scent of gardenias.

She tucked stray strands behind one ear. As she did so her evening bag, which was hitched over one shoulder by a thin gold chain, slipped to the ground. Muttering beneath her breath, she set the carry bag down and bent to retrieve the delicate lace evening bag that matched her dress.

Gabriel beat her to it. As he handed the evening bag to her, he checked out the contents of the much larger bag. The glint of foil was definitely the top of a bottle of champagne, and the trailing black lace and silk was not the wrap he had hoped it would be; it was lingerie of some sort.

The quick twist of anger settled into a cold moment of decision.

With a smooth motion, he picked up the bag. "I can take this for you."

With a startled glance, Gemma reached for it. "Thanks, but that won't be necessary."

Instead of hooking the strap of the evening bag back over her shoulder, she dropped it on top of the carry bag. The action effectively concealed the lingerie and champagne, which only succeeded in firing the edgy temper he hadn't known he possessed even further.

He had no problem putting a name to the burning emotion that lately seemed to continually overpower him.

Jealousy.

Annoyed with the fierce emotion and his inability to control it, he shifted position to shield Gemma from the wind. As he did so a flash of movement drew his eye.

Zane was walking from the Castello's front entrance in the direction of the garages.

Gemma's gaze caught his. "Is there another way we can go?"

Grim satisfaction filled him that instead of chasing after Zane, Gemma was now intent on avoiding him. It was progress of a sort. "If you don't want to go back into the Castello, I can take you back to your hotel. My car is parked in the lot beside the stables, just a few meters down the path and around the corner." He jerked his head, indicating the direction.

Gemma sent him a brittle smile. "Thanks. I will take you up on that lift."

Immediately, she started down the path.

Keeping pace effortlessly, because Gemma had to negotiate the path in high heels, Gabriel glanced back in Zane's direction. Relief loosened some of his tension as he noted that his cousin had already disappeared from sight into the garage.

Common sense told him that it wasn't likely that Zane had seen them. He had been walking through a floodlit area, while they were in semidarkness.

He probably didn't need to be so cautious. But now that Gemma seemed to finally be free of Zane, he wasn't about to give his cousin the chance to change his mind and entice her back again.

As they rounded a corner, Gemma tilted her head and stared at the impressive view of the seaward-facing side of the floodlit Castello where it perched high on cliffs. Some distance below, waves dashed on rocks, filling the air with the muted background roar of surf. "This place is amazing. I would have liked to have had a proper look around—" She stopped midspeech, her expression taut. "No, cancel that. I'm over castles and wealth. I'm especially over anyone holding a camera."

Gabriel logged the sound of a powerful car, the flicker of headlights through trees as Zane accelerated down the drive. Satisfaction that his cousin was finally removed from the equation drained some of his tension. "I thought you would have visited this place a number of times."

The hollow feeling that gripped him at the thought that over the past two years Gemma would have shared

Zane's bed on frequent occasions renewed his edgy, burning tension.

Gemma sent him a startled glance. "I visited Medinos quite a lot when I was Zane's PA, but I was never invited to the Castello. This was my first, and last, visit."

Gemma halted so suddenly beneath an ancient gnarled olive tree that he almost walked into her. "What I don't get is why you're helping me?"

Because he was tired of fixing everyone else's lives and wanted his own back. Because he wanted more of what they'd shared six years ago.

An acute awareness of Gemma's nearness burned through Gabriel. The rich, tantalizing scent of gardenias teased his nostrils again. The banked anger at Zane's cavalier treatment of her flared a little hotter, and he was abruptly glad for the intense pooling darkness beneath the tree.

As soon as he had an opportunity, he intended to track Zane down and confront him with his behavior. If he was getting engaged, that meant he had established a relationship some time ago and yet had still continued to see Gemma. "Maybe I don't like the way Zane's treated you."

Surprise flickered in her gaze, and he wondered grimly what had happened to her over the past few years that she hadn't registered how shabbily she had been treated.

Her chin tilted. "Zane hasn't treated me badly. He's been extremely kind to me." Her gaze dropped to his mouth, and for a moment the air turned molten.

Drawing in a sharp breath, as if she had been just as affected as he, Gemma looked quickly away. "I like Zane. He's been a good friend. I've just had a run of bad luck, that's all."

Before he could answer, she walked briskly on ahead, and paused at a fork in the path, the sea breeze molding the black lace of her dress against her slim curves, making her look thinner than he remembered, oddly solitary and fragile.

Gabriel indicated the correct direction. His annoyance leached away as Gemma walked quickly on, now clearly wary of his presence. He had ruthlessly pushed her, moving into her personal space and suggesting the kiss. After the electrifying heat of the kiss and her unmistakable response, he had expected her to back off.

What he couldn't understand was why she was protecting Zane. The only conclusion he could draw was that despite Zane's upcoming engagement and the callous way he had dumped her, Gemma still harbored a soft spot for his cousin.

It was a complication Gabriel hadn't anticipated, and one he was determined to eradicate.

If Gemma hadn't been attracted to him, he would have stepped back from the situation, but that wasn't the case. Her response had been immediate and clear. He had seen it in the way her gaze had clung to his, the heat rimming her cheekbones, and felt it in the softness of her mouth and the rapid thud of her heart as they'd kissed.

He might have been out of the loop for a while when it came to the murky area of relationships, but one kiss and the years had spun away. He hadn't mistaken her response, and his own had been just as visceral, just as powerful, the chemistry sizzling between them hot enough to burn.

As far as he was concerned, Zane had had his chance. If he hadn't been able to commit in two years, and with a child in the mix, then he couldn't really want Gemma.

But Gabriel did.

The concept, which had grown in him over the past twenty-four hours—ever since he had read the newspaper article—was powerful and irrevocable.

Gabriel knew his nature. He was a Messena to the bone, but along with the hot-blooded, volatile streak, from an early age his father had impressed upon him the need to develop a level head and a steely discipline. As a result, when it came to the stormy seas of romance and passion, it took a great deal to sway him.

He had never been in love; he couldn't imagine the havoc that would cause, but something significant had happened between him and Gemma.

Instead of dissolving with the passage of time, the attraction had stuck with him. In six years he had been unable to forget her.

The moment was clarifying. He realized that after years of avoidance, he had finally applied the deliberate, methodical process he used to weigh a business proposition, and he had reached a moment of clear decision.

In this case it was a definite *yes* to more than just passion.

A sharp thrill shot down his spine at the thought of picking up on the relationship that had been snuffed out before it had had a chance six years ago.

He filled his lungs with tangy sea air and felt more alive than he had in years. Six years to be exact, since the last time he had experienced genuine passion, in a small, sandy beach house in Dolphin Bay.

Six

A disorienting sense of déjà vu, an odd feeling of inevitability, gripped Gemma as Gabriel walked alongside her, as sleek and muscular as a big cat, easily keeping pace.

From the moment she had realized that the kiss had been a mistake, she had done her best to distance herself from him. The last thing she needed right now was a resurgence of the old crush, the old love, that had haunted her for so long, but the plain fact was that right now she needed his help.

The wind gusted off the dark expanse of sea that glittered beneath a half-moon, raising gooseflesh on her arms and intensifying the sense of reliving a past that was emotionally fraught with temptation and risk.

Setting her jaw, she tried not to shiver and wished she had thought to bring a wrap. Unfortunately, when she had left her room at the Atraeus Resort, her home for the past few days, she hadn't been in any state to remember sensible details. She had been too stressed with the whole crazy idea that Zane was the answer to her problems.

Acutely aware of Gabriel next to her, his brooding glance touching on her profile, Gemma skimmed the parking lot and wondered which of the vehicles belonged to him.

She expected him to indicate one of the sedans that gleamed expensively under the lights, maybe a BMW or an Audi, but when he depressed a key and the lights of a muscular, low-slung Maserati flashed, the impression she had gained earlier was intensified. As ordered and high-powered as Gabriel's occupation was, there was nothing either soft or conventional about him. Underneath the business suit, he was utterly male, with the sleek, hard muscle and seasoned toughness that was uncompromisingly alpha.

Even though she had known how he could be, how he had been six years ago, the car put Gabriel firmly in context. She had gotten used to viewing him as belonging in the past, no longer connected with either her or Sanchia's life.

Now, suddenly, that convenient fantasy had evaporated. Gabriel was here, now, larger than life and twice as potent.

She drew in a breath at a sudden thought. And like it or not, according to the press story that would probably be published in the next few days, he was now part of her life.

Gabriel opened the passenger-side door and waited for her to climb into the dimly glowing interior. Forced to throw caution to the wind, at least until she was safely back in her hotel room, Gemma settled into an ultralow seat that smelled expensively of leather and felt like a warm, very expensive cloud.

Chilled from the breeze and inescapably on edge, she

quickly fastened her seat belt before Gabriel could offer to do it for her.

She shoved the light-colored bag, which seemed to glow in the dark, against her door, as far from Gabriel's view as she could get it. When she got back to her room, she intended to throw the entire thing away, bag, contents and all. It would take her a long time to forget the embarrassment and humiliation of the evening; the last thing she needed was reminders.

Gabriel slid into the driver's seat, making the interior of the Maserati seem even smaller. Seconds later, they were accelerating past the floodlit front of the Castello with its soaring stone facade and circular drive and down a narrow winding road.

Twin stone posts glided past as Gabriel turned onto the coast road and headed into the township of Medinos. Cupped in a gently curving bay, backed by arid, ridged hills, Medinos glittered softly. Lights from rows of streetlamps that resembled glowing pearls and ultramodern high-rises splashed out across the water, illuminating the graceful lines of yachts.

Gabriel braked for a set of lights. "I take it you're staying at the resort."

His deep, cool voice made her start. "For the meantime. I fly back to New Zealand in a couple of days."

Although she intended to change her ticket and leave on the earliest flight she could get. Tomorrow, if possible.

After the episode with Zane, and the next media scandal looming, she needed to get home to Sanchia as soon as she could.

Her fingers clenched together in her lap at the way all of her plans had flown to pieces. The thought that the child welfare people could try to take Sanchia permanently filled her with desperate fear. Until she got home, and had Sanchia back in her arms, she wouldn't be able to relax.

"I heard you've quit the job with the Atraeus Group."

"That's right." Warily, she juggled how much to tell him. "I need to be closer to my family. And I need a more settled environment for Sanch—for my child."

She felt rather than saw his gaze on her. "I take it your mother is caring for—the child?"

She didn't miss his slight hesitation, and, out of the blue, wrenching guilt jabbed at her. The moment was disorienting. Sanchia was his, and he didn't even know he had a daughter.

When she had been nursing her hurt and bearing the pregnancy on her own she had managed to convince herself that it was for the best, but now, in Gabriel's presence, the full weight of the deception settled in. The very least she could do was to give him her name. "Mom was looking after Sanchia, until she had a heart attack. One of my sisters has her at the moment."

"And that's why you've left your job."

Surprise at his knowledge made her stiffen. The wariness that she'd felt back at the Castello returned full force. "That's right. I was going to bring Sanchia out to Medinos, but now a lot of things have changed and I…need to go home."

Gabriel smoothly overtook a slower vehicle. "And your mother, is she okay?"

The concern in his voice reminded her that as much as she had tried to ignore Gabriel's existence, that didn't alter the fact that back in Dolphin Bay they were practically neighbors. "Mom's recovering. It wasn't a serious attack, more a warning. She just has to take things easy for a while."

"If there's anything I can do, let me know."

"Thank you for the offer. Luckily Mom has medical insurance, so she's had no problem with meeting costs."

The conversation reminded her that Gabriel had lost his father suddenly. The car accident had happened shortly after the night they had spent together. She could still remember anxiously scanning the newspapers for news of him and his family, and checking the internet to see what details she could pick up.

With relief Gemma saw the resort's neon sign. Gabriel pulled into the lobby parking lot just as a tall, familiar figure strode out of the front entrance.

Gemma's heart almost stopped in her chest. Zane.

He was too intent on his own agenda to notice them as he climbed into the Ferrari parked at the curb and shot away. Gemma skimmed the lighted hotel entrance looking for press. She couldn't see any, but she wasn't taking any chances. If Zane was here, the media were bound to be, also. The last thing she wanted to do now was walk into the lobby and get snapped.

She directed Gabriel around to the parking lot at the rear of the staff accommodation. As he slotted the Maserati into a space, Gemma's stomach tensed as the reporter who had followed her at the Castello stepped out of a rental car, camera in hand. He was accompanied by a second reporter, who was holding a video camera.

Gabriel frowned. "It's getting a little crowded around here. What do you want to do?"

She absolutely did not want to run into the media again, tonight. "Leave."

Zane and reporters was a combination she couldn't afford, which meant she couldn't stay at the Atraeus Resort tonight.

She could try requesting security, which she had needed

on occasion in her job as Zane's PA. But after what had happened at the Castello and the fact that she had officially resigned, she had to consider the possibility that Zane had advised his people that as she was no longer on the payroll, her status was as a guest only.

Before she could suggest another hotel, Gabriel reversed and cruised across the parking lot. The cameraman turned at the low throaty growl of the Maserati, but by the time he had lifted the camera and aimed it in their direction, Gabriel had turned out onto the main highway.

Seconds later they were in the middle of town, with its milling tourists, street cafés and tavernas. Idling now, to avoid the occasional jaywalking pedestrian, Gabriel cruised along the waterfront. "Do you have a place you could stay? Any friends on Medinos?"

Still unnerved by the sighting of both Zane and the press crew that seemed to be stalking her, Gemma kept her gaze on the ranks of gleaming cars parked along the street, the brightly dressed tourists mingling with the much more conventional Medinians. "No. When I've stayed in Medinos, I've always been working. I've spent most of my time either at the airport or the resort."

And any spare time she had spent either studying, talking with Sanchia via the internet or troubleshooting endless problems with nannies.

Gabriel took a turn into a quieter section of town, dotted with villas. "I have a beachside villa with a security gate. If you want to stay the night you're welcome."

Gemma risked a glance at Gabriel's profile. With his longer hair and the faint shadow of stubble on his jaw, he looked far more broodingly dangerous and exotically Medinian than she remembered.

The thought of spending further time with him in a private setting with no one but perhaps an odd servant around tightened the tension humming through her. Although with the Ambrosi Pearls launch it was entirely possible there would be other family members staying. "I was thinking a small *pensionato*."

Gabriel pulled over against the curb and stopped. "Unless you've prebooked one, you might have trouble getting a room. It's the height of the tourist season, plus there are a lot of press and extra people on the island for the Ambrosi Pearls launch."

He lifted a brow. "And unless you've got some extra clothing, even if you find a room, you could still have a problem with that scenario."

Gemma's stomach sank. She had temporarily forgotten that Medinos was a place that hadn't quite shaken off its medieval traditions, particularly with regard to women. Caught halfway between the east and west, no bikinis, and no cleavage or overtly sensual clothing were allowed in public areas. Unless in a private setting, which the Castello had been, women were expected to dress modestly.

Until she could either get into her room at the resort, or go shopping, all she had to wear was what she had on. No respectable *pensionato*—and that was the only kind on Medinos—would rent her a room while she was wearing a black lace dress and high heels, and with no luggage.

Although her bag, despite holding champagne and a negligee, could pass for luggage.

Gabriel extracted his phone from his pocket. "If you want I can ring a couple of places."

"Okay."

Fifteen minutes and ten calls later, Gabriel set the phone down. "The offer of a bed at my place is still good."

Gemma stared out of the Maserati's window and tried not to feel a forbidden jolt of excitement that she would be extending her time with Gabriel. "All I need is a bed for a few hours."

It was the lesser of two evils.

Just one night. How dangerous could that be?

Seven

A small thrill shot down Gemma's spine as Gabriel's villa, which occupied the bay next to Medinos's central business district, loomed in the darkness. Set against the pure dark backdrop of sea and sky, it was an arresting mixture of ancient and modern. The crenellated stone tower of an old fortress blended seamlessly with the blunt addition of smoothly rendered walls, the windows stark sheets of glass.

The view slid away as Gabriel drove into a cavernous, empty garage. As the remote-controlled door came down behind them, Gemma unbuckled her belt and climbed out of the car, eager to assert her independence before Gabriel could get around to open her door.

Grabbing her bag, she tried to suppress a renewed surge of awareness. Desperate to at least give the appearance of normality, she examined the garage space, which was big enough to hold at least four cars. It was empty, but that could be because everyone was out for the night. "Does your family stay here?"

Gabriel closed the door of the Maserati with a quiet thunk. "No. This is something in the nature of a retreat for me. My family usually arranges their own accommodations."

Her heart beat once, hard. So they really would be alone.

Despite her determination to be brisk and superficial, to clamp down on the spellbinding intensity of the attraction, she found herself once again caught in the net of Gabriel's gaze. Despite the fact that, in theory, Gabriel shouldn't have the least interest in her, the sense of being herded was suddenly suffocatingly strong. "I guess that explains why your mother was at the Atraeus Resort."

His gaze sharpened. "You saw my mother at the Atraeus Resort?"

"I helped settle her and her friend into their room."

He opened a door that led out onto a covered deck and gestured that she precede him. "Mom mentioned she had seen someone who looked like you, but she couldn't be sure because you've lost so much weight."

Gemma frowned, remembering the awkwardness of the scene. Although most of that had been generated by the shock she'd received when she'd heard that Gabriel was about to be engaged.

The remembrance of that made her stiffen. In all the turmoil of the night, the tingling heat of the kiss they'd shared, she had managed to gloss over the fact that Gabriel wasn't free. "I didn't think your mother recognized me."

Feeling suddenly depressed, she stopped at a heavy door and looked upward at old fortress rock, weathered by time. "This looks like an old watchtower."

"It's the remnants of the Messena Fortress, given to an

ancestor during the Crusades. It was a crumbled ruin even before the bombing in the Second World War."

Without waiting for him, she grasped the heavy iron ring and attempted to open a door that looked ancient and clunky.

When the door didn't budge, Gabriel stepped in. "Unless you know the security codes, you're going to have to let me do that."

Lifting a metal flap fitted into a niche in the rock wall, he pressed in the key and alarm codes. The lock disengaged with a smooth click.

As she pushed the door open into pooling silence, despite her confusion another electrifying thrill shot up Gemma's spine. At the Castello there had been people everywhere. Now there were no reporters, no pressure, just the two of them and the night.

A sense of inevitability heightened all of Gabriel's senses as Gemma stepped into the ancient watchtower, now a wine cellar filled with extremely expensive wines. He flicked a switch. Soft golden light filled the room, highlighting the rich color of Gemma's hair, the creaminess of her skin, and he was gripped by the conviction that in the space of a few minutes his life had swung in a totally new direction.

He had felt that kind of internal shift before, the night his father had died. That night had been marked by grief and grim resolve. The way he presently felt was the exact opposite. The calm deliberation that had become his hallmark had utterly deserted him and in its place was a humming, restless energy.

A cliché or not, he knew the exact moment the change had taken place: when he had seen Gemma across the width of the crowded reception room.

Stepping inside, he swung the heavy door, with its medieval double thickness of timbers designed to stop both arrows and spears, closed behind him. The sound of the lock reengaging echoed.

Gemma, who was already at the far end of the circular room that opened out at one end into a large barnlike lounge, was busy checking out the impressive view across the sea. She swung around, her expression professionally brisk. Gabriel couldn't help thinking that it was a look he had gotten used to seeing from his own very efficient PA.

"If it was anyone else, I might suspect your motives in locking the door."

"I'll take that as a compliment." Although Gabriel's sense of irritation increased that, evidently, even Gemma didn't think he was capable of doing anything either remotely edgy or borderline. Strolling to the wine counter, he poured some of the water, which was still sitting there from his afternoon session with Constantine, into two clean glasses. "What makes you so sure I don't have motives?"

Gemma gave him a preoccupied look, as if her attention had just switched to something else. "It's been six years since we last met. I seem to remember you saying that we had very little in common, so I don't see how that's changed."

"We did have one thing in common."

She checked her watch, although her cheeks had taken on a pink tinge, so she wasn't entirely oblivious to their exchange. "I don't think sex counts."

It did in his world. "So any motives on my part other than chivalry are doubtful?"

Her blush deepened. "It's been six years. You never called. I think that about settles it."

Gabriel frowned. Thinking about what Gemma might have needed from him was not an aspect he had dwelled on, because he'd been so absorbed with fixing the scandal that had erupted after his father's death. But he was thinking about it now. "Did you want me to call?"

Her gaze locked with his for an electrifying moment. "I slept with you. That was not something I did lightly. Of course I wanted you to call."

Blinking, as if she couldn't quite believe that she had said the words, Gemma set the bag, which she was still keeping annoyingly close, down beside one of two leather chairs grouped around a coffee table.

"I thought about calling." And a couple of times it had been more than that. He had actually picked up the phone and started pressing numbers before he had come to his senses.

She sent him a level look. "It wasn't a problem. I understood why you couldn't afford to be involved with me. Banks and scandal don't really go together."

Gemma began investigating the racks of wine lining the walls as if she were riveted by his wine collection. Gabriel suppressed a surge of frustration. It was not the response he'd hoped for.

She pulled out a bottle of a rare French vintage worth a staggering amount of money. "I know for a fact that if anything about you appears in the papers, it's always in the financial, not the social pages."

Suddenly intensely irritated at the way Gemma insisted on reinforcing his image as a staid, boring banker, Gabriel drained his water and set the glass down on the counter with a click. "I didn't know you were interested in the financial pages."

She gave the label of the award-winning burgundy a distracted look and slipped the bottle back onto the rack. "When I'm stuck on a long haul flight, I've been known to read anything I can get my hands on, even the financial pages."

She glanced at the narrow watch on her wrist again, and despite the optimism that had gripped him when Gemma had agreed to spend the night at his house, his mood plummeted. "One step up from the classified ads."

"Only just." She abandoned her perusal of the wine racks and strolled over to the counter. "Speaking of finances, I read somewhere that you're a qualified economist as well as an accountant—"

"With a calculator for a heart, no doubt."

She accepted the glass he handed her. "I didn't say that. If you had a calculator for a heart you wouldn't have bothered to rescue me. Twice."

His pulse racing that she had mentioned the previous occasion that he had intervened to help her, he said, "Just a suggestion, but maybe you need to rethink the kind of guy you're dating."

The second the words were out, he wished he could retract them. Six years on from the one passionate night they'd shared and he was sounding like an older brother—worse, a father figure—dispensing advice.

"I intend to. As of tonight, I'm not dating anyone afraid of commitment—"

The distinctive chime of her phone distracted Gemma from a conversation and a simmering tension that was continually pushing her out of her depth. She had been worried because Sanchia was due to call her and she absolutely could not take the call right now.

Feeling under siege, she dug the phone out of her evening purse, intending to simply turn it off. Sanchia would understand. She knew that Gemma couldn't always answer, and that she would pick up on the missed call when she could.

The phone ringing was a sharp reminder that she could not afford another sizzling fling with Gabriel. Before she could hit the power button, the phone was whisked out of her hand. Incensed, Gemma grabbed at the phone, desperate to get it back. "That's mine."

"You can have it back once Zane's hung up."

"Why would Zane be ringing me?"

Gabriel's gaze was cool and flat. "I'm not prepared to take any chances."

The small silence that followed, the knowledge that Gabriel was not only acting unreasonably, he was behaving in a distinctly possessive way, made her stomach clench.

Although she refused to accept that Gabriel's disconcerting focus on her was either real or lasting. She knew now that Zane and Lilah had found the kind of deep, committed love she herself longed for. She wished them well with all of her heart, but that didn't change the fact that their togetherness underlined her single, lonely—and now desperate—state. "I'm not Zane's girlfriend or his mistress."

Gabriel's expression underlined his disbelief. Given that he had dropped her like a hot coal six years ago, his opinion shouldn't register, but tonight it did.

She was tired of being judged and dismissed and treated as if she was a pretty airhead just out for a good time. She was strong and independent; she had dreams and desires and plans. She certainly wasn't the good-time girl the tabloids had dubbed her.

Just the thought of that derogatory label made her feel sick. The only good time she'd ever had had lasted just a few short hours. "I am not interested in an affair with Zane. If only you knew, it's the last thing I want."

One final chime and the call went through to answer phone.

She drew an impeded breath. She should be angry that Gabriel was behaving so high-handedly in taking her phone and switching it off. That he could believe, even now, after everything that had happened, that she would try to remain in contact with Zane.

But she couldn't sustain the anger for one simple reason. Gabriel wouldn't behave in such an arrogant fashion if he didn't care. The thought clutched at her deep inside and refused to let go, generating a dangerous excitement she recognized only too well. She lifted her chin. "And if Zane does call, what then?"

"I'll deal with him."

"It's none of your business, but the number that flashed up was my sister's, in Dolphin Bay. She's looking after Sanchia until I get home."

She caught the flash of relief in Gabriel's gaze and in that moment a startling thought hit her. Gabriel was jealous. The revelation took root, spiralled through her on a dizzying wave of delight.

So it definitely wasn't chance that he had used the secret tunnel that had come out near Zane's door. He must have deduced where she had gone and had probably chosen the hidden way to avoid the press.

He let out a breath, dragged long fingers through his hair, his expression repentant enough as he handed her the phone that she had to resist the urge to smile. "Damn. Sorry."

And just like that they were back to the softness, the singular, sweet camaraderie that in tiny fragments they'd shared over the years, and which she had always adored.

She drew in a breath at the curious melting sensation inside, the crazy desire to step close to Gabriel and test out her theory by winding her arms around his neck, lifting up on her toes and kissing him again.

Feeling suddenly in need of air, she turned to the French doors behind her, fumbled at the handle and stepped outside.

The fresh, cool night air took her breath as she walked to the edge of the balcony and looked out to sea and a magnificent view of the nearest island, Ambrus. Anything to dissipate the perilous warmth, the heady tension that gripped her.

Below the balcony a sweep of floodlit lawn flowed to a wild, rock-strewn garden, then down to a smooth stretch of sand. Further out dark clouds blotted out the stars. A gust of wind, a forerunner of the distant storm, sent strands of hair drifting around her cheeks and raised gooseflesh on her bare arms.

In the instant she felt cold, Gabriel's jacket dropped around her shoulders, the weight of it deliciously warm, a hint of his clean masculine scent clinging to the fine dark weave.

Grateful for the warmth, she resisted the urge to meet his gaze and succumb to that particular madness again. She'd gone to the Castello tonight needing a knight in shining armor. Instead, she was here on an ancient watchtower balcony with the fascinatingly dangerous Gabriel Messena, the last man she had thought she would ever be alone with again.

Worse, she was feeling every one of the tingling symptoms of attraction that she had tried to feel for Zane, and failed.

Desperate to break what was becoming an uncomfortable silence, Gemma checked her wristwatch and quickly texted Sanchia. She knew it was late on Medinos and that Gemma could possibly be asleep, so she wouldn't be too worried if Gemma didn't call back right away.

She tried for a bright, relaxed smile as she hugged his jacket around her, soaking in the warmth. "Thank you. I guess I'm still acclimating."

Gabriel crossed his arms over his chest and leaned against the parapet, looking sleek and muscular and as graceful as a big cat. With his dark hair blowing around clean-cut cheekbones, he looked utterly at ease in the stark Mediterranean landscape. "If you want to know why I helped you, it's because I saw a piece about you and Zane in a newspaper. I felt responsible, since I was the one who originally recommended you for the job."

Gemma frowned at Gabriel's alleged involvement in her landing the Atraeus job in Sydney four years ago. Originally, it had been for a PA position in one of the Sydney hotels. She had thought at the time that it had been a minor miracle that she had beaten off a number of better-qualified applicants but she would never in her wildest dreams have imagined that Gabriel had helped her out. "I thought it was Elena Lyon who put in a reference."

Elena was a girlhood friend, also from Dolphin Bay, and well known to the Messena family, since her aunt had been the housekeeper who was supposed to have had the affair with Gabriel's father. Although Elena swore black and blue that the affair was nothing more than supposition and media hype.

Gabriel lifted his shoulders. "Maybe she did, but Constantine approved the appointment on my recommendation."

Gemma firmly suppressed a surge of pleasure that Gabriel hadn't forgotten about her altogether, that he'd cared enough about her to ensure she obtained a good job. "In that case, thank you, but I still don't understand why you thought you had to intervene then or now. I'm well used to looking after myself."

Gabriel was silent for a beat. "I'm sure you are. But what about the father you need for your child?"

Eight

Gemma froze. Her first thought was that he knew Sanchia was his, but then the way he had referred to her registered.

He had said "your child," not his child. Which meant he had probably read one of the gossipy snippets of information the tabloids had recently printed. Snippets which had implied that Zane was the father and thankfully hadn't included any real details about Sanchia, such as her age. The reporters had been more interested in repeating known facts about Zane rather than far less interesting facts about either herself or her daughter.

For a few taut seconds, the urge to confess to Gabriel that Sanchia was his was strong enough that she actually opened her mouth to speak, but the caution that had gripped her ever since the last nanny had accused her of being an unfit mother reasserted itself.

The custody situation was difficult enough without introducing the complication of Sanchia's biological father.

"That's why you intervened? Because you thought Zane wouldn't be interested in fatherhood?"

Gabriel frowned. "I intervened because I was the one who put you in a situation where you came into Zane's sphere of influence in the first place."

Gemma gripped the lapels of Gabriel's jacket, hugging it more closely against the wind, although that was a mistake, because the movement released more of his clean, masculine scent.

She went back to the issue of just how she had gotten her job. "What makes you so sure I wouldn't have gotten the job purely on merit?"

"Constantine wanted someone who could be trusted with confidentiality. I told him you could."

If Gemma had felt chilled before, she was warming up fast. Gabriel probably thought he was pouring oil on troubled waters, but as far as she was concerned it was more like pouring gasoline on a smoldering fire. "You mean I got the job because I kept quiet about sleeping with you?"

Her throat had automatically locked against the phrase *one-night stand.* Maybe it hadn't been special for him, but she had been caught up in the fairy-tale magic of the night, the indefinable feeling that the gorgeous man who had come to her rescue was special.

He shrugged. "A lot of people are affected by wealth. They have an agenda. That didn't seem to be the case with you."

She frowned at his summation of her character, even though it was on the positive side. Maybe it was simply that his view of her was so objective. She couldn't help thinking that if he had ever been even the tiniest bit in love with her, he wouldn't have seen her in such a cold, impersonal light.

Like an employee.

It highlighted an aspect of Gabriel's character that she had suspected had always been there. That in his heart of hearts, Gabriel valued control and slotting people into neat boxes more than he valued spontaneous love and affection.

It explained why his mother had thought he would accept a marriage to a well-connected, suitably rich and beautiful girl.

Suddenly, the idea that Gabriel could judge her for possibly wanting to make a good marriage, when it was obviously standard practice within the Messena family, made her bristle. "So you thought I had an agenda, as in trying to marry the boss."

His gaze narrowed warily. "It happens."

"And sometimes the agenda works the other way. There are plenty of employees who get sexually harassed."

"Point taken."

The piercing look Gabriel gave her made her feel distinctly uncomfortable and she hastily decided that it was time to drop this subject. He was referring to the relationship he thought she'd had with Zane, but the last thing she wanted him to do was remember back to what had happened six years ago and figure out that *he* could be the father. "Why should you care, anyway?"

He crossed his arms over his chest, and she had the distinct sense that she had been neatly maneuvered. "Because I have a proposition for you. You need a fiancé to get Sanchia back, and as it happens, I need one to short-circuit a clause in my father's will."

In clipped phrases he explained the glitch with the will that his uncle was presently exploiting in order to pressure Gabriel into a marriage he didn't want.

An absurd sense of relief gripped her at the explanation that Gabriel wasn't in love with some beautiful, perfect woman, but was trying to avoid an arranged marriage. It also cast a new light on his pursuit of her tonight that made a depressing kind of sense. He wasn't after her because of passion, but business.

Gabriel shrugged. "To cut a long story short, if you'll agree to be my fiancée for the period of time it takes me to gain full control of the bank, in exchange I can offer you an apartment, a job and whatever else you need to get your daughter back."

The offer was riveting, but tempted as she was to grab it, she couldn't ignore the danger of getting too close to Gabriel. "How long would you need me to pose as your fiancée?"

"A week at most. That should be enough time to convince the legal firm that handles the trust provision of the will."

Her mind was racing. She could do it. She could be Gabriel's fake fiancée for a week. After all, she was trained to act. How hard could it be? She drew a swift breath. "What kind of job?"

"The same thing you did for the Atraeus Group. The reason I came to Medinos was to meet with Constantine. He's starting up a new branch of Ambrosi Pearls in Auckland. I'll be taking care of the launch phase. We start advertising for staff next week."

Still feeling skittish and cautious, despite Gabriel offering her everything on her current wish list, Gemma took a deep breath and let the idea settle in. It was a new venture with an old established firm like Ambrosi, and the kind of opening she would have wanted to apply for anyway. The fact that Gabriel was only involved in the start-up phase meant that she could keep the job after their charade ended, which would be perfect.

With a new job and an apartment. It would mean that she could get Sanchia back immediately.

Before she could change her mind, Gemma said, 'Yes."

The momentary flash of surprise in Gabriel's gaze startled her. "You thought I was going to refuse."

"It crossed my mind, since the job combines a personal relationship with employment."

"I do believe there's a line drawn in the sand. It's called a personal contract."

A hint of impatience jerked his brows together. "Yes, but in this case we have a verbal agreement that the initial stages of this job involve some personal connection."

The startled recognition that Gabriel wanted more than just a charade set off alarm bells, although the alarm was almost totally drowned by a tingling heat that was dangerous.

She cleared her throat and tried to keep her tone smooth and professional. After all, Gabriel had just employed her as his PA. "Of course. Definitely. Within certain bounds."

And the first rule would be that if they were going to proceed, she needed to protect herself emotionally.

"Good." Gabriel's hands closed around her arms as he drew her slowly, mesmerisingly closer. "We have an understanding."

Gemma stiffened at the warmth of his touch, the instant fiery desire that swamped her. Somewhere in the back of her mind languished the concept that sleeping with the boss before they even got to the office was a very bad idea. "I'm not exactly sure what I understand."

"I guess what I'm trying to say is that I've always regretted what happened six years ago."

The words she had wanted to hear all those years ago shimmered through her, undermining every one of her reservations. "You can't be serious?"

Reaching out, he linked his fingers with hers and pulled her closer and, like a fool, unable to resist him, she went

The warmth of his breath drifted against her throat.
"Why not?"

Because it was too late for the luxury of the wild, fatal
attraction that was zinging through her. Too late for a replay of what had happened six years ago: the starry night,
the champagne. The rescue.

She drew a swift breath. And all of those things followed by the off-the-register lovemaking.

The kind of lovemaking she would in all likelihood
never again experience, because realistically, the type of
man she would end up marrying would be a dependable,
average kind of guy who placed a high value on family. He
wouldn't be either dangerously attractive or mega-wealthy.
First off, Sanchia would have to like him.

A deep feeling of depression hit her at the thought that
marriage with someone else would ultimately be depen-
dent on Sanchia's needs, not hers. That it would be an up-
hill struggle to find someone other than Gabriel who she
could settle for.

Until that moment she hadn't understood just how vivid
and exceptional her response to Gabriel was.

Resolutely, she reminded herself of the non-negotiable
list of things she needed to establish in her life over the
next few weeks. She could not allow herself to be sucked
back into a dream that had already proved to have no substance.

Lifting her chin, she met the cool determination of Gabriel's gaze. "I didn't think that what happened had meant
that much to you. After all, it was only one night."

"A night I've never forgotten."

The deep timbre of his voice shivered through her. One
more half step and he was so close she could feel the heat
flowing off his big body, catch the scent of his skin. He
cupped her chin, hesitated, then lowered his mouth to hers.

The kiss, his lips soft, was little more than a touch, a tester, but suddenly her heart was pounding and she was having difficulty breathing.

She considered what he was offering, right here, right now. Another passionate interlude.

But the sting of that thought was drowned out by another much more powerful consideration. Despite wanting to move on from the powerful attraction that drew her to Gabriel, she hadn't; she still wanted him.

Everything was in place, the starry night sky, the sea, the sense of isolation and privacy, and somewhere inside a too-comfortable couch or very large bed. It was a virtual replay of the night six years ago.

A gust of wind tugged at his hair, and the moon slid behind a cloud. As the gloom of the approaching squall deepened, he cupped her face.

The pads of his thumbs swept over her cheeks, sending rivulets of fire shimmering through her. "Say yes."

She froze in the rawness of the moment, the flash of need that melted her bones.

Her hair whipped around her cheeks. The night was turning wild and elemental. If she wanted to keep things on a professional basis, she should go, hand his jacket back and walk up to the road before the approaching deluge hit. She had her phone; she could order a taxi or ring the hotel concierge, who would send someone to pick her up. But she knew that she wouldn't be doing any such thing, and suddenly there was no air. "Yes."

In answer, Gabriel dipped his head and laid his mouth on hers. Emboldened, she dropped her phone in Gabriel's jacket pocket and braced her hands on his shoulders. The warmth from the muscle beneath her palms sent a quiver of heat through her, as flash after flash of memories from that long-ago night turned the air molten. Heart pour ing, she lifted up on her toes, wrapped her arms around his neck and kissed him back.

Her faint awkwardness, the fear that he would know just how unpracticed she was at this, disappeared as his arms tightened around her waist. The heat from his body burned through the thin lace and silk of her dress as she shifted closer still.

The fierce desire she couldn't afford cascaded through her along with a sudden clear memory of exactly what had seduced her six years ago. Apart from the dark and dangerous outer package, Gabriel had been unexpectedly gentle.

He had gone to some lengths to make sure that nothing happened that she didn't want. They had slow danced, they had laughed and then they had walked along the beach and ended up on the tiny adjacent island, which was reached by a causeway.

The only slip-up had been when they had both lost control and had ended up making love without protection. Even then, Gabriel had apologized. And when they had spent the rest of the night snuggled together just talking she had felt dizzyingly, almost terrifyingly, happy.

In some indefinable way they had connected. For want of a better word, Gabriel had been nice, which was why it had hurt so much when he hadn't ever followed up.

Out at sea lightning flashed and the damp pressure of the wind increased. Not in the least intimidated, instead drawn by the primitive fierceness of the storm, the clean, simple, uncomplicated nature of it, she fitted herself even closer to Gabriel.

Rain spattered, shockingly cold against her overheated skin. Gabriel lifted his head and muttered something short in liquid Medinian.

A split second later the heavens opened up, the deluge king. The world tilted as Gemma found herself lifted and cradled in Gabriel's arms. Two long strides and they were inside. The sharp thud of the door slamming behind them punctuated the wild turn the night had taken.

Gemma's feet found the floor and Gabriel's jacket slipped off her shoulders. She registered the faint clunk of her phone, which was in the jacket pocket. She dragged chilled fingers through her hair, which clung to her skin like damp seaweed.

Gabriel stayed her hand. "Let me do that."

In contrast to the fury outside, his touch, as he smoothed her hair back into some semblance of order, was gentle and deliberate. But it wasn't what she wanted.

It had been six years since they had made love, years in which she'd been busy and fulfilled with work, study and parenting, but where, essentially, she'd remained alone.

She had tried to resurrect her dating life, but somehow she just hadn't had the enthusiasm for any of the very nice men she had occasionally dated. As hard as she'd tried she hadn't wanted anyone, until now. One glance from Gabriel and every nerve ending in her body had been humming.

With fingers that felt clumsy and inept, she dragged at the buttons of his shirt until it hung open over a broad chest and mouthwateringly tight abs. He shrugged free of the damp shirt, tossing it on the floor, then pulled her close and kissed her.

His hands framing her hips, he walked her backward. The quality of the light changed as they traversed the lamp-lit sitting room and entered a darker, quieter room.

An enormous bed, piled with pillows and draped in an ornate, burnished coverlet, floated on a sea of dark oak floorboards, dominating a bedroom that was an arresting mixture of modern severity and lavish excess.

She felt the loosening of her dress as the zip released. Anxiety gripped her at the thought of being naked with

Gabriel after all this time, of the mechanics of making love after years of being emotionally and sexually closed down. She might have been stuck in a time warp, but he hadn't, and her inadequacies were abruptly choking.

She sensed his frown rather than saw it. "What's wrong?"

"It's been a while."

"How long?"

She ducked her head against his shoulder, her face burning. "Since—the pregnancy."

He pulled her close, fitting her against the muscled contours of his body and the awkwardness shimmered into heat. Soothed by the dimness, she eased her arms out of the shoulder straps and let her dress drop to the floor.

His fingers threaded into her damp hair, tilted her face back so he could look into her eyes. To her surprise, his mouth was quirked in a half smile. "Don't worry. You might have forgotten, but I haven't."

Nine

When he murmured that there was no rush, that they could take their time, she reached for a trace of the old levity, the fun side of her that had shriveled when the custody situation with Sanchia had blown up. "Are you telling me you're slow?" Her own experience was that he was fast, hot and selective.

"Not where you're concerned." He grinned as he dipped his head and nibbled on her lobe, and her brain temporarily froze.

Emboldened by the humor and the sweetness, she leaned into him, wrapped her arms around his waist and soaked in his heat, his delicious scent.

She felt her bra strap release. In a definitely slick move he dispensed with the bra, leaving her in just her panties, and cupped her breasts. Her breath hitched in her throat. "That was sneaky."

He grinned, making her heart flip. "You should know by now that all guys are sneaky."

Bending his head he took her breast into her mouth. Sensation hummed through her, coiled low in her belly, and any awkwardness sizzled out of existence.

Gabriel lifted his head, fierce satisfaction registering. A split second later he picked her up and placed her on the bed then peeled out of his trousers before joining her.

Gabriel fully clothed was impressive; naked, he was beautiful. And, for the moment, *hers*. He let her touch him and shape him and learn the intriguing planes and angles of his body, the hard muscle and hair-roughened skin.

Keeping her close against the furnace heat of his body, he reached into the drawer of a bedside cabinet and found a condom. Lightning jagged through the sky, illuminating the room as he sheathed himself. Seconds later, when she stretched herself on him, the tension that had been slowly building wound unbearably tight.

His gaze locked with hers as he gripped her hips and she logged the fact that, as controlled as he was, Gabriel had been keeping his desire rigidly in check.

With easy strength he rolled so that he was on top. Tension coiled as she felt him lodge between her legs, the heavy pressure, the weight of him anchoring her to the bed.

Rain spattered on the wall of glass, filling the night with the rhythm of the storm. Heat and dampness seemed to explode, and suddenly the deep, achy throb low in her belly, the humid heat of the night was too much. Coiling her arms around Gabriel's neck, she pulled him closer, pressing up against him. With a hoarse groan and one heavy thrust he was inside her, the night dissolving, one with the wild storm, as they clung together.

* * *

Long minutes ticked by while they lay entwined. The storm passed, leaving behind a dripping quiet and the heavy roar of surf hitting the white sand beach below the house.

Gabriel pulled her close. This time he took charge, making love to her with a slow intensity that took her breath.

Long minutes later, sleep tugged at Gemma along with the knowledge that now that they had made love, it was going to be impossible to keep Gabriel at arm's length for the duration of their fake engagement.

Heat shimmered through her at the thought that they could make love again, that Gabriel wanted her. Making love had been a mistake: she'd known it, but it was too late now. The damage was done.

Her priority now had to be to concentrate on the professional aspects of the new job, which meant no sex. She needed to establish a working relationship with Gabriel that would fulfill the part he wanted her to play but that would not compromise her new job or her emotions.

Creating a professional distance was going to be tricky, especially with her willpower at such a low ebb, but it wasn't as if she hadn't coped without sex before.

She could do it, but after tonight she was aware it would take all of her acting skills.

Her last conscious thought was that the first thing she needed to do was leave. If she woke up with Gabriel they would make love again, which would be counterproductive. For now she would sleep, just for an hour....

Gabriel waited until Gemma's breathing evened out before gently disengaging himself from the arm draped across his midriff and climbing out of the rumpled bed.

The room was filled with a pressing darkness, barely

penetrated by the glow of a single lamp out in the lounge, but even so, he could clearly make out Gemma's form. Against the burnished coverlet, her pale skin glowed like a pearl and the rich flood of red hair, leached of its color, looked like ebony on his pillows.

He studied the pure line of Gemma's profile and the fierce need that had overtaken him earlier reasserted itself.

He wanted her, and he now knew how much she wanted him. The minute he'd kissed her earlier in the evening, the intervening years had seemed to dissolve, the chemistry instant and explosive.

Snagging his pants from the floor, he padded through to the bathroom, freshened up and pulled on the trousers. After draining a glass of water in the kitchen, he found Gemma's canvas bag where she'd left it in the wine cellar and carried it through to his study.

Closing the door behind him, he flicked on a lamp and set the bag on his desk. Setting the bottle of champagne down on the glossy surface, he drew out the liquid soft mass of black silk and lace. His stomach tightened as his guess that it was lingerie, not a wrap, was confirmed.

As he pulled out what was without doubt a pretty negligee, he noticed something fluttering and white. A sales tag that Gemma in her impulsive haste to seduce Zane had clearly forgotten to remove.

His fingers tightened on the garment, elation gripping him.

The negligee wasn't the symbol of a seasoned sexual relationship. It was new and unused.

It was the final confirmation.

The craziness of the night now made perfect sense. He understood Gemma's position, her need to draw Zane into a committed relationship.

She had failed. Zane had already been committed to

another woman, for which Gabriel was profoundly thankful. Because, as of an hour ago, as far as Gabriel was concerned, Gemma now belonged to him.

He noticed a glossy magazine in the bottom of the bag. Frowning, he pulled it out. It was folded open at an article, "How To Seduce Your Man in Ten Easy Moves." He flicked through it, skimming a collection of articles on what men really wanted and a list of exotic tactical dating maneuvers that were "guaranteed to succeed."

The evidence of the off-the-wall solutions Gemma had come up with to solve her custody problem should have been a turnoff. Instead it only proved just how unprepared and unpracticed Gemma was at making love. The magazine further underlined her lack of experience with men in general. He knew from what she'd told him that she hadn't made love since she'd gotten pregnant.

The thought of Gemma with a baby made his stomach tighten. Heated tension hummed through him. If the explosive attraction between them was not simply an obsessive sexual attraction and blossomed into an actual relationship, Gemma could one day be pregnant with his child.

The thought was out in left field, and that was where it would stay, he decided, until he was certain. He would not repeat his father's mistake by risking the calm order he had worked so hard to restore to the business and his family by succumbing to a searing attraction.

Gemma surfaced from a restless dream instantly aware of the warmth and weight of Gabriel's arm where it lay draped across her waist. A small sensual shock brought her fully awake as she registered the delicious heat of his body, the sheer intimacy of waking up and finding him sprawled next to her.

Glancing at the digital clock on the bedside table she

discovered that, despite trying to stay awake until Gabriel fell asleep, at some point she must have slept deeply, because it was now after five in the morning.

It was past time to go, although she was finding it unexpectedly difficult to revert to the businesslike mode she had decided was the only sensible way forward with this relationship.

Knowing she shouldn't, she turned her head on the pillow and studied Gabriel's face in the dimness of the early morning light. Hair tousled, his lashes inky crescents against olive skin, he looked younger, and uncannily like the Gabriel of six years ago.

Her heart squeezed tight in her chest. In sleep, he looked oddly vulnerable and she had to fight the urge to simply cuddle up to him and immerse herself in the simple pleasure of his heat and warmth. She had to keep reminding herself that Gabriel was no tame pussycat; if she gave an inch, he would take a mile. If she was going to manage her way safely through the next few days, without falling in love with him all over again, she would have to be strict with herself.

And the first rule, now that Gabriel was her boss and her soon-to-be fake fiancé, was no more sex. She had given in to him tonight because she simply hadn't been able to resist. She had felt starved of affection, starved of love. Maybe because of all the stress and the shock of the custody battle she had been unexpectedly vulnerable.

Whatever the cause, if she wanted to enforce the no-sex rule, she would have to leave now, before she was enticed back into his arms and lost her willpower altogether.

She intended to leave him a note, outlining her conditions. She was certain, given the businesslike way Gabriel had couched her new job description, that once he adjusted to the fact that she would not continue to sleep with him, that he would be happy with the idea.

Shifting slightly, just enough to dislodge Gabriel's arm, Gemma inched nearer the edge of the bed. Fully awake now, the chill of early morning registered. The gray light of dawn pushed through the enormous expanse of glass that framed the panoramic view of the Mediterranean, revealing the hedonistic chaos of the bedroom. Her clothes and Gabriel's were scattered where they had discarded them, and at some point the silk coverlet had slipped off the bed and now lay tumbled on the floor.

Outside the piercing cry of a gull was loud enough that Gemma held her breath as Gabriel stirred restlessly. The rumpled silk sheet slipped low on his hips, exposing his long muscular torso and the intriguing line of hair that arrowed to his loins.

Setting her jaw against the instant tug on her senses, and annoyed with herself that after years of abstinence she was actually fickle enough to let herself be ruled by desire, Gemma worked her way free of the gorgeous, entangling sheets. Her feet landed softly on the bare expanse of the hardwood floor, the cool of the marble-smooth wood sending an involuntary shiver through her.

Overpoweringly aware of her nakedness and the faint stiffness that telegraphed just what she had been doing for half the night, Gemma was tempted to drag the silk coverlet off the floor and pull it around herself as a covering. Reluctantly, she abandoned the idea. It was a miracle she hadn't woken Gabriel up already, and modesty came a bad second next to her need to leave and reestablish her collapsed boundaries.

Padding silently, she found her panties. As she straightened, she caught a ghostly view of herself in a carved gold full-length mirror. Her mind instantly slid back to the riveting, addictive pleasure she'd experienced making love with Gabriel. Cheeks warming, she scooped up her bra, which was dangling over the arm of a chair, and a little desperately reminded herself of the downside of all this.

Six years, and she had made the same mistake with the same guy, and once again without settling any of the vital issues, such as love and commitment. The only saving grace was that this time they had used contraception so she was safe from a second pregnancy.

Despite the fact that she absolutely did not want to get pregnant, the thought was oddly depressing, because it brought home the fact that as irresistible as the passion they had shared was, love had definitely not been involved.

It impressed upon her the need to stick to her resolve that there would be no more sex, because giving in would only signal to Gabriel that she would happily accept sex over love and commitment, that she didn't require him to value her.

When the fake engagement was over, she could work on forgetting Gabriel. She had done it before; she could do it again.

As she bent to pick up her lace dress, which lay pooled on the floor, her fingers brushed Gabriel's discarded shirt, which was lying next to it. Irresistibly tempted, she picked up the shirt instead.

The faint, clean masculine scent that clung to the fabric made her stomach clench on a zing of desire. Out of nowhere a shimmering wave of emotion hit her. If she'd had any sense she wouldn't have done such a silly, sentimental thing as picking up his shirt, but now that she had, she didn't want to relinquish it.

It was silly. She didn't need a memento of their time together. She would see Gabriel again in just a few days when she started at Ambrosi Pearls, but by then their relationship would be back on a proper professional footing. Apart from the necessities of the charade, there would be no more intimacy, no more passionate kisses, no more snuggling in bed. And absolutely no more sex.

Although, it was a fact that the shirt would be a more practical piece of clothing to wear on Medinos in broad daylight than the sexy lace gown.

A rustling sound, Gabriel turning over in bed, made her freeze in place. She risked a quick look. He was now lying sprawled on his stomach on the side of the bed she had vacated. In the gray light slanting across the bed, the long line of his back looked muscular and sleek, his tanned skin exotically dark against the white silk. From the even tenor of his breathing, and his utter, boneless relaxation, he had simply turned over and was unaware that she had left the bed.

Letting out a silent breath of relief, Gemma padded quickly from the room. Minutes later, she had found her bag and retrieved her phone from Gabriel's jacket pocket. She located a bathroom off the main living area. After using the facilities and washing her hands and face, she quickly dressed.

As she fastened the buttons of Gabriel's shirt, she checked the effect in the large vanity mirror. Gauzy and white, the shoulder seams fell halfway to her elbows and the shirttails covered her to her knees.

She tried not to notice the wild tousle of her hair, or the fact that her mouth was faintly swollen and there was a faint red patch on her neck where Gabriel's stubbled jaw must have scraped her skin.

A tinge of misery edged through her resolve as she rolled up the trailing shirt cuffs until they were bunched just above her wrists. The result wasn't stylish, but it was acceptable. She could easily be someone who had gone for an early morning swim and had decided to use a shirt as a cover-up.

Her heart leaped in her chest as she checked her wristwatch and saw how much time had passed. She still needed to write her note. If she was going to get out of the house before Gabriel woke up, she would have to hurry.

Not bothering to finger comb her hair, she picked up her bag and padded to the kitchen. Finding a piece of notepaper, she quickly dashed off an explanatory note. She included her email and phone numbers, anchored it on the counter with a cup then padded to the front door. Remembering to turn the alarm off, she eased the door open and stepped outside. Her heart hammered as she gently closed the door. Simultaneously, her phone chimed.

Sending a brief prayer upward that she had gotten out of the house before Sanchia rang, she answered the call as she walked quickly, avoiding the drive and instead heading for the beach. The route to town was more direct and it would be easier on her bare feet.

The conversation was grounding. It was a relief to put her own needs aside and think of Sanchia's instead, and for her daughter the equation was simple—she needed the security of her mother back in her life.

Gemma checked her watch again as she said good-night and ended the call. She then rang the airline and changed her flight. The extra cost made her stomach hollow out, but now that she had a job, she would be able to replenish her bank account.

A fifteen-minute walk to the hotel, and hopefully any press would still be in bed after the late night. She had an hour and a half until her flight. She had already done most of her packing, so all she really needed to do was pile the few things she'd left out into her case, zip it closed then catch a taxi. She would check in and board straight away.

Once she got to Sydney, she would sort all of the furniture and possessions she had left in storage, dispose of the things she didn't need and have the rest freighted to New Zealand.

Number two on her list of things to do was change her appearance. The idea was extreme, but she was tired of the media sneaking around after her, and with her stylish clothes and red hair she was just too easy to spot.

As long as her welfare caseworker knew she was engaged, there was no need for a media circus. She was determined that the move back home would be a complete fresh start, in all ways.

Tears welled as she walked along the pristine beauty of the shore, waves curling into foam at her feet. Dashing the moisture away, she kept her gaze on the distinctive shape of the Atraeus Resort, midway along the misted curve of the beach, and resisted the urge to look back.

She'd had a wonderful night and had said her own private emotional goodbyes to the relationship, such as it was. The small kernel of hurt that not once had Gabriel mentioned any degree of emotional involvement was the most difficult thing to acknowledge. Maybe he felt he hadn't needed to because it wasn't as if it was the first time they had made love, but the lack mattered to Gemma.

It underlined the need to enforce her own rules on the situation, and one of those was that if they were going to be engaged for a week, then during that time Gabriel would have to play his part. He would have to value her as if he *did* love her.

It was a small point, but it was important to Gemma. A man valuing his fiancée meant a ring, flowers, dinner—all of the important elements of a courtship that he had happily bypassed both times because she had slept with him so quickly.

* * *

Gabriel woke with the sun on his face and the space beside him in bed empty.

The second his lids flipped open he knew that Gemma wasn't just missing from his bed; she was gone.

He should have seen it coming, read it in the quiet way she had tried to distance herself from him in bed after making love. A distance he had obliterated by the simple expedient of wrapping an arm around her waist and drawing her close.

The first thing he saw as he climbed out of bed was her dress and shoes still on the floor. Padding through to the sitting room he noted that the canvas bag was gone, and the shirt he had tossed over the arm of a chair was missing.

He muttered something short and flat under his breath. After pulling on a pair of dark pants, he walked out onto the balcony. His jaw tightened as he noted the trail of footprints in the sand. Sliding his phone out of his pants pocket, he dialed the hotel and asked to be put through to security.

A brief conversation later, he hung up. He had thought Gemma might disappear for the day, but it was worse than that. She had just left for the airport.

Moving quickly, Gabriel walked through to the kitchen and found a note anchored to the counter. The message was simple, politely thanking him for the night together and stating the new terms of their relationship, which from now on, owing to Gemma's status as his employee, would not include sex.

Gabriel's fingers closed on the piece of paper, crumpling it. She had ditched him, close enough, and he hadn't seen it coming.

Although, thinking back, it was not the first time. Technically, he had ended their last relationship, but Gemma had never at any point tried to cling to him or get him back.

Six years ago she had seemed unruffled by the fact that he had no space for a relationship.

He smoothed out the crumpled note and reread it, frowning at the businesslike language, the small P.S. that stated that they would both have to play their roles as an engaged couple to the letter.

He frowned. What did that mean?

He was not exactly au fait with the whole process of getting engaged. As far as he was concerned this was just a sham that would facilitate his control of his company.

And keep Gemma in his bed until he could figure out just where the relationship was heading.

He finished dressing, not bothering with a shower and shave. By the time he accelerated away from the house, only fifteen minutes had passed since he had first woken up. Even so, he was certain he was going to be too late to catch Gemma.

As he drove, he dialed the airport. Precious minutes ticked away while the call was shuffled to someone more senior and manifests were checked. He had thrown his weight around and used every bit of influence he had, but by the time it was ascertained which of the international flights Gemma was on, the plane had been cleared for takeoff.

Pulling over onto the side of the winding coast road with its stunning views, Gabriel climbed out of the Maserati. Gaze narrowed against the glare of the sun, he searched the blue arc of the sky and saw the jet in the air.

The sea breeze whipped his hair around his jaw and flattened his shirt against his torso as he watched the jet for long seconds.

Despite all of the unanswered questions he had about Gemma, his unwillingness to commit, it was an out he didn't want.

Too late to realize he should have cossetted Gemma more, treated her like a date instead of rushing her into bed. His approach had lacked finesse; it had lacked even basic good manners.

But the problem was, he wasn't certain how much more he wanted from this relationship. All he knew was that Gemma had fascinated him six years ago, and she fascinated him now. They hardly knew each other, and both times the passion had been too quick, the situations pressurized. What they needed was the one thing they had never had: time together.

Although he had ensured that they would have that now.

Relief filled him that he had tied her to an employment contract. He had time on his side. After last night he was certain that, despite the odds, Gemma was emotionally involved. No woman could respond as she had and not be.

The addition to the note about playing their roles as an engaged couple slid back into his mind and a small, salient fact registered.

When he had flipped through the magazine in Gemma's holdall during the night, he had noticed a large section on women being valued in relationships, with passages underlined in blue ink as if Gemma had read and reread the article, committing it to memory.

He had made love to Gemma, and now she wanted to be courted.

Sliding behind the wheel of the Maserati, Gabriel put the car in gear and drove back toward Medinos.

Now that he had some facts to work with, he could form a strategy. He was a little rusty with dating, and it was a fact that he had never courted a woman, but he had a major advantage. Gemma had slept with him twice, despite his utter lack of courtship, which meant that she had a definite weakness he could, and would, exploit.

Sexually, she couldn't resist him.

Ten

Five days later, Gemma walked toward the plush ground-floor offices in Newmarket, Auckland, for her first day of work at the newest Ambrosi Pearl House.

Gleaming glass doors slid open, flashing back the conservative new image—she hesitated to call it an actual disguise—that she was still adjusting to.

Alarmed by the attention of the press when she had arrived in Sydney, and their interest in the fact that she was now, apparently, having a hot affair with Gabriel, she had made a beeline for her hairdresser and changed the color of her hair to a low-key sable brown.

Once she had made the initial breakthrough of changing her hair color, she had distilled the reinvention process down to rummaging through good quality secondhand shops for shoes and clothing in neutral shades. It had been a productive exercise because she had found a number of exquisitely cut, designer-label items for very cheap prices.

Evidently, this season no one wanted to be seen dead in either oatmeal or beige.

Today, instead of her normal clear, bright colors and fun lace and ruffles, she was wearing a biscotti suit. She refused to call the color beige. Fake glasses and her hair smoothed into a prim French pleat added to the office look.

But as boring as the color of the suit was, it wasn't as low-key as she would have liked. The jacket cinched in at the waist, emphasizing the fullness of her breasts and the curve of her hips. The skirt was also a little on the short side, making her legs look even longer. She had added high heels to the outfit, because she had made a judgment call and balanced the need to start her new job incognito against looking frumpy.

So far her new image had worked like a dream. No one had hounded her at the airport or tried to photograph her, and it was no wonder. When she had checked her appearance in the mirror that morning, she had barely recognized herself.

A workman wearing a faded gray tank, tanned, muscled biceps on show as he painted a wall, grinned at her and clutched at his heart as she strolled past.

Gemma found herself grinning back as she headed for the elevators and the second floor, where the offices were based. She just bet the guy was married with children— they all were—but the harmless bit of fun was soothing and exactly the lift she needed.

Boring in designer neutrals, but not dead in the water... yet.

Aware that she had almost veered into forbidden territory in thinking sexually about Gabriel, she refocused in a more positive direction.

Just that morning she had bought Sanchia a tiny hot-pink tutu and a pair of ballet slippers. She was going to give them to her once she had gotten the all-clear from the welfare caseworker and was able to move Sanchia back in with her. Now that she had a guaranteed income, she could afford the ballet lessons Sanchia wanted.

She pressed the call button on the elevator then stepped inside as the doors swished open. The sound of a firm tread behind her signaled that someone else had just entered the building.

She heard the low timbre of a masculine voice as the doors closed and froze, certain it was Gabriel.

On edge, she exited on the second floor and walked to the front desk. The receptionist, an elegant blonde called Bonny, was expecting her. Gemma glanced around as she followed Bonny through a smoothly carpeted corridor, amazed at the speed with which the new Ambrosi Pearls venture had been put together.

By the time she had reached Sydney, the employment contract had already been in her email in-box. All she'd had to do was print it out, sign it and fax it to the number supplied. Within an hour of doing so, she had received a flight ticket, which had surprised her, as there had been no mention that her travel expenses would be paid. The following day, she had received the lease to her new apartment in the mail, and had sent a certified copy off to her welfare caseworker.

Bonny introduced her to another very efficient older woman called Maris, who took her through to Gabriel's large, sleek office, which was dominated by a large mahogany desk. Although the most notable feature by far was that one wall contained a collection of computer screens flashing up nonstop financial information.

Maris indicated she should take a seat while she fetched

coffee, but Gemma, her gaze glued to the screens, was too wired to sit.

Moments later, Gabriel, larger than life and broodingly attractive in a dark suit, a pristine white shirt and a red tie knotted at his throat stepped into the office and closed the door behind him.

Despite coaching herself for this moment, her heart slammed in her chest and a highly inappropriate image of Gabriel naked and sprawled in silk sheets popped into her mind.

"How was your flight?"

Before she could reply, his brows jerked together. "What have you done to your hair?"

The sudden switch in topic threw Gemma even more off balance. "I needed a change."

He was close enough now that she could see the fine lines fanning out around his eyes, the dark circles beneath, as if lately, like her, he'd been losing sleep.

"And it's not just the hair." His gaze raked over the biscotti suit. He frowned at her glasses. "Since when did you need glasses?"

She drew a breath at his proximity, the sheer energy of his presence, the knowledge that, just days ago, she had woken up in his bed. "Since last week."

Knowledge registered in his gaze. "The story in the press."

The one that very wrongly stated that she had jumped out of Zane's bed, but had unfortunately got it right by saying she had jumped straight into Gabriel's. "I got tired of being a target."

"So this is a disguise?"

"I prefer to call it a reinvention."

His frown deepened. "If you needed protection, you

should have asked me. I could have made sure you got home without being bothered."

Gemma's fingers tightened on the strap of her handbag. "The only reason I get 'bothered' is because of my connection to your family."

"That's regrettably true." Reaching out, he wrapped a finger around a tendril that had escaped the French pleat, his attention once more diverted by her hair. "How long will the brown color last?"

"Sable," she corrected.

The heated patience in his dark eyes told her he didn't care about the shade. "How long?"

For a split second, caught in the blatant possessiveness of the demand, as if he had a right to know intimate details about something as personal as her hair color, she was spun back to the night on Medinos. His intense focus on her then had been utterly seductive—the possessiveness of his touch, the way he'd held her after they had made love, even in sleep, as if he truly hadn't wanted to let her go.

Although that had been a sham. After she had left, Gabriel had not contacted her except in an official capacity, which had proved that their night of passion hadn't really been important to him. "Does it matter?"

"It does to me."

She drew a sharp breath, the proximity of his closeness, his intense focus weaving its spell as her breasts tightened against the fit of her jacket and the slow ache of arousal shimmered to life. Her jaw firmed as she cleared her mind of any crazy romantic illusions. Gabriel's attitude toward her appearance was purely about image. With her appearance toned down, she no doubt didn't quite fit his vision of a fiancée. "Well, it shouldn't."

He shrugged, let the strand of hair go and strolled around behind his desk. "Then I guess we should talk about what's really important. Why did you walk out on me on Medinos?"

She blinked. There it was again—the illusion that he was her lover, that he genuinely cared. "I left a note."

"I read it."

Heart tight in her chest, she rose to her feet, too tense to sit, and found herself staring blindly at the bank of screens flowing with financial data. "I can't have a relationship with you and work for you at the same time."

"But that's exactly what you agreed to do."

She frowned. "We both know I agreed to a pretense, not—"

"Sex."

She threw Gabriel an irritated look, but his face was oddly bland and devoid of emotion. "That's right."

A heavy silence descended on the room. Out in the next office she could hear a phone buzzing, and farther afield she could hear the blare of a car horn, the hum of city traffic. Suddenly Gabriel was close enough that she could feel his heat all down one side.

"You did agree to be my fiancée. We can't do that without touching." To illustrate, he picked up one hand and deliberately threaded his fingers through hers.

A new tension flooded her. She drew a deep breath and tried not to respond. "I've got no problem with appearing to be close in public."

"Good. And you're going to need to dress a little more—" His gaze skimmed the biscotti suit again as if something about it displeased him intensely. He shook his head. "Where did you get that suit?"

She snatched her hand back. "Does it matter?"

"Not really." He had his cell in his hand. He pressed a number to speed dial. A quick conversation later and he hung up. "I've just rung one of the twins, Sophie. She has a designer boutique at the Atraeus Hotel. She should be able to help us."

Gemma blinked at the fact that Gabriel was actually involving a member of his family in the charade. "What do you mean, 'us'?"

His expression was oddly bland. "'Us' as in an engaged couple. We're going shopping."

A brief tap on the door cut through the thickening silence that had followed Gabriel's pronouncement.

Gabriel clamped down on the edgy impatience that, lately, seemed to have become a defining characteristic as Maris walked in with a tray and set it down on the coffee table.

Gemma accepted one of the paper cups that Maris must have sourced from a nearby café as Maris chatted cheerfully. Jaw locked, Gabriel picked up the remaining coffee and stoically waited out the interruption.

Gemma, looking irritatingly unruffled and disarmingly sexy in her secretarial outfit despite the boring color, fielded Maris's superficial questions with a smooth expertise that reminded him that she had been Zane's very competent PA for some years.

As Maris left, he deliberately strolled to the bank of windows that overlooked the street, forcing himself to ease back on the pressure.

Before Gemma had arrived, he had done a standard security check on her. It had been simple enough, given that, courtesy of this temporary position as CEO of Ambrosi Pearls in Auckland, he had access to the Atraeus personnel database.

It shouldn't have been a surprise to find out that she had a degree in performance arts. He could see her creative flare in the scenario with Zane on Medinos and now in this morning's performance.

Finding out that Gemma was trained to act had cast a new light on the impression he had received that she could walk away from him easily. The knowledge that Gemma hadn't slept with anyone since she'd gotten pregnant told him that she didn't give her affections lightly. Put together, those two pieces of information suggested that the fact that he had gotten her back at all was significant.

Cancel significant. He was almost sure that beneath the brisk, professional facade Gemma was still in love with him.

It was the only thing that made sense of her allowing him to make love to her on Medinos.

Every instinct told him that if he messed up now and she walked out, he wouldn't get another chance. On Medinos he had blundered in, locked into his own need and been determined to get his way.

This time, he was determined to keep her close. For a week, maybe longer, he had carte blanche to spoil Gemma, and he intended to do just that.

He finished the coffee and dropped the cup in the trash can beside his desk. He began to outline what would be involved with the temporary engagement. "A week, at least—"

"You said a week on Medinos."

"It could take longer."

There was a small silence as Gemma digested his pronouncement.

Gabriel decided the best tactic was to continue on as if the gray area didn't exist. "Tonight we're having dinner with Mario and Eva. She's a wedding planner—"

Gemma's head came up. "Eva Atraeus? Is she the one your mother and Mario want you to marry?"

Gabriel logged the look of horror on Gemma's face

that his family was lobbying for a marriage between first cousins.

The whole idea was archaic, dynastic, downright Machiavellian in his opinion, and despite the tension amusement tugged at him. "Mario's pushing that one. I think my mother could be looking outside the family."

When Gemma appeared outraged rather than amused, he shrugged and gave up on the joke, although a part of him was loving it that Gemma was mad on his behalf. "Now you're beginning to see what I'm up against," he murmured. "High maintenance doesn't cut it with my family. But, to put your mind at rest, Mario's not trying to sell his daughter into an incestuous marriage. Eva Atraeus isn't a blood relative, she's adopted."

Her gaze flashed. "I'm relieved. If that's the case, I don't know why you didn't ask her—"

"No."

Gemma was silent for a long drawn-out moment, as if trying to gauge whether there was any flexibility in the one short word he'd used. "So why, exactly, do you need to take me shopping?"

Gabriel dragged at his tie, feeling suddenly way out of his depth. "Both Mario and Eva will expect you to be wearing designer clothes and jewelry."

Gabriel frowned as Gemma extracted a small diary and pen from her purse and made a note, as if she was an efficient employee following instructions. "What time is dinner, and where?"

"Eight. I had planned to cater the dinner at my apartment."

She frowned behind the glasses and he had to control the urge to pluck them off the delicate bridge of her nose.

"We're not going out to a restaurant?"

"Not tonight." He watched as she made another small, very efficient note. "Did you want to go out?"

"What I want isn't at issue."

The coolness in her voice informed him that he had made a mistake. It occurred to him, too late, that he had somehow blundered into what his twin sisters, Francesca and Sophie, termed "value" territory. "Mario's old. I didn't want to present him with a fait accompli in a public place."

Instantly, her expression softened and Gabriel found himself relaxing at the hint of approval.

Gemma placed the pen and notebook in her handbag. "What happens if you can't remove Mario as trustee?"

Back on familiar ground, Gabriel propped himself on the edge of his desk. "Mario can't interfere in the day-to-day running of the bank. His power of veto applies to big-ticket investments, which is affecting some of our biggest clients and almost every member of my family. If Nick can't obtain his financing for a big development, he'll have to pull out of the bank and go elsewhere. Both Kyle and Damian have large projects on hold until Mario agrees to release funds." He shrugged. "Their loyalty to me is hurting them."

"So this is hurting your family."

Something relaxed inside of him at Gemma's insight. Family was big with both the Messena and the Atraeus clans, which was the reason he had been reluctant to remove Mario with a psychological evaluation. He was old, but he was family, and until the past six months, he had been an asset. "That's right."

Setting her coffee down, Gemma rose to her feet and walked over to the windows, ostensibly more interested in what was going on down in the street than the tension that vibrated between them. After an interminable few moments, she turned. "Okay. I can do the shopping thing. But I get to choose what I wear."

"Just one proviso. No beige."

Gemma looked faintly disconcerted, as if she'd forgotten their conversation about her new repressed look. "No problem."

Her phone chimed, and Gabriel tensed as she fished her cell out of her bag. The call went through to voice mail and he wondered grimly if it had been Zane she had just ignored, or worse, some other man he didn't know about.

As annoyed as he was, Gabriel didn't make the mistake of pressuring her about the call, sensing that if he pushed too hard she could change her mind about the engagement. "As part of the remuneration package the bank can offer you a loan on any business you want to start."

The quiet way she turned and met his gaze told him that he had just made a further mistake with the offer of finance.

"I don't want a loan, but thank you for offering. All I'll accept is the salary agreed to in the contract I signed and the apartment, since that's part of the remuneration package."

His jaw tightened at her insistence on sticking strictly to the terms of the contract, and the new, quiet distance. In that moment he realized that since Medinos, something had changed. In the few days since she had left his bed, Gemma had become as closed down and crisp as the disguise she was wearing.

He didn't know what, exactly, had changed, but he was determined to find out. "The job itself isn't temporary, just the engagement. The position of PA is real. Maris works for me at the bank. Once Ambrosi Pearls is up and running, and I install a new CEO, she'll come back to the bank with me. Plus there are other positions in the design department and in retail management opening up. With your background with the Atraeus Group, you would be perfect for any one of them."

Her gaze brightened at the possibilities, although he decided he couldn't be sure about what had cheered her up the most: the possibility of her pick of a number of jobs, or the fact that he would soon be leaving.

Gabriel checked his watch and slid his phone out of his pants pocket.

He could sense the conflict that pulled at Gemma, the mystifying factor that constantly saw her applying the brakes to what she so obviously felt for him. But the fact that she had emotions she needed to control was key.

Something shifted inside him, settled.

One week, maybe two.

It wasn't long enough, but it was a start. Despite all the ploys, Gemma did still want him. And when she came back to his bed, like the night on Medinos, he was pretty sure there wouldn't be a lot of conversation involved and that the passion would be the same: searingly hot and mutual.

He punched a speed dial on his phone. The clerk in charge of the bank vault picked up the call. A brief conversation later, and Gabriel set the phone down and extracted his car keys from a desk drawer. "If you'll come with me now, I've arranged to get a ring out of the bank vault, then we'll drop by my sister's shop."

Gemma, in the process of slinging the strap of her handbag over her shoulder, froze. "A ring?"

Gabriel paused at the door, riveted by the combination of uncertainty and pleasure on her face. "I read your P.S. on the note you left in Medinos. Your condition was that we would both have to play our roles to the letter, and in my book that means a ring. Besides, Mario will expect to see one. So will the lawyers."

Before Gemma could argue, he opened the door, which brought Maris into view and earshot.

Pale but composed, Gemma walked past him on a waft of the warm perfume that still had the power to stop him in his tracks. Despite the horrible color, the tight little beige suit was distractingly sexy, and the short skirt made her long legs seem even longer.

His heart slammed against the wall of his chest as he strolled beside Gemma to the elevator. With every moment that passed, he was more and more certain that she cared for him in a deep, meaningful way. It explained the dichotomy of her behavior, the way she'd avoided him at first, but then had melted in his arms.

Relief mingled with a fiery elation coursed through his veins. She hadn't been able to resist him; they hadn't been able to resist each other. He would bring her around. It would take time, but time was a commodity he now possessed.

As he stepped into the elevator with Gemma at his side, a curious feeling swept over him.

For the first time in his life he realized he was approaching a point where he could commit.

Somehow, he had finally ended up in relationship territory.

Eleven

Gemma watched the elevator doors seal shut, closing her in with Gabriel. After spending the night with him, she had realized that she had to tell him about Sanchia. And she intended to do so…when she found the right time.

The fake engagement, as outrageous as it was, would at least give her a few days to find a way to break it to him.

She didn't know how Gabriel would react, or how the situation would work out. All she knew was that Gabriel deserved to know his daughter, and Sanchia needed to know her father. Given that marriage for her was looking doubtful, Gabriel could be the only father Sanchia would ever have. It would be difficult sharing Sanchia, but she knew that ultimately it would be the best thing for her daughter.

The doors swished open. Gabriel's hand cupped her elbow, sending a hot tingle clear up her arm and spinning her back to the night in his apartment.

As they strolled out of the elevator into an underground parking area, she forced herself to relax. For the next week she would have to get used to this kind of casual touching.

Gabriel stopped beside another low-slung muscular car and held the passenger-side door for her. "Did you get custody of your daughter back?"

"Not yet. Getting this job and the apartment sped things up. I should have her back within the week."

Gabriel closed her door and, thankful that he hadn't pushed for more information, Gemma fastened her seat belt.

As he slid into the driver's seat and negotiated the tight lanes of the parking building, she made an effort to relax.

The powerful hum of the car drew her attention as Gabriel accelerated into traffic. Happy to concentrate on anything but personal issues, Gemma examined the interior of what was, she realized, a gorgeous Ferrari. "Somehow I don't see you as a Ferrari kind of guy."

"Tell me, what do you think I should drive?" His gaze briefly connected with hers. His teeth flashed white against his bronzed, clean-shaven jaw, and there they were, back on that dangerous, easy wavelength.

She tried not to respond to the killer smile, the easy charm, and failed. She stared determinedly ahead, concentrating on traffic. "I guess I got used to seeing you in a Jeep Cherokee, like the one you used to drive in Dolphin Bay."

Sunlight flowed into shadow as he pulled into another underground garage. He pulled into a named parking space and turned the powerful engine off. "Maybe that's why I like them."

Feeling suddenly suffocated in the confined space with Gabriel just inches away, his clean male scent keeping her on edge, Gemma busied herself unfastening her seat belt. "Tired of being typecast?"

He shrugged. "When Dad died, overnight I became head of the family, with five siblings, two of them under twenty." He shrugged. "Parenthood at age twenty-five wasn't what I'd planned for my life. Damned if I was going to drive a Volvo or a BMW."

Gemma's fingers curled in on the soft buttery leather of her handbag. Parenthood hadn't been so great at twenty, either. "It's a shock if you're not ready for it."

"Were you?"

The soft question drew her gaze. "By the time I had Sanchia, I was. Now that I'm a mother, I couldn't imagine life without her."

A little annoyed by his probing and the blunt way he was steering the conversation, Gemma asked the one burning question that had kept her awake at night. "Is that why you didn't want any more than the one night we shared six years ago? You wanted to preserve what freedom you had?"

"The business and the family were under a lot of pressure. A relationship wasn't viable."

Even though she hated the answer, it was a reason she understood. Gabriel had had his choices taken away. He had shouldered the burden for his family, even though it had meant putting his own dreams and desires on hold.

Given the sacrifices he'd already had to make, she could understand his distaste for being maneuvered into a marriage not of his choosing.

More than ever, she was happy that she hadn't told him she was pregnant, that she'd chosen to take responsibility for the outcome of that night. For Gabriel, having an instant wife and family forced on him would, literally, have been the last straw.

Gabriel locked the Ferrari then led the way into the bank through a door with a security PIN.

The chill of air-conditioning was a relief after the humid heat, cooling her skin as they strolled through hushed, carpeted corridors, past offices occupied by beautifully suited executives.

Gabriel acknowledged staff as they walked past. When she asked how many people worked for the company, the number of personnel he employed took her breath. The bank was the hub of a financial community, and Gabriel was tasked with overseeing it all.

For the first time she understood the crushing burden taking over all this had been. While she had been struggling with a life-changing pregnancy, Gabriel had been fighting to control all of this.

He opened a door and allowed her to precede him through to an older part of the building possessed of beautiful mosaic floors and soaring ceilings decorated with intricate plaster moldings. Light flooded through high arched windows, imbuing the rooms with a lavish, Italianate glow, and dark paneled doors opened into large offices fitted out with state-of-the art electronics.

She stared at the painstakingly preserved gold leaf embellishing an already ornate ceiling rose, a hand-painted fresco depicting saints and sinners. Whimsically, she decided that with his olive skin and the fierce male beauty of his features, Gabriel could have been an angel lifted straight out of the fresco. And in that moment a part of Gabriel that she had never quite understood fell into place. In all the years she had known him, she had never seen him in his true environment, at the leading edge of a dynasty, and at the center of the Messena empire.

Gabriel didn't attempt to take her arm again, for which she was grateful, because she was still coming to terms with this new view of him and a whole host of contrary emotions.

Disappointment and regret, a crazy longing to follow up on the cues he was giving her and claim the ephemeral closeness of a temporary relationship, even if it meant she was going to be badly hurt.

Gabriel lifted a hand to a burly man dressed in a security uniform who had just stepped out of a side room. Minutes later, they were taken through another security door and shown through to the section of the vault given over to safe-deposit boxes.

Gemma shivered slightly at the cooler temperature as Gabriel extracted a box, set it on a table and waited for the guard to insert his key. He then produced his own to unlock the box. Inside there were a number of jewelry cases stacked one on another. He chose a case marked with a symbol that Gemma, through her years of working for the Atraeus family, recognized instantly.

She stiffened. "You can't give me that. It's Fabergé."

She looked around quickly, to make sure the security guard hadn't overheard, but he had already retreated to a small glassed-in office.

"As my fiancée you would be expected to wear significant jewelry. This set belonged to my great-grandmother Eugenie. She was Russian."

Gabriel flipped open the box. Inside was a gorgeous set, which included a diamond necklace, earrings, a gorgeous set of hair clips and a ring. The diamonds were large and shimmered with burning flashes of fire under the lights, signaling purity and perfection of cut. She couldn't imagine the cost of the diamonds, let alone the fact that they were designed and set by Fabergé.

Gemma shook her head. "No. Absolutely not."

"It's either this, or we have to go to a jewelry store in town." He checked his watch. "We're due at Sophie's shop in half an hour. If you want to shop for something else, we can do that afterward."

Gemma sent Gabriel a frustrated look. "There's no point in shopping for a ring when I only need it for a few days."

"Then wear this." Gabriel picked the ring out and insisted she try it on. "You need a ring for tonight. If this one fits, we'll take it."

"We could get a piece of costume jewelry, or else something smaller and cheaper—"

Gabriel's glance cut her off. "No Messena bride would wear anything but family jewels—it's tradition. Mario is a traditionalist to the bone. He'll want to see which set you've been given." The faint ruefulness of his glance softened the demand.

"There must be something smaller and cheaper in the box—"

"If there was, no Messena bride would wear it."

Despite herself the phrase *Messena bride* sent a small thrill through her. "I'm not a bride, not even close."

"And that's not even close to an excuse." Picking up her left hand, Gabriel slipped the ring on her third finger.

The warmth of his fingers, the faint calloused roughness against her skin sent another sharp little kick of sensation through her. The ring warmed against her skin. Her breath caught; the fit was perfect.

Gemma lifted her head, which was a mistake, because Gabriel was so close. Her gaze caught and held with his and for a long, drawn-out moment she thought he might kiss her.

She blinked, unexpectedly emotional, because the ring, this scene, was something she had never dared dream about. Yet here she was, and Gabriel had just placed the most beautiful engagement ring she had ever seen on her finger. It should have meant fidelity and undying love; instead it meant absolutely nothing.

The sharp little pang of hurt finally made her face something she should have known all along. She wasn't just fatally attracted to Gabriel; somehow, despite all of the things that had gone wrong between them, she was in love with him. Seriously, devastatingly, in love.

She felt the blood drain from her face. Straight-out warmth and friendship she could cope with, but she knew the extremity of her nature. It had gotten her into trouble often enough. Issues were black or white, emotions either hot or cold. If she was in love, that was it.

Gabriel's hands closed around her upper arms, steadying her. "Are you all right? You went dead white just then."

"I'm fine. A little tired." Even though she knew she would be compounding the situation by letting him touch her, she allowed him to draw her close. For a few moments she gloried in the anchoring heat of his touch, his concern, and examined the frightening truth: that even fighting and arguing, she would rather be with Gabriel than anyone.

She loved being with him now, touching him, wrapped in his warmth, the beat of his heart thudding in her ear. She loved him, and it couldn't be.

Misery wound through her. In that moment she recognized a stark truth. As much as she wanted to marry and settle down, to have a husband she could love and more children, it wasn't going to happen.

She wasn't going to fall for anyone else. She had been in love with Gabriel for years. If she was honest, since she was about sixteen years old and had volunteered to help her father at the Messena estate, just so she could catch a glimpse of Gabriel.

It explained how curiously content she had been not to

date or get involved with any of the men who had tried to entice her into relationships after she had gotten pregnant.

Loosening his hold, she sniffed, still ridiculously emotional. She glanced at the ring, which burned with an impossibly white fire, desperate for a distraction, because any moment now she was going to cry.

Surreptitiously, she dashed at one dampening tear, but the movement alerted Gabriel, who was busy repacking the safe-deposit box.

"Hey." He cupped her face and brushed his thumbs over her cheeks and pulled her close.

She stiffened for a moment, then gave in, wound her arms around his waist and leaned into him. Distantly, she registered the firmness of his arousal, although the hug was devoid of sexual demand. Gabriel just seemed content to hold her.

A sound from the small glass office made her stiffen.

The moment broken, Gabriel let her go. Automatically, she started to tug the ring off.

"Leave it on," Gabriel said quietly. "That's the whole point."

The security guard collected the box and as he did so he glanced at the ring. "Just got engaged?"

He beamed, his face pink as he shook hands with Gabriel. "I tried not to notice, Mr. Messena, but I couldn't help but see that something special was happening. Have you named the date?"

Gemma opened her mouth to protest, but a dark glance from Gabriel cut her short. "We haven't set a date yet."

Gabriel introduced her to the guard, Evan. When he heard her name, he frowned. "The name's familiar."

Gemma's stomach sank, but Gabriel forestalled any further questions by picking up the case that contained the rest of the jewels, slipping them in his jacket pocket then checking his watch again.

After asking after Evan's wife, who apparently suffered from arthritis, and successfully diverting him, Gabriel urged her from the room, one hand at the small of her back.

Gemma caught the reflected glitter of the diamond on her finger as the heavy vault door swung closed behind them. Another set of doors, these ones made of heavy glass, threw their reflection back at them.

Gabriel looked tall, broad-shouldered and darkly handsome; Gemma looked unexpectedly voluptuous and Italian in the biscotti suit. By some kind of weird alchemy the color had added a richness to her hair and invested her pale skin with an olive glow. With the flash of the diamond on her finger, she looked every bit the expensive, pampered bride.

As they turned a corner into the mosaic floors and gorgeous architecture of the lavish office suites, Gabriel indicated that he needed to collect something from his office.

He smiled as Gemma looked curiously around the light-flooded room. "One of the perks of the job. If you want to freshen up, there's a bathroom through there."

Bemused, Gemma checked out the cream marbled bathroom, which contained a walk-in shower and a heated towel rail draped with fluffy white towels. She was used to the Atraeus family and their extreme wealth, so she was accustomed to opulent surroundings. She guessed she just wasn't used to seeing Gabriel in the center of the same kind of elaborate wealth and power. In Dolphin Bay he had seemed attainable. Here he did not.

As she stepped back out into Gabriel's office and his gaze connected with hers, the tension she had briefly managed to leave behind returned full force.

While he checked his computer, she sank into a leather

chair that felt like a cloud and tried not to fall in love with the ring on her finger, or the shattering, improbable idea that Gabriel might want the engagement to be real.

Even if Gabriel did genuinely want her, the second he found out about Sanchia, everything would change. He wouldn't be happy that she had kept Sanchia from him and they would be forever linked in a way that took away his choice. There would be no more easy companionship or heart-pounding lovemaking. Nothing would be either simple or easy between them again.

A quick tap at the door and a husky female voice had her head turning. A pretty, blue-eyed brunette came in, a sleek computer tablet in one hand. Dressed in an elegant white suit that made her skin look like porcelain, and possessed of a delicate serene beauty, for a confused moment Gemma thought she was Lilah Cole, then the differences registered. Her hair was shorter, just brushing her shoulders in a sleek bob, and she was shorter and more delicately built.

Not tall and just a little lanky, or too forthright, as Gemma was.

Gabriel made introductions, but before Gemma could do more than acknowledge Simone, apparently one of the bank's investment analysts, Gabriel walked her out into the corridor, where he completed his discussion with her.

As the conversation ended, Simone glanced in the door and gave Gemma a long, silent look before turning on her heel and strolling back to wherever it was she had come from.

Gemma realized that somewhere along the way she had forgotten to breathe. As Gabriel collected a briefcase from his desk, she rose to her feet. The glitter of the gorgeous ring caught her eye again, and she wished, too late, that she hadn't hidden it in her lap while Simone was in the room.

Finally, she identified the emotion twisting in her stomach. Picking up her handbag, she waited for Gabriel and wondered if she could find something solid she could bang her head against.

If she'd had any doubts about the in-love diagnosis they were gone. After all of the progress she'd made in walking away from Gabriel and trying to neutralize the irresistible attraction, she had somehow managed to progress another step in the wrong direction.

She was fiercely, primitively jealous.

Twelve

Gemma dressed for the evening in a slinky tangerine gown Gabriel's sister Sophie had helped her choose. Gabriel arrived, still dressed in the suit he'd worn to the office, to pick her up, but insisted on coming in for a moment.

Reluctant to allow him in because the place was dotted with photographs of Sanchia, and the odd toy, she agreed, then rushed around, jamming photos and toys in cupboards.

She left one photograph of Sanchia as a chubby baby out, because it would be strange if she didn't have any. Even that was a risk, because with her dark hair and eyes Sanchia looked heart-stoppingly like a Messena.

When Gabriel stepped inside her apartment, she logged his instant, searing appreciation and felt suddenly self-conscious. The tangerine dress was much more her natural style—bright and pretty with an edge of sophistication. But after seeing Simone in his office, with her subtle, perfectly cut clothes and serene beauty, she wondered a little desperately what Gabriel found attractive about her.

He slipped the Fabergé case out of his pocket and extracted the diamond necklace. "I want you to wear this tonight, as well."

Gemma stared at the cascade of diamonds shooting off fiery sparks under her lights. "Because Mario will expect it."

Gabriel's gaze was abruptly soft enough to make her heart melt. "No. Because I'd like you to wear them."

"That is not a good answer."

"It's the truth."

She drew a breath and turned, lifting the weight of her hair away from her neck.

The oval mirror in the hall framed Gabriel as he fastened the necklace at her nape. She fingered the diamonds where they warmed against her skin. The pure, fiery light of the jewels was a perfect foil for the dress. "They look beautiful." Although almost all of her attention was on his hands where they cupped her bare shoulders.

"They suit you."

Taking a deep breath, she smiled brightly. "Diamonds suit anyone."

She moved away from his touch before she did something sillier, like turning into his arms and kissing him. Instead, she picked up her evening bag and the wrap, which was neatly folded on the small table in the hall.

Gabriel paused beside the small table beneath the mirror. "Is this a picture of Sanchia?"

Her heart banged against the wall of her chest as she saw Gabriel with the baby photo in his hands. "Yes."

A small silence formed as he replaced the frame on the table. Feeling worse than she had expected to feel, Gemma opened the door and pointedly waited.

Gabriel's gaze was enigmatic as he walked out onto her front porch, and she wondered a little anxiously if he'd seen any resemblance to photos of other Messena babies.

Gabriel held the car door for her then walked around and climbed into the driver's seat. As he accelerated away she sent him a fleeting glance. "So who's cooking tonight?"

"If you're asking me if I can cook, I can, but it's strictly survival stuff. Maris rang a local restaurant that caters dinner parties. They're delivering."

Warmed by the relaxed timbre of his voice, the way that he loosened off his tie as he drove, as if he was unwinding from the day's work, Gemma looked away from the clean lines of his profile and tried to focus instead on the neon signs and illuminated shop windows of downtown Auckland.

Gabriel ran the gamut of Queen Street and the series of traffic lights then turned along the waterfront. Eventually, he turned into a gated apartment complex in Mission Bay.

Opening the front door of an apartment that was the size of a small mansion, with ground-floor access and three stories, he allowed her to precede him into the hall then on into a large lounge with a towering ceiling. He checked his watch. "I need to shower and change before Mario and Eva get here. Make yourself at home."

He showed her the kitchen and formal dining room and invited her to help herself to the trays of drinks and nibbles the caterers had left out.

Setting her evening bag and wrap down on one of the stools that were grouped along the kitchen bar, Gemma decided to familiarize herself with the apartment before Eva and Mario arrived. Since she was supposed to be Gabriel's fiancée, it would look a little strange if she didn't even know where the bathroom was.

Gabriel had gone upstairs, so she figured it was safe

enough to open doors downstairs. On her second try she found a small gleaming bathroom. As she closed the door, the front doorbell buzzed.

Adrenaline arrowed through her veins as she walked to the door and opened it. She wasn't ready; she hadn't had time to look through kitchen cupboards or work out the stereo, but it was too late now. When she opened the door, an ultrasexy and quite lovely brunette stepped inside, carrying a frosted bottle of champagne.

A small frown pleated her brow when she saw Gemma. "Hello. Are you a friend of Gabriel's?"

Gemma took a deep breath. "Actually, I'm his fiancée."

Shock registered in her gaze. Her eyes dropped to Gemma's left hand. "He gave you the Fabergé."

When she didn't say anything more, Gemma calmly asked if there was anyone else to come in. When Eva indicated there wasn't, that her father was arriving later, she closed the door. "Gabriel's, uh, just in the shower. Come through and I'll get you a drink."

That was, if she could find the glasses.

Eva strolled to the kitchen, not waiting for Gemma. "How long have you known Gabriel?"

Gemma almost gave a sigh of relief. At least this part was easy enough. "Years. Most of my life, actually."

"Then you must be from Dolphin Bay."

Gemma began opening cupboard doors, looking for glasses. "Yes."

Eva frowned, somehow managing to look even more gorgeous. "You look familiar. Maybe I've seen you at a family gathering?"

Gemma pretended not to hear that one. Finally, she found wineglasses and set them on the counter. When she picked up the bottle of wine, thankfully it had a screw top so she didn't have to search for a corkscrew.

Eva took the glass of wine she poured and walked into the lounge to stare out at the view. "If you were at Constantine's wedding, maybe I saw you there."

Gemma studied the taut expression of Eva's face, the combative stance. "I wasn't at Constantine's wedding."

"But you know him?"

"Yes, I do." Gemma bit her tongue against the urge to supply more information, just in case Eva guessed who she really was.

Feeling stressed, and wishing Gabriel would hurry up and come down, she bypassed the wine and poured herself a glass of water instead. The way the night was going, she was going to have to keep her wits about her.

Eva returned to the kitchen counter and set her glass of wine down. "I hope you don't mind if I put on some music? Gabriel's got a great collection of jazz."

Gemma tried for her best neutral smile, the one she used to soothe prickly clients. "Be my guest."

As soon as Eva disappeared into another smaller lounge, evidently the place where the stereo system was to be found, Gemma started up the stairs. As she reached the top, Gabriel stepped out of the shower, a snowy white towel wrapped around his waist. "Eva and Mario are here?"

Loud music began to play. Gemma raised her voice. "Just Eva and a bottle of champagne. Apparently Mario's coming later."

He dragged the fingers of one hand through his damp hair. "Champagne? Damn, there must be something in the air."

Eva's voice drifted up from the bottom of the stairs, her face vivid and engaging. "Dad's got a meeting. He'll be here in half an hour." She frowned. "Gabriel...you didn't tell me you were getting engaged."

"It's only just happened," he said smoothly, and pulled Gemma close.

Her hands skidded over his damp abdomen as she found herself plastered against his side. His arm came around her, clamping her tight against him. Before she could protest, Gabriel dropped a light kiss on her mouth, then she was free.

If the drinks were difficult, dinner was worse.

Mario, an impeccably dressed older man, arrived with one of Gabriel's younger brothers. Kyle, like all of the Messena men, was tall and dark, with a sleekly muscular frame. Although instead of dark eyes, his were a cool, piercing shade of green. A short haircut and a tough jaw completed a look that was more than a shade dangerous and didn't reflect what he did for a living, which was investment banking.

As soon as Kyle saw her, he raised a brow. "Gemma. It's been a long time. The last time I saw you was in Sydney, at some art auction with Zane."

Eva paused in the motion of pouring a glass of champagne for Mario. She looked curious rather than annoyed, for which Gemma was grateful. However much Mario was pushing for a marriage between Gabriel and Eva, evidently Eva hadn't been over the moon about the idea, either.

She continued pouring champagne, although ever since Kyle had stepped into the room her manner had grown even more acerbic. "You didn't say you knew Zane."

"I'm from Dolphin Bay." Gemma looked around a little desperately for Gabriel. "I know them all—Constantine, Lucas, Zane—"

Eva frowned. "I can't remember Zane ever going to Dolphin Bay."

Gabriel, dressed in black trousers and a black gauzy

shirt casually open at the throat, intervened with a cool glance. "He came once, when he was fourteen or fifteen, before he went away to college."

Gemma breathed a sigh of relief and sent Gabriel a thankful glance. She guessed it didn't really matter if Eva found out that she was Zane's notorious ex-PA. If there had been a problem, Gabriel would never have asked her to pose as his fiancée in the first place.

Gabriel shook Mario's hand and formally introduced Gemma.

Mario's gaze was glacial, but he was polite. When he noticed the ring he met Gabriel's gaze for a long moment then inclined his head. "That's a very beautiful ring," he said with something like resignation. "Congratulations."

Mario turned to Eva with a frown. "You could have been wearing that ring!"

"Dad!" Eva sent him a reproving glance then rolled her eyes at Gabriel. "Sorry, Gabriel. Dad just could never accept that we aren't destined to be together."

Mario's reproving gaze was directed firmly at Eva. "You need a husband."

Eva smiled, although there was a definite edge to it as she poured herself another glass of champagne. "I'm wedded to my business."

Mario shrugged and sat down. "Women," he said repressively, "shouldn't be in business."

There was a tiny, vibrating silence, then Kyle jumped in to break it by taking Gemma's hand and studying the ring.

He sent Gabriel a curious look. "Great rock. Very historical."

Gabriel handed him a beer. "You're here to run interference," he murmured, "not start a fight."

Kyle released Gemma's hand and grinned. "Gotcha. Guess I'll go sit by Eva. That'll be fun."

Gabriel's hand landed in the small of Gemma's back, the warmth of his palm burning through the silk. A now familiar tingling heat shivered through Gemma. "Do you think it's safe to eat?"

"As long as we hand out plastic knives."

She glanced at her ring. "What is it with this ring? Everyone seems to recognize it."

"Which is exactly why I chose it." Gabriel went into the kitchen and opened a huge stainless-steel oven, where covered dishes were keeping warm. "It has a bit of history attached to it. Eugenie had a reputation for being elusive. My great-grandfather wooed her across two continents. She finally succumbed when he produced the jewels."

Gemma would have liked to know more, because the story sounded enchanting, but Gabriel was unloading hot dishes onto heat pads, so she grabbed a set of oven mitts and started carrying dishes to the table. It was a Mediterranean-style feast, with a platter of dips and antipasto and deliciously fragrant savory pastries.

Gabriel pulled out her chair at the table and poured wine. Mario said grace in his native Medinian, his voice soft and cracked with age.

The first course was rocky. Mario's conversation was stilted, and it was clear that at times he was having trouble remembering things. Eva seemed intent on drawing out more about just how and when Gabriel had proposed and when the wedding was.

It was a relief to get up from the table, help clear plates away and serve up the rich beef stew that had been sitting in a chafing dish, along with rice, spicy lentils and a green salad. By the time they reached dessert, a rich tiramisu, Eva had stopped asking questions. Gemma was uneasily certain, owing to the measuring glances that Eva kept sending her way, that despite the change in hair color she had finally realized who Gemma was.

Gabriel picked up on her unease and sent Kyle a steady look that was some kind of signal. Kyle immediately got up and offered to drive both Eva and Mario home. Mario had arrived by taxi and Eva had driven, but because Eva had had two glasses of wine, Kyle refused to let her drive.

As soon as they were gone, Gemma let out a sigh of relief and helped Gabriel clear up and fill the dishwasher. While she did that, he loaded all of the chafing dishes and large serving platters into a large box for the caterer to collect. When the kitchen was clean, she collected her wrap and bag.

Gabriel met her gaze, his own oddly somber and guarded, and she caught the subtext. She could stay if she wanted.

Despite the small amount of wine she'd sipped through dinner, she had managed to stay sober for the express purpose of avoiding moments like this. "I can get a taxi back to the apartment."

Gabriel frowned. "I'll drive you home."

The drive home was quiet, the streets mostly empty. When Gabriel braked for lights, Gemma studied his profile and tried not to remember the pulse-pounding kiss. "Did the dinner achieve what you wanted?"

His gaze touched on hers. "Mario knows his trusteeship is coming to an end. I spoke to him before he left. We have a meeting with the law firm in the morning."

"Then the legal situation should be wrapped up inside a week."

"It's possible."

He accelerated through the lights and pulled over into her street. Instead of staying in the car, he insisted on seeing her to her apartment. When she paused at her door, he took the key from her hand, unlocked the door and insisted on seeing her into the apartment itself.

When Gemma saw the baby picture of Sanchia, she thought again about telling Gabriel that he had a daughter, but he walked past the photo and the moment passed.

She set her evening bag and wrap down, suddenly on tenterhooks even more than she had been in his house. Somehow it seemed unbearably intimate to have Gabriel in her small apartment, with her bedroom just visible down the hall. "So, what else do we have to do with this charade?"

His movements deliberate, he linked his fingers with hers and drew her close. "This." Bending close, he touched his mouth to hers.

When he lifted his head, his gaze was dark and intense. "And maybe we could talk about the real reason you walked away from what we had in Medinos."

She closed her eyes, melting inside. "I didn't think you seriously wanted anything more."

He cupped her neck, his thumbs smoothing along her jaw. "It's been a long time, but I've never forgotten you. When we were on Medinos I realized I shouldn't have let you go all those years ago. Babe, I want you back."

The words, the husky endearment, shivered through her. For a split second she was unable to absorb the concept. Not when she had been engraving the exact opposite message on her brain for six years.

He kissed her again, this time taking his time.

He wanted her back.

A crazy, dizzying elation shimmered through her.

Underneath all of the reasons that she shouldn't make love with Gabriel again—number one being that she hadn't told him about Sanchia—she was completely, utterly seduced. All evening he had been attentive. Fake engagement or not, he had put that beautiful ring on her finger and she had felt like his fiancée.

She pulled back. "Why do you want me when we haven't seen each other for six years? It doesn't make sense."

"You're beautiful. I've always liked you. This is why." Cupping her face, he brushed his mouth across hers. The caress shuddered through her, evoking memories she thought she had buried, swamping her with emotions that were at once intense and painful and yet unbearably sweet.

One more night. What could it hurt?

Despite all the reasons to say no, temptation pulled at her.

A few more days and everything would change, because he would know about Sanchia.

Her stomach hollowed out. Once he found out she would never experience this again, the passionate highs and the desperate lows. And in that moment the decision was made.

One more night. She would tell him about Sanchia in the morning.

Lifting up, she wound her arms around his neck. "I want you, too, but you've always known that."

She kissed him back and his arms closed around her. She found herself being slowly walked back until they were in her room. He unzipped her dress. It puddled on the floor as she unfastened his shirt, fingers slipping on the small buttons in her haste.

He shrugged out of the shirt. The street lighting from outside shafted through her window shutters, tiger-striping his body with dim gold and inky shadow. As he unhooked her bra and took one breast into his mouth, she was spun back to the dark room on Medinos, the storm pounding on the windows.

Another step and he pulled her down onto the bed with

him. Gabriel eased out of his trousers then peeled her panties off in one smooth movement and they were both naked. "You're beautiful," he said softly.

Seconds later, he rejoined her on the bed. The next kiss tingled all the way to her toes. Groaning, Gabriel rolled, pulling her beneath him. Gemma wound her arms around his neck and pulled him closer still. Another kiss, and then there was no more need for words.

Thirteen

Gabriel came out of sleep as the first slivers of dawn light flowed through the shutters, aware instantly that Gemma was with him.

Broodingly, he turned on his side and simply watched her.

Despite the lovemaking there was something wrong, something he couldn't quite put his finger on. He would find out what was creating the cool distance and do what he could to eliminate the problem. It would take time, but he had plenty of that.

Now that he had her back in his bed, he didn't intend to rush things.

A sense of satisfaction filled him that she had his ring on his finger. In a day or two, he would suggest they make the engagement real. Maybe it was a bit early, but he couldn't see the point in waiting now.

He noticed the dark shadows beneath Gemma's eyes

and decided that now they were engaged, even if she saw it only as a fake engagement, he would intervene with the department that was giving her a problem with custody.

Gemma must have been worried sick about her small daughter, but all of that would end now. He would take care of her. As his fiancée she would be cushioned and cared for, and there would be no more financial hardship.

If she would accept the help.

The O'Neills were fiercely proud and independent. In their own way, just as stiff-necked and proud as his own family.

Despite the pretty clothes and the social veneer she had learned as Zane's PA, Gemma was an O'Neill through and through.

His decision to make the engagement real solidified. He had dated enough women to know that Gemma was different in a way that mattered.

Aside from the searing attraction, he liked her and he was no longer worried that the passion that bound them together was the obsessive kind that could prove destructive. The trouble he'd had getting Gemma back into his bed had proved that.

The ring on her finger glimmered in the morning light. The diamond was breathtakingly valuable, with a notable history. If he should ever choose to sell it there was a list of buyers registered at Sotheby's, one of them prepared to buy at any cost. Getting the ring from the vault was a significant move, which Eva, Kyle and Mario had recognized.

The fact that he had put that particular ring on Gemma's finger signaled that Gabriel was prepared to undertake a situation that was not entered into lightly by any Messena.

Marriage.

* * *

The flowers arrived later on in the morning as Gemma dressed for the meeting with Mario and the lawyers who dealt with the trust.

She wrapped herself in a robe and collected the enormous bunch of pink roses from the courier, then set about trying to find vases. She had just filled every container she had when a second delivery, this time of rich, deep red roses, arrived.

Dizzy with delight that Gabriel had thought to send flowers, she searched out jars and jugs from kitchen cupboards. She set containers of flowers around the apartment, on every available surface, and took a moment to breathe in the perfume before she had to dash back to her room and finish dressing.

An emerald-green silk dress with a sleek black jacket over top, which she had gotten from Sophie Messena's boutique, produced a look that was both stunningly feminine and businesslike.

After coiling her hair up in a loose, sexy knot, she dabbed on perfume and slipped into a pair of high heels. With the diamond on her finger, she looked and felt like the pampered, expensive bride-to-be of a very rich man.

She heard the throaty roar of the Ferrari and her stomach clenched on a jolt of pure, 100 percent in-love emotion. She was so happy she could cry, but at the same time she was aware that she was living in a fool's paradise.

Gabriel, who had left earlier to go back to his apartment and shower and change before coming back to pick her up, was parked out on the street. As Gemma walked out of the front door of her apartment block to meet him, he held the passenger-side door open for her.

Gemma couldn't stop smiling. "I got the flowers."

"Good." Pulling her loosely into his arms, he kissed her.

Long seconds later, Gemma slid into her seat and watched Gabriel as he strolled around the bonnet of the car. In that moment she was almost terrifyingly happy and content.

A short drive downtown and they walked into an expansive, leather-scented office. Don Cade, a lawyer who looked to be of the same vintage as Mario, got to his feet. While Mario appeared a little vague at times, Cade was as sharp as a rapier.

He eyed her ring as he shook her hand, his perusal discreet but thorough. Gabriel pulled out a chair for her next to his own, and the proceedings began.

A second, younger man entered the room and was introduced as Holloway, an associate of the firm.

Gabriel frowned at Holloway, and minutes later, when he began producing newspaper clippings and other evidence that proved that Gemma could not seriously be Gabriel's real fiancée, Gemma realized why.

Holloway was a private detective.

Cade directed all of his comments to Gabriel, completely ignoring Gemma, and she realized he had known all of the information that had been presented before he had met her. The gist of it was that Cade was erring on the side of retaining Mario's trusteeship. Gemma decided it was a setup if she had ever seen one.

Annoyed beyond belief, she found herself on her feet, confronting the lawyer directly. "The evidence you've amassed to prove there isn't an engagement is impressive, but unfortunately, your man didn't dig deep enough." She directed a scathing glance at Holloway. "Any investigator worth their salt would never rely on tabloid and internet reports, which are all lies anyway."

She ignored the surprised cough from Holloway and

ploughed on. "You're saying we're not engaged, but it didn't feel like that last night. In bed."

Cade frowned. Holloway opened his mouth to say something, but Gabriel cut him down with a glance.

Gabriel switched his icy gaze to Cade. "I suggest, if you want to retain my business, that you ask your man to leave now."

Cade turned to Holloway and advised him to go in a low tone, but Gemma noticed that Holloway left his report on the table.

Cade picked up the report and began intoning his verdict in a low voice.

Incensed, Gemma reached into her purse and extracted Sanchia's passport, which her sister had posted to her along with some other correspondence just the previous day. "If you think Gabriel and I don't have a real relationship, you're wrong." Her stomach twisted sickly at what she had to do, but there was no way past it.

Opening Sanchia's passport, she slapped it down in front of Cade. "Gabriel and I have a daughter. She's five years old. I think that's a bit more believable than a tabloid exclusive from a reporter named Lucky Starr."

She turned to Gabriel, barely able to meet his gaze. "I'm sorry."

Picking up Holloway's report, she ripped it into pieces, tossed it on Cade's desk and walked out.

Gabriel arrived at Gemma's apartment minutes later, Sanchia's passport in his pocket. He knew Gemma was here because he had followed her as she'd run out of Cade's offices and hailed a taxi. Keeping close to the taxi across town had been difficult because he'd gotten caught at a set of lights, but it hadn't taken long to guess her destination.

He buzzed her apartment, half expecting that she wouldn't let him in, but she did almost immediately.

The first thing he noticed when he walked into Gemma's lounge was a suitcase filled with brightly colored articles of clothing, which Gemma had placed on one armchair. Drawn by the intensely feminine pale pink fabric, he pulled the top item of clothing out...and went still inside.

His fingers closed on silk and tulle. He sat down on an adjacent seat, his heart pounding.

The tutu, because that's what it was, was somehow more real than the passport photo had been, because it was a practical object. Clothing for his child.

He took a deep breath, pinched the bridge of his nose.

Now it all made sense: Gemma avoiding him over the years. There was no other explanation as to why they hadn't bumped into each other.

No matter how often he had gone to Atraeus social events in Sydney, despite the fact that Gemma was part of the firm, she had never been present while he had been there.

Gemma sat down opposite him. "I was going to tell you."

"When, exactly?"

"Today. I just wanted one more night before you found out." She sat down in the armchair opposite him, gorgeous in the green dress, her face pale.

"What did you think I would do?" he said flatly. "Finish with you?"

Her expression was pale but composed. "Yes."

Like he had done six years ago.

He drew a deep breath, let it out slowly, his mind racing—a far cry from his usual disciplined process. "I'm not going to. We need to get married. It should have happened years ago." He stopped and remembered to breathe again. "Can I see a photo of her?"

Without answering, Gemma walked across to a sideboard and opened a cupboard. A mass of frames tumbled out, and suddenly the extent of the deception hurt.

Gemma had hidden the photos, hidden his daughter from him.

As Gemma collected the frames in a stack, her fingers quick and just a little clumsy, she knocked the top one and they all cascaded across the floor.

Gabriel moved before he could think, helping her pick up the quirky catalog of Sanchia: the chubby baby, the cheerful little girl with dark eyes and hair like his and the same lanky grace as her mother.

The colors of the frames were just as bright and whimsical as Gemma's clothes, pink and yellow, blue and green— candy colors sprinkled with a liberal amount of bling.

Gabriel's heart squeezed in his chest as he drank in the images and fell utterly in love with his daughter. It hit him just how much of Sanchia's life he had missed. Although as knee-jerk as that reaction was, he knew he couldn't afford to dwell on it.

The years at the bank and dealing with his volatile family had taught him the danger of allowing emotion to rule. He had a daughter—now, today.

He stared at a photo of Sanchia, a birthday hat jammed on her head, a smear of chocolate on one cheek, grinning straight at him. A perilous joy gripped his heart. No matter what, he couldn't afford to mess this up.

Gemma handed him a pink folder, flipped open to show a series of photos of Sanchia as a newborn, tiny and serene, all red skin and damp dark hair and wrapped in white. "When you rang to ask me if I was pregnant, I didn't think I was. I had periods until I was three months along and by then I was back at university, busy with exams. It didn't register that something was wrong until I reached four months."

Gemma indicated the first photo. "Sanchia was about five minutes old there. My sister took the photos."

Gabriel studied the tiny, exquisite baby, Gemma pale and exhausted as she held her. "Your sister was with you at the birth?"

"Yes. No one else." Her gaze connected bleakly with his. "There's been no one else. No other man."

For a long, drawn-out moment, Gabriel forgot the photos, his chest tightening as he absorbed the stunning fact that Gemma had only ever been his. "So why didn't you tell me you were pregnant? We could have gotten married."

"I didn't think that would happen."

He was silent for a moment. "You're right. After what happened with Dad my hands were tied. Damn, this is a mess."

"Apart from the fact that I knew you were busy with your family and the business, I thought that if you really did want me, you wouldn't be able to stay away from me, but you did. Completely. Not even a phone call." She sat back on her knees, creating a subtle distance. "I was in the same city as you, studying. You knew that. Some days I actually walked past the Messena building, trying to catch a glimpse of you. A couple of times I even saw you."

"You should have contacted me—"

"So you could come and see that I was pregnant?"

Her fierce frown told him how repugnant that idea had been to her. He shrugged. "We would have sorted something out—"

"Sorry. I didn't want charity." She gave him a quick neutral smile, the inner toughness he had always admired suddenly surfacing. "I could see why I was completely not what you wanted in a wife."

In that moment any uncertainty about Gemma's feelings for him evaporated. "You loved me."

"For a long time." Her expression was self-effacing. "Why else do you think I was so keen to help Dad with the gardens at your place? Why I slept with you?" Jerkily, she rose to her feet, gathered the frames and placed them on the coffee table as if she couldn't bear to talk about it any longer.

Grimly, Gabriel rose to his feet. Gemma's white face, her uncharacteristic clumsiness, hit him forcibly.

He needed time; they both needed time, but in that moment he knew he couldn't afford to give Gemma that kind of space. The minute he eased back, she would close him out.

He placed the folder of Sanchia's first hours on the coffee table. "I meant what I said about getting married, so what do you think about making the engagement real?"

Fourteen

Gemma unlocked her arms from around her waist and watched as Gabriel rose to his feet. With his dark gaze leveled at her, she felt exposed and vulnerable. Gabriel knew that he was the only one, that she loved him. She had no defenses left.

Pure white fire glinted off the engagement ring, reminding her of something else she didn't have: his love.

Gabriel wanted to marry her, but essentially she was still the same person she'd been when he hadn't wanted her in his life.

The things that had changed were all external. They shared a child, and marriage, even to someone like her, would help him solidify his hold on his family's company.

It wasn't the true, deep love, the fairy-tale relationship, she had always wanted. Gabriel was offering a practical solution. "You don't have to marry me, but if you want to go ahead with a wedding, then I accept. I've already told Sanchia about you, and she wants you in her life. She can't wait to meet you."

They reached Dolphin Bay at four in the afternoon. Gabriel drove straight to Lauren's house, which was situated in a little suburb one street away from the beach.

He parked the Ferrari out on the street. Gemma fumbled free of her seat belt and pushed her door open, her heart swelling with the straightforward joy of homecoming and the fact that any second now, Sanchia would burst out of the door.

The salt tang of the air hit her face. As she hitched her handbag over one shoulder, Gemma noticed a bunch of kids across the road openly staring at the vehicle.

Gabriel had already grabbed her suitcase of gifts out from behind the seats, along with a package of his own. As he straightened, expression remote behind a pair of dark glasses, he lifted a hand at the boys then glanced at her. "Aren't those the Roberts kids?"

Gemma reached into her bag and found her sunglasses. "How did you know that?"

He walked around the bonnet, looking more casual and sexy than she could ever remember in faded, glove-soft jeans and a white V-neck T-shirt that clung across his chest. "Their mother used to teach the twins piano after school. Her kids used to come over and swim in the pool. Pretty sure I recognized some of those faces."

He held the front gate to a weatherboard house with bikes and assorted toys littering the front yard. As he did, the front door was flung open and a small, dark whirlwind burst out.

Gemma braced herself for the impact and wrapped Sanchia in her arms, soaking in the feel and smell of her, tears squeezing past her lids. Yesterday she had gotten the all-clear from the welfare department, but the relief of that was now tempered with this new situation.

Sanchia pulled free and turned her attention to Gabriel. Her likeness to Gabriel was acute, even down to the quiet, assessing way she regarded him before speaking, a trait that was Gabriel's own.

She frowned, her gaze intense. "Are you the dad?"

Gabriel dropped down on his haunches. Even so, he was still taller than Sanchia. "Yes, I am."

She darted a quick look at Gemma. "Does that mean you're married?"

Gemma sniffed and swiped at her eyes. "Not yet, but soon. You can be a bridesmaid."

Sanchia resumed her fascinated focus on Gabriel's face. "Are you really going to be my dad?"

"I am, and when I promise something, I do it."

There was a considering silence. "Okay." Sanchia beamed and slipped her hand in Gemma's. "You have to come inside now. Aunty Lauren's got a cake and Benny and Owen are driving her crazy 'cos they can't have any till you come."

Sanchia bounced as they walked. Now that the introductions were over, all her solemnity was gone. "It's chocolate. My fav'rit."

"Mine, too." Gabriel's eyes met Gemma's, his expression unreadable, and in that moment it clicked that Gabriel was at his most expressionless when he felt the most.

It wasn't much to go on, it didn't change the limbo they seemed to be caught in, but finally she had a kernel of hope to cling to. She didn't know if Gabriel could love her back the way she needed him to—she knew she couldn't make him love her—but for Sanchia's sake she had to try.

Just before they reached the steps, Gemma saw the moment Sanchia slipped her hand into Gabriel's and closed the small distance between them.

Her heart squeezed almost painfully tight as she saw Gabriel's fingers gently tighten around his daughter's, saw the expression on his face.

He loved her already.

At least that part was right.

After a walk on the beach, during which Gabriel got to spend some one-on-one time with Sanchia, who insisted on wearing the pink tutu over her orange bike shorts, they collected their daughter's things. Lauren and Sanchia's cousins waved them off, and ten minutes later they drove between the gates of the Messena estate.

Gabriel's gaze touched on hers as he braked on the gravel outside the front entrance. "Mom's still on Medinos, so we'll have the house to ourselves for a day or two at least."

Relief eased some of Gemma's tension. It was an odd enough feeling to be staying at the Messena's palatial family home, but she definitely wasn't looking forward to facing Gabriel's mother. As well as she knew Luisa Messena, she couldn't forget that she was not the bride Luisa had been certain Gabriel was waiting for.

Gabriel showed her and Sanchia to their rooms, which had been made up for them by the housekeeper, a Mrs. Sargent. Sanchia's room contained a collection of soft toys and a large wicker basket of toys that looked like it had seen hard service over the years. Gemma left Sanchia happily sorting through the toys while Gabriel showed her to her room, which was next door.

Pushing open the door, he stepped back so she could enter first. Gemma's heart pounded just a little faster as she walked into the room. Instead of the masculine setting she had expected, the room was pretty in white with touches of pink and green that created a fresh springlike effect. Clearly a room designed for feminine occupancy.

Gabriel carried her case over to an elegant freestanding wardrobe. "My room is at the end of the hall."

Gemma dragged her gaze from the way the white T-shirt clung across Gabriel's shoulders, revealing tanned biceps, the faint mark of Sanchia's sticky fingers on the pristine white interlock. Despite the hot afternoon at the beach, sand and ice cream and kids running in every direction, Gabriel's gaze was just as remote as it had been that morning when he had found out about Sanchia.

She set her handbag down on a pretty padded blanket box at the foot of the bed and watched while Gabriel unlatched the French doors that led out onto a terrace that ran along this side of the house.

Instantly, a warm breeze wafted inside, bringing with it the rich scents of the wisteria and the climbing rose that clambered up over the wrought-iron balustrade.

After hooking the door back, Gabriel stepped back inside the room, long lean fingers raking windblown hair out of his face. "Sanchia's door is locked, so she can't access the terrace, but even if she does, the balustrading is childproofed and the climbing rose has serious thorns. Most kids won't go near it."

"Thank you for being so good with Sanchia."

"It wasn't hard." He leaned one broad shoulder against the frame of the French doors, looking broodingly introspective and ultrasexy as he turned his head and stared out at the hot blue sky and the cool green of the trees in the distance. "Thank you for showing me those photographs of Sanchia this morning."

She shrugged and ran her hand over the pure white waffle duvet cover and a gorgeous quilted throw patterned with cabbage roses. "I have a lot more, and all the negatives if you want copies—"

"Since we'll be living together, I won't need copies."

The quiet timbre of his voice shivered through her, and in that moment it hit her forcibly that she was in a situation she thought she would never be in. She was engaged to Gabriel and staying in his mother's beautiful house. When they went back to Auckland after the wedding, she and Sanchia would be moving into Gabriel's apartment. Although he had made it clear enough that, for now, at least, they wouldn't be sharing a bed.

A wedding.

Disorientation mixed with a potent shot of misery made her mood drop like a stone. She had gotten through the day, smiled for Lauren and the kids and gotten over the hump of explaining that she and Gabriel not only had a future, they had a past. But the happiness she had tried to project over her engagement had been an empty thing.

The engagement was now real, but that special something, the possibility of a once-in-a-lifetime passionate love that had made her heart pound and her mood spiral crazily, as if she was a dizzy teenager, had gone.

They were together, but the relationship felt stiff and forced. She was miserably uncertain if Gabriel even wanted her anymore, and she guessed that was the essence of the problem. She needed to be loved and nurtured, to be the center of Gabriel's life. Most of all, she needed *him* to fall head over heels in love with her, but that was hardly possible if Gabriel felt forced to love her.

Gabriel straightened away from the doorjamb. "Hey. Don't look so depressed."

She drew a quick breath as he strolled toward her. "It's hard not to."

"I've made some preliminary arrangements for the wedding. Money's no object. Anything you want, we can do. The only constriction is time. For the dress, we can fly you anywhere you need to go, or have the dress, and the designer, flown to you."

The thought that Gabriel had the power to bring not only a dress, but the designer, to her briefly diverted her. She had been brought up to sew her own clothes, and that had always been a passion, but with the wedding so close she would have to buy dresses for both her and Sanchia.

Gabriel pulled out his wallet and extracted a platinum card. "You should take this. Order in what you want, and if you have any trouble let either me or Maris know."

The card, access to Gabriel's personal bank account, brought home both the reality and the underlying wrongness of their wedding.

She had agreed to marry Gabriel, but she was still shaky about the whole idea of marrying without the in-love factor. Using his credit card somehow seemed another big step into the relationship that she wasn't prepared for, another cold layer of necessity. "How do I use this?"

"Since you're not a signatory on the account yet, I'll have to give you my PIN."

He checked out a small writing bureau in one corner of the room, found a pen and a piece of paper and wrote a series of numbers in strong, slanting strokes.

"What if I lose the PIN? Or the card?"

He went curiously still. "I guess I'll try and weather the loss."

She suddenly felt a little ridiculous. Of course, he was a banker. He owned a bank. He could lose a thousand platinum cards and not notice it.

He handed her the slip of paper. "If you don't want to keep a written record, you'll have to memorize it."

She studied the four digits. Gabriel may be a banker,

but she had been a PA. "I have a good memory. I can still remember Zane's PIN, although he's probably changed it by now."

Gabriel's gaze narrowed. "Do we have to talk about Zane?"

A sharp little tingle ran through her at the irritable note in his voice.

Was that a hint of jealousy?

She took a deep breath and let it out slowly. "Zane who?"

He grinned quick and hard and caught her hand, drawing her close, and suddenly the terrible cold distance was gone. "Zane's a relative. When we're married, we'll bump into him from time to time."

Her palms flattened against his chest, and she found herself staring into the dark, chocolate-brown depths of his eyes, happily mesmerized by the gold striations that gave them an amber gleam, the long silky curl of his lashes. "You don't have to worry about Zane. He was my boss, and a friend, that's all."

"Good. Because I don't share."

The possessive note in his voice sparked even more hope. That morning she had thought Gabriel would end up hating her for keeping Sanchia from him, that with their engagement charade morphing into a marriage of convenience he would have a difficult time even wanting her. But for the first time since she had walked into Gabriel's sitting room and realized that he knew Sanchia was his, she thought they really did have a chance.

He brushed the delicate skin beneath one eye with a fingertip. "You look tired. You should get some rest."

Cupping her face, he dipped his head and touched his mouth to hers, but to Gemma the kiss felt perfunctory and forced, as if his mind was on other things. Despite the positivity of a few seconds ago, her doubts came crashing back.

If Gabriel had found her so easy to resist six years ago, what were the chances that he would really, honestly fall for her now?

The reality was that the only solid link between them was Sanchia.

On cue, Sanchia skipped into the room. Instantly, Gabriel let her go. All shyness gone now, Sanchia produced her phone from a small zip pocket in her jacket and requested Gabriel's number.

Sending Gemma a bemused look, Gabriel extracted his phone and sat down on the blanket box. Automatically, Sanchia clambered up beside him, her legs dangling, inches short of the floor.

Sitting together, Gemma couldn't help noticing that they looked heartbreakingly alike. Once again feeling ridiculously vulnerable and isolated, Gemma busied herself unpacking while Gabriel and Sanchia swapped numbers. As she hung a dress in the wardrobe, she was aware of Gabriel leaving then Sanchia's stifled giggle.

Out in the hall a cell phone buzzed, and Gabriel's footsteps stopped dead. Gemma heard the low timbre of his voice as he answered the call, followed by Sanchia's delighted answer.

Gemma kept hanging clothes then walked through to Sanchia's room to help settle her in.

Gabriel had bonded with Sanchia in the space of a few hours. And he had kissed Gemma. There was hope.

More than hope. Last night with Gabriel had been beyond sublime; it had been heartbreakingly special. There was no reason it couldn't happen again, and the way things had gone today, it needed to.

She pulled out a silky peach chemise pooled in the bottom of her case. Unzipping a side pocket, she removed the magazine with the article on seduction that she'd kept.

If she could talk herself into seducing Zane, a man she had only ever liked, not loved, she could seduce her husband-to-be.

Tonight.

Moonlight gently illumined the night sky as Gabriel strolled out onto the balcony, the soft black cotton pants he'd pulled on after his shower clinging low on his hips, a towel draped over one shoulder.

Without the benefit of the slowly swishing ceiling fan in his room, it was hotter outside than in, the scents of wisteria and roses and night jessamine infusing the air with a cloying richness. A far cry from the stormy night on Medinos he was having trouble forgetting and the passionate hours from last night that were still etched on his brain.

He paced restlessly along his end of the deck, taking care to avoid Gemma's room.

He wasn't desperate—yet.

Although that was a mantra that was rapidly losing its power.

Soft music drifted on the night air, the low throaty sound of a blues singer. Frowning, he glanced in the direction of Gemma's room and noticed that both of her French doors were open.

Jaw tight, he strolled toward his room, which just happened to take him closer to Gemma's.

A rich, musky scent that reminded him of a dark, expensive little souk he'd once walked through in Morroco—and which had been filled with filmy lace garments, interesting bits of leather and shelves of aphrodisiacs—caught at his nostrils, drawing him past his door.

Gemma stepped out onto the balcony, almost stopping

his heart. Dressed in a sexy little chemise that revealed an enticing swell of cleavage and left her long legs mostly bare, she took his breath. "I thought you were tired."

She shrugged. "I had a nap earlier—" She frowned. "Darn, that didn't sound good."

Another step and he could see that the scent came from flickering candles set on almost every available surface of Gemma's room. "What's wrong with taking a nap if you're tired?"

Although he could barely concentrate on the conversation. The musky scent from the candles and the seductive setting they created were distracting him, but not as much as the fierce response of his body.

"Because it sounds like something a tired mother might do."

"And you're not that?"

"Not tonight." Stepping close, she grasped both ends of the towel draped around his neck and pulled him into her room, step by slow step. Every muscle in his body tightened at the slumberous seduction in her gaze, and then he saw the magazine.

It wasn't folded open, but he recognized that it was unmistakeably the same one that contained the article "How To Seduce Your Man in Ten Easy Moves."

Relief that they had finally moved past the awkward silences of the day eased some of his tension.

From memory, Gemma had settled on the section headed Slow, Heated Enticements.

If he wasn't mistaken, he was about to be embroiled in technique number six: setting the scene for seduction with erotic scented candles.

Despite his arousal, the fact that Gemma thought she needed to seduce him didn't please Gabriel. It reminded him of her seduction attempt with Zane, that when she had needed a husband, and a father for Sanchia, Gemma hadn't approached him.

He was fighting jealousy, pure and simple. He wanted Gemma to be upfront with him and spontaneous. He wanted the same heart-pounding passion he had gotten just days ago on Medinos, and last night in Gemma's apartment.

His stomach tightened on the thought that maybe this seduction wasn't for his benefit so much as Gemma's. She had agreed to marriage but, despite admitting that she had loved him in the past, he didn't know how she really felt now.

Gemma let go of the towel. "What's wrong?"

He picked up the magazine. "This." Stepping out on the balcony, he tossed it over the side. "We didn't need that six years ago. We don't need it now."

Gemma, who had followed him out onto the balcony, stared over the side as the fluttering magazine hit the pavers around the pool. "You went through my bag on Medinos."

"While you were asleep. And before you ask why, it was because I was jealous." He caught her around the waist and drew her close. "If I'd found condoms I would have punched Zane out."

He saw the instant glimmer of relief in her eyes and his mood lightened. That was spontaneous and her relief that he was jealous was definitely real.

Her palms, which were spread on his chest, slipped up as she coiled her arms around his neck. "I'm sorry about the magazine. It was a dumb idea all around. I should have tossed it on Medinos."

Her body slid against his, and his hands closed on her hips. News flash, he thought grimly, she did not need the magazine.

She frowned, her gaze startlingly direct. "Do you still want to make love?"

"Just as long as you don't think you're giving me some kind of consolation prize," he growled.

She smiled, the kind of wide smile that stopped his heart.

He pulled her close enough that she could feel just exactly how much he did want to make love to her. "Just promise me one thing." He picked up a handful of silky hair, threading his fingers through it. "Do whatever it is you do and make this red again."

"You don't like brunettes?"

Swinging her up in his arms he carried her to the bed, set her down and joined her. "Not for six years."

"Then I might consider it."

He watched as she slipped out of the chemise, restraining himself from simply grabbing her and taking control. His patience was rewarded as she slowly peeled his soft cotton pants over his hips and down his legs.

When he was finally naked she straddled him and produced a foil packet and ripped it open. He almost grinned when he saw the condom, which was color coordinated with the candles, although the desire to smile disappeared as she ripped open the foil package and began to fit the condom. The feel of her hands on him and the small fumbling movements she made almost drove him insane.

When he was completely sheathed, she gently lowered herself onto him. Taking a deep breath, he fought for control as she accustomed herself to having him inside her then began to move, slowly and smoothly, closing her eyes as she did so.

Exquisite pleasure rolled through Gabriel. He framed Gemma's hips, steadying her as the tension coiled and built on endless waves of heat until, with a muttered expletive,

Gabriel moved, rolling her beneath him as the shimmering heat and intensity coiled tight and the scented, candlelit night dissolved in a blaze of light.

Fifteen

The wedding was set for the following weekend, the reception booked at the Dolphin Bay Resort, which was adjacent to the Messena estate.

Luisa arrived home after two days, but happily Gabriel had already explained the whole situation to his mother over the phone. Sanchia took care of any other awkwardness. As the long-awaited first Messena grandchild, she was always guaranteed center stage for Luisa. Gemma was more than happy to take a quiet step back and let Luisa come to terms with the impending marriage.

The following day, after another night of lovemaking and physical closeness, during which the distance she couldn't seem to close was just as present, just as frustrating, Gabriel had to go back to town for an appointment he couldn't cancel.

Already dressed for work in a dark suit with a blue tie

that made him look formal and distant, Gabriel pulled her close for a kiss, then picked Sanchia up and hugged her.

Standing on the forecourt, waving goodbye as he drove away, Gemma couldn't help comparing his response to Sanchia with his response to her.

With Sanchia there was no ambivalence. Gabriel loved her unconditionally; it was there in the teasing exchanges, the way he relaxed with his daughter. His response to her was guarded; there was no other word for it. No matter how hard she tried, the tension hadn't entirely dissolved.

While Gabriel was away, Gemma threw herself into ordering the dresses for the wedding. Luisa, who was expert at all forms of entertaining, took over the organizing for the pre-wedding dinner and the ceremony and reception the next day.

Expecting the wedding to be very small because of the short notice, Gemma was a little dismayed to see the Messena social network come to immediate vibrant life. Family and friends were not only coming from distant places in New Zealand, Gabriel had organized charter flights to bring cousins and relatives from overseas.

As she spent time with Gabriel's mother, Gemma came to the conclusion that, in her own way, Luisa was trying to make her feel at home and accepted as Gabriel's bride.

Warmed, when the dresses were delivered by helicopter on the front lawn, she unwrapped the parcels and showed Luisa the wedding and flower girl dresses she had selected.

Luisa touched the silk and exclaimed over the workmanship. "I trained as a seamstress before I got married, so I know how much work has gone into these. They're beautiful. If you need any help with the fitting, I can do the alterations."

Touched by Luisa's kindness, the days passed almost too quickly.

* * *

Gabriel returned from Auckland the day before the wedding and an hour before the pre-wedding function Luisa had planned at the Dolphin Bay Resort was due to start.

His cell rang as he walked into the front hall. Setting down Sanchia, who had rushed out to chatter excitedly at him, he fielded the call, his expression grim.

By the time he got off the phone, Gemma was on the phone talking to her best friend, Elena, Zane's current PA, who had just arrived in Dolphin Bay.

The private moment she had been hoping to share with Gabriel slipped away. Instead, Gabriel sent her another one of the neutral glances that frightened her to death because they made her feel that, emotionally, he was growing even more distant, and strode up the stairs to his room.

Ten minutes later, he appeared, showered and dressed in a pair of dark trousers and a gauzy dark shirt worn loose, the two top buttons undone. The effect was casual, devastating. Hot.

When he got close to her, instead of kissing her, he reached into his pocket and brought out a pair of diamond earrings. "You should wear these tonight."

The earrings were beautiful, part of the Fabergé set that matched her engagement ring and necklace.

He cupped her bare shoulders, the warmth of his palms sending a hot tingle through her as he turned her so she could see herself in the large oval mirror that was hung just inside the door.

Lifting her hair away from one ear, sending more shivering-hot whispers of sensation through her, he dangled an earring so she could see the effect. "Perfect."

Although, Gemma wasn't looking at the earring. It was Gabriel's gaze she was most interested in, but the emotion, the warmth she longed to see, wasn't there.

Misery twisted in her as she took the earrings and began very carefully putting them on. Originally they would have been clip-ons, but someone had thoughtfully had them converted for pierced ears.

They dangled, scintillating with the same pure fire as her ring, perfectly matching her pink dress and making her look like a million dollars. "They're beautiful, but you don't have to give me gifts. The ring is more than enough."

He turned her around, and this time he did kiss her. "You're going to be my wife. You'll have to get used to wearing expensive jewelry." His mouth quirked at one corner, the first hint of humor she'd seen from him since he'd arrived and in that moment she realized how grim he'd been. "Unfortunately, as a banker's wife, it's part of the job."

The party was elegant but casual, held mostly outside under an enormous white tent that would also be used for the wedding reception the following day.

Gabriel circulated with Gemma, introducing her to the family and friends she didn't know and keeping a wary eye on Sanchia, who was running wild with a couple of her cousins. As night fell, the music got a little louder and the resort lights glowed to life, shimmering off a huge curvaceous swimming pool and spotlighting clumps of graceful palms.

As they walked together, Gemma seemed more than ordinarily quiet, but he put that down to tiredness. According to Luisa, Sanchia had been fretful at night, so Gemma had missed sleep. Add to that the workload of organizing the wedding and he would be surprised if she was in sparkling form. Still…

Movement registered in the parking lot. He frowned as he noticed the dark head of a new arrival.

Zane Atraeus. Fury gripped Gabriel. He could hardly believe it. Moments later, Zane disappeared, swallowed up by the crowd spilling out of the marquee.

Excusing himself, he left Gemma chatting with her friend Elena as they watched the kids playing and strode toward the last place he had seen Zane.

He found him standing at the bar with Nick. Suppressing the primitive urge to grip Zane's shoulder and spin him around, Gabriel contented himself with asking Zane if they could have a word in private.

Zane lifted a brow, but didn't argue. "If you're worried about Gemma, I never touched her."

"I know that." Gabriel clamped down on his impatience. "What I wanted to know is what you plan on doing next."

Zane's gaze narrowed. "That would be marrying the woman I love, in about two months time."

Gabriel let out a breath. He knew Zane; he was a straight shooter and not given to displays of emotions. If he said he was in love, he was in love, period. "Did Gemma ever date anyone other than you?"

"Not that I know of."

A stunning brunette Gabriel recognized as Lilah Cole strolled toward them and slid her arm around Zane's waist. He pulled her in close.

Zane made introductions.

Gabriel noticed the engagement ring on Lilah's finger. "Congratulations."

Lilah smiled. "Likewise. Looks like weddings are in the air."

Zane tucked Lilah in more snugly against his side. "I do know one thing about Gemma. She had plenty of opportunities to date. Guys hit on her all the time, and I mean all the time. Usually, she didn't want to know. If you ask me, she's waiting for that once-in-a-lifetime special love."

Gabriel didn't miss the challenge in Zane's words, or the steely glance that went with them. Not quite a warning, but close.

In that moment, he warmed to his cousin more than he ever had. Zane had genuinely cared about Gemma, and he was sending Gabriel a curt message that he would hear about it if she got hurt.

Zane's opinion that Gemma was looking for true love reverberated through Gabriel as he watched his cousin and Lilah stroll over to the buffet, and suddenly he got her.

Gemma was an idealist and a romantic. Nothing else explained the extremity of her actions. She was looking for true love, but she was also wary of being hurt.

For years he had tried to keep tabs on her. He had been constantly frustrated, because she would disappear overseas with Zane, or she wouldn't be at the social event he had decided to attend because she was there.

It hadn't been pure coincidence that he had never managed to connect with her. She had been actively avoiding him.

He hadn't understood why. Now that he knew about Sanchia, he did. Gemma hadn't wanted to be forced into a compromised relationship. She had been protecting herself, her daughter *and him*.

Not because she didn't love him, but because she did.

"Gabriel."

A familiar feminine voice that lately had started to intrude just a little too often into his life jerked his head around. "Simone." His stomach sank. "You weren't supposed to come here."

A movement at the periphery of his vision distracted him. He frowned, for a moment certain he had seen a flash of the ivory-toned dress Gemma had been wearing. Although he had probably been mistaken. With the number of women and men wearing light, cool colors, it could have been anyone.

Simone placed a hand on his arm. "I couldn't stay away. I had to see you."

His jaw tightened at her sudden intensity. An intensity he had been avoiding at work for weeks now. He removed her fingers. "You were supposed to be on holiday this week."

"I am." She smiled with the same kind of steely determination he had seen on her very wealthy father's face when he closed a deal that he wanted. "I'm here, in Dolphin Bay. I just checked into the resort."

Gemma froze in place behind the tree she had ducked behind when she had seen Simone. Her cool, light voice, and the words, "I couldn't stay away, I had to see you," kept reverberating through her mind.

And it wasn't just the words, but the way they were spoken, with an edge of desperation.

She shifted back into the shadows at the side of the tent as Gabriel walked with Simone into the resort.

Simone looked as cool and perfect as she had at the bank, although distinctly bridal with the white shell dress and discreet pearls. Gabriel was being careful not to touch her, but his distance and stiffness was revealing.

"You weren't supposed to come here."

The words indicated that there had been a conversation, probably during the important appointment Gabriel hadn't been able to miss in Auckland that week. He would have had to tell Simone that they could no longer be together because he was marrying the mother of his child.

Feeling numb, she went into the hotel lounge that was open to the party, turned down a corridor that led to the ladies' room, which also contained a business center.

Pushing the door of the business center open, she stepped inside and walked to one of the desks. Extracting her phone from her bag, which had a sizable screen and an internet connection, she went online and did a search using Simone's name.

The second hit was all she needed. It was a gossip columnist's piece about a charity event Simone had attended with Gabriel, ending with speculation about an expected engagement before the end of the month.

Gemma stared at the photo of Gabriel and Simone together and the caption beneath—The Perfect Couple.

The article explained the conversation she had overheard on Medinos, when Luisa Messena had talked about an engagement by the end of the month. The date of the charity event was less than three weeks ago.

She did a further search and found more information. Simone's family was rich and connected, which made sense of why Gabriel hadn't asked Simone to pose as his fake fiancée. He probably hadn't gotten to the stage of proposing, so to ask that of Simone would have been totally wrong.

Gemma didn't think Gabriel was in love with Simone, otherwise he wouldn't have made love with her. But neither had he ever said he was in love with Gemma.

What really mattered was that the very thing Gabriel hadn't wanted to happen, had. Six years ago he'd had to put aside any plans and dreams he might have had to take over the business and responsibility for his family. Now she had taken away the one free choice he had left.

She'd dreamed of marrying him six years ago, but because he loved her, not because he was fulfilling yet another duty, another obligation.

And if she didn't do something, they would get married tomorrow and head for an even bigger disaster.

Closing down the page and her internet connection, she tucked the phone back in her bag and walked slowly back through the lounge and out onto the hotel terrace.

The sound of the music, which before had seemed just right, now seemed overloud, sparking a sharp ache at her temples, and the number of people at the party seemed to have swelled.

Fingers tightening on her clutch, Gemma searched the laughing, chatting groups of guests and tried to think. Gabriel was nowhere in sight; neither was Simone.

The thought that they could be in Simone's room, since she had checked into the resort, sent a sharp pain straight to her heart, although she quickly vetoed the idea. She knew Gabriel, and he was honorable. She wouldn't love him if he were a low-down sneaky womanizer.

He would be talking to Simone and trying to get her to leave without making a scene. Maybe he would even be helping her check out, then he would make sure she left.

She knew from the things that Luisa had said that Gabriel was meticulous about detail. When he took care of a situation he left no stone unturned. That was why he had made such a success of the bank, despite being thrown in the deep end when his father had died.

He would be finishing things with Simone so that there would be no repercussions within their marriage. But it was too late, because the one flaw in her thinking had been exposed. Her own emotions were the problem. The second Gabriel had suggested they get married, she should have vetoed the idea and suggested they just share custody of Sanchia.

But no. She'd seen Gabriel fall in love with Sanchia and crumbled and selfishly grabbed at what she had wanted.

Walking quickly, she made her way back to the last place she had seen her sister Lauren and asked her if she could have Sanchia for the night.

Lauren frowned. "What's wrong? You're white as a sheet."

Gemma made an effort to smile. "I'm okay, just a little tired."

Lauren shook her head. "What am I saying? Of course you're tired. You helped organize this lovely party, and you're getting married tomorrow. Of course we'll have Sanchia."

Finding Elena was a little more difficult; she seemed to have melted away. Gemma checked her wristwatch. It had been a good fifteen minutes since she had seen Gabriel and Simone disappear into the resort lobby. By the time she had searched the marquee another good ten minutes had passed. She didn't know how long Gabriel would spend with Simone, but if he was trying to check her out of the resort it wouldn't take too long.

Eventually, she saw Elena, distinctive in her red dress, her hair a dark swath down her back, in conversation with a shadowy masculine figure at the deserted end of the pool nearest the resort parking lot. For a moment, she thought it was Gabriel, and her stomach tightened until she recognized one of Gabriel's brothers.

As she approached, he dragged long fingers through his hair, as if frustrated, then turned, letting her know that he was aware his conversation with Elena was no longer private.

Light glanced off one taut cheekbone and a stubbled, obdurate jaw, and highlighted caramel streaks in his tousled dark hair. Super-sexy and hot, but not Gabriel. It was his younger brother, Nick.

Taking a deep breath, Gemma broke into a conversation that looked unusually fraught.

Elena shot her a turbulent look, her dark eyes still lit with the remnants of some fiery emotion. The display of temper was distinctly out of character, because normally Elena was ultracalm and controlled: She was the kind of woman who had a walk-in closet for shoes and bespoke designed hangers for scarves and belts. When put against the cheerful chaos of Gemma's wardrobe, that kind of control spoke volumes.

Gemma glanced at Nick and wondered what she had walked into. "Hello, Nick, sorry to butt in, but I need Elena."

His normally warm green eyes were glacial. "Join the queue."

Elena shot Nick an irritated look. "Last time I looked there wasn't a queue." Pointedly, she turned to Gemma. "It's okay, I can come now. I'm all finished here."

Nick frowned. "We need to talk."

Elena gave him a bland smile Gemma recognized only too well—the pacifying smile of a PA for a difficult client. "It's too late for another discussion tonight."

Nick sent her a cool, measuring look. "Then save me a dance at the wedding."

Gemma led the way into the parking lot and found a quiet spot under the deep shadow of a pohutukawa tree.

Elena made a seat for herself on the low plastered wall that separated the parking lot from the sweeping lawns. "One night and he thinks I'm a doormat."

Gemma almost dropped the diamond earrings she had just carefully extracted from her lobes. "You slept with Nick Messena?"

"It was a long time ago. A youthful mistake. Everyone's entitled to one."

Her thinking exactly. One mistake was allowable, not two.

She took a deep breath. "I need your help."

Sixteen

Gabriel checked his watch as he saw Simone into her car and waited until her taillights disappeared down the drive. Feeling grimly annoyed at the pressure both Simone and her socialite mother had brought to bear, both personally and through the press, he headed back to the party.

After several minutes of walking through the crowded marquee and pool area, he stepped into the lobby of the resort and saw Elena.

The minute he started to ask her if she knew where Gemma was, he knew something was wrong.

Gemma had seen him with Simone and totally misread the situation. "Where is she?"

Elena reached into her evening bag and took out a folded envelope. "I don't know. I'm sorry I can't be more helpful. I tried to stop her, but she said she needed some time. She gave me this to hand to you."

Gabriel opened the envelope. His stomach dropped

when he saw the engagement ring and the earrings. "How long ago did she leave?"

"A few minutes."

Gabriel headed straight for the parking lot. Gemma wouldn't leave without Sanchia, which meant that they could have gone to the house to get some things before they left Dolphin Bay.

He climbed into his car, thumbing a number on his phone as he slammed the door. A quick conversation later and he knew that neither Gemma nor Sanchia had gone to the house.

As he accelerated down the drive, he tried Gemma's phone, without much hope. Even if her phone was turned on, when she saw his number she probably wouldn't answer it. When the call went through to voice mail, he tossed the phone on the passenger seat and continued driving.

He turned into Lauren's drive on the off chance that Gemma's sister would know something. When Lauren answered the door and told him that she had Sanchia tucked up in bed, all the breath left his lungs.

"Are you all right?"

He met Lauren's concerned gaze. "She's left."

"Left?" Lauren frowned. "She wouldn't. She loves you. She always has."

Gabriel's fingers curled into fists. "What makes you say that?"

As far as he was concerned, apart from the one mistake he had made years ago in leaving Gemma, she had been the one walking away.

"You do know she's only ever slept with you, right?"

Gabriel's jaw clamped. "Yes."

"Do you know why a girl as gorgeous as Gemma has only ever slept with you? It's because she fell in love with you when she was about sixteen and, somehow, being Gemma, she just never fell out of love."

There it was again, the extremity. He knew about it, had tried to reason it out, but in a blinding moment he realized there was nothing to reason.

She loved him. It was black and white, an absolute truth.

He stared out into the moonlit night, edgy frustration eating at him because he needed to find her now. "Have you got any idea where she would have gone?"

Lauren frowned. "If she's running out on the wedding, I'd say back to Auckland."

Not with Sanchia still here.

And suddenly he knew. Gemma was a romantic and an idealist. *She loved him.* There was only one place she would be.

He drew a deep breath. "I think I know where she is."

Gemma carried her shoes as she waded the last few yards to the island that sat just south of the resort.

The tide was on its way in. As she'd walked, waves had kept splashing against the narrow causeway, gradually soaking her. To make matters worse, a thick bank of cloud had moved in, obscuring the moonlight so that she'd had to pick her way carefully, in case she missed the causeway and fell into the deeper water on either side.

The water now almost entirely covered the causeway. A few more minutes and it would disappear under the waves and the island would be cut off from the mainland.

Stepping onto the pretty, hard-packed shell beach, she set down her evening bag and the bottle of water she'd taken from the marquee drinks table, and used the resort towel she'd borrowed from the pool house to dry herself off.

As she straightened, her phone chimed. Taking the

phone out of her clutch, she checked the number, her heart thumping hard in her chest when she saw that Gabriel was trying to call her.

The call went through to voice mail.

Resolutely she turned the phone off. Slipping it back into her bag, she picked up her shoes, the bag and the water and kept walking, and wished she had thought to borrow a flashlight.

Ten minutes of careful negotiation of the rock-strewn beach later, she rounded a small headland and found the pretty resort beach house. Although in reality it was little more than a pavilion that was used for day-trippers and sometimes for evening events like champagne picnics.

She stepped into the trellised shelter with its graceful pergola-style roof and padded daybeds and sat down. Silence enclosed her, broken by the gentle rhythm of the sea as waves broke on the sand, and more distantly, the lonely cry of a pukeko, a native swamp bird that roamed the area around the resort.

Now that she was here, the idea of escaping to a place where Gabriel could choose to come and find her if he truly wanted to seemed desperate and hopelessly flawed.

For one thing, she hadn't thought about the tide. Walking here wouldn't be an option until the small hours of the morning. Even if he did remember the place where it had all begun for them, he wouldn't be able to get here unless he managed to borrow a boat.

She was going to have a long, lonely night, and then she would have to face the music tomorrow.

Sanchia was expecting to be a bridesmaid. There were people coming from Sydney, Florida, London and Medinos for the wedding. Luisa had insisted on ordering a hopelessly extravagant and utterly gorgeous six-tiered cake, with chocolate layers for the kids.

Gabriel would be… She drew a sudden breath. Gabriel would be hurt.

The lonely quiet seemed to seep into her skin. Maybe she wasn't Gabriel's dream come true as a wife, but he had been ready to commit, and he wanted to be a father to Sanchia.

Pushing to her feet she walked back down onto the beach and began to pace. No matter which way she looked at the situation and the decisions she'd made, first to agree to the marriage, then to get cold feet and run out on it, she had made a mess of things.

Half an hour later, beginning to feel desperate because now she wanted off the island and there was no way that was going to happen, she walked back to the pavilion and looked for her phone.

She thumbed through to contacts and pressed Gabriel's number. Holding her breath, she listened to the ring tone, her mood plummeting even further when the call wasn't picked up.

She gave it a couple of minutes while she walked down to the break line and tried again. The phone rang several times. Misery gripping her, she stared up at the dull, leaden sky. "Pick up, Gabriel. Where are you when I need you?"

"I'm here," a low rough voice said. "Talk to me, babe, before I go crazy."

Gemma spun. Gabriel was just meters away, hair slicked back, bronzed torso gleaming with moisture as if he'd not long ago walked out of the surf. His dark pants were just as wet, clinging to his narrow hips and sticking to his skin where they touched.

For a bleak moment she thought she was hallucinating. "You swam."

"It was farther than I thought." He pulled a dripping cell out of his pocket. "No point in ringing that number again. The phone's dead."

And suddenly she didn't care about Simone or any of the other beautiful, intelligent women in his life, and she didn't care about the old inferiority complex that had crippled her for so long. Gabriel was here, now, for her.

He was soaking wet and his phone was destroyed *because he'd had to swim to get to her*.

And suddenly she saw him, not the wealthy banker with platinum cards and gleaming Maseratis, but the gorgeous, beleaguered, beautiful man she loved.

He just had time to toss the phone in the sand before she caromed into his chest.

His arms closed around her, hauling her in tight. "I wasn't sure that you wanted me to follow."

"I did. I do. I'm sorry I ran out on you like that. I can't believe you came after me."

His gaze locked on hers, dark and emotion-filled. "Then you don't know me very well. I haven't seriously wanted anyone but you for years. Why do you think I'm still single?" He paused for breath. "Marry me."

"In a heartbeat."

He cupped her face. "Promise?"

"On my heart. I love you, no one else. I've loved you for years." And finally she blurted out the problem that had hampered her all those years ago. "I thought I wasn't good enough. I was an employee."

He gave her the kind of mystified look that told her that she had been completely wrong on that score. "I'll admit that the employee thing was a problem just after Dad died, because of the press. But the real reason I stayed away from you was because what I felt was so addictive, I was afraid I'd make the same mistake my father had. I knew I couldn't do the job that needed to be done and have a relationship with you at the same time."

Compulsively, she ran her hands over his shoulders, curled her fingers into the damp hair at his nape. Despite the fact that he was wet and should be cold, his skin was warm, the life in him burning bright and indomitable.

She cupped his jaw, loving the grim masculinity of his five o'clock shadow, needing the reassurance of touch. She was hardly able to believe that he was here, when she had done her level best to mess everything up.

He held one hand captive and turned his mouth against it in a gentle caress. "I know you saw me with Simone. She was trying to maneuver me into a relationship. I wasn't interested, but she couldn't take no for an answer."

"I thought you wanted her. I felt like I'd trapped you into marriage. I wanted to give you the choice."

"Where you're concerned, there's only been one choice for a long time. I'm sorry I let you go all those years ago. I won't let you go again." He paused, his voice husky with emotion. "I love you."

And in that moment the moon came out, spreading a molten silvery glow over sea and wet sand, glimmering on the damp, muscular curve of his shoulders and allowing her to see the softness in his gaze. Closing her eyes, Gemma lifted up on her toes and kissed him.

When she opened her eyes, Gabriel smiled, picked her up with the easy strength she loved and carried her into the pavilion.

When he set her down on one of the daybeds and joined her, she saw the time glowing on his watch. It was after midnight.

Their wedding day.

* * *

Hours later, Gemma woke to find the first gray light of dawn illuminating the pavilion. Shivering slightly, she cuddled in closer to Gabriel.

They'd made love, slept and made love again, then finally dragged two daybeds together for comfort, found a store of towels and beach blankets in a locker, and made a bed of sorts.

Gabriel caught a strand of her hair and tugged it lightly. "About Simone. I didn't have an appointment with her. We did have a discussion, but it was about the loan structure for a major development she was working on. She offered to bring it down personally for my signature. I told her not to bother. The reason I had to go back to Auckland was to sort out the legal paperwork dissolving Mario's trusteeship."

Gemma turned on her side and propped her chin on the heel of her hand. "I forgot completely about that."

Gabriel pulled her close and kissed her softly. "Forget the bank. I have. It's our wedding day."

Giddy delight shimmered through her. She could still scarcely believe that she and Gabriel were getting married after all, that she would wear her lovely wedding dress and walk down the aisle toward him. That Gabriel loved her with passion, and had for years.

The wedding was held in a pretty church on top of a hill, with a breathtaking view of Dolphin Bay.

Gemma was ready early. Her mother, Lauren and the kids and Elena had arrived just minutes before the influx of hairdressers and beauticians. She'd deliberately hurried each stage because the last thing she wanted to do was to make Gabriel wait.

After everything that had happened, all she wanted to do was get to the church early and get married to her man.

Her gown was gorgeous, dove-soft ivory silk that made her skin glow like honey and made her hair look even richer. The Fabergé diamonds went perfectly with the dress.

While she had dressed, Luisa had filled her in on the history of the jewels. Apparently, Gabriel's grandfather, Guido, had fallen in love with a Russian girl during the war. Separated by the conflict, he had continued to woo her with letters. When the replies had stopped, worried, he had gone to Russia and found her.

Destitute after the losses of the war, Eugenie had decided he wouldn't want her anymore. Guido Messena had proven otherwise. The jewels had been his wedding gift to her.

Luisa had given her a smiling glance at the end of the small story and Gemma had picked up on the subtext. Gabriel had known the romantic history of the jewels. He had chosen them for that reason.

When the bridal limousine arrived at the church, it was so early guests had to be hurried inside. Gabriel, who was outside the church talking with Nick and one of his other brothers, Kyle, glanced across at her and met her gaze for a heart-stopping moment.

Mesmerizingly handsome in a gray morning suit, instead of going inside the church with his brothers, Gabriel helped her out of the limousine, smiled into her eyes then took her arm.

When they reached the nave and the music began, Gemma stopped and waited for Elena to organize Sanchia, who was the flower girl.

When Gabriel didn't walk on and join Nick and Kyle at the altar, but stayed with them, waiting for the wedding march to begin, she sent him an anxious look. "They're waiting for you at the altar."

In response he took her arm, drawing her close to his side as Sanchia began her careful trek to the altar, tossing rose petals. "They can wait. Right now I'm going to walk up the aisle with my two girls."

* * * * *

MY FAKE FIANCÉE

BY
NANCY WARREN

USA Today bestselling author **Nancy Warren** lives in the Pacific Northwest where her hobbies include walking her border collie in the rain and watching romantic comedies. She's the author of more than thirty novels and novellas and has won numerous awards. Visit her at www.nancywarren.net.

For my Mom,
the best amateur caterer I know,
who taught me how to cook.
Thanks, Mom!

1

THE ELEVATOR DOORS opened like welcoming arms as David Wolfe crossed the marble floor of the office building in downtown Philadelphia. Not having to wait for an elevator during the Monday morning rush was always a good sign. It was going to be one of those great days when everything went his way.

When the doors opened again to deposit him on the twenty-first floor and the offices of Keppler, Van Horne Insurance Co., he was already moving.

Life had never been better. After six years of hard work in the prestigious family-owned-and-run firm, he'd had a few subtle hints dropped his way about a vice presidency coming vacant when Damien Macabee retired. David was so ready to be the youngest VP in the company's history.

As he strode to his office, he greeted his assistant, "Morning, Jane."

"Morning, David." Jane was a middle-aged career secretary and probably the closest to a stroke of sheer luck he'd ever had in his career. They respected each other's work ethics, operated as an efficient team and he knew that one day when he was president of Keppler, Van Horne she'd still be his right hand. A partnership like that didn't come along very often.

"I made a couple of changes to your schedule today. The Belvedere group asked if you can make it at four instead of three, so I shuffled some things around."

"Great, thanks."

He scratched his nose. It was itchy with sunburn after a weekend sailing where he'd played doctor with a nurse from Boston who'd kept him too busy to think about sunscreen.

"Oh, and you had three calls from some woman named Gretchen."

"Gretchen leave a last name?"

She smiled thinly. "I don't think she's interested in an insurance policy."

"Oh, that Gretchen." She was a flight attendant he'd had some fun with, but who clearly wanted more from the relationship than he was willing to give. "I told her not to call me at the office." He never gave out his office number to women he hooked up with, but it wasn't hard to track him down. A simple Google search did the trick. "If she calls again, tell her—"

"If she calls again I'll put her through. Maybe you should tell her yourself."

"Right. You're right."

"I take it you didn't get sunburned with Gretchen."

"No. I sailed with a woman named Claire." He chuckled in memory. "She's a lot of fun, in fact—"

Jane was looking over his shoulder, and suddenly interrupted, saying, "No wonder you're going to marry her. You two are perfect for each other."

If Jane was talking about his fiancée, it could only mean one thing, which was confirmed when an older man's voice hailed him. "Ah, David. Do you have a minute?"

He turned to greet the president and CEO of the company, Piers Van Horne. "Sure, Piers. Come on in."

"You're sunburned," the older man remarked. "Where were you and your fiancée off to this weekend?"

David felt Jane's eyes burning into his back like twin laser beams of disapproval. Sure, it wasn't a good idea to tell lies—even little white ones—to the boss, but David was confident his reasoning was sound.

"A little sailing off Cape Cod. The weather was gorgeous."

He led his boss and the CEO of the company into his office, where they settled around the small conference table. David kept his space uncluttered. The only personal touches were his framed MBA degree, his current insurance industry designations and on his desk a photo of him hugging a dark-haired woman. You could only see the back of her head, but David was laughing into the camera and they were clearly having a good time.

Piers gestured to the photograph. "How's that lovely girl of yours?"

David had been talking about his fiancée for months, ever since he'd heard rumors of Macabee's imminent retirement. He knew that Keppler, Van Horne had an unwritten rule. No one got promoted to VP who wasn't married. The VPs were expected to entertain clients both at home and abroad, and for that reason, Piers and his brother who ran the company preferred that the VPs, both male and female, be part of a couple. David figured he'd fudged the lines on a few rule books and he was determined to do the same with this. So, he'd started talking about his fiancée. Casually. He'd come to work on a Monday and talk about the weekend he and his fiancée had spent in New York. Or the quick trip they'd taken to the Caribbean.

"She's wonderful," he answered. "Gives my life meaning. And Helen and the kids?"

They chatted about college decisions and braces and then Piers said, "We'd like to celebrate your engagement. We're a family business and, let's face it, we're all involved in each other's lives, especially at the executive level. We've got a board dinner coming up. I want you to come along and bring your fiancée with you."

For him to be invited to a dinner with the members of the board was a huge honor. It meant he was being looked over by the board members before he was offered the VP spot.

Yes! It was really happening. He was going to be the youngest VP in Keppler, Van Horne's history.

And that's when David got it.

It wouldn't be *him* under scrutiny. Piers and the board wanted to make sure he was marrying the right kind of woman to be a Keppler, Van Horne VP's spouse.

David considered himself a glass-half-full kind of guy, but right now he felt like that glass had fallen off the table and smashed to pieces on the floor, spilling all his hard work and dreams of promotion with it.

"An engagement dinner?" His voice sounded a little higher-pitched than usual as he frantically tried to think of a way out. "I'm not sure, she's got a pretty hectic schedule, I'll—"

Piers rose and clapped him on the shoulder. "Don't worry about it. Since you two are the guests of honor, we'll work around your schedule. We've got plans for you, son. Big plans."

"Thank you, Piers."

After his boss left, he should have plunged into the day's work. Instead, he tried not to panic and started to think.

He was staring out his office window, watching the

pedestrians scurrying like so many ants way down on Arch Street. The hub of the city center was as busy as always as workers scuttled along hot sidewalks before diving into air-conditioned high rises.

Jane entered. "Here are the—" She stopped when she noticed he had his forehead pressed against his office window. It was possible he may have groaned. "What's the matter with you?"

He turned. "Piers and the board want to have an engagement dinner for my fiancée and I. We get to set the date so I can't pretend she's not available."

Jane dropped a stack of papers on his desk with a thump. "If you're looking for sympathy, you came to the wrong person. Didn't I warn you?" She shook her head. "What are you going to do? Break up with the love of your life before the dinner?"

He ignored the sarcasm and shook his head.

She crossed her arms and drilled him with her pissed-off gaze. "How long have you got?"

"Couple of weeks, tops."

"No problem. I'm sure you can find some nice, respectable woman to agree to marry you in a couple of weeks. Should be easy as pie. There's Gretchen, for instance, or... what was her name? Claire?"

"Look, the women I choose to spend time with are not the kind of women Piers and the board would approve of. We both know that." He picked the first file off the desk, then put it back down. "I'm not the marrying kind."

She snorted, but she didn't know his past and he had no intention of sharing the most humiliating interlude in his life. If she wanted to peg him as a player who was having too much fun to get serious, which was essentially true anyway, then that was fine with him.

He made the decision then and there. "You're half-right.

I'm going to find a woman to pose as my fiancée for a couple of months. All I need is a nice, decent woman. She'll meet the board and then after I get the promotion, we'll break up, faster than you can say irreconcilable differences. If I'm up-front about it, nobody will get hurt. How difficult can it be?"

"Let me count the ways. David, this is a terrible idea."

"It's only for a couple of months. All I have to do is find a nice woman."

"Do you know any nice women?"

He scratched his itchy nose again. "Yes. Lots. But none are corporate-spouse material." He glanced at the woman who had almost as much riding on his promotion as he did. "I don't suppose you know anyone?"

"All the women I know are too mature for you. And that includes my twenty-year-old nieces."

He'd been charming women for more years than he could count. He hiked a hip onto his desk, certain he could pull this off. "Care to make a small wager on my chances?"

"What is a guy like you, who loves risk so much, doing working in insurance?"

"Insurance is all about odds, Jane, you know that. The client pays a small premium in case catastrophe hits, the insurance company essentially bets that it won't and keeps the money. Risk, safety, reward—it's all tied up. And this risk? I think I can safely take."

Jane opened her mouth, closed it, opened it again. "You are so going to hell."

CHELSEA HAMMOND WAS in the mother of bad moods when she met her friend Sarah Wolfe for a drink after work at a trendy restaurant in Old City. Usually, she loved being here near the river and in the center of the city's history, but not today. It was all just too cute and seemed full of annoying people. Summertime tourists, mostly, she suspected, here to see the Liberty Bell and eat cheesesteak.

William Penn himself seemed to disapprove of her bringing her bad mood into his space. He hulked over her and his great statued hand seemed to be wagging reprovingly down at her.

She should have canceled her drink with Sarah and gone home to sulk. But Sarah was her oldest friend. They'd grown up in houses that faced each other and were the same age. Amazingly, in spite of the fact that their mothers practically shoved them at each other, they'd ended up friends.

As she approached the restaurant she saw that Sarah was already there. Her old friend was wearing one of her tough female lawyer power suits, holding a briefcase in one hand and yelling at someone on a cell phone she held in her other hand. Chelsea sincerely pitied whoever was on the other end of that call.

Their different personalities were represented by their respective clothing choices. Chelsea was snugged into well-worn jeans she'd bought in Paris and her blue-and-green top was an impulse purchase from a weekend trip to fashion-forward Barcelona, as were the leather boots on her feet. Her silver jewelry was all flea-market finds. If her passion was cooking, fashion was a rival love.

As she approached, Sarah caught sight of her and her stern expression vanished in an impish grin. "Okay, yeah. We don't want to go back to court, either. Uh-huh. Good. Talk to him and get back to me." Then she sighed. "Yes, we're still on for dinner."

And she flipped her phone shut without so much as a goodbye. "Cretin," she said, then dropped the phone in her bag and leaned over, opening her arms for a hug. "How you doing?"

"*Cretin* is the word of the day," Chelsea affirmed, hugging her old friend.

They walked into the bar section and settled at a table. Sarah ordered a martini and Chelsea asked for a Pernod.

"You are so French now, it's weird," Sarah said when the drinks arrived and Chelsea poured a little water into the Pernod, clouding it.

"I guess you're right. I got used to Pernod when I was living in Paris. Now I'm hooked."

She pointed at her friend's glass, olives fat and smug in the bottom. "And I know that your poor date tonight won't get far."

"How?"

"You never drink before you have sex with a guy the first time. It was always your rule and I'm betting you haven't changed."

Sarah's teeth flashed in the grin that Chelsea privately thought she should show more often. It revealed her soft, fun-loving side. "We know each other way too well. I missed you. I'm so glad you're back." They toasted each other.

"I missed you."

"So, who's the cretin in your life?"

"My boss. Fabulous at yelling and insulting staff. Which you might forgive him for if he was a genius restaurateur, but he treats food as badly as he treats his employees." She wasn't sure which aspect of her boss's behavior irked her more. "He acts all Gordon Ramsay but he cooks like a caveman who just discovered fire."

"Not a cretin. A troglodyte."

"Exactly. I hate my job. I hate my boss." She dropped her head in her hand and sighed. "Working as a sous chef in a restaurant was the only job I could find when I came home. It's been three weeks of hell."

"Want to sue your boss for harassment?"

She snorted. "No. It's not only me he harasses, it's everyone. I don't even want the job. I want to start my own catering company, but with no capital and no kitchen it's hopeless." And with her debts from training in Paris, as well as the lowly sum she was now earning, it was going to be quite some time before she could open her own shop.

"Don't say that. Of course it's not hopeless."

Chelsea was in no mood for a pep talk. "Shut up. I don't want a rah-rah speech. I want to whine. So, to recap, my job's crap, my boss is crap and oh, yeah, my sublet is about to expire. I'm twenty-eight and all I have is a talent I can't afford to use, cooking equipment I have no kitchen for and a Paris wardrobe. I am such a loser."

"You are not. Look at you. You're gorgeous. I'd kill for your body, men fall all over themselves for you." She squinted at Chelsea's chest. "You were such a late bloomer. It's like you got to college and suddenly sprouted boobs."

"And hips."

"So, work sucks. You've only been home a few weeks. Give yourself a break."

"I guess." She sipped the licorice-flavored liqueur reflectively. She'd had such great plans to open her own catering firm. She knew she had the drive, the talent and the recipes. What she didn't have was capital. Damn, reality sucked.

"I don't even need much money. A decent kitchen would do me to start. I'd complain about the hot plate and bar fridge in my sublet, except that soon I'll be homeless."

"But you went to Paris! To Le Cordon Bleu. It's the dream of a lifetime."

Her forehead creased. "Do you think I might have watched *Sabrina* too many times?" She'd introduced Sarah to the classic movie where Audrey Hepburn, the prettiest chauffeur's daughter ever, fell hopelessly in love with her father's employer's handsome son, William Holden, who barely noticed her. Her father shipped her off to cooking school in Paris to get her over her hopeless crush. Naturally, in the movie, Audrey ended up with the smarter, richer, older brother, Humphrey Bogart, and lived happily ever after.

Sarah laughed. "We loved that movie, didn't we?" She tilted her head and studied Chelsea. "You are a dead ringer for Audrey Hepburn, but you're no chauffeur's daughter."

"I'm the next best thing. I was only living in that neighborhood because my aunt and uncle took Mom and me in after the divorce." She made a wry face. "And I did have a big crush on a guy named David, your brother, who didn't know I existed."

"Hah! You did. You were so shy around him. You'd only ever open your mouth to ask him about homework. He thought you were a total brain. Never knew you had a personality. Or a pretty face under all that long hair you hid behind."

"Don't remind me. He always helped me, though." Her fond memories of the godlike creature darkened suddenly. "Then one of his fluffies would drop by and he'd forget all about me, calculus, everything."

"He still dates fluffies, if you can believe it. The guy never grew up."

It had been more than ten years since she'd seen her teen crush. "Please tell me he's bald now. And a beer belly wouldn't hurt a bit."

"I'd love to, believe me. But the guy's still a major hottie.

Of course, inside, he's the same shallow teenage frat boy. Tragic, really."

"Mmm. He never married?"

Sarah chewed an olive off her pick before saying, "You have to double-pinky swear not to tell anyone I told you, but he was engaged once."

"Really? What happened?"

"I'm not completely sure. But she was smart, pretty, athletic, nauseatingly perfect, really, and then suddenly she decided to go back to her old boyfriend. David acted like it was no biggie, but he was devastated."

Her eyes were round with amazement. Imagine, having a guy like David and letting him go. "He must have been so hurt."

"Yeah. Now he's back to his little fluffies. He's only interested in women who share his comfortable worldview that he's the center of the universe. Who don't challenge him. He puts all his real focus into his career. Thinks he's going to be running his company by the time he's forty. Cretin."

"I see you two still have that love/hate thing going for you."

"I do love him. You know I do. But I'm pissed over the little prank he pulled on me at Christmas."

"You still play tricks on each other?" It sounded to her like neither of them had grown up yet.

"He started it," Sarah exclaimed, pretty much confirming her opinion. "He signed me up for one of those online dating sites. With the stupidest profile you could imagine. Made me sound like a fifties virgin looking for Mr. Right. Took me days to figure out why I was getting personal e-mails from all these conservative stiffs."

She had to force herself not to laugh. Those two had

been punking each other for years. "And what did you do to retaliate?"

"I haven't found anything rotten enough." She smiled a cunning smile and stabbed the last olive in her glass. "Yet."

"Who's your hot date with tonight? Another divorce lawyer?"

"You really do know me too well." She shrugged. "I can't help it. A good argument gets me all riled up. Trouble is, usually when we're not fighting the chemistry fizzles. You know?"

"Oh, I know all about fizzling chemistry. In two languages."

Sarah chuckled. "Look, why don't I blow off this guy and we can hang out?"

She shook her head. "Can't. I have to look for a place. Or a homeless shelter."

"You're welcome to stay with me for as long as you like."

"And I would, if I wasn't allergic to your cat, but thanks."

Sometimes she wondered why she'd even come back to Philly. Her mom had remarried and moved to Florida, her aunt and uncle had retired to Palm Springs. Yet, somehow this was home. Her friends and all of her memories were here. As much as she'd loved Paris, she'd always known she'd come back.

Philippe had begged her to stay, convincing her that they could open the best restaurant in Paris together and if the authorities gave her any trouble with visas, then he would marry her.

But home had called to her, and now here she was, back home, ironically, without a home.

2

DAVID WAS PRETTY GOOD about staying cool under pressure. In his experience, things usually worked out fine. Maybe he needed to work a little longer, push a bit harder, find a way around a blocked path. But he worked a problem until he found a solution.

This was different. He'd stretched out the date of the engagement dinner as far as he could, but it was fast approaching. Having to produce a suitable fiancée in a few days? How was he supposed to do that without stumbling across a magic lantern or selling his soul to the devil?

And not just any girl would do. This one would be under scrutiny from the top brass, the board and their spouses. He'd mentally reviewed every woman he could think of, scoured Facebook, his personal contact lists, but none of the women he knew were the kind of women Piers and his brother would consider corporate-wife material.

Mainly because he was attracted to certain assets in a woman that had nothing to do with long-term plans.

He should have been spending this whole weekend tracking down high-end matchmakers who might know a suitable woman who wanted to be his fake fiancée for a few months. Somebody serious, maybe a little dowdy, who could hold her own in a conversation. Also, she'd have to be discreet. Then, once the VP job was in the bag, he and his wife-to-be would discover she didn't want to marry him after all. He'd get all the sympathy of a jilted man and the job would be his.

However, instead of interviewing suitable candidates, he was heading home for brunch at his parents' place before they headed off on summer vacation for a few weeks.

He pulled in to the driveway of his parents' Cape Cod, noting that his sister's car was already there. Suck-up.

He got out of his vehicle, leaned in for the huge bouquet, part send-off and part guilt gift since he hadn't seen his folks in weeks.

As he walked by his sister's car he saw that she was still in it, arguing on her cell phone as usual. He sent her a cheery wave and walked on, only to halt and head back a slow step or two until he was level with the driver's door. He knew it was desperation driving him now, but Sarah was a lawyer with a ton of women friends, many of whom went to Vassar. One of them might impress Van Horne. Sarah was four years younger than he, so most of her friends were in the right age range. Of course, Sarah's friends tended to be way too serious and definitely too feminist, considering a man's balls not as one of his chief erogenous zones, but as the handiest place to kick him. Hard.

However, he was desperate.

She clicked off the phone, then gave a purr of satisfaction. His sister rarely lost an argument. Or backed down. As he knew from painful experience. She was the perfect divorce lawyer. "What poor schmuck are you screwing over this time?"

"You want to talk about screwing over? The guy hid millions of dollars overseas and now he's suing the wife, a high school teacher, for alimony." She tapped her phone against her chin, "We'll get him."

"Do you ever represent men?"

She gave him a scornful glance. "As if."

Then her gaze sharpened on him. "Well, aren't you the dutiful son?" she crooned, getting an eyeful of the blooms. Then she stepped out of the car and gave him a one-armed hug. "How's my big bro?"

Winning an argument always made her mellow, so he decided to ask for her help, assuming he wouldn't be any further behind if she laughed in his face, which she'd probably do. But maybe, just maybe, she had the perfect woman for him.

"In a jam, as it happens. I need your help."

Her glance softened and a look of concern crossed her face. "Oh, honey, what is it? Not trouble with the law?"

"No. Nothing like that. Woman trouble."

Her crack of laughter nearly wilted the roses in his bouquet. "Here's your problem, lover boy. Those aren't women you insist on going out with. They are emotionally stunted fashion dolls."

"Exactly." He grinned at her shocked expression. "I need to meet a real woman. Someone like you. Who obviously isn't a blood relative." He considered her. "Or a man hater."

"I don't hate men."

"Okay." He wouldn't get anywhere by insulting her, he reminded himself. "Honestly, Sar, I really need your help."

"Tell your counselor everything."

So he did. And watched her eyes grow rounder as the story progressed.

"You lied about having a fiancée for career advancement?"

"You make it sound like that's a bad thing."

She shook her head at him. "What were you thinking?"

"Obviously, I wasn't. Wasn't thinking they'd want to meet this woman, anyway."

She slammed her car door shut with her hip. "I cannot believe any firm in this millennium thinks it's okay to withhold promotions based on a person's marital status." She shook her head. "It's antiquated and wrong."

She was clearly thinking deep legal thoughts. "The whole thing's all but illegal. Want to sue them?" She looked so hopeful he almost laughed.

"No. I don't want to sue my employer. I want the VP job."

"Why did you say you wanted my help?"

"I was hoping you might know a nice, unattached woman, somebody smart and classy who would be good wife-of-the-VP material. Who might enjoy coming out to a few business occasions and posing as my fiancée. Then, after I get the VP job, we'd quietly split."

Her face creased as though she'd tasted something bad. "If I knew any women like that I'd—"

He put up his free hand to stop her. "Never mind. It was a long shot. I really don't need a lecture, either. Let's forget we had this conversation and enjoy a nice family brunch."

He turned to head inside when her hand shot out and grabbed his arm. "Wait."

He turned back.

"Believe it or not, I do know someone who might just be desperate enough to do this, if you help her in return."

"Really?"

She nodded. "You know her, too. Or you used to."

"Who is she?" If he knew this woman, he'd have thought

of her by now since he'd gone through every contact he'd ever made searching for a suitable candidate.

"Chelsea Hammond."

"Chelsea Hammond?" The name rang a vague bell, but he couldn't picture her.

She glared at him. "Chelsea? My best friend? Who lived right there in the Dennises' home while she attended high school?" She pointed to a white two-story that shared a back fence with his folks' place. "She was always over here. She used to bake the most amazing cookies and cakes and stuff."

His confusion cleared. "Oh, you mean Hermione?"

"Nobody called her that but you," Sarah reminded him.

He remembered her well. She was so serious. Always had her nose stuck in a book, often a cookbook, masses of long dark hair and eyes that were too big for her face. The minute he'd read the first Harry Potter book he'd thought of Sarah's serious friend and from that moment on had called her Hermione, after Harry's best friend, the superbrainy Hermione Granger.

Before he could ask more, the front door opened. "I thought I heard you two outside," their dad said, beaming at them. He raised his voice and bellowed, "Meg, the kids are here," and his mother came out from the kitchen with her arms spread wide.

Meg and Lawrence Wolfe were like the poster couple in the early retirement ads. They were exactly what they looked like. Successful, healthy and still—as far as he could judge—happily married. They traveled, got away in the winter to somewhere warm, golfed, gave dinner parties and attended church regularly. His mom volunteered at a soup kitchen and his dad had recently, to his and Sarah's eternal embarrassment, involved himself in amateur theater.

Their only disappointment, as far as he could tell, was that neither of their children was married.

The minute they'd said their hellos and got the initial chitchat out of the way, Sarah went to the shelf of photo albums in the walnut bookcase beside the gas fireplace, chose an album and flipped through. She brought the album over to him.

"Here's a picture of the three of us. Chelsea, you and me."

He squinted at the album his sister shoved under his nose. The event was Sarah's birthday and the three teenagers stood together. He had his arm around both girls. The cake read Happy 15th Birthday, Sarah, and they'd posed beside it. He'd have been nineteen, he supposed, and he towered over the two girls. A slight, thin girl, Hermione had shiny dark hair, he remembered, that was like a curtain, hiding her face. She used to blush when he was around, which made him suspect she had a bit of a schoolgirl crush on him. She'd been a nice kid, though. He was pretty sure he'd helped her with her homework a few times.

"What's she doing now?" he asked, trying to sound casual.

"She studied at Le Cordon Bleu in Paris. She only got home a few weeks ago and is looking for a kitchen. She plans to start her own catering company."

His mother came and looked over his shoulder. "She was such a nice girl. I'm glad she's back. We'll have to have her over when we get back from vacation." Then she asked his next question for him. "Is she still single?"

"Yep."

Meg sighed. "I don't know what it is with you young people. Doesn't anybody get married anymore?"

"Sure we do, Mom. David and I are selective, that's all."

David was still staring at the photograph, trying to imagine Hermione all grown up. He studied her at fifteen. Nice hair, big eyes, clear skin. He could imagine her older. He pictured a librarian type with her hair in a bun. Maybe glasses from all that reading. He really liked the image. He had one fear that Sarah's update had raised. "Catering, huh. Has she gained a lot of weight?"

Both women sent him identical withering looks.

"What? I'm just asking."

"I had drinks with her on Thursday. She's not as skinny as she was at fifteen. She's filled out a little. She looks the same only twelve years older. If anything, she's prettier than she used to be. Otherwise, she's exactly the same," she assured him. "You'd know her anywhere."

David felt like his world had suddenly transformed from a bleak black-and-white European film into a bright, happy Technicolor blockbuster. Chelsea Hammond was bright, studious, a little shy, which was fine. She'd been to Paris, which suggested a level of sophistication. And if she could cook? The old boys were going to wet themselves.

Chelsea Hammond didn't know it yet, but she'd just become his perfect fake fiancée.

3

"So? Am I a genius or what?" Sarah exclaimed, sounding ridiculously pleased with herself.

Another long second of silence passed. The coffee shop was busy with midmorning traffic, moms with kids in strollers, older folks with crossword puzzles, a large noisy table that seemed to be some kind of walking club. The babble of voices was punctuated by the steaming hiss of the espresso machine.

"Are you kidding me?" Chelsea finally managed to respond.

She'd spent the morning looking at two hopeless places to rent in the South Street area, one where a cat came to greet her at the door and her eyes started watering before she could even cross the threshold, and the other with a supposed nonsmoking roommate who seemed to think marijuana didn't count. They'd met at a coffee shop in the area, Sarah pleased with her purchase of an old book of art deco photographs from an antiquarian bookseller. She'd bought Chelsea an old Pennsylvania Dutch cookbook, with recipes for things like schnitz pie and young duck with sauerkraut. So she hadn't fully paid attention when Sarah promised she had the answer to Chelsea's prayers.

When she glanced up, Sarah's eyes were alight with mischievous laughter. She shook her head. "On the level. Dead serious. My brother wants you to pretend to be his fiancée."

"I don't believe it." She'd had a hopeless crush on David Wolfe since the first moment she saw him, out in the back of his house shooting baskets. Her attention was caught by his long, athletic teenage build, his fierce focus and that face. She'd never forget that moment as long as she lived. She and her mom had just moved in with her aunt and uncle, since her parents, not content with messing up her young life with their divorce, couldn't even work out an agreement that let her stay in her home, near her school and friends. She remembered feeling lost and lonely and hopeless. Then she'd looked out her window, seen that boy leap into the air, sun gilding his hair, and fallen hopelessly, madly in love.

She'd been fourteen years old and to this day no man could match the impact on her of first seeing David Wolfe.

Of course, as in all cases of unrequited teenage love, he'd barely noticed her existence. Now the grown-up David wanted her to playact the part of his lover?

"You haven't heard the best part."

"There's a best part?"

"Because I am your lawyer—"

"No, you're not."

"I would be if you needed a lawyer. Quit interrupting. I negotiated terms."

"Terms? I'm about to be homeless, I'm in no mood for your tricks. Play them on your brother."

Sarah shook her head so violently her hair flew all over the place. "I'm not messing with you. I told him that if you were going to do him a huge favor and save his ass, then he had to do you a favor."

"Which is?"

Sarah favored her with a huge smile. "You're not homeless anymore."

"What?" As the possible implication of what her best friend was saying sank in, her eyes opened wide.

"I told David you had to give up your sublet. I suggested that if you're going to do him this huge favor, then he has to do you one and let you live in his guest room."

Shoofly pie and the best way to cook a young pig were both forgotten. "You're suggesting I move in with your brother?"

"Sure, his place is fantastic and there's lots of room. The guest room's professionally decorated, has its own TV, you'll love it. But wait," she said, sounding like a late-night TV commercial, "there's more."

"I can't imagine."

"He's got this amazing kitchen. Designer everything, top-of-the-line appliances. All he ever uses is the microwave and the ice dispenser. I told him you'll be running your catering business out of his kitchen until you can afford your own place."

In spite of every rational brain cell—of which she used to have a lot more—she was starting to get excited. "And he said yes?"

"He said, 'Thank you, Sarah. You are a goddess among women and I am privileged to be related to you.'"

"In other words, you told him he has to put up with me in his house or the deal's off."

"Pretty much."

She sat back in her chair and sipped her latte as visions of stainless-steel appliances and a bedroom to call her own faded. "I don't think so."

"Are you crazy? This is everything you want. On a silver platter. I admit, having to pretend to be in love with David is going to be hard, and if I had to live with him again I'd kill myself, but you're much nicer than I am."

"It's not that. I would be an unwanted guest in his house. It would be weird."

"Believe me, that man is so desperate I could tell him he has to move out while you live there and he'd start packing."

She chuckled. "How is it possible that an attractive man in his thirties doesn't know any nice women?"

"He knows lots of nice women. They're fluffies. Honestly, I don't know where he finds these women. It's like he orders them online. Point is, they aren't the type of women you parade in front of your boss as corporate-wife material."

"And you think I am?"

She made a scornful, half-laughing sound. "Hell, yeah. You're nice to everyone, have good table manners, keep up with current events and you love to cook. Also, you're hot, which is definitely a plus." She stole the uneaten croissant off Chelsea's plate and took a bite. "I'm half in love with you myself."

"It would be nice to have a real kitchen again," she said.

"Atta girl." And before Chelsea could say another word, Sarah had whipped out her cell phone and hit speed dial. "Hey, bro. It's the world's greatest sister."

Chelsea couldn't believe it. Her friend was confirming the deal and she hadn't even said yes.

"I talked to Chels and she says she'll do it. She'll need a three-month commitment, of course, since she needs that kitchen, so even if you get offered the VP job in a week, she still has a place to stay and a kitchen."

Chelsea was shaking her head and her hands, she couldn't believe Sarah was making her sound so self-serving.

Her friend ignored her. She was in total business mode now. "Deal? Excellent." She laughed again. "Of course there will be a contract. I'll get it drawn up before the big date on Friday. Where should she meet you?"

Chelsea opened her eyes wide. They were meeting for this date?

He obviously had some objections, too, because she heard Sarah say, "No. You can't get together with her ahead of time. Because she's not here." Her friend winked at her. "She's on location catering. She'll be back Friday. Don't worry. I guarantee she'll be there. You remember Hermione—she was always completely reliable. Now, tell me where and when."

Chelsea wondered what on earth she was letting herself in for. And what sort of game was Sarah playing? She'd almost forgotten the Hermione nickname. She'd pretended to hate it, of course, but secretly she'd been thrilled that David had noticed her enough to give her a pet name. Even if it was because she reminded him of a too-smart, socially inept nerd girl.

"No. You can't call her. Remember, she's working on location, I told you. Her cell phone is still on some European plan. Way too expensive. No. I'm not giving you the number. You'll have to trust me."

Her tone changed. "Hey, I wouldn't let you down, not about something important." It seemed like David had a lot more to say, and Sarah did little talking for a minute or two, merely saying things like "yes" and "of course" and finally, "Look, if you want me to tell Chelsea to forget it, I will. We only want to help you out." Her friend continued, "Okay. She'll see you Friday at ten minutes before seven."

He said something else and Sarah rolled her eyes. "Don't you remember her at all? Chelsea is the most punctual person you'll ever meet.

"Call me Saturday and tell me how it all goes. Good luck, future veep." And she hung up.

Her brother obviously had some misgivings and Chelsea realized she had a few of her own. Also a heavy dose of suspicion. "Why aren't you letting him see me or even talk to me before Friday?"

"Little grasshopper, you must learn to be wise. Would you rather this little high school crush you haven't seen in forever sees you at work up to your armpits in flour and food gunk in your hairnet or wearing one of those gorgeous Parisian dresses you bought home with you, hair all done, makeup perfect?"

She had to admit the woman had a point. If she had to see the teen god of her youth again, she wanted to look her best. "And the reason you won't even let him talk to me on the phone?"

"'Kay, that was for me. On behalf of all women, he deserves to be a little bit nervous, don't you think?"

Chelsea took the remaining half of her croissant back again. "Frankly, right now, I don't know what I think."

"This is going to be fantastic. Oh, one thing, David asked that you wear something sexy." She shook her head. "You know what men are, they love to show off a gorgeous woman. Like it gives them extra points in the boy game or something."

"Sexy, huh?" In a deep part of herself, she had to admit the idea of having David actually look at her as a desirable woman instead of a shy teen was appealing. She reviewed her options. "I've got just the thing. It's red, pretty tight-fitting and kind of low-cut. You don't think that's too sexy for a corporate do?"

Sarah looked delighted. "That will be perfect."

4

HE SHOULD BOOK AN appointment with a psychiatrist right now, David thought as he headed out for possibly the most important evening of his entire life, where his escort was not only a woman masquerading as his fiancée, but to add a little extra spice to the evening, was also essentially a blind date.

As he exited his Rittenhouse Square town house, which he'd had his cleaning service freshly clean today, including making up the guest room for a woman he barely knew, he contemplated just how much could go wrong tonight. He passed a street vendor selling soft pretzels and the scent reminded him that he'd eaten nothing for lunch but Tums. Not for the first time, he wondered what he could have been thinking. How arrogant to suppose he could pull off a scam like this. Why hadn't he listened to Jane? She was right, she was always right. This deception had been a bad idea from the beginning.

Kids played in the wide green spaces of the park, horsed around the lion and goat statues. He wished he could go join them, anything but show up at this dinner.

If the big brass found out, he probably wouldn't lose his job, but he would lose all possibility of promotion.

Never mind the respect of people who had come to matter to him.

He walked by a few couples, normal-looking twosomes who obviously belonged together, and his collar grew even tighter. Long before he was ready, he found himself in front of a big hotel where he'd arranged to meet Chelsea. He was a couple of minutes early so he prepared to wait for his date.

He sauntered over to stand beside the entrance to the hotel, and as he did so noticed a stunning brunette looking like she was waiting for the World's Luckiest Man. Every cell in his body zinged to attention. The woman was hot, hot, hot. On a scale of one to ten she was a fifty. Her hair was a sleek bob, dark and shiny, and her huge brown eyes looked out on the world with what he could only think of as a sophisticated innocence. Glorious mouth. Painted in rich, I-could-talk-dirty-all-night red. Red to match the body-hugging dress that outlined her centerfold curves. She took a step toward him on do-me-baby stilettos, and the sway of her hips almost did him in. He took one step forward himself, closing the gap between him and paradise, when he suddenly remembered why he was there.

"Sorry," he said, with true regret. "I'm meeting someone."

That killer mouth curved into a smile. "I think you're meeting me." Even the sound of her voice was a turn-on. Rich, slightly exotic, somehow.

Ooh, great line. He really wished he'd met her some other time. He laughed. "I wish." Then took a quick look up and down the street, hoping Hermione would get there soon.

The smile disappeared and a puzzled frown took its place. "David! It's me. Chelsea."

"Chelsea?" He gaped at the sexiest woman he'd ever

seen. He felt like a man having a sex dream that insanely turns into some horrible nightmare. This amazingly desirable woman? Hottie on heels was supposed to be his fiancée? What happened to drab, shy, smart girl Chelsea? Introducing this woman to the executives and board of directors of his firm would be like introducing nitroglycerin to gas.

Boom.

And he'd be the one exploding up in the air.

He could hear the echo of his sister's words now. "She's the same, David. She's gained enough weight to fill out a little, but she's exactly the same."

And that's the moment that he realized he'd been conned. He never should have signed Sarah up for that online dating site. In retaliation, she'd ruined his career.

"You're Chelsea?" He looked her up and down, unable to believe the gawky teenager was now a goddess.

A delighted smile lit her eyes. "You didn't recognize me."

"I, uh, no. Honestly, I didn't." He felt aggrieved. "What happened to Hermione?"

"She grew up," the woman said softly.

And wasn't that the understatement of the year. If only it was winter, he could huddle her in her coat—hell, he'd buy her one. A nice wool trench coat that would cover her from neck to ankles. But it was July, hot, sultry July, and there was no way to cover her up.

She picked up on his doubt. "Am I dressed okay? Sarah said to put on the sexiest outfit I own."

"Of course she did."

Rapidly, he reviewed his options. Five minutes until they were supposed to meet for dinner.

He could either tell her to go home and make up some tale about his fiancée being sick, or he could go through with this charade. Maybe he could break up with her much sooner than planned, since the fiancée he'd imagined would help forward his career seemed in imminent danger of destroying it.

He forced a smile. He didn't have any options. "You look fine." He stepped forward, leaned in and gave her a kiss on the cheek. "Thanks for helping me out."

"I could say the same. I guess we're helping each other out."

He almost groaned. He'd forgotten his sister's conditions. Not only was she single-handedly destroying his career, but she'd also finagled him into allowing this woman to stay in his house for three months.

No doubt there were morality tales about the consequences of telling lies, tales that would terrify children into behaving perfectly. He felt like he was living a morality tale right now. *The Liar is Punished.*

"Can you walk in those heels? The restaurant is a couple of blocks that way."

"I think I can manage."

They headed off to the restaurant. He had five minutes to prime her, when he'd planned to spend hours telling her everything he figured a fiancée would need to know. But she'd so addled his brain he couldn't think of any of the things he'd imagined would be so important.

What did it matter, anyway?

He was doomed.

Chelsea didn't seem to appreciate she was his doom. As she walked beside him, her body seemed to dance to the tap of her shoes on the pavement. "Who are these people I'll be meeting tonight?"

"Right." Luckily she was smart, and obviously not as thrown off stride by seeing him again as he was by seeing her. He gave her a quick rundown of all the players and she listened intently, with a tiny line between her eyes, reminding him for the first time of the girl he'd known.

"Is there anything in particular I should say or not say?" she asked, as though she were cramming for an exam. But he'd pretty much already accepted the failing grade.

"Just be yourself," he said, "and if you're unsure of anything, defer to me."

"What have you told them about me?" Her hair swung against her jaw, sleek and sophisticated, and he noticed how long and elegant her neck was.

"Nothing. They didn't even know your name until a couple of days ago. Oh, we went to the Caribbean in March. You got sunburned."

"Foolish of me."

"I might have told them you love skiing."

"Foolish of you."

"Yeah. I think we went to Vail in February."

She turned to stare at him. "From Paris?"

"I didn't know you were in Paris when we got engaged." He threw his hands up in the air. "You know what I mean. We'll wing it."

"I'll do my best," she said.

Even with her in those ridiculous heels they made good time and before he was remotely prepared, they were standing outside the restaurant. He drew in a quick breath. "Ready?"

"As ready as I'll ever be."

"Okay." He reached for her hand. "Hope you don't mind. We should act like, you know…"

"Lovers," she replied, wrapping her fingers around his. The clasp was perfect. Her hand felt surprisingly reassuring in his. Even if the word *lovers,* and the way she'd said it, had him conjuring up a vision of the two of them in bed, hot and sweaty and orgasmic. Which was not what he wanted to be thinking about when he saw his bosses.

They walked into the restaurant, an upscale French place, and were directed to the upper floor, where a private space had been reserved.

There weren't many people there yet. Only the key ones. Piers and his wife, Helen. Piers's brother, Lars, and his wife, Amelia, and several board members and their wives. Damien Macabee nodded to him affably, and David was already so rattled he barely thought about any awkwardness that might be attached to him coming to dinner with the man he planned to replace. Macabee's wife also nodded and under her scrutiny he felt even more uncomfortable. But then, the woman was a judge, and he was always convinced she could see right through him.

Not only were he and Chelsea the youngest by a few decades, but bringing Chelsea into this room was like bringing a gorgeous parrot into a flock of drab pigeons.

For a second total silence fell over the assembled company. Piers recovered first. He walked forward with a welcoming smile on his face. "Well, David, good to see you. And please introduce me to your lovely lady."

"Glad to, Piers. Piers Van Horne, this is my fiancée, Chelsea Hammond." His tie was choking him again. He'd been engaged once and never, ever planned to put himself in the same position again, where a woman had the power to gut him. Not that this one did—obviously, he didn't love her. Barely knew her, but still, introducing her as his fiancée left him feeling like he needed to down a bottle of Maalox.

She held out her hand and shook her host's. "Thank you for inviting me," she said.

"We're so glad to finally meet you. We've heard a lot about you."

"David's told me a little about you, too." But not nearly damned enough to prevent disaster, he was certain.

"Come and meet some of the other people we work with."

He ushered her forward. "My wife, Helen. Helen, this is Chelsea."

Helen was not what you'd call well-preserved. She'd let her hair go gray long before it was fashionable to do so, and always wore the same hairstyle, a simple bun at the back of her head. She was on the heavy side and wore clothes and shoes that were comfortable rather than stylish.

Helen and Chelsea shook hands and he couldn't imagine two women in the world who could have less in common.

"Let's get the women drinks, shall we?" Piers said.

He hated to leave them, but what choice did he have. "Sure. Honey? What do you want to drink?"

"I'll have my usual Pernod, if they have it," she said. "White wine, if they don't."

Pernod. Why the hell couldn't she drink something normal. Scotch or a martini or something.

"Pernod," he heard Helen say and inwardly cringed. "I remember my brother used to drink that. He picked up the habit when he was living in France."

"That's how I started, too. I was living in Paris until recently."

"Really? We took the children to visit Bob one Christmas. He was with IBM and it was a great treat for us all to go over there. Were you on holiday?"

"No. I studied at Le Cordon Bleu. I'm a chef."

"Really? How interesting. Oh, how I envy you. I married so young I never…" And then they were out of earshot and he didn't know what Helen had never done. At least the first five minutes of his ordeal were going better than he'd hoped.

He and Piers picked up the drinks and returned to the ladies, by which time the women were talking about pastry. Pastry!

David downed his scotch-and-soda. He wasn't much of a drinker, but he definitely felt the need for some false courage if he was going to get through this night.

More board members began to arrive and if Chelsea still stuck out as the most glamorous and sexy woman at the party, he began to realize that she wasn't the embarrassment he'd feared. She was still the same intelligent, well-read, curious person she'd always been. She also seemed to have grown out of her shyness.

By the time dinner was served, she'd charmed most of the board members and their spouses. She had the rare ability to converse on a wide range of subjects and seem as interested in talking about cooking and fashion as about politics and current events. The only time she seemed lost was when talk turned to sports.

He was beginning to think that maybe this night wasn't going to be the disaster he'd imagined when they sat down to dinner. Given the number of people, they were arranged at a long table. He and Chelsea were seated side by side, and Piers and a couple of the senior board members were closest to them.

She ordered the day's fresh fish and he ordered the same. It wasn't planned, but it definitely made them look more of a couple, he decided.

When the first courses arrived, Amelia leaned forward and said, "I asked Lars where you and David met." She shook her head. "Men are so hopeless. They work together every day, and do you know, he couldn't tell me?"

David swallowed. He and Chelsea exchanged a glance. "You didn't tell him anything?" she asked.

He shrugged. "It's a guy thing. You tell them, honey."

She really had the most amazing eyes. Sparkly, brown like rich chocolate cake, and the most incredible combination of innocence and mischief. "Well, the truth is, David and I have known each other since I was fourteen."

"Really, were you high school sweethearts?"

She laughed, easily. "No. He was several years older than I was. The brother of my best friend. He didn't even know I existed." She gave an exaggerated sigh. "And I had a hopeless crush on him."

Everyone laughed. She continued. "We moved away after I finished high school and I didn't see David again for many years."

He picked up the story. "Then we bumped into each other one day on the street, and I couldn't believe how beautiful she was."

Even though they were only acting a part, they'd both managed to tell the truth. He caught her quick glance and saw that she was flattered by his words.

"Oh, that's so sweet," Helen said. "When is the wedding?"

He and Chelsea exchanged a glance, but she didn't speak, letting him field this one.

"We haven't set a date," David said quickly. Then, realizing how that sounded, he said, "Probably next spring."

"You should get on it ASAP if you are planning a spring wedding," Amelia warned him. "The good places all get booked. When my daughter got married, we had a full year to plan, and still, she only got her second choice of venue."

"That's something to think about, honey," he said. Then he dug around desperately for a topic that would move the conversation into a new direction. But before he'd been able to think of anything, Amelia was at it again.

"I see you don't wear a ring, dear."

He stared at Chelsea's left hand, with its short, buffed nails and no jewelry whatsoever. Damn it, he'd totally forgotten. Of course he should have given her a ring. A fake diamond for his fake fiancée.

He opened his mouth with no idea what he was going to say, when Chelsea put her hand over his. "He wanted to, but I work with food all day. Honestly, a ring would only get in the way. I'd be terrified I'd take it off to wash my hands and wash the ring down the drain or something. Once we're married, I'll wear a wedding band, though, of course."

A few of the board members at the other end of the table got a little rowdy as the night went on. And suddenly, to his horror, he heard a spoon begin to bang against a glass.

"We want the engaged couple to kiss," somebody shouted.

Piers started to protest, but his wife said, "Oh, don't spoil the fun. It's nice to see young people in love."

By now, other spoons had joined in the din. What could he do?

He leaned forward and caught the laughter in Chelsea's eyes as he closed his lips on hers.

For a second he forgot that he was in a corporate setting with a group of people who held his future in their hands. All he knew was that she tasted like chocolate and sex and a hint of licorice from her earlier Pernod.

He pulled away slowly, seeing the shock in her eyes. He imagined her look must have mirrored his own. Slowly, her tongue slipped out and she licked her lips as though trying to catch the elusive flavor of that kiss.

He wanted to say something that would lighten the

sudden tension, but he couldn't think. Rockets were exploding in his brain. Or maybe they were Mayday flares warning him that he was in deep, deep trouble.

5

OH, NO. THE WORDS bounced around Chelsea's brain like a pinging dot in one of those annoying computer games. *Oh, no. Oh, no, oh, no, oh, no, oh, no!*

If she'd had one rule for herself—if she'd thought any of this through enough to have created some rules for herself, which would have been a pretty damn good idea—rule number one would have been no kissing. Well, no physical contact of any kind, obviously. But it was too late for that, so maybe if she pulled herself together long enough to list a few rules for personal conduct, she had a tiny possibility of getting through this charade without making a fool of herself.

Maybe.

She got through the rest of the night somehow, but she was always conscious of David's presence beside her, of the feel of his arm when it brushed hers. Even through the summer-weight jacket he wore she felt his body heat the same way she felt the insistent attraction that thrummed between them.

She wasn't sure whether she was glad or sorry when they finally left. Sure, it had been stressful to play a part, but at least the mental effort had kept her from thinking about the fact that soon she'd be going to David's home.

With David.

Alone.

"What are you thinking about?" David asked her. They were seated in a cab speeding to his place. She was sure he lived close enough to walk, but in deference to her heels, he'd insisted on a cab. And the two of them were headed for his place for all the wrong reasons.

No! She corrected herself hurriedly. For all the right reasons. Sex was a bad reason and they weren't going to do that. Clearly no sex was the new rule number one.

Good reasons for heading to David's place included a nice place to stay rent-free for a few months and use of a kitchen that Sarah insisted was top-of-the-line.

She had to keep reminding herself of that, especially since breaking rule number one of the former rules list, the one where no kissing held top spot. Because any fool could see that once a woman started kissing a man like David, she was never going to stop.

How many times had she dreamed about that first kiss? A thousand? A million? Ten billion? She'd been a quintessential shy-girl nerd. Not even a geek, which was starting to be cool when she hit high school. No. She didn't mess with computers, she read classics and she cooked. She supposed, looking back, that she was trying to recreate the home she'd lost by becoming a great cook. With the three adults all working, she was usually the one to cook dinner, and she found that she loved to experiment with new recipes, to refine old family favorites.

Other kids played video games and watched *Friends* when they got home from school. She watched Jacques Pepin and Martha Stewart. She wore the wrong clothes. She was plain and shy and studious. And the perfect fodder for a hopeless crush on the guy most likely to do whatever the hell he pleased.

But even in the fantasy realm where David suddenly noticed her and drew her slowly to him and kissed her, she'd never imagined that it would be quite so earth-shattering—and like most shy, bookish girls, she had quite an imagination.

Who'd have believed that now, now that she was no longer that shy young closet romantic, when she had plenty of experience of life and love, a simple kiss could rock her world.

But it had.

And so she was obsessively thinking about not thinking about that kiss—and about rules.

"I'm thinking about rules," she said at last in answer to his question.

"Rules?" In the dim light of the cab, she thought she caught the interest on his handsome face. "What kind of rules?"

He said the words in the low, sexy tone of a man who brought women home to his place more often than she cared to think about, and not so they could sleep in the guest room and cook in his kitchen. Oh, no. He thought she was about to invent some sex game with rules. Even as the thought hit her, heat flooded her body.

No. Oh, no, oh, no, oh, no, oh, no!

"Rules of conduct," she snapped, knowing she must sound like a kindergarten teacher on the first day of school.

"Maybe you'd better explain exactly what you mean."

"If we're going to be, um, sharing the same apartment, I think we need some guidelines."

"If this is a toilet-seat-up-versus-down conversation,

you can relax. There are two bathrooms. You'll have your own."

"I wasn't thinking of those kinds of rules, though I suppose we'll have to work around each other's preferences. I was thinking more of…" She had no idea how to phrase this, and suddenly felt incredibly foolish. "Rules between you and me."

Did he have to sit so close? There was plenty of room, but David had positioned himself so his leg was touching hers, thigh-to-thigh, and she felt the heat pulsing between them in a way that did not bode well for her peace of mind.

David, as she knew well, was a player, and she had no interest in being one of his playthings. At least, not in the sensible, self-protective part of her.

"Rules between you and me," he echoed, sounding a little confused but also hopeful.

"Like no kissing," she blurted.

He chuckled softly. And it was such a sexy sound she wanted to throw herself at him and break all the rules she'd thought of and a bunch she hadn't. "Looks like we already broke the first rule."

"I know. That's what started me thinking. I can't live in your house if we're going to be, you know…"

"Kissing."

"And so on."

"I'm willing to negotiate here. What if we skip the kissing and stick to 'and so on?'"

"This isn't a joke. I barely know you."

"What are you talking about? We've known each other for years."

She could feel her red dress riding up her thighs and she tugged it down. "You didn't even recognize me."

"You grew up and got all sexy on me, that's why." His

hand came down to rest on her knee, warm and confident. "We're going to be spending a couple of months living together. Under the same roof. Based on that kiss, I'm guessing we've got pretty amazing chemistry. Are you seriously going to ignore it?"

The question hung in the air far too long before she found the strength to say "Yes."

His hand moved up and down, not exactly a caress, but the next closest thing. "I think you're getting pretty serious about something that doesn't have to be."

And that, right there, was the very reason that she had to have rules, and force both of them to stick to them.

Turning her body so she was facing him, and that thigh-to-thigh contact was broken, she said, "Sex is serious to me," knowing he had to understand her position or they'd never make this thing work.

"Why?" He seemed genuinely curious.

"Because it matters."

"Of course it matters. Sex feels good, is fun, doesn't hurt anybody and could definitely help reduce some of the tension you're carrying."

"Is that really what you think? That sex is only a recreational sport, like a game of tennis?"

"Maybe not exactly like tennis, but a game that feels good, gets your heart rate up and relieves tension. What's wrong with that?"

"Not for me. For me sex goes together with love. I can't give myself to someone I don't have deep feelings for."

There was silence for a few beats. Then he removed his hand and said, "Okay."

That was it? Okay? She had no idea why, but she felt let down. He hadn't tried very hard to argue her out of her position. And not that she'd have caved, but it would have felt good to know she was so desirable he'd make an issue out of wanting to sleep with her.

She supposed he'd find another willing partner to play his games easily enough that not getting into her bed wasn't going to bother him very much.

How depressing.

She hadn't even been entirely honest. She'd slept with men she knew she didn't love, but she'd always felt more than mere friendship, she supposed. And more than simply lust. And she hadn't been sharing living quarters with them at the time.

Fortunately, since she couldn't think of anything to talk about and her companion didn't seem interested in starting a new subject of conversation, the cab pulled up in front of a brownstone on a quiet, tree-lined street. The area was one of the nicest in the city, and full of up-and-coming hotshots like David. She could walk everywhere from here, which was great, she reminded herself.

He paid off the cab and climbed out, then held out his hand to help her navigate high heels and a short skirt.

"Thanks," she said, when she reached the pavement.

He let go of her hand and dug out his keys.

They walked up a few steps to a glossy black door with a leaded window embedded in the upper half, and when he opened the door and flipped on the lights, she followed him in and instantly fell in love.

His town house combined the best of the nineteenth century, when it had been built, with its original wainscoting and gleaming hardwood floors, fireplace and high ceilings, with completely modern furnishings, including the art and lighting.

The designer had stayed with a masculine palette, painting the rooms in burgundies, grays and some greens, but she liked it.

"It's beautiful," she said.

"Thanks. The kitchen's through here," he said as though he'd known she'd want to see that room before anything else. He led her through the living room, pointing out a powder room on that level, and then he opened double doors and she found herself falling in love all over again.

"It's huge," she said, not able to come up with anything more original.

"I had the dining room taken out and one big kitchen put in. I'm not the dining-room type. I figured this was more practical. Not that I cook much."

She walked forward and ran her fingers over dark gray granite counters the way she'd touch a lover's face. A breakfast bar had four high-tech stools pulled up to it, but an old farmhouse table that just begged for a jug of fresh flowers to sit on it provided sit-down dining. Most of one wall was windows.

She glanced back at David. "Are you kidding me? Look at these appliances," she crooned, running her fingers over sleek industrial stainless steel. "Gas oven, perfect. And a six-burner stove." The fridge was double-sided and if the pull-out freezer wasn't large, she didn't think that would matter. She intended to buy fresh and cook fresh. David could fill his entire freezer with ice cubes for all she cared.

Clearly, Sarah hadn't lied about David never using his own fancy kitchen. There was a sterility to the space that suggested not much cooking went on here.

She opened the oven door, picturing her trays inside. Peeking into the fridge, she found it a bachelor cliché. "There's nothing in here but booze and a few take-out containers."

He shrugged. "I'm not home much." He seemed to enjoy

her excitement as she dragged open every cupboard and drawer, gauging how much she'd have to buy and where she'd put her supplies. She was delighted at how relatively empty his storage spaces were and knew that wouldn't last for long.

"This is so perfect," she said, looking up to find him regarding her with amusement.

"You haven't even looked at your bedroom."

"Who needs to sleep when you have a kitchen like this? Oh, the things I'll be able to create in this space."

But she followed him down a short corridor and up a flight of stairs.

"My bedroom," he said, opening the first door. *Ah,* she thought, *here's where he spends most of his time when he's at home.* The bed was huge, and the room, although neat, sported stuff. Including a TV he could watch from his bed.

He crossed the hall and opened the last door. "And your room."

Like everything else in this town house but his bedroom, her room had obviously been staged by a decorator and never touched since. It was done in neutral shades, contained a queen-size bed, a dresser, mirror, some not very interesting art on the walls and its own en suite. A neat stack of moving boxes on the floor told her her stuff had arrived okay.

"It's beautiful. Thank you."

"Don't thank me. Remember, we're helping each other out."

She looked up and saw him regarding her with a mixture of longing and frustration. He shoved his hands in his pockets. "There's one more floor where I keep a home office."

"Okay."

A beat of silence ticked by.

"You did good tonight. Thank you."

"You're welcome. I enjoyed myself. They seem like nice people."

"They are." He stood there, leaning against the door-jamb. "I wasn't sure where you'd want your stuff, so I put the boxes in your room, but unpack however you like. My house is your house. I put the box labeled 'bathroom' right in your bathroom, but everything else is here."

"Oh, right. Good." She was so busy thinking about how good he tasted that she'd forgotten she didn't have so much as a toothbrush with her. Sarah, who thought of everything, had told her to pack all her stuff up and have it sent over to David's.

His gaze dipped to her mouth and she knew he was reliving their kiss just as she was. "You really serious about those rules of yours?"

Oh, it would be so easy to shake her head, let herself go. So easy.

And such a truly, monumentally terrible idea. Maybe, if she didn't have to live here for the next couple of months, maybe she'd throw her own sense of what was right for her out the window. She'd take one step and be in his arms, then his bed.

And tomorrow? He'd have a new partner. For all she knew, he played doubles. She really didn't think she could stay in his guest room while he carried on his carefree bachelor existence. Not once she'd been intimate with him. She wasn't built that way.

So, with some regret, she nodded. "I'm serious."

He shook his head. "Okay, then. Good night."

She heaved a sigh of combined relief and frustration when he exited, leaving her alone in a tasteful, neutral guest room.

She used up some of her restless energy in unpacking her suitcases, putting her clothes away in the closet and dresser. Then she organized the bathroom and unpacked her toiletries and prepared herself for bed.

It was late, and she was tired but she wasn't sleepy. She dug out one of her favorite cookbooks and crawled into bed with Chef Patricia Yeo. She read cookbooks the way some people read Dickens or Shakespeare. She could dip into the same books over and over again and always find something new.

At last, she flipped out the light and settled herself in the big, empty bed. It had been a lot of years since Chelsea fell asleep thinking about kissing David.

In truth, she wasn't thinking about kissing. Her imagination had moved on. And she wasn't anywhere near sleep.

She sighed and punched the pillow.

It was going to be a long couple of months.

6

"I THINK MY TONGUE just had an orgasm," Sarah moaned as she bit into the tiny lime-and-pomegranate tart, fresh from the oven. Her fourth in less than a minute.

Chelsea couldn't remember when she'd felt so gratified.

Four days since she'd moved into David's place and already she was experimenting, cooking with recipes she knew as she got comfortable with the stove and playing with local ingredients to try new combinations.

"You are a food genius." Sarah swallowed, tried to control herself and gave in, reaching for another tart. "This is my last one. Stab me with that chef's knife if I even try to reach for another tart." She popped the treat into her mouth and closed her eyes as she devoured it. Opening them again, she said, "I am going to have to spend the next week at the gym to make up for it."

"You can't leave before you try these and tell me what you think."

She gazed at Chelsea, busily piping chocolate ganache into the rest of the tart shells. "How do you do it? You create this amazing food and you're not seven hundred pounds. I don't get it."

"Well, I'm not skinny like you, either." She glanced down at herself. "I should lose a few pounds."

"Get out. You have womanly curves." Sarah stared at her in frank envy. "I'd kill for those boobs."

She watched Chelsea add a sliver of almond and pipe a flourish of crème fraîche then obediently raved.

Sarah wasn't the kind who said what you wanted to hear. Chelsea knew her bliss was unfeigned. Good, two of her recipes were as good as she'd hoped.

"How did my deviant brother react when he saw you the other night?"

"He didn't even recognize me."

Sarah snorted with laughter. "Really? He didn't know you at all?"

"It wasn't all that funny. He thought I was trying to pick him up. On the street."

"Only an egotist like David would ever think a woman like you would pick him up on the street. As if."

"I wouldn't pick anyone up. On the street or off it."

"I know you wouldn't. Oh, I wish I'd seen that first meeting. After you got over that little misunderstanding, how did the fake fiancée thing go? All right? Or were you busted?"

"No. I think we pulled it off. They all saw what they were expecting to see and of course I've known David long enough that I was able to improvise." She grinned. "They thought we were high school sweethearts. Which is pretty funny considering your brother didn't know I was alive."

"I bet he knows now."

Chelsea made a wry face and glanced down. "Amazing what a few pounds of cleavage will do for a girl."

"It's not that. It's the whole package. You were a late bloomer. It's like you grew into your sexuality a few years after everybody else. Probably in Paris."

"Maybe."

"So?" She put both elbows on the granite counter, pushing away a pastry bag to do so. "What happened? I want no gory details, obviously, because we're talking my brother, ugh, but did you, you know? Get down and dirty with my bro?"

"No. Of course not. This arrangement is strictly business for both of us."

Sarah looked both relieved and disappointed at the same time. "I guess that's for the best, but I sure would like to see him with someone who wasn't a fluffy."

"I guess he's a late bloomer, too, emotionally."

"Or a stunted stick who will never bloom emotionally," said his loving sister. "It's a great arrangement, though, huh? Can you believe this kitchen?"

"I know. I was so happy to quit the restaurant and start really working toward my own business."

"And he's an okay roommate, right? He's a bit of a neat freak."

She shrugged. "I might as well be living alone. I never see him."

Sarah nodded. "He works hard and plays hard." She gave a wry grin. "We're alike in that way."

"I've noticed."

She had, too. "When I left for Paris, you were killing yourself at work as an articling student. And trying out men like they were shoes."

"Now I'm an associate in the firm and I'm killing myself to make partner." She began rearranging the ingredients on the counter. "How many men do you have to try on before you find one that fits?"

"I don't know."

"I don't have time to waste, you know? Mom's always on about what a hard time she had getting pregnant. It's her favorite story these days and she always gives me this look, like it probably runs in the family and I'm not getting any younger."

"You're only twenty-eight."

"I know. But I want to have a kid by the time I'm thirty. It's stupid, but it's on my list and you know how I am about my lists."

Chelsea glanced up from her task. "I can't believe you still have those."

"A goal that isn't written down is only a dream," she replied, sounding like a talk-show guest with a new self-help book to promote.

"But some things you can't control. Like love. Or even when you'll make partner."

"I know. I know." Her cell phone buzzed. She looked at the call and ignored it. "I don't want to end up one day realizing I'm thirty-five and still single and making an appointment at the sperm bank, you know?"

Chelsea couldn't help laughing. "You won't end up at the sperm bank."

"The thing is, I need a partner. I can't raise a baby by myself. Not with my schedule."

"Maybe you should relax and not push it."

"I push everything. It's my personality. I'm Type A," she announced, like that was news. "I can't waste time."

"I'm your best friend and I have to tell you that you are sounding kind of neurotic. Even for you."

"It's all David's fault. I am going to kill him!"

"What's he done?" And when, she wondered. He'd barely been home in the last four days. She sometimes heard him come in at night, usually around midnight when she was already in bed, and then he was up and gone by seven. She had no idea how he got by on so little sleep. And also she had to wonder why he'd invested in this beautiful home. He rarely saw it.

"You remember I told you my emotional retard brother signed me up for an online dating site?"

"Yes. You said he made you sound like a girl from the fifties."

"He did. And these ridiculous men started e-mailing me."

"You know, you can cancel your subscription or membership or whatever it is."

"I stayed on it for a joke, I'd get all whupped up about what Neanderthals men are, and I admit I've had a few laughs with some of the other women in my firm." She looked as though she were truly in pain.

"Right. And?"

"And I met someone."

"You met someone."

She nodded, her eyes squeezed shut.

"Someone who thinks you are a traditional girl with traditional values?"

"Yeah. I mean, I haven't 'met him,' met him. But I e-mailed him back."

"Why?"

"Because he's frickin' gorgeous. At least, his picture is. And we've been e-mailing. Kind of a lot."

"Oh, dear."

"And now he wants to meet me."

"What do you know about this guy?"

"He's a school guidance counselor and he teaches yoga on the weekends."

"Yoga?" If she'd been asked to pick the top qualities Sarah would hate in a man, practicing yoga would be right up there.

"Yes."

"As in Zen, meditation, the sitar."

"Yes, yes, yes!"

Her next batch of tart shells was ready, so she slipped them out of the oven and onto the cooling tray. "And do you want to meet him?"

"I don't know. He's gorgeous, and he writes these really great e-mails, but it's not enough, is it?"

"It's a start."

"I can't even have him for a while just for sex because the reason he's on that site is that he's not into casual relationships."

"You'd do that?" She looked at Sarah, wondered how she and David and half the people she knew could engage in hookups that meant nothing.

Her old friend shrugged. "My life is hectic. I don't have a lot of time and I need sex like anybody else. There's a lot of people who use those sites to hook up, you know."

"I hadn't thought about it."

"Anyhow, he's really clear that he has no interest in that. He wants to get to know a woman before he has sex with her."

"How unusual," Chelsea said. And how ironic. She was interested in David, who only wanted casual hookups, and the unknown school counselor had the same issue with David's sister.

"What do I do?"

"Why don't you have coffee with the guy? It can't hurt. Or go to one of his yoga classes. Maybe the whole relaxation thing would be good for you."

"Maybe. And it's not like I'm looking to get laid, I'm not. But I don't want to be with some guy who won't do it until he's married, either. You know?"

She couldn't help but laugh. "What do you talk about on e-mail?"

"I don't know. Dumb stuff. Traveling, books, movies we've seen. We both love movies. And biking."

"You bike?"

"No. But he does, and he tells me about it."

"So? Meet him for coffee. It can't hurt."

"I guess." She shook her head and a lock of black hair flopped onto her forehead, a little the way her brother's did.

"It's only coffee."

"I just hope he doesn't end up being a bore. I don't have that kind of time to waste."

"You know what? I think maybe I do see a sperm bank in your future."

7

"HI, HONEY, I'M HOME." David felt like an idiot announcing his presence in his own house, but he didn't want to startle his temporary roommate.

He stepped inside and felt his nostrils quiver. What was that amazing smell?

"Hi," a cheerful voice answered him. "You're home early."

He put down his briefcase. He'd never thought of his home as cold before, but walking into it now he noticed a difference. The space felt warm, lived-in, and whatever that woman was cooking, his stomach wanted some.

He'd never thought a woman could look sexy in an apron. The image reminded him of moms and old ladies at Christmas dressed as Mrs. Claus, but on Chelsea? The blue-and-white striped apron was about the sexiest thing he'd ever seen.

Dragging his tie off, he moved closer to his kitchen. Never had there been so much activity in it so long as he'd lived here. He'd grilled the odd steak, and a woman or two had cooked him dinner, but mostly he ate out. He stared in amazement. Little blue flames danced under copper-bottomed pots that certainly didn't belong to him, and the air was scented like the best French restaurant, only somehow cozier and more familiar.

As he looked at the number of dishes spread out he experienced an uncomfortable scratchy feeling behind his breastbone. "Are you entertaining tonight?"

She'd been quick to make up rules about how he couldn't have sex with her, or even kiss her, and naturally, the minute he was faced with rules like "no sex," what else could he think of but taking that lush body in his arms and making love to her all night long?

Why hadn't he thought to institute a few rules of his own? The first of which would be no entertaining other men in his house when she was supposed to be engaged to him.

She laughed, a deep, sexy sound. "No, I'm not. Well, your sister did drop by earlier, but I wouldn't invite people here without your permission. And I certainly don't intend to invite men over while I'm supposed to be engaged to you."

Even though he was relieved to find she saw the situation exactly as he wanted her to, he also saw how unfair it was. He dashed upstairs into his bedroom, changing into jeans and a shirt before emerging once again into the kitchen.

"I've been thinking," he said, "that this deal isn't exactly fair on you, is it?"

She was stirring something on the stove, critically studying the contents. "What's not fair?"

"That you can't see anyone else, I guess."

She glanced up at him, her cheeks slightly flushed from the heat of the stove. "I went into this arrangement with my eyes open. I won't do anything that would embarrass you." She considered. "At least, not on purpose. And I really don't have time for a man in my life right now, I want to get my business going." She wiped her hands on a towel. "There's so much to do. Licenses—oh, that reminds me, I need to make an appointment for a health inspection of the premises. Are you okay with that?"

"Sure. I guess."

"I'm not completely sure yet what I'm doing. I mean, what my menus will be. I don't want to start too big and ambitious and turn your apartment into a catering company, but if I start too small, then it's going to take ages to build a reputation. So far I'm just cooking."

She'd pushed her hair behind her ears at some point and the ends brushed her jaw. He had no idea why the sight was so hypnotic but he wanted to kiss that spot, trail kisses along her jaw and to her mouth, that glorious, sexy mouth. It took an effort to concentrate on her words.

"Who is all this food for?"

She looked around as though she hadn't realized how much food she'd cooked. She shrugged helplessly. "You, if you want it."

The itchy feeling behind his breastbone subsided. "Oh, if it tastes half as good as it smells, I want it."

She found one of the ridiculously expensive black-and-white plates his designer had chosen. "You have to be honest, though. I want a critique of every bite. I'm determined to be the best caterer this city has ever seen."

"And I respect your position. But I really don't want to eat alone with you hovering over me with a scorecard. How about you take off that apron, grab another plate, I'll open a bottle of wine and we can eat like regular people." He glanced around. "Only with a lot more food choices."

"You're laughing at me. But I can't help myself. This kitchen is wonderful and I start cooking and can't seem to stop. I went to the Reading Terminal Market today and got a bit carried away. I'd forgotten how great it is there. So many fresh fruits and vegetables, and an excellent assortment of fish, and artisanal cheeses and—" She laughed. "Well, I don't have to tell you, you live here."

But he didn't think he'd ever in his life got all excited about a food market.

"I may be laughing at you just a little bit, but I'm not complaining. What's on the menu?"

"We have about three different appetizers to start with, then duck with fresh cherries—I hope it tastes good—and a little lamb that we should probably have later, grilled simply with fresh herbs and fresh vegetables, and two kinds of tart for dessert."

Whistling softly, he went to the wine fridge that he kept stocked even though he was rarely home to drink wine. While he selected a decent bottle that he hoped would complement a few of the dishes laid out, his roommate set the table. She knew his kitchen far better than he did, unerringly finding table mats he'd forgotten he owned and placing everything neatly on the table.

He noted a big vase of daisies on the table and thought how much they brightened up the place. His roommate wasn't quite as neat as he was, but the few things she left around made the place seem more lived in. There was the book she'd been reading, set on a side table by the window. Today's newspaper, open to the half-finished crossword puzzle.

As he moved it off the chair he was about to sit in, he said, "Amputate."

Chelsea blinked. "I beg your pardon?"

"Six across. Eight-letter word, to cut off," he explained, smiling at her. "Amputate."

"Oh, right. Thanks. I hope you don't mind that I did the crossword. It didn't seem like something you enjoyed."

"No. I never do them. No time."

She shook her head at him. "You and your sister with your no time."

"Oh, come on. You can't compare me with my sister. She's so driven it's insane."

She set a plate with about seven kinds of appetizers on it in the middle of the table. Under a short cotton skirt, her summer-brown legs were bare. Her feet were in sandals and besides noting that she'd painted her toenails purple, he saw a little silver toe ring. "She's not so driven that she'd pretend to be engaged in order to further her career."

He grinned at her. "She would if she'd thought of it."

When she'd settled herself on the other side of the big farmhouse table, he poured wine, then raised his glass. "A toast to our mutual success."

She smiled at him and they both drank.

"You were a big hit at dinner the other night, by the way," he told her.

"Really?"

He reached for a tiny pea pod stuffed with crab and some kind of sauce and popped it in his mouth. "Oh, wow, this is fantastic," he said thickly. "Yeah, they all loved you. Piers is convinced you'd be the perfect hostess at any company function. He's beside himself with excitement." Piers wasn't the only one beside himself with excitement, and he got the feeling his fake future wife had picked up on it. She leaned forward, looking eager.

"So, did you get the VP spot?"

He savored the moment, conscious that he'd pretty much rushed home to tell her, knowing she should be the first to know. "He said they can't make anything official until Macabee retires, but he offered me the job."

She shrieked and jumped up and ran around the table. He rose and as she threw her arms around him he caught her against him. Her body felt as good in his arms as he'd known it would. Her smell entranced him, like wildflowers and woman all mixed up with the scent of a great restaurant.

Through the thin cotton of her cherry-colored tank top, he felt her body, warm and luscious.

Her lips were curved in a smile and they were absolutely the sexiest, most kissable lips in the universe. His mouth was on hers before he had time to register what he was doing. Instinct took over, and a kind of need, to taste and hold and savor.

He felt the softness of her breasts crushed against his chest, the fine bones in her back as he held her, and the magical feel of her mouth against his.

Heat pulsed between them and the need to touch her, to take her, pounded in his veins.

As he moved in to pull her even deeper into him and take the kiss to the next level, she put her hands on his shoulders. It took him a second before he realized she was pulling away.

There was a moment of total awkwardness as they stood facing each other. Her eyes were a little wide, her breathing fast.

He wanted to kiss her again; it seemed the most natural thing in the world. He wanted to peel off her clothes and take her to bed, and he could see in her eyes that she was tempted.

But she shook her head, a quick no. Backed away. And then he remembered her stupid rules. Like the no-kissing rule that rattled around in his head like a penny in a tin can.

She sat back down in her seat and made a fuss out of offering him more appetizers, which he ate to keep his mouth busy. Since her food was amazing, the flavor distracted him, but still, he couldn't entirely stop thinking about kissing her and all the places that could lead.

"I have news, too," she said, looking pretty pleased with herself.

"What?"

"I got my first catering job."

"You did?"

"Mmm-hmm. It was through your sister, actually. Some friends of hers are getting married. They've been living together for a while and are expecting a baby so they suddenly decided they want to get married in three weeks' time. And I'm catering the wedding."

"That is fantastic." Married in three weeks, he thought. Well, the lucky couple were probably doing it like rabbits, getting so much sex they'd be exhausted by the time they got to the wedding night. That's what it should be like when you were engaged to a sexy woman. And here he was, engaged to the sexiest woman of all, and he ached, literally ached from the lack of sex.

She beamed at him across the table. "I couldn't have done it without your kitchen." She reached for a tiny round of crispy cooked potato topped with goat cheese and some fancy green stuff. As she bit into the appetizer he thought of how much he liked her mouth and how much he wanted her. "We could be the making of each other."

He had to get a grip!

Stop thinking about sex and Chelsea. Think about something else, anything.

Business, that was it. He was genius at business and maybe if he focused on that he could get his mind off sex.

Temporarily.

"Maybe I could help you in your business," he blurted.

One sexy eyebrow rose. "You can cook?"

He shook his head. "You're a genius in the kitchen, but how's your marketing coming? Have you got a Web site set up?"

She wrinkled her nose. "I was planning on waiting until I have a proper kitchen."

"Mistake a lot of people make," he said around another fantastic bite of heaven topped with goat cheese. "Get your advertising and marketing going right away." He licked his thumb. "Product quality is important, no question, which you definitely have here, but you've got to get people buying it or you won't have a successful business. Bottom line, you won't have any business."

"Yeah, I guess."

"I can help you with that. I've got great contacts through my work. I know a woman who does fantastic Web sites and she owes me a favor. I bet I can cut a good deal. I've got a good printer who turns things around fast."

"A printer, but—"

"You need it all. If you want to be a top caterer, present yourself as a top caterer. You can print off menus on the computer, that's cool, but have a fancy folder to put them in. And some decent business cards."

"Business cards?"

"Business cards." He pictured something classy but forward thinking. "What's your business name?"

"Hammond and Co." She got that line between her brows that she always got when she was concentrating on something. "I thought of a bunch of cutesy names, but the more I thought of it the more I wanted my food taken seriously."

"Sounds like a good strategy to me."

She beamed at him. "Thank you."

He was glad she was in such a good mood, and already

profiting from their little arrangement, because he had another piece of news for her. One she might not love as much.

"Even though it's not official yet, I've been invited to my first leadership retreat."

"Leadership retreat? Sounds like a Bible study camp."

"It's more a work/play weekend where the top brass of my company plan the future, work on the strategic plan, play a few rounds of golf, that kind of thing."

"You are so in there," she exclaimed.

"Yeah, I know. I'm pretty stoked." He paused, took another sip of wine. Worked up his courage. He'd been selling since his first job in a steakhouse. He was brilliant at sales, he reminded himself. "So, what are you doing weekend after next?"

She stopped chewing and her eyes grew all squinty and suspicious. "Why do you care what I'm doing weekend after next?"

"Because it's the corporate retreat, and, naturally, the significant others are invited." He rushed on before she could speak. "It's going to be great. It's in a five-star resort in the Poconos, with a spa, excellent meals that you will appreciate. There's horseback riding, I think, and shopping—" he racked his brain "—and golf."

"I believe you mentioned golf." She stared at him for an uncomfortable moment. "I didn't realize weekend retreats would be involved when I agreed to this charade."

"I didn't, either. I mean, I didn't know it would all move so fast." He gave her his best winning grin. "It's all because of you. They liked you so much they've fast-tracked things."

She did not appear to be won over.

"I thought it would be a few dinners and cocktail

receptions. I never imagined having to pretend to be in love with you for an entire weekend."

"Is that so tough?" he asked, stung.

She put down her wineglass. "Yes," she answered at last. "Tougher than you can possibly imagine."

8

HE LOOKED SO HURT AT her words that she wanted to take them back, but Chelsea was essentially an honest person and *tough* didn't even begin to describe what it was going to be like to spend an entire weekend with David when everyone thought they were an engaged couple. It was bad enough sharing a town house that he was rarely in. What would it be like if they had to share a room?

The kiss was still tingling on her lips and in truth she'd barely tasted the food she'd worked so hard preparing. All she could taste was David. If she could turn the experience of kissing him into a flavor she'd be the most successful caterer in history. Who could resist the taste of passion?

Why hadn't she said no when this ridiculous charade was first suggested to her? Why hadn't she run far and fast to avoid an impossible situation?

It was hopeless for her to pretend to be in love with David when the truth was that she'd been in love with him since she was fourteen years old.

Sure, she'd enjoyed the company of other men, gone to bed with a few of them, but no one, however nice, good-looking, funny, or charming, had ever come close to winning her heart. Now she knew why.

She didn't have a heart to give. She'd given it to David all those years ago. He had no more clue of her feelings now than he'd had then. He looked at her like she was a monster to tell him it was horrible to be expected to spend a weekend with him. But it was as close to the truth as she could come without making a fool of herself.

"I see," he said at last. "Well, I'll tell them you're sick, or working or something. I'm sure they'll understand," he said, with no conviction whatever.

But she discovered that what the poets said about love was true. It was self-sacrificing. For she could no more imagine him at a couples retreat all alone, when it was so important for him to make the right impression, than she could imagine walking past him if he was sick or injured.

The truth was, he needed her. And because she loved him, she said, "No, it's okay. I'll come with you. Of course I'll come." She forced a smile. "We made a deal, and I'll stick to it."

"We never negotiated for weekends because frankly I didn't think there'd be any."

She tilted her head to one side, thinking he was going to have a few surprises, too. "I never imagined that I'd have actual catering gigs while I was living here, either. I'm guessing your kitchen may be busier than you'd expected."

"If you can live with corporate retreats and God knows what else, I guess I can live with a commercial kitchen in my house for a couple of months."

He raised his glass. "Deal?"

She clinked her glass against his. "Deal."

"You know, we might just squeak through this thing after all."

He'd barely finished the sentence when the phone rang.

He checked the call display, seemed to hesitate, then he picked it up. "Hello? Mom, hi. How's your vacation? How's Poland?"

He looked a little concerned. "You sound kind of funny."

One of the things she'd always liked about David and Sarah's family was how close they were. He sounded genuinely pleased to hear from his mother and if he could tell she sounded funny when she was half a world away, he had to be a good son. She got up and started clearing the table, aiming to give him a bit of privacy.

But, even as she tried very hard not to eavesdrop, she couldn't help but hear David's side of the conversation and, since he didn't bother to leave the room, she supposed he didn't care if she heard him. Then she heard a snatch of dialogue that had her turning to stare.

"Got an e-mail from Norma in your book club? Is that the nosy woman who lives in my block?"

At that moment they locked gazes.

"What did she say?" She caught a note of panic.

"That's ridiculous. Of course I don't have a woman living with me. Naturally, you'd be the first to know if I had a girlfriend."

She glanced at him and found him looking pale, like he was in the middle of a really powerful horror movie.

His face twisted. "I'm not saying she made it up, it's—" He glanced up at her in appeal. "I—"

She could hear the upset, almost hysterical babble coming from the receiver. Oh, this was so not good. She knew David's parents. They didn't deserve this.

She walked over and whispered, "Tell her the truth."

David ignored her. Nothing new there, he'd been ignoring her for years.

"Mom, no. Look, it's not what you think." He grabbed

his wine and gulped down half a glass. "Mom, it's Chelsea
Hammond, you know, the nice girl who lived with the
Dennises? She needed a place to stay and Sarah asked if
she could stay here for a while. It's great. She's a fantastic
cook and it's only temporary."

His mother spoke again and she saw David turn his head
in the direction of the windows and glare. "That woman
was hanging out her windows watching me and Chelsea
come home all dressed up? Does she never sleep? Maybe
she should read one of the damn book-club books instead
of spying on the neighbors."

She shook her head at him. He was hopeless. Hopeless.

"We were not kissing. I don't care what she thought she
saw." He let out a huff of frustration. "I might have had my
arm around Chelsea, I can't remember, but—" His mouth
dropped open. "How can you say that about your own son?
I do not use women."

"Hah," she said, and not nearly as quietly as she should
have.

He looked panicky and kind of sweaty and finally
cracked like a guy who'd spent the night in police inter-
rogation. "Okay, okay, so we're seeing each other. Just
casually, Mom. It's not serious."

The hysterical babbling was calming down now,
sounding more like a happy fountain from Chelsea's
perspective.

"Yes." He laughed, a short, sharp snort. "Oh, she certainly is the nicest girl I've ever gone out with."

So he knew that, did he? And found it ripsnortingly
funny.

She wanted to smack him.

To control the impulse she turned back to the kitchen.
One thing she really, really missed was having an

underpaid grunt to clean up after her, sweep the floor every few minutes and, best of all, wash her dishes. It seemed, when you were a one-woman catering firm, that you washed your own dishes.

She was going to have to get successful enough fast to hire a grunt. She started stacking dishes that needed hand-washing. At least it gave her something to do with the energy burning within her. Behind her, David and his mother continued chatting and she made enough noise that no one could think she was eavesdropping.

"Just a second. Ah, Chelsea?" He looked up, appearing more guilty than when he'd forced her to agree to a weekend corporate retreat. "My mom wants to talk to you."

For a moment she considered refusing. But then she remembered how nice to her Mrs. Wolfe had always been. It was sad that she'd given birth to the spawn of Satan, but that wasn't her fault.

She stalked forward and grabbed the phone he was holding out.

"Hello?"

"Oh, Chelsea, I heard you were back in town, but I only just found out you and David are seeing each other. Of course, I haven't seen you in years, but unless you've changed a great deal, you were like a second daughter to us when you lived next door."

Chelsea felt emotion swell in her chest. "Oh, Mrs. Wolfe, I feel the same way. I mean, you were always so nice to me, exactly like a second mother."

"When Lawrence and I get home, we're going to have a family dinner and get all caught up."

"A family dinner sounds wonderful. Enjoy the rest of your vacation."

"Don't run away now, will you? Not before we get back.

I'm so happy to think of him with a good woman for a change."

"Thank you."

When she got off the phone she realized that she loved David's parents almost as much as she loved him, and for a lot better reasons.

They exchanged glances. "I cannot believe that woman's been spying on us and reporting to my mother. Internationally. It's like living across the street from Interpol." He sipped the last of the wine in his glass. "You don't know what my mother's been like since they both retired. It's like she's obsessed with weddings and babies. Her finding out about you living here is not good news."

"She's happy to think of you with a good woman for a change."

He looked outraged. "She said that? My own mother?"

"Her very words."

"I—"

"'Oh what a tangled web we weave, when first we practice to deceive,'" she quoted.

"What?"

"Sir Walter Scott. On the dangers of lying. I'm pretty sure you helped me with my homework back in sophomore English. Remember?"

9

WHAT'S STOPPING YOU from meeting me?

Sarah stared at the words glaring at her from her computer screen. What was stopping her?

She left the cursor blinking and went in search of something to eat.

There were all the obvious reasons, like men in general being bad news. The men her clients ended up divorcing, men like the current scumbag who'd hidden his assets offshore along with his current girlfriend. Or the male lawyers she spent too much time with, or David, her own brother who'd rather invent a fantasy fiancée than try to have a relationship with a real woman.

Returning with a doggie bag of Chelsea's treats, she sat back down at her computer desk. Clarence, the black-and-white cat she'd found rooting around in the garbage two years ago, leaped into her lap and she patted him absentmindedly.

She stared at the words. Took a breath. Because he was essentially an anonymous penpal, she'd been able to be honest with Mike in a way she never was with real men in her life. So, she told the truth. Typed:

You seem so perfect. I love talking to you like this, all anonymous. You could be anyone. A man I work with, a guy riding past me on a bike as I go to work. The cute guy in line at the bank. I don't know, so I can tell you anything and know you'll answer me honestly. How many relationships like this do you have? I have none.

She pushed Send.

He replied almost as soon as she could have expected him to.

I've never had a relationship like this one. Believe it or not, I'm not an online dating guy. A friend was posting and it sounded like fun at the time. Mostly I've found it's time-consuming and wastes hours I could be outside on my bike. It would have been a total waste if I hadn't met you. Maybe this is stupid, but I sort of believe things are sometimes meant to be. Maybe the reason I posted a profile that day was because I was destined to meet you. Who knows? We could have absolutely nothing in common if we meet, I know it's a risk, but how long do we play this game of e-mailing secrets? Wouldn't it be nice to know each other for real?

She read the words. Read them a second time. *For real.* Those words haunted her. There was the problem, right there. In those two little words. *For real?* What was real about this? Nothing. It was fantasy. Glorious, delicious, secret fantasy.

She e-mailed back, What if we don't like each other

in the "for real" world? We can't ever have this back once we come out of the shadows.

A couple of minutes later came his reply. I don't want to live my life in the shadows. Do you?

Some parts of it, she thought she did.

She was debating how to answer him when her doorbell rang. Swiftly, she shut off her e-mail and put the cover down on her laptop.

A peek through her peephole revealed one very stressed-out big brother.

She put her grin away before opening the door.

"Hi. This is a surprise."

"You set me up!" He was so outraged, so full of blustering innocence. She couldn't believe it had taken him this long to blast her. She'd essentially done him exactly the favor she'd promised in setting him up with Chelsea. Except for the part where she'd encouraged her old friend to look her sexiest. That, she had to admit, was for revenge.

She stuck a hand on her hip and recited, from memory, "I am a childless professional woman seeking a man who can see beyond the workaholic to the soft, caring mother within."

He had the grace to look guilty for about a nanosecond, then went on the attack. "That online profile was a Christmas prank. All you had to do was remove yourself from the site. Compared with this? You ruined my life."

"Oh, come on. You were desperate. You did all the lying yourself, remember? All I did was provide the perfect woman."

"I never knew Mom was going to find out."

She snorted with laughter. "What? Are you kidding me? How could Mom find out? She's in Poland."

"One of her cronies lives on my street. Seems she saw me and Chelsea come home together the other night and has had binoculars trained on my house 24/7 ever since. She e-mailed Mom that I'm living with a woman."

"Okay, that blows." Then her sense of the ridiculous overcame her once more. "I have to say, you getting busted by Mom was an unexpected bonus."

He stormed past her and started pacing her apartment.

Sarah studied him for a moment, a puzzled frown on her face. "I don't get why you're so upset. Mom and Dad will understand if you put up an old friend for a few weeks. In the meantime, you've got exactly what you want. Chelsea told me herself that the dinner thing went really well. In your wildest dreams you couldn't have come up with anyone who would be more perfect as a corporate wife than Chelsea. She cooks, she speaks French, she dresses well, has good table manners, no tattoos, addictions or her own YouTube porn video."

"Nannette was a performance artist."

"Whatever. I'm just saying, Chelsea's fabulous. So why rip up at me?"

But it seemed he hadn't come to her only to storm at her. He started speaking, a little like a witness on the stand, like the words were forced from him. "My firm loves her. They want us both to go to a weekend corporate retreat. This is totally out of control."

"Well, don't yell at me. What were you thinking would happen?"

"I thought a couple of dinners, maybe the Christmas party and we'd be done. I never imagined she'd infiltrate my life this way."

"Infiltrate your life? Chelsea's not a spy, David."

"No, but she's changing everything. My house is full of food and there are flowers in vases all over the place, and suddenly I'm going to a corporate retreat with a woman. Everything's all mixed up."

She hadn't seen him this upset since his engagement broke up. She began to grow hopeful. "What are you going to do about it?"

"I don't know."

"Why are you here?"

"I had to get away. It's like frickin' domestic bliss. We had dinner together in my house, and she told me about her day, and I told her about my day, her stuff is all over the place, there are flowers in my living room—I think I already said that—and my family likes her and, and..."

"And you can't handle it."

He paced a little more. "I don't even know why I came here. You know what?" He turned to her as though he had something profound to say and then suddenly said, "The one greatest benefit to living with a woman is denied me. She has these rules. No sex, no kissing... Oh, never mind." And as quickly as he'd appeared, he was gone.

She didn't want to feel sorry for him, he was in a mess of his own creating after all, but for some reason she did. He was just so clueless about his own needs and feelings.

She opened the door and shouted down the hall, "Do you even know how many years that amazing woman was in love with you? Clueless, you're clueless." He didn't answer, was probably already riding the elevator down, and so she slammed the door and retreated back to her apartment.

She stomped back into her home office, pulled her laptop open. People who played games with their love lives were idiots. Then, as she thought about what she was doing e-mailing her mystery man, she realized that she had more in common with her clueless brother than she wanted to admit.

She took a deep breath, knowing she was about to risk losing something that had become special to her over the past months.

Okay, she replied. I'm in. Let's meet.

She looked at the words for a long time. And then she closed her eyes and pushed Send.

Do you even know how many years she was in love with you? The words spun round and round in his head like song lyrics that wouldn't quit.

Of course he'd known. Did his sister think he was completely stupid? Not love, that was Sarah the drama queen talking, but he'd known Chelsea had a thing for him. So, her friend had had a crush on him in high school. That was a long time ago, and the woman David had met in front of the hotel was not the kind of woman who pined after an old school crush. A woman with a body and face like that? She could have any man she wanted.

Love. What did love have to do with anything anyway? It was the talk of an engagement that got everyone's emotions on hyperdrive. What he and Chelsea had going was a simple business arrangement.

But he halted in his tracks as he recalled Chelsea's really strange reaction to the weekend away together. She'd said it would be tough to have to spend a weekend with him at a luxury resort. At the time he'd thought she was just yanking his chain, but with Sarah's words still dancing in his head, he began to wonder. Was it possible that she still had…feelings for him? After all these years?

A strange warmth flooded him at the thought. She'd been a sweet kid, too smart and serious for her own good. Now? Now she was one of the sexiest women he'd ever seen. Was it even possible that a woman like that had never overcome a high school crush?

He didn't want it to be true, of course, but if it was, he could see he needed to treat her carefully. He didn't want her thinking there was any more to this engagement than a chance for both of them to get ahead in business.

Still, he wasn't entirely able to quench a certain flattered pride that persisted when he returned to the town house they were now sharing.

Everything made more sense. Especially her completely bizarre refusal to sleep with him when you could cut the sexual tension between them with a knife. Every time they touched he ended up weak-kneed. He wasn't so full of himself that he could have mistaken the honest lust that had flared between them. She'd felt it as strongly as he had and he'd been surprised when she refused to take their wild attraction to its obvious conclusion and let them both enjoy each other.

But maybe he'd misunderstood the situation. Maybe she had feelings for him.

If that was the case he was going to have to tread warily. Still, he was grinning to himself when he walked back into his own home.

The grin died a sudden death when he heard little Miss High School Crush laugh—a deep, sexy laugh that no woman would pull out for just anybody.

He closed the door quietly; she was sitting back on a big comfy chair with her back to him.

"Philippe, *c'est impossible. Non.*" Another ribbon of sexy laughter floated to his ears. And then she continued speaking.

He had no idea what she was saying, but it was in French and that made everything sound dirty. He understood one word very clearly. Philippe. Yeah, no girls he knew were called Philippe. Obviously, Chelsea had a French boyfriend. No wonder she was willing to forgo any dating activity in Philly. That was why she didn't want to sleep with him, that was why she didn't want to spend a weekend away with him. It wasn't because she was still hopelessly in love with him. It was because she was hopelessly in love with another man.

He couldn't wait to tell his sister how wrong she'd been.

Chelsea wasn't in love with him anymore, if you could even call a high school crush love. She'd moved on.

He pictured some guy in a striped T-shirt and floppy hair smoking Gitanes and quoting Proust. The vision made him mildly queasy.

He made a noisy production of entering his own home so she wouldn't be startled. She glanced up, sending him a smile and a cheery wave. Her legs were crossed at the ankles, feet resting on the arm of his couch. Long, lean legs and the toe ring winking at him. And then she went back to cooing sweet nothings in French.

David wasn't a jealous man; he didn't believe in an emotion that caused nothing but pain.

However, he'd really, really love to have his own personal UN-style interpreter right now so he could understand exactly what his fiancée was cooing to another man.

10

"THERE'S ONLY ONE BED." It was probably the stupidest thing she could have said, but the two of them were standing there inside the door of the suite on Friday night of the corporate retreat, both staring at the mammoth bed that dominated the room.

Seemed like someone should mention it.

"Looks like it." He sent her a half guilty, half pleading look from under eyelashes that were far too long and lush for a man. "I could request two beds, but word would get around."

"No. Don't do that."

He glanced down at the floor dubiously. "I suppose I could sleep on the floor."

"It's slate. You'd be miserable. No, the bed's huge. You stay on your side, I'll stay on mine. We'll work it out."

The room was gorgeous, the resort fairly new and built in a style she thought of as eco-chic. All natural materials, stone and wood, big natural rock fireplaces and natural linens for bedding and towels. Huge French doors led to the woodland retreat outside. There were trees and wildflowers out there and plenty of privacy.

"I am really sorry about this. I had no idea they'd put us in the bridal suite."

She giggled. "It's not the bridal suite," she said, glancing over a brochure that was on the desk. "It's the romance package."

They'd left early in the day to avoid Friday night traffic and enjoyed a leisurely drive through rolling hills, past lakes and forests of trees that would be turning every color of fire come autumn, but for now were a deep, placid green.

"I used to come up here a lot to go hiking and camping," David said. "There are some great trails, waterfalls and good views." He glanced at her sideways. "And not too many snakes."

She rolled her eyes.

"We should come up with a tent sometime," he said, and then as though realizing that he was talking as though they had a future, added, "With a group or something. You know."

Piers and his wife had been so excited when they arrived, they'd all but accompanied Chelsea and David into their room. "We thought you could combine the corporate retreat with a bit of fun time to yourselves," Piers had informed them.

The double Jacuzzi bathtub in the middle of the suite, for instance, could no doubt be fun if you were in fact in love, and not faking it.

There was a basket of goodies on the table that included champagne, chocolates and massage oil and a few more intimate items. Oh, dear.

"I had no idea they'd do something like this. Honestly, I figured we'd get a standard hotel room with two queen beds."

"It's fine." Hoisting her bag onto the edge of the

enormous bed, she began unpacking her case into the wooden drawers. "I trust you."

"What about Philippe?"

"Philippe?"

"Your French boyfriend. I overheard you talking to him on the phone."

She glanced up at him. "I didn't know you could speak French."

"I can't. But I picked out a few words."

"I see. Well, you don't need to worry. Philippe knows he can trust me."

Philippe had studied with her and they'd bonded over béchamel sauce. Neither of them could stand the thick white sauce and tried to avoid using it in their own cooking. If David had picked up on passion during their conversation it was a passion for food, since Philippe was happily living with Raoul, a financial analyst from Nantes.

She thought about disabusing him of his mistake, but stopped herself. A little consideration was all it took to make her realize that Philippe was the perfect excuse to keep her distance from the all-too-attractive and far-too-accessible David.

She hadn't had sex in months and the lack was getting to her, especially while living under the same roof of a man who reminded her she was a woman with a woman's needs. Plus, with the stress and anxiety of opening a new business, some good recreational sex and a few laughs were exactly what she needed, but she wasn't built that way. And with David, she didn't think she could have a few laughs and walk away unscathed. She really needed to keep her distance.

He was staring at her while she neatly put her clothes and things away. "You unpack for a weekend?"

"Yes. I suppose you jumble everything together in your suitcase and wonder why your clothes end up creased."

"No," he said in a constricted voice. "I unpack for a weekend, too."

She bit her lip. "Oh."

She hung her dresses neatly in the closet; he hung his jacket and slacks beside them. How intimate they appeared, those clothes, cosily snuggled up like lovers.

They moved around each other fairly efficiently until she noticed he'd stopped and seemed to have turned to stone. She was unpacking her lingerie—she hadn't even considered that he'd ever see it, and here she was with all her frilly, girly French silks and laces. Sexy lingerie was an indulgence she'd picked up in Paris. No matter how yucky her day with food, how utilitarian her apron, she always knew that underneath all that she was feminine and sexy.

It seemed he'd noticed. For a second she stood frozen, a black lacy bra and panties in her hand burning like a handful of live coals. He didn't move, either; it was as though he couldn't. Their gazes connected and she felt the scorch.

He took a step forward then halted. Swallowed.

He glanced at his watch. "We've got an hour until we have to join the crew for dinner." He gestured behind him to the walking trails that meandered behind the lodge. "Think I'll take a walk."

Oh, this whole place was altogether too romantic. A long walk seemed like a good idea, because if he took one step closer, they'd be cracking open the massage oil and champagne.

"Okay. I think I'll finish unpacking."

He nodded. "See you later."

It was going to be a long weekend, David thought as he strolled among the pines and birch, enjoying the fresh air, the softness of the path beneath his feet and the fresh air. Fresh air. Right. If he kept repeating that thought, breathing in deep lungfuls of the stuff, he might keep his thoughts off the sexiest wisps of nothing that women considered as underwear.

All he could think about was that glorious body covered in dabs of silk that he was pretty sure were designed more to enhance than reveal.

This weekend was going to be torture. Pure torture. Between the stress of spending a sexless weekend in the sex palace and trying to impress the execs, he thought a three-day migraine might be easier to handle.

He wandered aimlessly, wanting to go back and make love to that woman so badly his teeth ached, knowing he couldn't. He reached a summit where a view of gently rolling hills seemed to stretch to New Jersey.

He could do this. He could share a bed with a beautiful woman who wore sexy undies and not touch her. Fresh air, he reminded himself. Breathe. He kept up a fast pace until he barely had time to dress for dinner, then reentered their room through the French doors.

He was in time to see Chelsea poke her second earring in her ear, otherwise she was fully dressed, and every cell in his body yelled *Wow*. "You sure do have some nice clothes," he said. She was wearing a simple black dress but it had a kind of attitude to it somehow. He didn't understand women's fashion, obviously, but he knew when a woman had style and Chelsea had it from the top of her sleek shiny hair to the soles of her black high-heeled shoes.

Of course, while he didn't have X-ray vision, he did have a vivid imagination, and based on the lingerie he'd seen in her suitcase earlier, she was wearing some sinful confection underneath that dress.

She looked down at herself as though she might have forgotten what she was wearing. "Thanks. Clothes are my weakness. I think it's because I'm cooking or preparing food all day, in a uniform and aprons. When I get a chance, I love to dress up."

"Lucky me," he said, and he realized how true that was. Also, she wasn't one to keep a man waiting, another quality he admired. "Give me five minutes and I'll be ready to go."

The dinner was exactly what he would have predicted. A private room, good food and a partner a man could be proud of.

They'd barely walked in when Piers's wife, Helen, gestured them over to a table. "Come and join us. I've got something to show you."

She sounded so excited that his heart sank. Not more romance. He couldn't take it.

When they reached her, Helen pulled out a brown envelope and opened it, spilling out an array of photographs of a wedding. "These are some of the pictures from my niece's wedding. Not sure if you've booked a photographer yet, but if you haven't, this company is excellent. He's done a lot of the big society weddings, so he's top-notch."

"Wedding photographer..." He couldn't even formulate a sentence.

The sight of that camera-perfect couple, the bride in her white gown and the groom tricked out in a monkey suit, made him feel like he couldn't get enough air. They'd studied photographers, he and Suzanne. They'd planned to get married at her mother's house, where the grounds were bigger than a park and there were sixteen bedrooms to accommodate overnight guests.

The elegant invitations had even been printed, and then Suzanne, who was as cool and organized about details as she was about running her family's business, kept forgetting to put them in the mail.

Two weeks later, she told him she'd made a mistake and was going back to her former boyfriend.

A guy who hadn't even been on the invite list.

Pick another wedding photographer? Not in this lifetime. David had no idea what to say.

Luckily, Chelsea picked up the dropped ball.

"These pictures are amazing," she said, flipping through them. "Oh, I like the one here, by the fountain. And your niece is gorgeous. Where did she get that dress?"

And soon he found the women discussing wedding details. Amelia joined in and the women talked about everything from engraved glassware to bridal headgear as easily as if Chelsea and he were actively pursuing a union. He didn't know what he'd do without her.

Afterward the evening was free; some headed to the bar, some to their rooms and some to other parts of the lodge. Knowing he didn't want to expose Chelsea and himself to any more scrutiny than necessary, he challenged her to a game of Ping-Pong, which she laughingly accepted.

The games room wasn't very busy and one of the two Ping-Pong tables was free. He slipped off his jacket, she stepped out of her shoes and they faced each other across the green table.

"I remember we used to play this game in my parents' rec room," he said, surprised at how clear the memory was of teenage Chelsea and him battling it out. His sister, even then, hadn't seen the point in wasting time on games, so if no one else was around he dragged Hermione into the rec room where they enjoyed some spirited competition.

Of course, he usually won, but she always put up a good fight.

"I haven't played in years," she said, laughing as they volleyed to get into the swing of things.

"Then I guess I'm going to kick your butt," he informed her.

"A gentleman would give me a head start."

He grinned at her. "If you see any around, challenge them to a game."

She shook her head at him. "You know, you really haven't changed."

"Oh, you have," he said softly, glad that the bouncing plastic ball covered his comment. Watching her move and sway, jump forward and back as they began the game for real, he wondered when shapeless, studious, not at all stylish Hermione had turned into one of the sexiest, most beautiful women he'd ever seen.

He got so carried away watching her body move in that dress that she'd scored six points to his two. Clearly it was time to focus.

In the end, he won, but it was a squeaker.

"Best of three?" she asked and he said, "Sure."

He suspected she was as anxious as he was to drag the evening out so they wouldn't be stuck spending too much time in that huge bed pretending they didn't want each other.

Or maybe that was just him.

AFTER HE WON THE first two games, she surprised both of them by winning the third. It had helped that a few of the other people from David's company had wandered in to see the match, and after watching for a few minutes, Helen Van Horne had bet her husband five dollars that Chelsea would win the last game.

In spite of Chelsea's horrified protests, Piers had taken the bet and suddenly you'd have thought they were laying bets on the Super Bowl. All the women got behind Chelsea, which she really appreciated since she was obviously the weaker player, and then Helen had insisted the guys "man up" and support David.

Maybe it was the support of a group of women she was starting to really like, or maybe it was simply the heat of competition, but Chelsea decided that David wasn't going to win the third match, and concentrated all her energy on the little white ball.

She knew all of David's weaknesses from playing against him so often in the past, and she exploited every one of them. He liked to stand back from the table and smash balls so they bounced too far for her to return them. But he wasn't very good when she dropped the ball softly just inside the net, so that's what she did whenever possible.

His backhand was also a little weak and he wasn't as agile as she, all of which she exploited ruthlessly until they were both panting with effort.

Finally, to a chorus of feminine cheers, she won the game.

She felt like an Olympic gold medalist. David, a drop of sweat rolling down his hairline, leaned across and shook her hand, giving her his crooked grin. "Nicely played, Hermione. Didn't know you had it in you."

"Come on, don't be a sore loser, kiss the girl!"

As their gazes connected, she saw the heat spark and felt the answering burst of passion within her. She leaned in, kissed his lips. She tasted sweat and felt the warmth of his mouth, the thickness of his hair as she cupped her hand around the back of his head. Suddenly, he pulled her in to his body and she was so startled she dropped her paddle so it clattered to the table.

Oh, he felt so right against her, so hot and gorgeous and hers. She felt as though he'd always been hers, he simply hadn't known it.

Sadly, she thought, as she eased carefully away amid the laughter and catcalls, he still didn't know it.

They turned the table over to the next challengers and decided to turn in.

Now was the moment she'd dreaded. How would she ever resist him if he picked up where that kiss left off?

The rules, she reminded herself.

She simply had to remember the rules.

Once in their room, however, David didn't turn on the charm. Instead, he politely asked her if she'd like the bathroom first. She deferred to him with equal politeness, and after he disappeared into the bathroom, she clicked on the news.

David emerged a few minutes later wearing pajamas that were so obviously never worn she had to assume they were a gift he'd never before used or that he'd bought them specially.

They were navy cotton with tiny white stripes, slightly stiff where they'd never been washed and still bearing the crisp creases where they'd been folded.

He looked adorable.

She disappeared into the bathroom on the same task, brushed her teeth and slipped into her much more worn pajamas. Also cotton, but purple and covered with printed recipes written in French.

"Great pj's," David said as she flipped back the covers and eased herself into her side of the bed, leaving at least an acre between them.

"Thanks. Philippe bought them for me. He said I was

so passionate about food that I should wear it to bed. It was kind of a joke present."

"You must miss him."

She thought about Philippe and how they'd laughed and helped each other stay sane through the rigorous training program. They called and e-mailed to give each other advice and support, but it wasn't the same as talking in person. "I do. I miss him every day."

David got into his side of the bed and pulled the covers up to his chin. "Okay, then, good night. If I snore, just punch me."

If he snored, she'd lie awake all night listening to him, but she didn't say so, merely nodded. "I don't think I snore, but if I do you're welcome to punch me, too."

"You don't look like a snorer, but you can never tell. Okay if I turn out the light?"

"Yes."

He plunged the room into relative darkness. As her eyes adjusted, she realized there was a sliver of light slipping between the curtains from the outside lights of the hotel.

She turned away so her back was to David and tried not to think about the man she'd reconnected with. She still had a terrible crush on him, and he still had no clue.

11

SHE'D BEEN EYEING that beautiful, deep soaker tub built for two since they'd arrived yesterday. It was the most decadent tub she'd ever seen, with a view to a private garden area outside and candles and bath products galore.

She'd had a surprisingly fun day, beginning with a strenuous walk after breakfast with several of the wives. The two husbands of female execs and a couple of the women who golfed had taken to the greens, but she'd preferred the hiking.

After lunch, they'd been given the option to choose among the spa services and she'd gone for a facial and a body wrap involving seaweed.

After another group dinner, she was in need of some alone time. David and the other execs were safely off doing some kind of team-building exercise, so she skipped the movie-and-popcorn social and slipped away.

Oh, this room was nice. Imagine if she and David were really a couple in love. How much fun they could have.

Oh, well. A nice decadent soak in a tub was all the fun she needed right now. She poured herself a bath, watching the steam billow into the air, and, after she dumped a jar of bath salts into the tub, the scent of lavender filled the room.

They'd shoved the champagne in the fridge, and she didn't think that she and David were going to have a romantic champagne breakfast together or anything so she might as well sample it as let it go to waste. Besides, she figured David owed her for making her come with him for an entire weekend of fakery.

She undressed slowly, putting her clothes away as she did so, and drawing on the oatmeal-colored linen bathrobe and slippers the hotel provided.

She lit the candles around the tub, lovely fat beeswax candles, and flipped off the lights. The French doors were open to the forest outside, fading in color as evening advanced.

She eased off the champagne cork and poured herself a bubbling glass of wine.

Then she slipped off the robe and stepped into the bath, sliding down into the scented water that felt like undiluted pleasure. She sighed. The candlelight danced off the water, gilding her body and the champagne. She sipped, approved. Tilted her head back against the headrest and closed her eyes.

For a woman who spent so much time on her feet, this was pure bliss.

DAVID WAS MORE THAN happy to have been let off tonight's event early. Since he wasn't officially a VP yet, he'd been perfectly willing to take the hint offered by Piers, who suggested he'd probably be more interested in spending a Saturday evening with Chelsea than in spending hours with the board. He understood and appreciated Piers's tact.

He nodded. "Can't complain about spending more time on that romance package."

The older man chuckled, delighted with his surprise. "That's the spirit. I envy you, you know. A beautiful woman, your entire future ahead of you. Make some memories, son. I'm not saying you won't still be making them at my age, but those early years…" he said with fond nostalgia. "Well, I wouldn't give up those memories for anything."

He'd never had such a personal conversation with his boss and he was mildly uncomfortable to hear anything even this close to the details of Piers and Helen's sex life. "Yes, sir," he said. "I'll see you in the morning."

He didn't have much choice but to head back to the room when Piers so obviously expected him to. He couldn't hang around in the lobby or bar without arousing suspicion, but he thought that an entire evening in a room that had been designed with sex in mind was going to be torture when he was cooped up with a woman who seriously could have been designed with sex in mind.

And he'd promised not to touch her.

What a cruel, cruel joke.

At least she was off on some movie-night thing. He'd throw on sweats and head to the gym for a couple of hours, work off some of the lust that had kept him wakeful and longing in the night.

He opened the door with his key and walked in, and then stood stupidly rooted to the spot.

It was like somebody had opened up his brain and looked into his fantasy vault and pulled out a good one. There, naked and golden in the bath, was the most glorious woman he'd ever seen. Candlelight licked lovingly at her wet skin, making him want to follow suit. Her breasts seemed to float, begging him to put his mouth on them. Even as he stared, dumbfounded, her nipples puckered, making his mouth water.

Their gazes caught and held. She was so beautiful, her eyes dark and huge, her hair pinned back to reveal that long, beautiful neck and the perfect round breasts. All this happened in the space of a couple of eye blinks and then they both reacted like actors in a bad farce.

"Hell," he said, shielding his eyes from paradise. "Sorry, I should have knocked."

He caught her movement as she dragged her knees up and pulled her arms in front of her glorious breasts. "I thought you were in a meeting." Water sloshed and candles flickered.

"I was supposed to be." He turned back to the door. "Look, I'll go get a drink or something. I'll come back later."

"No…" He heard an edge of laughter in her voice. "It's okay. This is just the most ridiculous situation. Whoever heard of putting a bathtub in the middle of a bedroom?"

"The folks who brought you the romance package." He didn't even let himself think about how much he wanted to shuck his clothes and climb into that tub with her. He'd show her a romance package all right.

"Give me a second to put on my robe and—"

"Are you sure? I could go to the bar and come back in an hour or so."

"No, it's fine. I've been in here long enough—I'm turning wrinkly. Besides, we don't want them thinking we had a fight. I don't think I could handle a lot of well-meaning advice from all those matchmakers out there," she said, sounding mildly panicked.

"Yeah."

He heard more water dripping and sloshing and tried very hard not to think of her standing up, naked and wet and fragrant. He heard her feet running across the slate floor and then the sound of the bathroom door. "It's safe to come in," she called out.

"I am so sorry about that," he said again when she emerged from the bathroom a few minutes later, wearing soft sweats, her damp hair brushed off her face.

She looked mildly embarrassed and he knew they were both picturing the moment when he'd walked in and seen her naked. He wasn't sure if she was more embarrassed about being caught in the buff, or if it was that strange moment before they both panicked when the pull of attraction had been too strong to ignore.

Maybe he'd gone into this thing by not telling the truth, but other than telling a little white lie to get ahead in his career, he tried to be an upright guy. If she didn't want to sleep with him while they were living together, he had to respect that. And now he'd learned there was another man in the picture, he knew he'd try even harder.

This arrangement, he reminded himself, was strictly business. It wasn't personal.

If seeing a fantastically gorgeous woman naked in the bath in his hotel room felt kind of personal, he supposed that was his problem.

"So," she said, "do you want some champagne?"

"Might as well." He got up and poured himself a glass, topping hers at the same time. "I thought we might watch an in-room movie." He caught her expression and grinned. "Not porn. I'm thinking something highbrow and depressing that will not make me think about sex. Especially, since—" he glanced significantly at the huge bed dominating the room "—you know, we have to sleep together, but not, ah, sleep together."

He knew his honest admission had done the trick when she laughed and seemed to relax.

"Good plan."

So they put on a movie that had been a big award contender even though it had done poorly at the box office. Neither of them had seen it and after forty minutes, he could see why. He was crammed in a chair and she was very carefully on one side of the king-size bed.

"If one more person offs themselves in this movie, I'm seriously going to need therapy," he said.

"It's the most depressing thing I've ever seen," she agreed. Then after a minute she said, "But the acting's amazing."

"You enjoying the movie at all?"

"No. I like uplifting stories with happy endings."

"Me, too." He thought for a second. "Or a lot of action."

"Do you think that makes us shallow people?"

"Probably. But well-adjusted."

For something to do he started turning over the items in the gift basket. He opened the mixed nuts and offered her some, then took a handful and while he was munching, pulled out the massage oil. "Chamomile and bergamot. Cool." He tossed the bottle in the air and caught it. "I had a girlfriend who was totally into reflexology. I could give you a foot massage if you like." He glanced at the screen. "It would be a lot less depressing than this movie."

She glanced up at him. Her face was scrubbed free of cosmetics and her hair had had the style damped out of it. He thought she was one of the prettiest women he'd ever seen. "You can give a foot massage?"

"Yep. Pretty good one. You game? I feel like I owe you something for interrupting your bath."

"I'd rather do that than watch any more of this movie," she agreed.

He was more than happy to flip off the depressathon and crawl onto the bed beside her.

"Normally, I'd soak your feet in warm water and Epsom salts, but I guess you were soaking them in the tub, so we can skip that part."

He jumped off the bed and went to the bathroom, returning with one of the thick, fluffy bath towels the hotel provided.

He settled the towel under her feet, then poured some of the massage oil into his hands. Lifting her left foot, he spread the oil carefully, then, starting at her ankle, ran his hands in long, smooth strokes to her toes. He did this over and over, as Melinda had taught him, until the oil was warm under his hands and he could feel the skin and muscles in her feet begin to warm and soften.

She even had beautiful feet, he noted. Shapely and long, but they were hard-working feet, too. He felt the gnarled spots and calluses where she stood on them all day. She'd left the toe ring at home and he sort of missed it.

Starting with the top of her foot, he worked between the tendons, then he moved to the sole of her foot, running his thumbs in slow, firm circles around the pressure points, one at a time.

She was a little stiff with him at first, but as the massage continued and he clearly wasn't trying to touch anything but her feet, he felt her relax and give herself over to him.

"Oh, that's wonderful," she moaned at one point.

"People don't realize how much stress they place on their feet, especially people like you who stand a lot."

He found her most sensitive spots were on the balls of her feet, so he put extra effort there, rubbing and smoothing.

He was on the outer part of the ball of her left foot, rubbing, when he felt a constriction and she sighed. "That feels so good."

"You know what part of the body that corresponds to according to the foot reflexology chart?"

"What?" Her voice was a sexy murmur.

"The heart."

She opened her eyes and regarded him. "Are you saying my heart's in pain?"

"No. Confused maybe."

She chuckled. "Maybe."

"Your foot could be telling you that Philippe's not the man for you."

"A foot can tell you so much?"

"You'd be surprised."

And if he was as lucky as Philippe, he sure as hell wouldn't be wasting his time in France while a woman like Chelsea was a continent away getting her feet rubbed by another man.

If Frenchie didn't watch out, he was going to be ousted by some good old American grit and determination.

12

WHY ON EARTH HAD SHE let David come near her with
a bottle of massage oil? Chelsea wondered in horror. It
wasn't like he was touching her sexually, because all the
man was doing was rubbing her feet, but somehow there
seemed to be a strange correlation between her toes and
more intimate regions of her body.

Warmth was spreading where warmth had no business
spreading. And it wasn't in her foot.

Him and his damn foot-map. He probably had the cli-
toris spot memorized and he was working it for all he was
worth.

Certainly, he seemed intent on his task. His black hair
flopped forward on his forehead in a way that made her
long to brush it back. His entire focus was on the bottom of
her feet and she had to admit it felt good. Far too good.

She watched him, his hands slick with oil, his long
fingers working with steady strength. She'd never known
she carried so much tension in her feet or that it could feel
so good to have that tension relieved. Except that it only
seemed to move the tension to other parts of her body.

As though he were aware of her growing excitement,
even as she tried to hide it, she felt his hands begin to

move, slowly sweeping up and over her ankles, pushing the sweatpants up a little as he did so.

"You feel so good," he said with a note of huskiness that told her he was as turned on as she was.

"You give a good massage."

"If the insurance thing doesn't pan out, it's good to know I've got a backup career." He pushed her sweats up even higher.

"What are you doing?" she whispered.

"Hell if I know, but I can't seem to keep my hands off you. If you tell me to stop, I'll go spend the night in the tub."

His fingers were magical, making her crazy with desire, and this was only from stroking her feet and lower legs. She could barely think straight.

"What about the rules?" she managed to ask.

His lovely, slick hands paused and she wanted, like a cat, to rub herself against him until he stroked her once more. "I've got a new rule that says the rules only apply in Philly."

"So, once we get home, we go back to our own rooms?"

"If you want to."

Dimly, she suspected this was a terrible idea, but she was only human, and he was altogether too amazing. So for one magical night she'd have him. "Okay," she said. "For this one night, the rules don't apply. But when we get back…"

"Got it."

He eased her out of the sweats as easily as if she wore nothing but a peignoir. Off came the top and he made a little growling sound at the back of his throat. "I am so glad you're wearing that crazy sexy lingerie," he whispered. He leaned forward, kissed her breasts through the filmy silk.

Already aroused, she found herself almost embarrassingly excited as his mouth closed around her nipple.

She wrapped her arms around him, ran her hands down his back and into his hair, all the places she'd wanted to touch him were hers to explore for this one no-rules-apply night. Her body felt light, magical, sizzling with desires and needs she'd been tamping down for all of the days and nights she'd been sharing his life, his home, everything but his bed.

His hands tracked down her belly with barely controlled haste. She smiled to herself, glad his actions suggested he'd been wanting her as badly as she'd been wanting him.

He began kissing his way up her legs, when suddenly he reared up. "Hell. I didn't pack condoms. I mean, I thought about it, but I didn't want you thinking anything." He stared up at her. "I guess we could just—"

"I think there are some in the romance gift basket," she said. She'd found them earlier when she'd unpacked the champagne and tucked them deep into the basket.

He snorted with laughter, but she heard the relief, as well. "Damn, I love this hotel."

He rose and she watched him rummage through the basket and retrieve a duo of condom packs, then he picked up the box of matches and began lighting some of the candles that had been placed around the bath, moving them to the bedside tables and leaving several around the bath, so the room flickered with the soft, romantic glow of candlelight.

He returned to the bed, stripped off his clothes with impressive speed, and then settled himself beside her.

She had the impression of strong shoulders, a hairier chest than she'd imagined and an impressive erection, before he was so close that feeling took over for seeing.

He began touching her, stroking her, everywhere from her shoulders to her belly to her thighs.

His hands were still a little oily, and they left tiny patches of sparkle that lit with candlelight where he touched her.

Kissing her deeply, tormenting both of them, his touch grew more intimate. Slipping under the wisp of silk at her crotch, he began to play with her, taking her up, up, impossibly up. "You are so beautiful," he breathed into her ear.

While he caressed her, she took her own tour of his body, loving the hard belly, the even harder erection that sprang into her hands as she stroked him softly.

When they couldn't stand tormenting each other any longer, he stripped off her panties and she unsnapped her bra and then naked they rolled together. It wasn't as though he entered her or she guided him inside, it was as though they simply fit together, as easily and naturally as though they'd been together for years.

Except that this was brand-new.

"Oh, you feel so good," she said, as he began to move, stroking her inside, pushing her to the limit.

"You have no idea," he muttered. They were side by side and he hooked her leg high over his hip so he could reach between them and play with her clit. Deciding to do a little playing of her own, she took his balls gently in hand, making him groan. They teased and played, and knowing they only had one night made them both want to take every second they could, she thought. They rocked back and forth, driving each other higher. Their breathing grew ragged, she felt the sweat build on his skin, and then suddenly he flipped her to her back, driving up and hard into her until her head fell back and she cried out as her climax swamped her.

Moments later he echoed her cry and then slowed his pace, stroking her through her aftershocks.

A little later, once their heart rates had returned to normal, he reached for the second condom package, flipping it up in the air and catching it like a coin. She almost expected him to call "Heads or tails?" Instead he glanced at her with the trace of a wicked smile. "Only one left."

She reached up and snatched it out of his hand. "Then let's make the most of it," she said, and taking matters into her own hands, she did.

CHELSEA HAD NO IDEA what time she finally fell asleep, only knew she'd actually been asleep when she wakened and for a second couldn't think where she was, or with whom.

Clearly she was in bed with a man, that much she could tell from the warm weight of a body pressed against her back and the amazing contentment of a woman who's had a night of great sex. She felt sleep-deprived and gloriously well-used. His arm was around her with the casual intimacy of lovers, his long fingers cupping her naked breast. He was sleeping, his warm breath wafting against the nape of her neck.

She leaned back against him, enjoying the lazy warmth of his body, and noticing the morning erection prominent against her hip.

As the night came back to her in detail, she considered waking him with her mouth, but it was morning, their one night was over and if she had any hope of walking away from this guy, she had to get back to the very sensible rules she'd instituted.

Even if he felt amazing and she wanted him with every cell of her tired body.

One more moment she gave herself to enjoy the fantasy

that he was hers, then carefully she began to disengage herself, sliding out from under his arm so she almost fell onto the floor.

She rose carefully, but he was still asleep, a slight smile on his face. How boyish he looked when he was unconscious. It was all she could do not to smooth back the hair flopped onto his forehead and kiss him softly. Instead, she crept to the bathroom, where she showered and prepared for the day.

DAVID SMELLED THE FRAGRANT scents of a woman on the pillow. He woke slowly, wondering where the woman who smelled so good had disappeared to, and as his faculties sharpened, he realized he was sleeping on Chelsea's side of the bed. And that there was a very satisfied smile glued to his face.

He'd known from the moment they first kissed at the dinner where he'd introduced her as his fiancée that he and she would have chemistry. But he'd had no idea. The woman was hot; she gave and took pleasure with honest enjoyment.

Even after a night where they'd worked around the limited supply of condoms by pleasuring each other with mouths and hands, he still wanted her.

Her and her damn rules. When this thing was over and she no longer lived with him, then maybe they could forget about the rules and have some fun.

It was something to look forward to.

By the time she emerged from the bathroom, fully dressed, made up and hair done, he'd put coffee on and scanned the day's agenda.

He wasn't entirely sure how to greet her, a fiancée who wasn't, a lover who was—at her insistence—a one-night stand. Did they go back to the casual way they'd acted together before? Was there need for one of those horrendous "talks"?

He glanced up, their gazes connected and heat and sizzle arced across the space between them, pulling him to her with no thought at all.

He kissed her. She tasted toothpasty and cool, but he felt the heat simmering beneath, waiting to bubble over.

She started to melt into him, and his cock rose immediately, nudging her to attention.

Even as he started to pull her back toward the bed, she resisted and pulled away. He saw that her color was heightened and that her lips were swollen and wet from their kiss.

She pressed them together as though trying to clamp down on her own passion. Then she showed him a bright, happy face. "That was great last night. I had a really good time."

He couldn't believe it. It was such a guy line. *His* line!

The subtext was clear as he knew from delivering some version of the same line countless times in the past. *Thanks for a few laughs and some good sex, and don't expect anything more.*

Which left him stuck with mumbling, "Yeah, me, too." Which somehow didn't begin to express how great it had been.

But he could play the casual game, he'd been playing it for years. He handed her the schedule.

"Good news, honey," he said with false heartiness. "You've got your choice of a photography session or flower arranging."

"Well, it's nice of them to invite spouses, it must cost the company a lot of money."

"Haven't you heard? Significant others are our support network. You're part of the success of this company, too."

She thought about it for a moment, pouring coffee for both of them as though she did it every day.

"I guess that makes sense in an odd way. I mean, if you're married, you need someone you trust to bounce things off. Somebody who looks after you when you're sick and helps you pick out tasteful ties."

"Tasteful ties? Are you speaking metaphorically?"

She gave him a pitying glance, fashionista to fudster. "No."

"What's wrong with my ties?"

"Nothing that a woman of taste couldn't fix."

"Huh."

"But I'm not that person in your life. Obviously."

He was certain she'd brought up the tie thing to keep them from falling back into bed, but he had to ask. "Do you like any of my ties?"

"Not any that I've seen so far."

"Maybe you don't have any taste in menswear."

"That could be it," she said in a tone calculated to make him feel like a big zero in the fashion department.

"I try to look young."

"Juvenile is young, I suppose." She smiled brightly at him, but the humor was definitely of the laughing at him rather than with him kind.

He had to go or he'd drill down and figure out what exactly was wrong with his ties. Juvenile? He wanted to be a VP, juvenile ties were not going to help. If it was his sister talking he'd ignore her, but Chelsea wasn't the kind of person to shake a man's confidence for no reason, and no one could look at her and doubt her fashion sense.

Over a business breakfast, he found himself glad this

wasn't a tie-wearing occasion or he'd have kept his suit jacket on and his shoulders hunched.

They worked steadily through the morning, and at the break he walked by the lobby gift shops. They were linked stores, sort of like an arcade where one merged into another. He'd noted the menswear shop before idly, the way he'd notice an umbrella stand. Now, though, he headed into the shop the way he'd bolt for the umbrella stand in a downpour. Only to look, he told himself. Did ties come with age ranges? He'd always been so afraid of looking like one of his father's colleagues that he'd gone for bright colors, and avoided anything in maroon or with stripes on principle.

Had he gone too far? It wasn't like all his ties featured Disney characters. Maybe Chelsea simply didn't have a sense of humor.

He pored over the display case of men's ties—paisleys and dots and stripes and ensigns in colors ranging from bright yellow to black.

"Is there anything I can help you with, sir?" a well-dressed clerk asked him.

"No, thanks, just looking." He was paralyzed with indecision, his confidence so shaken that he knew he couldn't purchase a scrap of silk to hang around his neck without Chelsea's approval. And maybe a short training course so he'd know what to look for in future.

Wandering out of the men's store led him into a boutique featuring high-end giftware, fancy china and jewelry. A display case of rings caught his eye and he found himself peering down into a forest of engagement rings.

There were diamond solitaires matched with wedding bands, rows on rows of them like a platoon of little sparkling soldiers. How could there be so many variations of something so simple? And how would a man who couldn't even manage to pick out a decent tie ever figure out how to please a woman who was to be his wife?

He suspected that he wouldn't be the kind of man to offer a ring on bended knee. If he ever got married, which wouldn't be for a long time yet, he imagined his intended would pick herself out something and he'd put it on his credit card. That's what Suzanne had done. Not the most romantic scenario perhaps, but he and his only actual fiancée had agreed that if a woman had to wear that ring for the rest of her married life, she should get something she liked.

He was about to turn away when a hand clapped him on the shoulder and he heard a familiar voice. "Oh, good. You're looking at rings. I thought the other night that you were making a mistake," Piers said with fatherly friendliness.

"Well, actually, I was just—"

"Chelsea may say she doesn't want to wear a ring because she works with food, but what about when she's not working? Of course an engaged woman wants a ring." He glanced down at the glittering display. "And, quite frankly, it's a sign to other men that she's taken. With a girl as beautiful as yours, I certainly would plant the 'out of bounds' sign as soon as possible."

"You know, Piers, I was thinking that my future wife should probably choose her own ring. What if she didn't like my choice? She'd be stuck wearing it for years and years."

"Nonsense. She's a modern woman," the man replied. "If she doesn't like the ring, you can bring it back and exchange it." He patted David on the back once more. "This is so exciting. Good thing I saw you here, I can help advise you. I know a lot about diamonds, you know. I've been insuring jewelers for decades. Fascinating business."

"May I help you gentlemen?" a woman who reminded him a little of a teacher he'd had in fifth grade asked.

"Yes," Piers said. "David here wants to buy an engagement ring. A good quality one, mind."

"Of course, sir."

So David, who didn't know a VVS diamond from his elbow and didn't care to know, got a lesson in gemstones and very little choice but to buy one of them for a woman he had no intention of marrying.

Since Piers was not only a self-proclaimed diamond expert, but also a shrewd businessman, he negotiated a nice discount on the ring they both agreed would look perfect on Chelsea's hand. It was a simple solitaire containing a diamond that wasn't the largest one in the collection but was of the highest quality, Piers assured him. He'd been drawn to that ring from the start because the minute he'd seen it he'd pictured it on Chelsea's hand and knew it was the one.

Lunch was the final event where everyone would be together and he knew Piers and his wife, and probably every other person there at the retreat, would obsessively check Chelsea's hands every time they saw her if he didn't shove this rock on her finger pronto, so he called her on her cell phone and asked her to meet him in their room before lunch. She answered him in a whisper.

"Is everything okay?" she asked him when he'd made his request.

"Yes. Why are you whispering?"

"I'm in a flower-arranging course. I stepped outside but I don't want them to hear me."

"Flower arranging? That sucks."

"It's not bad. Actually, it could be useful for my business."

"That's good." He couldn't help but add, "And an asset if you ever become a corporate wife."

"Did you call to tease me or are you wasting my friend-to-friend minutes for nothing?"

"I can't tell you on the phone. Can you sneak away early and come up to the room before lunch?"

"Yes, of course. I'll see you at eleven forty-five."

He felt weird and a little sick as he waited for Chelsea in their huge room dominated by that bathtub that evoked the sight of her naked and golden when he'd walked in last night.

Of course, if he didn't look at the tub, he ended up staring at the bed where they'd spent some of the best hours of his life.

Since they'd be checking out in the early afternoon, both of them had packed up this morning. With all their personal belongings tucked away in the two weekender bags standing sentry by the door, the suite seemed particularly impersonal and only reminded him that after they got back to the city their wild night of passion would be nothing more than memories.

He found himself pacing. He was glad they'd drunk the champagne last night or he might have been tempted to open it for tradition's sake, which would totally send the wrong message.

The thing of it was, how did you give a diamond ring to a hot woman you'd just had sex with while asking her not to marry you?

13

"WHAT IS IT?" CHELSEA asked as she entered. David stood on the other side of the room looking a little pale and his forehead seemed damp. She resisted the urge to rush to him and place a hand on his fevered brow. "You're sweating. Are you sick?"

"No. Of course not, I'm fine. I was outside and it's a scorcher."

"That's good." They stared at each other across the huge span of the suite, across the enormous bed and the massive bathtub. Memories of the night before rushed at her, and she felt heat begin to flood her body. All the way here, she'd been debating whether she'd say yes if he'd asked her here for a prelunch quickie. Technically, they could still have sex without breaking the amended rule, but she wasn't sure it was a good idea. Now that she saw him she knew she wouldn't be able to resist, but ironically, he didn't look like a guy bent on seducing a woman. He was as far away from her as he could get without actually going outside.

"Igotyouaring," he said.

"Pardon?" Maybe he was sick. He wasn't even making sense.

"I got you a ring." He blurted out the words, still a little too quickly, so she had to work it out in her head before understanding him.

"A ring."

"Seems more authentic."

He tossed a jewelry box at her like he was pitching softball and she caught the black velvet square in midair.

"What kind of ring?" But she had a sinking feeling that she knew.

"Engagementring."

"I see. Should I open it?"

He nodded. Still looking green.

She eased open the black velvet box and her mouth opened in an "oh," even though no sound came out. "David," she said, "it's beautiful."

Even though she'd known what was in the box, catching the sparkle and fire of a "will you marry me?" type ring, presented by the man she'd fantasized about during her prime fantasy years, was a little overwhelming.

And it was exactly the ring she'd have chosen. Square cut, the large, incredibly clear diamond surrounded by smaller diamonds was exquisite.

"If you don't like it, you can change it, obviously."

She glanced up, seeing all his fear and all the reasons why he was still single and likely to remain that way. "But I won't be keeping it."

"Sure you can keep it." He grinned weakly. "You just can't keep me."

As if she'd want an infantile boy-man who still played tricks on his sister and assumed he could lie his way into a promotion and who wouldn't know a woman who was the best thing that ever happened to him even if he was engaged to her.

"Should I put it on?"

He took a step back, bumping into the French doors.

"Yeah. Piers helped me pick it out and you can bet they'll all be pouncing on you to see it."

She blinked. "Your boss helped you choose an engagement ring?"

"I know! Honestly, this used to be a kick-ass company, now it's like a sorority."

She removed the ring from the box and slipped it onto the fourth finger of her left hand, trying hard not to imagine what it would be like if this were real. If David was on bended knee offering her his heart and a lifetime together.

She held her hand out, glad she'd sprung for a manicure before coming away on this weekend, and admired the flash and sparkle. "It's really beautiful."

She fished in her bag and brought out a flat box. "Strangely enough, I have a nonengagement present for you, too." She held out her hand with the package, then the humor of the situation struck her, him standing close to the French doors so he could make a quick exit, tossing the ring across the room at her.

"You'll have to walk over here if you want it."

"Right. Sorry." He came over and took the box. Opened it. Glanced up and there was something warm and sweet in his expression. "A tie. You got me a tie."

"This is the tie of an up-and-coming vice president," she told him. "It's youthful yet powerful."

"I'll wear it tomorrow to work. Thanks."

"You're welcome. Thank you for the ring."

She thought he might kiss her, could all but see the notion spinning in his head, but he didn't. He took the tie box and zipped it into his suitcase.

"We should probably go down for lunch."

"Yes, we should."

He gestured and she walked ahead of him, turning just before she reached the door. "Oh, David?"

"Yeah?"

"A piece of advice. If you ever get engaged for real? You might want to work on your technique."

And with the friendliest smile she could muster, she preceded him out of the room.

14

WHAT AM I DOING HERE? Sarah wondered, astonished at herself for even showing up. Sunday afternoon, her only real day off, and here she was with a bunch of families, tourists speaking every language on earth and animals, also from every corner of earth. All week she'd scoffed at the very notion that she, an intelligent, educated, sophisticated professional woman would be seen at such a place.

I'll meet you at the orangutan exhibit, he'd written.

She was having her first date with a man who'd excited her on both a deeply personal and an intellectual level. And she was having it at the zoo.

What was she thinking? She couldn't even believe she was here.

As she paid for admission, she wondered when she'd last been here, and couldn't remember. What if she got to the orangutan habitat and couldn't recognize him?

Horrified at the entire situation, she grabbed a map and found the meeting spot.

There was only one man there.

And he wasn't looking at her, he was looking at a shaggy, brown, overgrown monkey as though it were his son, with fondness and a sort of parental pride.

He was the right age, early thirties, definitely looked like a man who rode a bike all the time since he carried a soft-sided pack and had a hard-bodied outdoorsy look about him. Monkey man was so not her type.

She took a step back, thought she'd quietly head out of here when the man turned. "Sarah?" he asked.

What was she going to do, lie?

She gulped. Nodded.

He smiled at her. He had brownish-blond hair that was bleached to straw from the sunshine. He was taller than she'd imagined, over six feet, and he had eyes so clear and blue you'd think he'd never seen anything unpleasant in his life.

Considering this was a first date, he hadn't knocked himself out in the wardrobe department. He wore biking shorts and a T-shirt. If he'd combed his hair in recent history, there was no evidence of it.

"It's great to meet you at last. I'm Mike."

Not knowing what else to do, she stuck out her hand, and, after looking at her outstretched palm for a moment, he shook it. He had strong, tough hands. She could feel the calluses on his palms when he touched her. "Hi." Then, as he studied the expression on her face, his eyes began to twinkle. "Not the place your dates usually take you, huh?"

Since she'd paid for her own ticket he could hardly be said to have "taken her" anywhere, but she kept her mouth shut.

"Come here. I want to show you something."

And reluctantly she moved to his side, mentally preparing a whole list of reasons why she had to leave, and soon.

"See this guy?" He pointed to a mangy-looking creature

currently engaged in scratching his privates. "That's Mike Junior."

Oh, good. She was on a date with a lunatic. Excellent. And, based on her track record, exactly what she should have expected. "Mike Junior? Your son?"

He laughed, as though they were sharing the joke instead of him being one. "Yep. I adopted him."

Already she was too irritated to be polite. "Is there some medication you forgot to take this morning?"

"No." He still seemed to be amused by her for some reason. "I'm aware he's not my biological kid. It's the adopt-an-animal program. Haven't you heard of it?"

Her blank look obviously answered for her.

"It's a charity thing. You pay to help feed an animal." He shrugged. "I'm not a big zoo fan, but I like the conservation program so I got involved. Mike Junior is a Sumatran orangutan and my adopted zoo animal. I like to visit on a regular basis, not that he appreciates me or anything. But he's a teenager, what can you expect?"

He was right. What had she expected? Someone normal? She'd e-mailed a stranger, told him things she'd never told another living soul. Of course he'd turned out to be a monumental wacko.

The gaze he turned on her was surprisingly sympathetic. "You think I'm deranged, don't you?"

She'd been honest with him on e-mail, and wasn't about to lie now she'd met him in person. "A little."

"Come on. Let's continue with our date. Maybe I'll grow on you."

"Like lice on Mike?"

He laughed. "Like a new idea, an acquired taste, an understanding of music."

"I'm tone-deaf."

He shook his head at her. "You're not this difficult on e-mail."

"Actually, I am, but I use the delete key a lot." She made a wry face. "Maybe we should have brought our computers with us. We could have edited ourselves before speaking. Would have been easier."

Still, she allowed him to guide her deeper into the zoo. And, after looking at birds and reptiles and endangered animals from all over the world, she found herself relaxing and, strangely, beginning to enjoy her day.

Yeah, the kids were noisy, but they were excited, too. Sure, it was hot, and sometimes there were smells she really could have done without, but she'd never seen a lot of these animals before, not the rare shy ones, like the blue-eyed black lemur from Madagascar who stared at her with his huge marblelike eyes from the safety of a tree branch, looking so cute she wanted to tuck him into her pocket and take him home.

Or the birds who lived around the lake in the middle of the zoo.

"I guessed from your stories about your cat that you're an animal lover."

"One cat. Clarence. He was a stray. I'm usually more into history than zoology."

"Ah, but this is a historical zoo. Ben Franklin founded it, you know. It's the oldest zoo in North America."

She had to laugh. "Points to you."

"I brought a picnic," he said.

She stared at him in shock. A family of Russians passed them, jabbering excitedly. "You did?"

"I did." He glanced at her. "When was the last time you went on a picnic?"

She thought back. And back. And further back still. "I must have been a kid last time I went on a picnic. How weird is that? It's not like I intended not to eat a meal outside on a blanket, it simply didn't happen."

"I guessed right again, then."

He found them a spot on the grass, and from out of his battered pack he produced an old threadbare beach towel to sit on, sandwiches so inexpertly wrapped she assumed he'd made them himself, cheese, crackers, apples and soft drinks.

Not exactly the champagne and strawberries and gourmet fare she somehow associated with a picnic, complete with a fancy straw basket, checkered cloth and cutlery, but it was fun to sit down outside and munch sandwiches. Casual and easy so a person could enjoy eating in the great outdoors with a minimum of fuss.

"What kind of sandwiches?" she asked when he offered her a packet.

"I wasn't sure what you'd like so I made ham and cheese and peanut butter and jelly."

"Peanut butter and jelly?" What were they, eight years old?

"It's what I had in the house. Besides, I wasn't sure if you ate meat. Wouldn't want you starving."

He'd gone to a lot of trouble and there was something endearing about a man who brought a PB&J to a grown woman on their first date. "I'll have one of each," she said. On impulse, she removed her shoes for the pleasure of brushing her feet over the grass. Even though it was midsummer, her legs and feet were pale, and not because she religiously applied sunscreen, but because she was working so much she rarely saw the sun. She'd even had to run out to Banana Republic for some new shorts when she couldn't find any but an ancient pair of cutoffs at home. Now she realized the cutoffs would have been perfect with her current date.

He passed her a soda and for a few minutes they occupied themselves with unwrapping sandwiches and opening soft drinks. It was the oddest experience to be a stranger to someone who knew her so well. She needed to connect to the online person, so she said, "Tell me more about your new yoga studio."

He'd explained on e-mail that he was going to be teaching at a new place. They'd talked about a lot of things but the yoga studio seemed the most impersonal, the most like get-to-know-you chitchat.

"It's going to be good, I think. Location's right, plenty of stressed-out people who need to slow down, reconnect with their bodies and spirits." He stopped to swig from his can of soda. "You should come."

"Because I'm stressed out and need to reconnect with my body and spirit?"

"Maybe. But mostly so I can see you again."

Incredibly, she realized she did want to see him again. She liked his easy way, his loose-limbed walk, the fact that he hadn't dressed to impress her but he'd been thoughtful enough to pack a picnic. She was used to men in suits who took her to fancy restaurants and, if they could manage it, to bed. Guys who were as time-crunched as she. Not guys who showed up in biking shorts and treated her to lunch on the grass. Now that she was used to him, she even liked that he'd adopted a teenage monkey.

However, there were things she needed to get straight now that Mike was no longer some faceless Internet confidant. Like the fact that they'd met under false pretenses.

"What made you e-mail me the first time?" she asked him. There'd been no photograph accompanying her profile; even David wouldn't stoop that low.

Mike thought for a few minutes. "I don't know. That was a while ago. I liked your profile. How straightforward you were. Like, this is who I am and what I want. No apologies. It was straight-up. You communicate directly, almost like a man."

She looked into his frank, innocent eyes and knew she had to tell him. "The truth is, a man did write my profile."

He finished chewing a bite of sandwich and swallowed. "Why didn't you write your own?"

"It was my brother who put up the profile. He did it as a joke."

Mike didn't seem particularly shocked by her admission. She got the feeling that he liked to think things through, see all sides of an issue and come to conclusions slowly. Not jump to judgment like she did. "If it was a joke, why didn't you take your profile down when you found out?"

Which wasn't the first question she'd have asked if their positions were reversed, and one she found difficult to answer. Yet, if they were to continue, she supposed they needed to be honest with each other, even if it made her feel uncomfortably vulnerable. "You e-mailed me. I liked what you said, so I stayed on for a while." She shrugged. "Once I felt comfortable giving you my personal e-mail address, I deleted my profile."

"That's cool."

"It's not completely cool. You see, the part that was a joke was the way my brother described me." She felt hotness creep into her face. "Like I was a frustrated spinster looking to get married and have babies, and not interested in sex before marriage."

She wrapped up the remains of her sandwich and put it neatly into the bag he'd brought along for garbage.

He watched her as though waiting for her to go on. She didn't. So he said, "So, are you?"

A laugh shook her. "Am I what? All those things my

brother said? Of course not." She thought for a moment. "Well, in the legal sense, I am a spinster. It simply means unmarried woman. And of course I plan to get married some day and probably have kids, but it's not the top thing on my agenda."

Which left the sex thing hanging out there in the breeze like the muted sounds of animals from nearby enclosures. Again, Mike didn't speak but waited for her to tackle the subject she'd so rashly brought up. She fought cases in court, argued down some tough opponents. She didn't blush and dither. Yet now she felt an urge to do both. Finally, she said, "Let's just say I'm not saving myself for my wedding night."

"I see." Carefully, he packed away his garbage. Unlike her, he'd eaten every scrap of his sandwich, left only the barest core of apple. "So, you want to go somewhere and have sex now?"

"No!"

A tiny rumble that could have been a laugh shook his frame. "Then, I guess, somewhere between a first date and marriage is when you'd feel comfortable having sex with a new partner?"

"Why are we talking about my sex life?"

"You seemed to want to. You brought it up."

"My point is that I'm not as conservative as that profile made me out to be."

"You know, we've been e-mailing for a while now. Don't you think I might have figured out a few things about you for myself?"

"Like what?"

The sun shone through whatever those fancy, lacy trees above them were, casting snowflake-shaped shadows on his face and body. "Like you work pretty hard making sure people see you the way you think you should appear.

But when you relax and let down your guard, there's another Sarah in there. A softer woman who doesn't get out much."

And there it was, the thing she'd dreaded from the beginning. "So, you're interested in soft, squishy Sarah. Sarah the pining mom, Sarah the—"

He interrupted her for the first time since they'd met. "I'm interested in all of you," he said with unaccustomed firmness. "It's your contrasts that appeal to me. I like that you're smart and driven and take pride in your work. I also like the person inside who yearns for some things her tough exterior doesn't think she should. It's what makes you interesting."

"Oh." She was rarely speechless, but she felt close to it right now. Naturally, she turned the tables. "What about you?" He'd obviously gone to that site for a reason. "If I'd said, yes, let's go get naked in the bushes and do the deed, would you have gone along with me?"

He really did have the sexiest mouth, especially when he gave her his slow smile. One that sent her temperature up a notch. "I'd have been tempted. I won't deny it. I find you very attractive. But no. I wouldn't. I don't do that anymore."

Good to know he'd at least have been tempted. "Don't do what anymore?"

"The casual-sex thing. It gets old."

"Does it? It's been so long since I even had sex I can barely remember." She could have slapped her hand over her mouth. What was wrong with her?

Mike appeared quite intrigued by her blurted comment. He leaned back on his elbows as if he had all day and nothing much to do. "How long?"

"This is the weirdest first-date conversation I've ever

had." She huffed, scrubbed her bare feet a little in the grass to get rid of an itch. "About a year."

"Eight months for me."

"Somebody break your heart?"

He rolled lazily onto one elbow and contemplated her. "Maybe me."

"You broke your own heart?" Probably just as well he was confining his progeny to zoo animals.

"You really want my story?"

"Sure." She had a million things to do this afternoon, but it was a gorgeous day and no matter how hard she worked she'd always have another million things waiting.

"I was living in California, working as a surf instructor and a yoga teacher as well as working in a school. The thing is, when people do sports they tend to get a nice endorphin rush going. And I had a lot of female students."

A picture was starting to form. "Tanned California girls in bikinis."

He grinned. "Sometimes. And yoga wear. All these lithe, fit women and I know I'm going to sound like a conceited jackass here…but some of my students would come on to me. Seemed pretty harmless. I was flattered, we'd built up a bit of a good vibe from surfing or yoga or whatever and next thing you know I'd be having sex with these women." He shrugged, seeming uncomfortable. "After a while, I started to feel like the pool boy."

She had to suppress a laugh. "You mean these women were using you for sex?"

"Let's just say I didn't form a lot of long-term relationships." He rolled to his back. "I think I like sex as much as the next guy, but I'm looking for more than casual hookups."

"So you moved to Philly. A lot fewer girls in bikinis needing surf lessons here."

"I got offered a permanent teaching job out here. And I decided it was a chance for a new start. I made some rules for myself. So far I've followed them."

"Don't you miss it?" she had to ask. He was such a physical guy. She thought of David giving up sex for eight months and her mind couldn't contain the thought.

"Do I miss sex?" He rolled to his side so he was facing her again. "Absolutely." He reached for her hand, the most intimate gesture he'd yet made. Linked their fingers together. She was shocked at how sexy it felt. How good. "How about you?"

"I keep pretty busy. Most of the time I don't think about sex, but when I do?" She thought of the warmth coursing between them from the simple touch of their linked hands. "Yeah. I miss it."

They stayed like that for a minute, comfortable, easy with each other and yet with a current of sexual tension that was buzzing through their linked hands.

"About these rules you made for yourself…" She didn't know how to continue. "How long…?"

"Look, I'm really not into rules and rigid structures, I'm not saying I have to know someone a certain amount of time or anything, I'm just saying, I'm not a scratching post for every woman with an itch."

An unexpected snort of laughter erupted from her mouth. "That is some image you just put in my head."

He grinned at her. "I want to sleep with someone because I genuinely like her and want to get to know her better, and I want her to feel the same. No timeline."

"Got it."

"Does that work for you?"

"Yes, I think that could work for me."

They cleaned up the rest of their picnic and she shook out the beach towel and rolled it up neatly before handing it to him. They walked to where she'd left her car, the sun scorching. She pulled out her sunglasses and slid them on. "Do you need a ride somewhere?"

"No. I've got my bike."

"Right. Well…" She had no idea how to say goodbye.

He handed her a flyer. She was so surprised she looked down to read it. Saw a trio of distorted bodies and it took her a minute to make the connection. "Oh, it's your yoga studio."

"The schedule's on there. I teach Saturday mornings. Be great to see you."

"Aren't you afraid I'll try to seduce you after class?" she teased.

"I hope you will," he replied, then with a swift kiss— so quick it was over before she'd realized he was about to kiss her—he turned away and left. Her lips felt tingly and alive. And, she realized, the rest of her felt pretty good, too. Maybe they were both about to end their sexual dry spells.

She drove away with a smile on her face. Who'd have thought. One thing she was determined on. David was never, ever going to find out that she'd met a great guy through his bogus profile.

Never.

15

"ARE YOU GOING TO BE home for dinner tonight?" Chelsea called to David as he headed off for work.

He paused. "What's for dinner?"

"I'm trying out a new recipe with stuffed chicken breasts in a wine sauce."

"My pants are getting tight. I skip my workouts so I can eat your food."

"You make it sound like that's a bad thing."

"I feel like I'm living on the set of *Julie and Julia*. People aren't meant to eat so much butter and cream and wine."

"Nonsense. Julia Child and her husband both lived into their nineties. I'll take butter and cream over a bag of potato chips any day. Healthier and tastier."

"I don't eat potato chips."

She put her hands on her hips. "If you're going to be grumpy about this, I'll toss you a green salad."

"I'll be home for dinner." He walked by her and his lips quirked. "And stuff me a chicken breast."

When he got to work he realized he was going to have

to do something about the routine they'd fallen into. It was too easy, too comfortable, too damn domestic.

But, oh, that woman could cook. It was strange because she looked like one of those women who lived on carrot juice and celery sticks, but she didn't. She not only cooked the way Mozart created music, but she also had a hearty appetite and enjoyed food so much it was a pleasure to watch her eat.

He figured she was blessed with a fast metabolism, plus, she wasn't one for sitting around. She always seemed to be busy doing something. All that food was getting burned off all right. Sadly, not on hot sex.

He'd promised to keep his distance, but that woman was becoming an obsession to him. Having slept with her once, it was like she was a drug he couldn't get out of his system. He fantasized all the time about what he'd like to do to her in an apron, and nothing but an apron. Never in the past had he thought of a kitchen as more than a place to store beer and reheat pizza. Now he thought of it as the most erotic room in his town house.

And the more he wanted Chelsea, the more she treated him like a cross between a business coach and the big brother she'd never had.

An unaccustomed frown settled on his forehead and wouldn't budge.

When Jane had to remind him of a scheduled meeting off-site with an important client, he knew he was losing the laserlike focus that made him so successful.

David wasn't a man who got distracted by women, or one who kept glancing at the clock, willing the day over so he could run home and see the woman waiting for him at home.

And when he got there what did he get? Hot, crazy sex?

No, artery-clogging meals that were shortening his time here on earth.

On his way to the client's his scowl deepened. Seemed to him that little Miss Cordon Bleu was setting all the rules in this relationship. She didn't want sex. Fine. They didn't have sex. She wanted to cook constantly, start a business from his kitchen. Fine, he'd been decent about that. But using him as her test-kitchen guinea pig? No, that one wasn't going to work.

Not without some serious concessions on her part.

He wouldn't mind eating rich food and enjoying decent wine if, at the end of it, there was somewhere for all that decadent pleasure to go.

Of course, she had Philippe. But Philippe was in France, very far away. He wasn't the one eating all of her food, he wasn't the one sharing a home with her. If he didn't want another guy poaching his territory, why wasn't he here? David knew for damn sure that if Chelsea was his woman he wouldn't be letting her shack up with another man. And, knowing what her food did to a guy, he wouldn't be letting her cook for her roommate, especially if said roommate was a red-blooded male who wasn't getting any.

As he went over his sales pitch for the meeting, the pitch where he convinced the owner of a local record label that his company was large enough now to institute a corporate insurance plan, he realized that he'd been handling the whole Chelsea thing all wrong.

He'd lived by her rules so long he'd forgotten that rules were meant to be bent until they broke.

What did he do best in all the world?

He was a salesman.

If he couldn't sell a woman who was young, attractive and also not getting any—oh, yeah, and living with him—to have sex with him, then he might as well find a job in an anonymous cubicle somewhere because he had no place on the executive level of any business.

He spent the drive out to the record label mentally sharpening all the weapons in his seduction arsenal.

Like closing any sale, the prospect of getting Chelsea into bed filled him with excited anticipation. He couldn't wait for tonight.

A bit of compunction hit him as he stopped for a red light. What if she and Philippe were serious? When he arrived at the record company a few minutes early, he called Sarah.

"Sarah Wolfe," she barked when she answered.

"And that's going to scare any business away."

"I knew it was you. And I'm in a pissy mood."

"You can hardly tell."

"Do you want something?"

"Yeah, actually, I do. You got a minute?"

"Sure."

"It's about Chelsea."

"What did you do to her? I swear to God, David, if you upset her in any way, I'll kill you. She's vulnerable, you know? She's still finding her feet back here at home, she's trying to start a new business and that's not easy. So if you're giving her any trouble, I'll come over there and pack her up myself and she can move in with me and you can look after my cat."

For a few seconds there was silence. He could hear her aggressive breathing and waited until it had calmed a bit. "That was quite some rant. Feel better now?"

She laughed, which was a good sign. "Damn you, yes. Sorry. I'm having a personal issue."

"You're not getting any, either, are you? I know the signs."

"This whole sex thing is the worst evolutionary invention."

"Speak for yourself. As a matter of fact, that's what I'm calling about."

"If you want the birds-and-bees talk, sweetie, you want Dad. He and Mom are back next week. I hear a family barbecue is on the agenda."

Oh, she was definitely starting to feel better. "I am calling about Chelsea. There's this guy she talks to a lot on the phone. Philippe. You know anything about him?"

"Her gay friend in Paris? The one she went to cooking school with? What about him?"

The birds began to sing, the sun had never shone brighter, life was a magical feast and he was about to chow down. "Her gay friend Philippe? Yeah, that's the one. I was just wondering if he knows the truth about the fake engagement. I mean, can we trust him?"

"The guy's in France and doesn't speak English. Frankly, I think you have a whole lot of bigger problems to worry about, bro. Like that family barbecue. You better hope Mom hasn't been knitting baby booties on her trip."

"You're right. Listen I gotta go, I'm late for a meeting, but we should get together real soon. Hey, maybe we could all go out one night. You and me and Chelsea and I'll find a fourth."

"I can find my own date, thanks."

He was surprised. "Really? I didn't think you were seeing anyone."

"You're wrong."

"Shouldn't that put you in a good mood?"

"Wrong again." She muttered something and then "Later," and she was gone.

He shook his head as he got out of his car. Women in general were difficult enough to figure, but sisters? Or maybe it was just his sister.

16

"I LOVE YOU, STOVE," Chelsea cooed as she removed a tray of absolutely perfect profiteroles from the oven. Maybe the saying "You get what you pay for" wasn't always true, but in this case, the expansive range was a dream to work with.

Her hair was still slightly damp from her shower, and an apron covered the skirt and blouse she wore. She'd always taken time to freshen up and dress in her nice clothes when she'd been working in restaurants, and now that she was working from home she saw no reason to change her ways. If she made sure to shower and change and put on makeup before David got home, that was purely coincidental.

She heard the key in the door and her foolish heart fluttered. She was really going to have to do something about this little problem of hers, since they seemed to be spending a lot of time together and familiarity wasn't breeding contempt. It was breeding a longing that was all too painfully reminiscent of her teenage years.

Not for the first time she cursed herself for sleeping with the man. Before she'd only imagined what she was missing. Now she knew, in glorious, ohmygawd-it-was-fantastic detail.

The door opened and a familiar voice boomed, "Hi, honey, I'm home."

"Your martini is mixed and dinner's almost ready," she teased.

"You are my dream woman," he announced.

"Well, I might have lied about the martini, but I do have food."

And he had flowers. A mixed bouquet from a street vendor. Her heart fluttered once again as he presented it to her.

"Thank you. What's the occasion?"

"Just my way of saying thanks for all these great meals."

What happened to him complaining about his arteries and his waistline, she wondered.

"Everything smells fantastic," he told her, gazing at the array of food all over the counter.

"I got a little carried away. I decided to cook up everything I'm planning to serve at the wedding I'm catering, and time it all. It's a sweat, but if I hire a kitchen helper as well as servers, I'll make it."

"Does it all taste as good as it looks?"

"You'll have to tell me."

"Cool. Do I have time for a quick shower before dinner?"

"Of course," she said, mildly surprised. He didn't usually shower when he got home from work.

As though aware of her surprise he said, "I was running all over town today. I got hot and sweaty. I really need to cool off."

He emerged fifteen minutes later in shorts and a shirt, but not too casual, the kind you might go out in. He was freshly shaved. Something twisted in her belly when he walked by and she smelled the scent of freshly showered and shaved male.

The food was delicious, every single bite. But in truth she barely tasted any of it. David was so different than his usual self. He was attentive, making sure her glass was filled, kind of flirty, and he seemed completely fascinated by every word she uttered.

After he'd eaten every bite of the stuffed chicken breasts with never a single complaint about cholesterol, she said, "I've got these little strawberry puffs for dessert. Do you want to try some?"

He shook his head. "No wedding night couple would ever make it that far. You've cooked nothing but aphrodisiacs."

"I have not."

"Then why do I feel like I need to make love to you every time I glance across at you?"

She gulped. Glanced down. Then up...and caught the smolder in his gaze. Felt the temperature soar even in the air-conditioned room. "You do?"

He nodded, serious for once.

"But, we agreed we wouldn't—"

His head shake was a vigorous negative. "You set the rules and I agreed to live by them. It was never my idea. I can't see the point of living with a beautiful, desirable woman and going to bed frustrated every night."

She bit her lower lip, "You've been frustrated?"

"Every. Single. Night."

"I—I don't know what to say."

"How about, you've been frustrated every night, too."

She could barely stop the smile that tugged at her lips. "Not every night." But far too many for her own good.

"If there was even one night that you lay awake thinking about me, then I don't feel so inept."

"Inept?" It was such an odd word to use.

"There was a time when I used to do quite well with women. You wouldn't know it, but—"

"Of course I would. When we were in high school? You had girls falling all over the place to get your attention. And who did you bring home? Fluffies. They were all fluffies."

"Fluffies?" He appeared outraged.

She giggled. "That's what Sarah and I used to call them, those girls you brought over. Big-breasted, mostly sweet, with big hair and small brains." She tilted her head, regarding him. She hadn't snooped or anything, but there had been several vacuous phone messages, a couple of poorly spelled postcards. "I get the feeling you haven't changed much."

"You'd be wrong. My taste has changed." He shot her a calculated glance from under his ridiculously thick lashes. "Unless you consider yourself a fluffy."

"I most certainly do not."

"Well, I'm attracted to you, and it seems to me that in the interests of weaning me away from these so-called fluffies you should take a more active role in my personal improvement."

She couldn't help the smile that bloomed. "Do lines like that usually work for you?"

"Frankly, I don't normally have to work this hard."

"What a refreshing change I must be."

He moved. One moment he was across from her and the next he was scooping her out of her chair. "I'm not a bad guy, you know? And you're beautiful, and you look so good—" he touched her hair "—smell so good." He leaned closer so his nose touched the sensitive spot below her ear, where a pulse began to thump. "And you taste good."

She didn't think, she simply leaned forward, threw her

arms around his neck and kissed him. In the back of her mind she supposed this would turn out to be a mistake, but she wasn't having any luck protecting her heart. Her rules hadn't made her immune from falling for him all over again.

At least an affair would give her some spicy memories that would hopefully keep her warm when she looked back on the past.

As their lips met, the sizzle that had been part of their chemistry since the night he'd mistaken her on the street for a stranger burned hot and bright. She'd taken him by surprise—she could tell by the tiny moment of stiffness in his body, as though he'd been expecting a rebuff and wasn't ready for her to throw herself at him, in spite of him practically begging her to make love with him.

Good, she thought, with a tiny inward smile. She wanted to surprise him, and keep on surprising him until he realized that he didn't need any fake fiancées or elaborate hoaxes in order to get ahead in life. The woman in his arms was the perfect partner. Not corporate wife, or disposable fluffy, but a woman who complemented him, who challenged him and most importantly, who loved him.

She couldn't tell him any of this in words, but she could, and did, tell him with her body rubbing sensuously against his, with her lips moving against his with increasing urgency, with the heartbeats pounding through every pulse point.

He pushed her up against the counter, then hoisted her up so her butt hit the cold granite and he stepped between her thighs.

She had the odd experience of coming to him with a virgin's heart, one she'd so foolishly given to him years earlier, in an experienced woman's body. Even as she knew how to give and receive pleasure, she'd never given as she did now, to the man she'd loved since she was fourteen years old. The old flutters of nervousness danced over her skin even as her hands moved surely, tracing the contours of his back, his shoulders, his arms.

He was doing his own exploring, touching her hair, the curve of her face, her neck, and tracing patterns up and down her side, coming closer to her breasts but not quite reaching them, building heat within her as she waited and longed for his touch where she was so exquisitely sensitive.

Her nipples began to throb in anticipation. He kept kissing her, as though now he had possession of her mouth he would never let it go. He kissed with the finesse of a man who truly loved kissing. He licked, explored, teased, pleasured her mouth in a way that let her know he would take as much delight in every part of her, and he was in no hurry.

Oddly she found she didn't have all the time in the world. A strange urgency gripped her, compelling her to tug at his shirt, needing quite desperately to get her hands on his naked torso.

He helped her tug the thing off, and her urgency seemed to fire his, for suddenly she found—even as she was running her hands over his chest—that her own top was being tugged at. She helped him, four hands all pulling at once, and when the blouse went sailing through the air she heard the deep growl of satisfaction in his throat as he gazed at her.

Not that she'd had any inkling of tonight's activities, but she had selected one of her prettiest sets of underwear. Seemed David was also a big fan of French lingerie.

He helped her off with her skirt and then hoisted her up and into his arms, making her laugh. "I need more room," he panted. "I definitely want you in the kitchen, but right now, I want you in my bed."

She had no objection to the plan, hugging her legs around his waist, enjoying the stiff evidence of his arousal as he jogged them upstairs to his bedroom and tossed her back onto the big bed.

He was so very dear to her. Their night in the Poconos had been wild and fun, but they'd tried to pack everything into a night. Now she felt that she had time. Time to get to know him, to pleasure him and receive pleasure in return, night after night.

She liked the combination of familiar and exotic. She knew his moods, the sound of his voice, his quirky sense of humor, his intelligence and ambition, but she didn't know he was ticklish on the inside of his elbows until she stroked her fingers over his skin and he jerked away. She'd known he had freckle fields on the tops of his shoulders, but not that his skin would taste like toast and butter.

His fingers were bold and knowing, and yet there was an almost boyish eagerness to him that made her feel incredibly special. The flop of dark hair across his forehead was so endearing, and as she stroked it back off his forehead, their gazes connected and she thought in that moment they were more intimate than two entwined bodies could ever be.

When he finally stripped off her bra and thong, she was so aroused she thought she was going to explode. From the sweat-slick and engorged look of him he was close to exploding, too.

But he held himself back. Touching her breasts gently when he discovered how sensitive they were, tasting the nipples and rolling them on his tongue, he kissed her belly, and when he began to kiss her thighs she gasped, "Wait, I want you inside me first."

He glanced up at her, dark devils dancing in his eyes. Shook his head. "Not yet. You are my tasting menu."

Whether it was his words or the touch of his tongue on her clit she had no idea but he'd barely licked at her when she went off like a rocket, crying out and shuddering and quaking.

"Oh," she said, putting her hands over her eyes. "That was sort of embarrassing. You got me all worked up and—"

"Shut up," he said and went back to what he was doing. She'd have argued that she couldn't possibly climax again so soon if he'd let her catch a breath, but he didn't, merely went back to making a meal of her and from deep within, heat and pressure began to build again. When he pushed two fingers inside her and rubbed her G spot while pleasuring her with his mouth, she had to grab at the sheets on either side of her to fasten her to earth. As she rose, higher and higher, she heard her own cries, and suddenly nothing could keep her tethered any longer. She soared and went flying.

She came back to earth to find David kissing his way up her body, but there was an ache inside her that needed to be filled, and now. Grabbing at him, pretty much wordless with need, she pulled at him until he understood her need and, after reaching for a nightstand drawer so well-stocked with condoms that she didn't even want to think about it, he readied himself and then plunged inside her.

A shock of surprise rocked her. She'd imagined he'd be all gentle and take his time entering her, but his clumsy speed indicated that he was as needy as she was. His bucking haste rocked her back up again.

They rolled and reached and she felt something magical happening to her that she did not want to experience. Something soft, and gushy and sweet. She couldn't help the emotions that pummeled her as she held him to her and they found their perfect rhythm. When they climaxed together, as though they'd been working up to a perfect union for years, she wasn't a bit surprised.

It wasn't oysters or lobster or any of the other contenders that were the most powerful aphrodisiacs.

In her experience, the only true and potent aphrodisiac was love.

And unfortunately, she knew of no cure or antidote.

17

"Wow." THE WORD CREAKED out of his throat so hoarsely that he coughed and tried again. "Wow." He'd used the expression "That rocked my world" a ridiculous number of times. For everything from a great sports play to a tough-to-bag client signing on the dotted line. He now knew he'd been grossly misusing the phrase.

What had just happened in his bedroom with Chelsea was the first thing in his life that had truly rocked his world—seriously, like earthquake tremors, shaking his foundations.

How was it even possible that a woman he liked so much, had liked since she was a kid, who wasn't particularly mysterious to him, had uncovered a part of him he hadn't known existed?

He felt like a blushing girl in some bullshit teen movie saying, "I never knew it could be like that."

She smiled at him, trusting and sweet, her big brown eyes full of emotion. *"Je t'aime,"* she whispered.

He kissed her, to block out the messages in those big eyes, then rolled to his back, willing his breathing back to normal and his world to right itself. He wasn't sentimental. It was this whole bizarre scenario that was making him act strangely. He'd never lived with a woman before, and after his failed engagement he had no intention of it. Yet here was a woman living in his house, filling it with the homey scents of cooking and walking by him wafting girlie smells of flowery shampoo and all those gels and cosmetics and things they used. No wonder his brain was permanently fogged.

She reached out and rested her hand on his chest, as though she didn't want to break the connection. As though watching from another part of himself, he saw his own hand move to rest on top of hers. It felt so right.

It felt so terrifyingly wrong.

He didn't want to live with the world's greatest cook, who was also gorgeous and sweet and amazing in bed.

Especially not one who whispered *"Je t'aime."* Maybe he hadn't studied in Paris, but he knew what the phrase meant. *I love you,* that's what.

Only a fool would want to live with someone like that. She'd suck all of him into her world. He could see it happening already. He scurried home, lured by her food and her presence. It was classic taming behavior. Feed the wild animal and soon it relies on you, then you lure it into a cage, put a red leather collar around its neck with some cutesy nickname on a metal tag.

His heart had started to slow and suddenly it was speeding up again.

Worst part was he had nobody to blame but himself. He'd needed the fiancée, then when his sister made her living here part of the deal, he'd started sniffing around her. She'd said no sex.

Because she was a very smart woman. Much, much smarter than him.

But had he listened? Had he followed the one simple rule she'd laid down? Of course he hadn't. He'd done everything in his power to break that rule, because that's what guys like him did when confronted with stupid rules. They broke them.

Hah. He was the stupid one. Now he'd broken through that barrier, what had happened?

The Poconos had given him a taste, a raunchy, fun, sexy night that had felt good. Had he left well enough alone? Hell, no. He'd decided he needed more. And he'd got more, all right.

The best damned sex of his life, that's what. And with a woman who had *forever* written all over her, from her homemade cookies to her big brown happily-ever-after eyes.

Je t'aime.

He'd known the moment their bodies joined tonight, when she'd gazed up at him and he'd felt something inside him shift, that he was in the deepest trouble of his life.

Not all animals were meant to be tamed. He'd heard of trapped animals who chewed off their own feet to escape. Thanks to Sarah and her PETA membership he knew a bunch of things like that he wished he didn't.

Well, he wasn't going to chew off a body part, but maybe metaphorically it wouldn't be a bad idea.

He glanced down at their joined hands resting approximately over his heart. He picked up her hand, kissed the fingers. "You are amazing," he said, truthfully, because she was.

Her head turned to him, those big brown eyes slumberous and sexy. "So are you." She shifted even closer. "It was so much better this time."

"I, uh…" He couldn't look into those eyes and do what he had to do, so he turned back to look at the ceiling again. "I need to get back to the office for a couple of hours."

"You do?" She sounded sleepy and surprised, not remotely outraged.

"Yeah. But this was great." He leaned over and kissed her sweet, swollen mouth once more. "Don't wait up."

"Okay." She didn't seem to get the point, but he couldn't throw her out of his bed any more than he could throw her out of his home. Since she was living in it.

Getting out of that bed took a lot of determination, especially as she hadn't bothered to pull the covers up to her chin, but was lying, happily sated, her gorgeous body all curves and warm, silky skin, inviting him back in.

It took a physical effort to drag himself into the shower. When he emerged from the bathroom, she was exactly where he'd left her. Mild irritation surged through him, but then he saw she'd dropped off to sleep. Her face was so innocent, and for a moment he remembered the shy, serious girl she'd been. An unexpected and unwanted tug of tenderness drew him to her even as he struggled against it.

Her lips were parted, still swollen from passion.

Quietly, so as not to wake her, he grabbed a clean pair of jeans and a polo shirt, socks and underwear. He dressed swiftly and soundlessly, then, unable to stop himself, leaned over and kissed her gently on the mouth.

She made a tiny sound, kind of a sigh and an *mmm* joined together.

He crept out and left her sleeping.

There was no reason for him to go into the office. He wasn't one of those twits who dashed in to send e-mails at three in the morning so it looked like they were good company men. He believed in working hard during regular office hours and that productivity was how you proved your worth. Not stupid suck-up tricks.

Sure, he worked late when he needed to and if a

weekend was required, he gave a weekend. Right now, though, everything was under control. But he said he was going to the office and he felt bad enough about breaking the rules and having sex with Chelsea. He didn't want to add lying to his conscience.

He nodded to the night watchman and signed in, then took the deserted elevator up to his floor. To his surprise, he wasn't the only one at work. Damien Macabee was typing away at his computer, his gray head bent over his work. Probably cleaning up some things before he retired.

David popped his head around Macabee's door to be polite. They weren't particularly friendly, but he had a great deal of respect for the man who'd been in the business more than forty years. "Hi, Damien."

Macabee blinked his eyes and, taking off his glasses, rubbed them. "Hello, David. What brings you here so late?"

Even though he hadn't prepared an excuse, not dreaming anyone else would be here, he said, "I'm trying to land a record-label company. Had a good meeting with them earlier, but I think their top brass are hesitant to commit to an employee benefit plan."

Damien Macabee nodded as though he'd been in that position scores of times, which, of course, he had.

"The issue they're having is fear of change. They know they're ready, but our job is to help convince them that nothing but good can come of looking after their employees better." He leaned over and opened a filing cabinet beside his desk, pulled out a thick file and handed it to David. "There's a report in there that contains some excellent research on the benefits that accrue to a company with a good benefits package. Take a look at it and see if it helps."

"Thanks, Damien. I appreciate it."

David didn't have trouble concentrating during the day, but he had to admit it was nice in the quiet office with no distractions. Nobody popping their head into his office to ask him something, no phone calls, meetings, nothing but him and his computer.

And his thoughts. Even as he studied the research—and Damien had collated some fascinating statistics collected from studies from around the world, and pulled together facts and figures that he thought were relevant to a record label—his body felt relaxed and sated. If only his mind was as easy.

He discovered Macabee wasn't the only one working late when a soft knock fell on his door and a second later, Piers entered.

"Don't mean to interrupt, David, but since you're here, I think you're the very man I want. I want to talk to you about employee morale."

"What about it?"

"I think we should raise it."

David bit back a smile. Easier said than done. "I don't think there's anything wrong with the morale here. It's a good company, you pay well, nobody's been laid off that I know of. People are happy to have the job."

"I appreciate hearing it. I believe you're right, but you know it never hurts to throw a bit of fun into people's lives."

David wondered what management book he'd been reading, or what article he'd perused at his barber's. Piers was steady as a rock most of the time and good at looking into the future. He and his brother had made some strategic moves that had helped the company flourish during tough times. But he had his odd hiccups and this sounded like one of them.

"What did you have in mind?"

"I was reading an article about those bulls you can ride. You know, like that fellow did in that movie back in the eighties I think it was."

"Urban Cowboy?"

"That's the one. I understand that riding a mechanical bull is quite popular again and is a good morale booster. I thought we might try posting such an evening. Say in a week or two on an evening after work. We could have prizes and it would be a chance for people to get to know each other outside of work. And we'd invite spouses and partners, of course. I'm sure Chelsea would enjoy it."

"Riding a mechanical bull? I'm sure she'd love it." He paused. "But do you think it's wise? What if people have back issues or neck trouble and give themselves whiplash? That would pretty much dump a bucket of water over the morale boosting."

"Let's look into it anyway. I think it would be fun. I've always wanted to go to a dude ranch. Never got the opportunity. I like to think there's a little cowboy in all of us."

And that's when he knew that nothing he said was going to change Piers's mind. It was already bucking a mechanical bronco.

Maybe that's why he loved the company so much. They combined solid business acumen with a dash of the crazies. A mechanical bull. He shook his head and packed up his desk.

He returned home, having done some useful work that could have waited for the morning, but at least had given himself some space. A few more hours of intimacy with Chelsea and they'd have woken together in his bed. Officially, he'd have been in a Relationship. The kind that always had a capital letter to it.

This way, they'd enjoyed each other and he'd made

the separation. Maybe it was a subtle distinction, but it mattered to him. A little sex, a few laughs, they slept in their own beds and got on with their lives and this thing ended when he got the promotion. Her business would be launched and she could move out. He hadn't said anything but he'd already decided to invest in her business, thinking it was the least he could do when she'd helped him out so much. He refused to contemplate the possibility that he was planning to bribe her not to hate him.

The town house was quiet when he entered it. A single lamp burning in the living area. The kitchen was back to spotless, the way she usually left it, so he knew she wasn't still sacked out in his bed.

Now his only worry was that she'd misunderstood the situation and had moved all her stuff into his room. He crept upstairs to take a look, but when he stuck his head into his own bedroom he found that the bed was neatly made and all trace of Chelsea gone. There was no sign she'd even been there.

Strangely enough, no sooner did he have confirmation that she hadn't misunderstood the situation, that she was gone, than he found himself wanting her in his bed, wanting her warm, willing body.

He shook his head. Dragged off his clothes and flopped into bed. And found her scent clinging to the pillow. He turned his back resolutely and went to sleep. But when he woke in the middle of the night, half dreaming that she was back in his bed and in his arms, he realized he'd shifted to "her" side of the bed, and his nose was pressed into the pillow that held her scent.

18

CHELSEA WAITED UNTIL she knew David had left for work before venturing out of bed.

The rat bastard.

She'd felt so good. So good. Against her better instincts she'd let herself go, let him seduce her.

Frustration at her own stupidity rose like a scream. She'd known since she was fourteen years old that David Wolfe was bad news for her. At fourteen there'd been some excuse for her naiveté. At nearly thirty? No excuse.

And now what was she supposed to do?

She showered and dressed and quickly considered and discarded such ideas as packing up and moving out before he got home from work. She'd made a bargain, devil's bargain though it had turned out to be, and she wasn't the kind of woman to renege. Besides, part of the deal was this amazing kitchen and she had no interest in giving it up, not before she had another lined up. Not before she'd proven herself.

Speaking of which, she had a wedding to cater, and moaning and bitching wasn't going to get it catered.

And on top of today's work, she needed to make dinner.

She stopped, realizing that she did not have to make dinner. That the cozy evenings she'd been creating were part of her problem.

The truth struck her with the cruelty of a whiplash.

She'd been playing house.

She'd fashioned her own personal dream house complete with picture-perfect food, clothes she loved to wear and the final prop to any girl's dream home—an idealized male she could bend and pose around the house. Maybe there'd been some exclusively adult activity that wouldn't have been part of her child's playworld, but other than that, she'd been indulging fantasy.

And it had to stop. She needed to get real.

David had managed to survive for thirty-two years without her to fuss over him and cook for him. He could do it again.

Having that decision out of the way, she started working. She had a meeting with the wedding planner this afternoon and needed to get going. Beating the eggs into the flour-and-water paste for the choux pastry was remarkably satisfying. It was physically strenuous, since she preferred beating by hand with a wooden spoon to whizzing the confection in a machine. She liked to "feel" the dough so she knew by instinct when it was ready. After piping tiny puffs onto a cookie sheet and placing them in the oven, she filled tart shells with a selection of exotic mushrooms and goat cheese, then grilled prawns to go with her signature dip and prepared asparagus foam to squirt on top of the vol-au-vents. She added a couple of seviche in miniature martini glasses. It wasn't the complete line of appetizers she planned to serve at the wedding, but she thought she'd included a good selection.

She'd already pulled together lists of wedding menus she'd created for different budgets, times of the day and themes. She placed the sheaf of pages into one of the folders she'd had printed, complete with her new logo. She had to admit David was responsible for spurring her on to get her marketing materials together before she had much of a track record.

However, she had a great product she believed in. That had to count for something.

So, she readied a pretty tray of goodies, dressed in one of her favorite outfits, a simple black dress with a short red-and-black jacket, stepped into black heels and grabbed her folder. She supposed she ought to have a briefcase, but she didn't.

As she was leaving, a flash caught her eye. Her engagement ring. She'd fallen into the habit of wearing it. One more prop in her adolescent dream life. She slipped it off and placed it in the dish David used for his keys by the front door.

Even though she already had the job catering for the Sloane/Franco wedding, she wanted the wedding planner, popular in the area, to like her and hopefully hire her again.

So it was with some trepidation that she entered the renovated brick warehouse where If You Can Dream It was located. She walked in and immediately felt bridal. The reception area featured a photo gallery of happy couples at their weddings. Everything from Chinese dragon-inspired ceremonies to eco-conscious weddings were represented.

A young blonde woman was seated at the reception desk. "May I help you?" she asked in a British accent.

"Yes. I have an appointment with Karen."

"I'll let her know you're here. Would you like to set down your tray?"

"Thanks," she said gratefully, placing the tray carefully

down on a handy tabletop displaying bridal magazines. She'd had no idea there were so many magazines devoted to weddings.

In a very short amount of time a short, curvy woman in a floral-print dress came out of a back office with her hand held out and a professional smile painted on her lips like lipstick. "You must be Chelsea. Thanks for coming in. I always like to meet the caterers to make sure we're on the same page. You do understand."

"Of course."

"We'll talk in my office. I've got the Sloane/Franco binder in there."

Chelsea picked up her tray and followed. Since Karen was leading the way, she didn't see the tray until Chelsea had placed it in the middle of her desk.

To Chelsea's horror, a cry of distress slipped out of the woman's mouth when she eyed the tray, and she threw her hands up.

"No." She shook her head and took a step back. "No, no, no."

Chelsea had no idea what to do. She'd worked so hard and she thought she'd done such a good job. "You haven't even tasted anything."

Stricken blue eyes met hers. "I can't. I'm on a strict diet. Twelve hundred calories a day. It's killing me."

But she gazed at that tray like a gambling addict at a slot machine.

"And I'm so hungry, I'm hungry all the time. I'm thirty-five years old, wouldn't you think by now I'd have learned willpower?" She took a step forward and then sharply back. "Oh, get those things out of here."

A diet. Of course. Her confidence rushed back. "I can, of course, but that seviche is only thirty calories. I wish you'd try it. It's only fish marinated in lime juice and spices, no fat at all, and it's high in protein and potassium."

Karen's bright blue eyes grew round. "Seriously? Something that looks that delicious is only thirty calories?"

"Yes. In fact, if you can afford two hundred calories, I can also suggest these four canapés."

Karen almost snatched the seviche from the tray and, using the tiny cocktail fork, tasted the delicate concoction. "Mmm," she moaned. "Delicious."

Licking her lips, she motioned Chelsea to a seat.

"Really? I can eat four of them for only two hundred calories?"

Chelsea smiled, holding up her right hand. "I swear."

It was a pleasure watching a stranger devour her food with such obvious enjoyment. The woman didn't simply chow down, though, Chelsea could tell that she was tasting the food with a critical palate, closing her eyes as she ate each selection, then nodding approval.

When she'd finished the canapés, she pushed a button on her phone. "Dee, honey, come in here."

When Dee appeared Karen motioned to the tray. "Take these away and eat them before I succumb. Then report back on what you thought of them."

"Certainly." The young woman carried off the tray and Karen watched the way a dog watches a steak being eaten by its master.

"Pastry," she whispered. "I love pastry, and cheese. And ice cream. And chocolate." Then she shook her head. "I hate diets, but no one wants to hire a fat wedding planner." She sighed. "Now that you've proven you can cook, let's see your menu for the wedding."

Chelsea withdrew the menu sheet from her folder and placed it on Karen's desk. "The appetizers on that tray will be part of the predinner selection, and then for dinner, here's the menu. Wherever possible, I've sourced local produce."

The wedding planner scrutinized the menu. "Vegetarian options?"

She nodded. "And kosher. I can also work around pretty much any food allergy."

"This looks great. I approve." She started to rise, clearly getting ready to move on to the next thing on her agenda.

Chelsea knew she had to start selling herself if she was to make a success of her business, so she said, "I've also brought you some other sample menus and services I'll be offering, in case we get a chance to work together again."

She offered the folder and Karen opened it, scanned several of the menus and then, pushing the open folder away from her, stared at Chelsea for an uncomfortable moment. "Why haven't I heard of you?" she finally asked.

"I've been in Paris, training at Le Cordon Bleu. I only returned six weeks ago."

The woman tapped her manicured nails against the table top. "So you haven't catered any weddings here in Philadelphia?"

"No."

"What are you doing for a kitchen?"

"I'm working from home right now. The kitchen's been inspected and approved, of course, but I'm looking for a commercial space."

The woman nodded again. "I might be able to help you there."

"Really?"

"Tell you what. Let's see how you do with this wedding. Then we'll meet and maybe we can help each other out." She shuffled the menus back into the folder. "In the meantime? I don't want you talking to any other wedding planners."

She was about to agree. She had no time to meet with anyone anyway, but maybe she'd been listening to David too much. She copied Karen's professional smile. "I have a business to run."

The woman nodded, seeming not at all put out by her blunt speaking. "Okay. Cards on the table. Here's what I'm thinking. If I like your work at this wedding, and I don't only mean turning out more of that heavenly, delicious food like you brought in today, but also being able to run a kitchen and an event without losing your cool, and if the client is happy, then I'd be interested in using you as my exclusive caterer. It would mean you couldn't cater for any other wedding planners." She leaned forward and said, "And I've got more business than anybody in town. You want to take the deal. Ask around."

Chelsea was so excited she wanted to jump up and kiss Karen right on her calorie-hungry mouth. But she held on to her cool composure with both hands. "I could probably live with that. What about the commercial kitchen you mentioned?"

"There's a café near here that went bankrupt a couple of months ago. It's got a fantastic kitchen. I have a cake-maker who does the most amazing wedding cakes. I suggested it to her, but she can't afford the space on her own. I was thinking maybe if you two could work around each other that you might be able to share the space."

Her heart began to thump. She'd have the same problem until her business got off the ground, but if she could split the rent, it could work.

"You say it's got a storefront?"

"Yes. The location's not great, which is why it went bust and why the rent's reasonable, but you might want to open to the public. Sell ready-made dinners and nibbles for people planning their own parties. Could be a nice side business."

"Yes," she said, bubbles of excitement rising behind her sternum. "Yes, it could."

Karen opened a drawer and withdrew a notepad, then she hit a few buttons on her computer. She scribbled a few lines and passed Chelsea the paper. "That's the address and the name of the Realtor who's handling the property. Why don't you check it out? I have good instincts about people. I think you and I are going to get on fine."

"Me, too."

"Great. You'll get to meet Laurel on Saturday. She's the cake-maker. See if you two like each other. Who knows? Maybe we'll all end up working together."

Chelsea left the meeting filled with excitement. As she walked by the front desk, her empty tray awaited her, not as much as a stray crumb left.

The receptionist was on the phone, but when Chelsea walked by she gave a thumbs-up sign and mouthed, "Fantastic."

She knew she was a good cook, but it was nice to have strangers taking such obvious pleasure in her food.

She had to admit, David had been right. If she hadn't come ready with her list of menus and what looked like an operating business, Karen might never have taken her seriously. The thought of catering all the weddings for If You Can Dream It was amazing. The weddings would cover a huge proportion of her business.

She was certain of one thing: if she could pull off the catering event on Saturday, she was on her way.

And that much closer to being free of David.

David. She didn't even want to think about him. And she wasn't rushing home to make him dinner.

There were a lot of old friends she hadn't had a chance to see since she returned home. Having spent a few minutes this morning on Facebook and the phone, she'd arranged to see a few of her old girlfriends tonight for dinner.

Staying away from David had nothing to do with her sudden urge to organize a girls' night out.

Nothing at all.

19

DAVID HAD NO IDEA HOW to handle the situation he now found himself in because nothing like it had ever happened to him before. He had a gorgeous, sexy woman staying in his house, one with whom he'd had the best sex of his life, and he was trying to figure out how to ease out of the sex part.

Without hurting her feelings.

At least she had no idea he'd freaked out last night.

Why hadn't he kept it zipped? He'd have saved himself a world of trouble. Now he couldn't stop thinking about her naked and how she'd felt in his arms last night, the little noises she made, the French phrases she'd whispered in his ear. He didn't even speak French and they'd practically made him explode. Except that last one. *Je t'aime*.

The one thing he knew for damn sure was that he couldn't go home for another one of those cozy dinners tonight or all his determination to keep his distance would dissolve like her amazing food on his tongue. He'd phone her, tell her he wouldn't be home for dinner. That would be a good start to his mission to ease out of sleeping with Chelsea.

But when he called, no one was home. The thought

that she was probably at the market buying ingredients for another intimate dinner for two filled him with a combination of remorse and panic. He called her cell and when she picked up he could tell from the background noise she wasn't in any market shopping for food.

"Hey," he said easily, "what's up?"

"I'm out with some friends." From the noise there seemed to be a lot of them. There was a silence. She didn't invite him to meet up with them, he noted. Fine. Good.

"I was checking you weren't cooking tonight. I'm probably going to play squash and grab a bite."

"No. I'm not cooking tonight."

"Okay, then. Have a good one," he said, feeling suddenly foolish.

"You, too."

So, she wasn't home cooking for him. This was excellent. He should be elated. Why did he have a bad feeling in his gut all of a sudden?

Trying to put all thoughts of Chelsea and women in general out of his mind, he met up with his buddy to play some hard, sweaty squash where the rules were simple, and when you left the court you left everything about the game behind you.

WHEN CHELSEA SNAPPED her phone shut, she glanced up to find Sarah's gaze on her, too sharp and too smart. "Uh-oh," she said.

"What?" she snapped. "What do you mean, 'uh-oh?'"

"I've known you for half our lives, kiddo. You slept with him, didn't you?"

There were a dozen women crowded around the table, friends from high school and college. The drinks were flowing and so was the laughter and chatter. She leaned across the table to where Sarah sat and said, "I can't tell you. It's about your brother."

The other woman made a sign—her thumb dragging across her chin and pointing to the back—that took her back years. They were in high school again, and Sarah had big news to share, or wanted some private girl talk. Her best friend got up and headed to the restroom. She gave Sarah a minute then got up and followed her to the bathroom.

But they weren't in high school anymore. So, when she entered the ladies' room and found Sarah standing beside the sinks waiting, she said, "I am not discussing this with you. He's your brother. It's too weird."

"But you're my best friend. We tell each other everything."

"I know. I hate not talking about stuff with you. I really need to vent."

"I need to talk to you, too." Sarah thought for a moment. "I know. We'll pretend it's not my brother. Let's call this guy Frederick and you can tell me all about him."

"Frederick?"

"First name I thought of."

"I am sleeping with Frederick." She breathed out slowly. Sister or no sister, she had to squeal. "And last night it was amazing. Honestly the best sex of my life. I think he felt something, too…well, he must have. So we're curled up in the afterglow, you know?"

"I'll try and remember that far back in history to when I last had sex, but I get the point."

"I'm just feeling absolutely amazing, still a little tingly, like maybe we could take a little break and go for round two, and I whisper, *Je t'aime*. Not even thinking. It just slipped out. And suddenly Frederick goes batshit on me.

He gets this terrified look on his face. Makes up some excuse about having to go back to work."

"Are you kidding me?"

"No, I've been staying with the man for weeks and he never had to go back to work once he got home. Not one time. And suddenly he's gone. Doesn't get home until after midnight."

"Are you kidding me? You love my brother?"

"I didn't say I love you. I said *Je t'aime*."

"Right. Stupid me. It only counts in English."

She put her hands over her eyes. "Oh, what have I done? I told him I love him and he ran a mile."

"Cretin."

"We need a stronger word for guys like your brother. I mean Frederick." She banged her fist against the counter. "I could kill him. We've been fighting this attraction since I first moved in. And then suddenly, yesterday, for no good reason he went out of his way to seduce me. And then this?"

"Even for Frederick, who, let's face it, has the maturity of a toddler, this is pathetic."

"I know. We've been living together like friends. Besides, he heard me on the phone to Philippe and figured he was my boyfriend. I didn't let on that Philippe and I are only friends."

Sarah's eyes widened. "Oh, no. I think I might have messed things up." Sarah said, "I had no idea. Dav— Frederick called me yesterday and started talking about Philippe. I was in a bad mood, I've got man problems of my own, frankly, and I was busy at work and he asked me something about Philippe and I said, 'Who? You mean Chelsea's gay friend Philippe?'" She made a face. "And usually I'm so smart. I really screwed up. Sorry."

"So that's why he came home looking so cheerful." She

scowled as another part of David's infamy came back to her. "Oh, yeah. And he brought me flowers."

"Pig. He was so planning to get into your pants."

"And then once I blurted out a few words in the heat of passion, did he talk about it? Give me a chance to explain? No. He runs a mile."

"What did you do after he ran like the scared little baby he is? Did you empty all the trash in the middle of his bed?" she asked with glee.

"No."

"Something better? Smear peanut butter inside all his fancy Italian loafers?"

"I made his bed and cleaned up the kitchen. Then I went into my own room and put myself to bed."

"You are so much better a person than I am."

"True."

Sarah fake-slugged her but there was real sympathy in her eyes. "What are you going to do now?"

"Stay out of his way, do a great job at the wedding this weekend and move out as soon as possible."

"Move out? Where are you going to go?"

"I looked at that café the wedding planner put me on to, turns out it has a small apartment above the premises. The last renter used it for storage, but I could live there until I get my business off the ground. It's small and not exactly glamorous, but the location's perfect. Soon I'll have my own business up and running in a good commercial premises and a new place to live." She smiled cheerfully. "I only have to get through the next couple of days."

But Sarah could see through her act. "Perfect would be if somebody took out my brother's heart and replaced it with a working model." She scowled, then brightened. "I know, we could sneak home and pour itching powder in all his tighty whities."

"Not until after I move out." They exchanged glances in the mirror. "Then you can do anything you want."

A young woman came in to use the facilities so Chelsea took a lip gloss out of her bag and looked into the mirror to apply it.

"Speaking of the wedding, Becca Sloane thanked me for recommending you. She loves your menu. Giving her and her mother those tasting samples was genius."

"Good. I have a lot riding on this wedding. I really want them to be happy."

"Don't worry. What can go wrong?"

She didn't even want to think of all the things her imagination could come up with. So she changed the subject. "How about you? How's it going with Biker Boy?"

Sarah fiddled with her hair in the mirror, rearranging the black curls around her face. "I want you to come with me this weekend. I'm going to his yoga class Saturday morning. Will you? I feel like I need the moral support."

"I can't. The wedding's Saturday and I'll be working all day. Besides, you've been to his yoga class a few times."

"Yeah, but the guy's right. I see him in his yoga clothes bending his gorgeous body and I just want to crawl over to him and lick every inch of him. I'm as bad as all those women he moved from California to get away from."

"No, you're not. You're in a budding relationship and you have feelings for the guy. Plus, the fact that he's not trying to get into your pants is making you want him. Which is a good thing, right?"

"I guess."

She hid her smile. It was nice to see Sarah so interested in a man. It had been a while. And Chelsea liked the sound of this one. "Are you bringing him to the wedding?"

"I don't know. Should I?"

"Absolutely. So I can check him out."

"He'll probably show up in biking shorts. That's the kind of guy he is."

"I'm sure he won't."

"Maybe I'll ask him. It's not like we've had any real dates. Coffee after yoga a couple of times. Then he bikes off and leaves me so frustrated I want to eat the coffee cup." She sighed. "Why can't men be easy to understand? More like women?"

"I wish."

Sarah put an arm around her shoulders. "Come on, let's go back to the table and I'll buy you a drink." As they left the washroom and went back to their friends, she continued. "We'll give up men and move in together. You'll cook, we'll become more and more successful and we'll live happily ever after."

"What about sex?"

She sighed. "I didn't say it was a perfect plan."

20

WHY COULDN'T WOMEN be more like men? David fumed. Men were simple, direct, easy to understand.

If he'd done something to piss off a male roommate he'd get a direct response. Say he'd left the place a mess, he'd expect something like, "Do your dishes, asshole." That he could understand. Easy. Out in the open, clear communication.

But did Chelsea bother with anything clear and direct? No.

Did she come out and say, "Don't have sex and walk out on me, asshole?" So he could apologize and they could move on? No. She did not.

She acted like the entire incident had never happened. She was cheerful as always, and treated him exactly like a platonic friend and roommate. The only change in their routine, the only way she let him know that she was pissed off with him, was that the cozy dinners had stopped. She said she was too busy getting ready for the big gig on Saturday to cook, but he knew better. She was punishing him, denying him food the way, he supposed, he was denying her sex.

Not that he could be sure of this, because she hadn't said anything.

He should be jumping for joy. She'd got the message. He was up for casual sex, but none of that *je t'aime* stuff.

Except that now that she'd accepted there was nothing between them at all, getting her naked again was pretty much all he thought about. He was becoming embarrassingly obsessed with his roommate. He watched her move when they were home at the same time, which was rarely if either of them could help it, and he recalled the way her limbs had wrapped themselves around him in bed.

She'd taste a morsel of food, smile approvingly and all he could think about was her lips on his body.

Being in his own home was such torture he was certain that he was being punished. If only he'd never made up the stupid fiancée in the first place. Hell, if his company didn't want him to be a VP without having a suitable partner, then maybe he didn't want to be VP at this firm.

What business was it of his company's whom he married or if he married?

Nothing more had been said about him being made a VP in any case, and he didn't think he could stand this arrangement much longer. He was going to have to find his own place. He'd made an agreement that Chelsea could stay in his town house, and he was going to stick to his promise, but he couldn't stay here night after night and torture himself thinking of her lush body in the next room. A man could only take so much.

Saturday, while she was catering the wedding, he'd start looking for a short-term rental.

Even as the idea took hold he was conscious of a sinking feeling in his gut. He didn't want to move out of his own place. He didn't want to come home to an empty house, one that smelled of stale air instead of fantastic food.

They were nothing to each other, so why did the sight of her engagement ring in his key dish annoy him every time he saw it there?

Friday night, when after a tough day at work when it seemed like Macabee had spent a lot of time with clients and none whatsoever getting ready to retire, he came home to a town house that smelled like heaven where there was nothing for him to eat.

The sight of the diamond sparkling all alone in his key dish added the final insult to his mood.

"Why don't you wear that ring I got you?" he snapped when he stomped into the kitchen.

Chelsea looked up from piping some kind of filling into tiny little tomatoes. A smudge of flour decorated her cheek and he wanted to sweep her off her feet and drag her into the bedroom so badly it physically hurt him to stand still.

"I only wear that ring when we're going to see people from your firm."

"What if you bumped into one of the wives at the grocery store? Or saw Piers in the street or something?"

"I'd say hello. And if they asked why I wasn't wearing my engagement ring I'd explain that I'm working and I didn't want to get it dirty." She was so cheerful it set his teeth on edge. She also looked like she was getting plenty of sleep, which made one of them.

He watched her in glowering silence for a full minute. Then he said, "Guess I'll go out and grab a burger for dinner." He sounded like a grouchy three-year-old and knew it. What was wrong with him?

Chelsea didn't bat an eye. "I can make you a sandwich if you wait a few minutes."

He was being a pig and she didn't call him on it. And she had her big day tomorrow. "Have you had dinner?"

"No time. I've got so much to do for the wedding. I want everything to be perfect."

"It will be, but you have to eat. Why don't I get takeout for two?"

She filled a few more tomatoes. "That would be great, thanks."

"Thai okay?"

"Anything." He got the feeling she was barely listening.

He called for Thai food and went and showered and changed. But when the food arrived, she was in the middle of something and too busy to eat. "Put mine in the fridge, will you? I'll have it later."

So he took his lonely plate of takeout upstairs and into his bedroom so as not to bother her, and flipped on the TV. He hated eating in his bedroom. He didn't like crumbs and spills getting on the bed and the smell of food that seemed to linger. He should have eaten dinner out, but he'd wanted to make sure she had a meal. Fool.

When he took himself to bed at midnight, she was still at it.

"Hope it goes well tomorrow," he said, realizing he meant it. She'd worked so hard, he wanted her to achieve her dream.

A distracted smile greeted him. "Thanks. I've hired a bartender who conveniently owns a van and hired two waitresses and a kitchen helper. I've done everything ahead that I possibly can. Everything else I have to do tomorrow." She put a hand to her heart. "I so badly need for this to go well."

It wasn't only so she could impress the wedding planner, he realized, but for her own confidence.

He was suddenly filled with warmth and tenderness for

this woman. "You'll do great," he said. Then he looked around the kitchen. "What can I do to help?"

"Nothing. You've done so much already, lending me this kitchen and giving me a place to stay." She met his gaze frankly for the first time since they'd slept together the other night. "I've rented the café and there's an apartment above it. I'll be moving out next week."

And just like that, his conviction that it was a terrible idea for them to continue sharing his place was gone. His mouth opened and words he'd had no intention of saying spilled out. "But you can't move out. We have an agreement."

Her smile was sweet and a little sad around the edges. "I'll still be your fiancée whenever you need me to be, don't worry. But I think it will be better for both of us if I don't live here. Don't you?"

Now that she was actually doing the direct-communication thing, he realized he didn't like it at all. What was he supposed to say? Admit that he was confused as hell?

"I... There's no need."

"I think there is." She wiped her hands on a damp towel.

"If you're talking about the other night, it was just two friends getting extra friendly."

She nailed him with her gaze, so clear he felt that she could see right through him. "Really, David? Is that all it was?"

He gulped. If he'd been wearing a tie he'd have loosened it. "Sure. It happened, it was fun. Felt great. No reason to make a big deal about it."

"Then let me ask you one question."

He didn't like her tone and was wary as he answered, "What?"

"If it was no big deal and felt so great, then why haven't we done it again?"

He swallowed, felt like a spider was stuck in his throat and trying to crawl up. "I don't know. You've been busy. I've been busy."

She shook her head and looked at him almost as though she felt sorry for him. "I don't think that's the reason at all."

"Yeah? Then what is?"

She turned her shapely back to him. "You figure it out."

21

CHELSEA HAD BARELY gotten to sleep after working until the small hours preparing for tomorrow when she was woken by something ringing. She'd set the alarm for six, but it was so dark outside, she was certain it couldn't be six yet.

She rubbed her eyes and only then realized it was her phone ringing. She grabbed at it, at the same time squinting at the clock. Four a.m. "Hello?"

"Chelsea?"

Oh, great, some drunk calling her at four in the morning. "Who is this?"

"It's Tom."

She sat up in bed, no longer even sleepy. Tom was her bartender and the guy with the panel van. And he sounded strange. "Tom? Where are you?"

"The hospital. I was coming home from work and got into an accident. My van's a write-off and I'm going in for an X-ray to see if my leg's broken. I'm really sorry, Chelsea, but I can't help you today."

She wanted to scream, to rail and curse, but it wasn't Tom's fault that he'd had an accident, so she pulled herself together. "It's okay. You take care of yourself."

"I hate to let you down."

"It's fine," she lied. "There are other guys I can call, they just aren't as good as you. Call me later and let me know about your leg, okay?"

"Sure. Yeah."

"Is someone with you?"

"My wife's on her way."

"You take care."

She hung up and took a moment to wallow in her own panic, then she flipped on the light and tried to think what to do.

It wasn't a disaster, she told herself. Not yet. She had time to rent a van and hire a bartender. All she needed to do was find a rental place that was open at four in the morning and start calling everyone she knew in the business, which wasn't very many people.

As she crawled to the kitchen to put on coffee, she wondered when it was too early to start phoning around for an emergency bartender.

She'd taken her first sip of coffee when a sleepy male voice said, "What's going on?"

She turned to find David naked but for a pair of shorts she suspected he'd just put on for her benefit. "David, I'm so sorry I woke you."

"You didn't. I got up for a drink of water and saw the light." He scratched his head, which made his hair stand on end adorably. "You look seriously stressed. What's up?"

"My bartender, the one with the van, got into an accident last night. He crashed the van and probably broke his leg. I am trying really hard to be sympathetic but mostly I'm trying not to panic." She wasn't exactly thrilled with David these days, but just for this one moment, it felt so good to vent her problems. "Do you have any idea where I can rent a van at this time of the morning?"

He yawned hugely. "Pour me a cup of that coffee, will you?"

"But, you don't have to…" She stopped talking when she realized he was walking away from her and back upstairs.

By the time she had his coffee poured and the dash of milk and one sugar, which was exactly the way he liked it, he'd added jeans and a T-shirt to his outfit and returned.

He sipped his coffee and plopped himself on one of the kitchen stools. "What kind of van do you need?"

"It has to be big enough to carry trays of food and boxes of supplies."

"I can think of a few options. A few of my buddies have kids, and they all have the mom vans. But my squash partner, Mark, he coaches a soccer team and I'm pretty sure they had a van specially fitted out with shelves and stuff. That would probably be our best bet."

"That would be ideal, but honestly, any kind of van would be so amazing." She sipped her coffee, feeling panic start to subside. "Now all I need is a bartender."

"I could be your bartender."

She was so surprised she gaped. "You? A bartender?"

"Sure. I put myself through college bartending. I might be a little rusty, but I can still make any cocktail you can throw at me."

"It's a simple bar. Beer, wine and highballs. No fancy cocktails."

He spread his hands and sent her his killer smile. "Then your problems are solved."

"But I can't ask you to—"

"You didn't. I volunteered." His grin disappeared. "Unless there's somebody else you'd rather have. I could be your last-resort bartender if you want."

"No. You'd be perfect. I mean, I'd be thrilled to have you if you really don't mind."

"Don't mind at all. I didn't have anything planned for today anyway."

By six they were both showered and, in spite of her protests that it was too early, David called his squash buddy. She had no idea what words were exchanged or how unhappy the man was to have been woken so early on a Saturday, but the good news was that the team had no game that day so the van was theirs to borrow. The only stipulation being that they returned the van with a full tank of gas.

She was so happy she threw her arms around David in an impulsive hug. "Thank you."

The second their bodies touched she realized her mistake. Even at six-fifteen in the morning with a stressful day ahead of her and a night of very little sleep behind her, she couldn't help but feel the current of attraction between them.

She backed off immediately but not before catching the look of baffled longing on his face. Fool he was, but a good-hearted fool who was helping her out in her hour of need.

He was also muscular and cheerful, and she discovered that when he put himself into a project, he put his whole being into it.

Not only did he pack along a bartender's guide "just in case," but he also went and got the van, unloaded all the soccer paraphernalia and stopped at a car wash to get the inside of the vehicle thoroughly vacuumed and washed.

Then he helped her load the food and supplies and drove her to the mansion where the wedding would be held.

The wedding planner was already there, supervising the sound system setup, when they arrived.

Karen appeared as competent and in control as when Chelsea had met her in her office and she tried to act as nonchalant, as though she catered weddings every day of the week. As David came in behind her, hefting a box, Karen said, "Hello, gorgeous."

Chelsea had no idea how to introduce David. As her friend? Fiancé? The guy who was helping her out since her bartender had crashed his van? There was a split-second pause as she scrambled and then he stepped forward and held out his hand. "Hi. I'm David. The bartender."

Karen shook his hand. "I haven't seen you before. I'd have remembered."

"I work exclusively for Chelsea," he explained.

"Excellent. Well, let's pull off another wedding miracle, shall we?"

"We shall," Chelsea said, suddenly certain that everything was going to go fine. She'd prepared fabulous food, had timed her day exactly so that everything would run smoothly. And she was toting along the world's most gorgeous bartender.

When they were alone in the kitchen she said, "Thanks. I owe you."

He sent her a scorching glance. "I'll collect later."

It was a light, foolish comment, but it still sent a sizzle right up her spine.

YOGA WAS SUPPOSED TO be relaxing, Sarah reminded herself as the class ended and she and the rest of the participants settled into Savasana. Corpse pose. You were supposed to lie on your back with your arms and legs flopped out, body in total relaxation mode while Mike talked softly, reminding them to quiet their thoughts and let the world go.

Hah. Quiet her thoughts? Was he kidding? All she could

think about was how much she wanted him and how crazy-making this whole situation was.

As for letting the world go, she'd never been so conscious of the world, of the hardness of the floor and the soft wash of air across her stretched and limbered body, the beat of her heart and the flow of her blood. And the burning heat between her thighs.

She spent so much of her life in her mind, behind a desk, barking on a phone, staring at a computer. How often did she bother to connect with her body? Now that she'd started, her body seemed obsessed with sex, and with one bicycle-riding, orangutan-adopting, yogic school counselor in particular.

She wanted to jump off her mat and drag him out of here to the closest place where they could get naked and she could use this newfound awareness of her body's needs and wants.

But they were "taking things slow," she reminded herself. If she was lucky, she'd get coffee. Again. Big deal. She was sick of slow.

At least she'd worked up the courage to invite him to the wedding and he'd agreed to be her date. It was a start, she supposed.

When the ten eons that five minutes of meditation and relaxation felt like were finally over, she jumped up and began rolling her mat. However, as quick as she was, a lithe, supple redhead, who wore more makeup than anyone could consider appropriate for a yoga class, had uncoiled herself and was asking Mike something.

Sarah felt a scowl beginning to form. She wasn't going to compete for Mike. Not on any playing field. In fact, she was sick of games altogether. He and the redhead were talking softly, closer together than was necessary, way inside each other's personal spaces.

She grabbed her clumsily rolled mat and left the studio for the showers.

When she emerged, her hair still damp from her shower and her temper almost under control, Mike was waiting for her, his bag hanging from his shoulder. He ambled up to her, in no hurry, kind of how he did everything. "I'm done for the day. You feel like a coffee or something?"

Tilting her head back, she looked him right in the eye. Enough already. "Or something."

He grinned down at her. "Come on. Let's go."

The studio was in the art gallery area, an up-and-coming neighborhood, as Realtors liked to say. As they left the studio, she found herself slowing her steps to avoid ending up blocks ahead of him. "You sure are in a hurry," he commented.

"I hate wasting time," she snapped, trying to control her urge to speed ahead so as to catch the walk signal before it turned red.

"But time just is," he said in his slow, deliberate manner. "Whether you pack a hundred things into an hour or take care over one thing."

"I never understand that argument. Why wouldn't a person want to accomplish a hundred things rather than only one?"

He shook his head at her. "It depends on the one thing," he said in a slow, sexy drawl. "Maybe I should give you an example of what I mean." His eyes crinkled in that sexy way he had. "That is, if you've got an hour to spare?"

"As it happens, all I have to do today is get myself dressed up and go to my friend's wedding. So, I've got a couple of hours to spare."

"Even better. Come on." He headed off walking and she struggled to stick to his slow pace. They passed her car, but he declined a ride, telling her instead to look around her and take in the scenery. He headed in the opposite direction of the coffee shop where they'd gone the last few Saturdays.

"Where are we going?"

"It's not the destination, Sarah, it's the journey."

"Are you deliberately trying to sound like a Buddhist calendar?" She could even imagine the photograph. A pair of sandals, walking through a desert, leaving a track of prints.

"I like to challenge your beliefs a little."

"What about you? Don't you think you should be challenged?" Why was it always her who needed to change?

"Oh, believe me, you challenge me every time I'm with you."

She had no idea whether that was meant to be a compliment. Somehow, she didn't think so. They were walking down a quiet street of older, residential homes. Nothing fancy, but there was a nice sense of community here.

Before she could ask him to explain what he meant, he'd turned and indicated steps leading up to the front entrance to a row house.

"This isn't a coffee shop."

"No. It's my house."

"Your house? You've never invited me to your place before."

"Today I am. Would you like to come in?"

22

FOR SOME REASON SARAH felt nervous. Which was ridiculous. She was a grown woman who'd been longing to get him alone for weeks. Now that he seemed to want to let her into his house, she wondered what other intimacies were in store, and whether she was as ready as she thought she was.

Trying not to let him see her feelings, she nodded and followed him inside.

It was always interesting to get inside a single man's house. Was he a slob? A sports junkie? Did he have a collection of comic books? Had he decorated his space? Were the legacies of girlfriends past to be found? All this was yet to be discovered as she walked into his living room. And felt a strange sense of peace.

There was very little in the room. A few pieces of comfortable furniture, some black-and-white photographs hanging on pale gray walls, a tidy stack of books. Mostly there was space. No carpets covered the refinished wood floors, no ornaments cluttered the fireplace mantel or the single table.

He didn't immediately flip on music, so she was conscious of the quiet as well as the feeling of calm in the room. "I don't have coffee. Would you like some green tea?" he asked her.

Why was she not surprised?

"Yes. I would."

She followed him into the kitchen and it was as neat as the living room. A couple of green plants in the window, bare countertops, four cookbooks in the space where a microwave was meant to be. "Don't tell me you don't possess a microwave?"

His eyes gleamed with self-deprecating humor. "I'm more into the slow food movement."

She felt like banging her head against the gleaming, naked countertop. What was she doing here?

Then he turned and walked toward her. He raised his hands to cup her chin and slowly leaned in, kissing her in the slow, unhurried way he did everything.

And in that moment, she had an inkling that some things were really much better done slowly.

His lips were warm, gentle, and his hands moved slowly from her face to her hair, still slightly damp, she imagined when she felt his hands push into it.

He kissed her for a long time, standing in the middle of his kitchen, while the kettle sighed softly on the stove and her body grew increasingly aroused. She wanted to rip his clothes off him and take him right here on the kitchen floor, but she understood that he wanted them to take their time, and for once she was willing to give over control, fairly certain she'd be rewarded for her patience.

And it was taking all the patience she possessed and some she thought she must be borrowing from somewhere to stand still and let him diddle-daddle around, playing with the earring in her lobe, tracing patterns on her fully clothed back.

All the while her pent-up excitement grew. When the

kettle finally blew its whistle she knew exactly how it felt. The noise startled them both, and he pulled away, saying, "Maybe the tea can wait."

"I think so."

Then he took her hand and led her upstairs to his simple, sleek bedroom. No television, one book on the nightstand, no clothes scattered everywhere. A black wardrobe, one chair and the bed. It would look like a monk's cell except for that bed. A king size with nubby linen sheets that had the ecofriendly expensive look. She got the feeling that while he didn't have a lot of stuff, what he bothered to own he treasured and chose carefully.

Dappled light played through his window, patterned to lace shadows by a tree outside. He resumed kissing her. Right where he'd left off, as though he'd forgotten the taste of her and needed to start all over again.

Time seemed to drift as she stood there, feeling lazy and special. When he'd explored her mouth fully, he finally got around to helping her off with her hoodie, making such a production of it that she felt like she was doing the dance of the seven veils. Mysterious and sexy.

Under it she wore an athletic shirt—not the one she'd sweated in earlier, but a much nicer one that made the most of her meager curves. Besides that she wore only jeans, a black lacy thong and leather sandals.

He took half a century peeling her top up over her belly, stopping to kiss and caress the skin he revealed. When he pulled it up over her breasts, she heard his breath catch. *Hah!* she thought. *Surprise.* One of the nice things about being small-breasted was that she could easily forgo a bra when she felt like being casual.

Clearly, Mr. I'm In No Hurry had been expecting a bra and the way he couldn't seem to take his eyes off her breasts, or keep his hands off them, told her he wasn't nearly as Zen as he pretended to be. From the pace of his breathing, she thought he wanted to rip off her clothes and take her right here, right now, as much as she wanted him to.

But he didn't.

Controlling himself with an effort she had to admire, he went back to his slow, meandering exploration of her body.

He sat her down on his bed, reached down to tug her sandals off her feet before stroking up her legs.

"Could you do something for me?" she asked, trying not to pant.

"What is it?" She was pretty sure he was trying not to pant, too.

"Would you take off your shirt?"

The slow, sexy smile dawned. "Yes, ma'am." And he peeled his T-shirt over his head.

Even though she'd watched him contort himself and had seen the muscles in his arms, she'd never seen his torso naked. The man was gorgeous. Hard-muscled and yet lean, with a subtle six-pack. Copper-penny nipples and a delicious arrow of hair that pointed to hidden treasure.

His skin was beyond warm, so hot he felt feverish.

He reached for the button of her jeans. "You going commando everywhere?"

"No. I'm wearing panties."

He undid her jeans and eased them down over her hips. When he raised his gaze to her hips he groaned. "Those are not panties. You can see everything," he complained in mock horror.

He raised his gaze until it connected with hers. "I bet those don't even cover your butt."

Feeling silly and sexy and delicious, she rolled over. "See for yourself."

He not only looked, but he also touched, and then he removed the last of his clothes and climbed into bed with her. He took her into his arms and kissed her.

"You are such a good kisser," she murmured against his mouth.

"Glad you think so, because I am going to kiss every inch of your beautiful body."

And he did.

She lost track of time. For a woman who billed by the hour, whose schedule was blocked in fifteen-minute increments, who had clocks all over her home and office so she always knew what the time was, it was an extraordinary experience. But she truly did lose any sense of where she was in her day. And as her body trembled, and the man who'd made her wait finally entered her body, she decided that there was a lot to be said for taking the time to do one thing well.

He didn't rush her, or himself, seemed content to make love for hours, as though climax would come to them when it felt like it. She'd never been with anyone like that before and instead of focusing on achieving orgasm, she found herself experiencing her body and this new man's, enjoying every thrust and slide, every moan and soft whisper, how her skin felt against the soft cotton sheets, how his skin slid against hers. When she climaxed, he didn't treat it like an event, but like a wave, and there were plenty more waves out there, so they drifted and crested and played until, deeply satisfied, she dozed, wrapped in his arms.

When she woke, satisfied and smug, she said, "I lost track of how many orgasms I had."

He opened one eye, a blue gleam against his tawny skin, and mumbled, "Do you usually keep score?"

She nodded. "Of course I do. I track everything. My

time, my expenses, my billable hours, it's like my whole life is one big tally sheet."

"Good thing I came along," he informed her.

She was about to sling him a stinging retort when she considered that if she'd remembered to keep track of her orgasms, she was pretty sure she'd have needed more than the fingers of one hand. Most of the time, she was lucky to have one. She wasn't going to call him on his attitude. Not yet, anyway.

Instead she gave his delectable round butt a resounding slap. "Come on, gorgeous. We have a wedding to go to."

He turned onto his back and regarded her with a gleam of speculation. "You know, they'll still get married whether we're there or not."

"But they're my friends. Besides, my best friend is catering the wedding and I promised I'd be there." Since there was no clock in his room—how did the man get up in the morning?—she dug out her cell phone and gave a squeal of alarm. "We've got to get going or we'll be late. I'll run home and change and be back in, oh, crap, an hour."

"Hey, Sarah?" he said, not moving.

"What?" She was almost out the door.

"Bring your toothbrush. I want you to stay tonight. We barely got started."

23

"THE CANAPÉS ARE A huge hit," Giselle, the long-legged waitress Chelsea had met while working at the restaurant said, running into the kitchen with another empty tray. "One of the older men made me stand there while he ate seven butterflied prawns. I'm not kidding. I counted."

"Good thing I made lots," Chelsea said.

Amazingly, she was actually having fun. This was the work she loved, what she felt she'd been born to do. She took pleasure in food and loved to share that pleasure with other people. Maybe not to the point that some guy would gobble up seven prawns in a row, but she supposed his greed was a compliment of sorts.

Since this was a second marriage for both bride and groom, they'd arranged for hors d'oeuvres and drinks before the ceremony, then they were having the actual wedding in the conservatory, and afterward a sit-down dinner in the dining room.

After sending Giselle out with another tray, she checked on her bartender. And had to smile. David was having the time of his life, she could tell. He was laughing and joking with the customers while pouring drinks with deft assurance.

She glanced at her watch, which told her that the scheduled cocktail hour should be over in a few minutes, and exactly on cue, she watched Karen whisper into the MC's ear and the next thing, he was announcing that it was now time for everyone to head to the conservatory.

While the couple was getting married, she had time to get the first course ready to go and for David to open and place bottles of wine on all the tables.

She passed Karen on her way to the dining room and the woman beamed at her. "You're doing a fantastic job. I knew the minute I tasted your food we were going to be great together."

"Thanks," she said. "I feel the same." She did, too. She and Karen shared a perfectionism about event planning that ensured neither would let the other down. She hurried on.

"Everything fine in here?" she asked David.

"Couldn't be better."

Returning to the kitchen, she passed the conservatory and paused for a moment to enjoy the spectacle. She loved weddings. The hope and dreams of a couple promising to love each other for all their lives. Filled with hope and the support of their friends and family.

These two had written their own vows, she soon realized. Facing each other and holding hands, they promised to offer each other friendship and support through good times and tough. Maybe they weren't the most poetic vows ever written, but even so, Chelsea felt emotion catch at her throat. She felt a presence behind her and knew without turning that it was David.

Rock solid, standing at her back. He'd been there today when she'd needed him. She thought that if he ever grew up and got over the fear of commitment that was holding him back, he would be a terrific husband.

While they stood there, close but not touching, the bride said in a clear but tremulous voice, "I promise to love you every day of my life."

Chelsea felt the echo of those words in her own heart, repeated them silently to the man standing behind her. Then she felt him move. Not away, but closer, so his front was touching her back. For a timeless moment they stood there, while two strangers promised to love each other for the rest of their lives.

Then he moved away.

She turned and hurried to the kitchen, acknowledging the ache in her chest. She didn't have time for unrequited love, she reminded herself sternly.

She had a wedding to cater.

THE DINNER WAS EATEN, the toasts drunk, the speeches spoken, the wedding cake cut, and the dancing was beginning.

Chelsea's part was played and she thought with simple pride that she couldn't have done better. Karen was delighted, and the bride's mother had made a special trip to the kitchen to thank her, bringing a bottle of the good champagne as a gift.

"You did a wonderful job," the woman gushed. "And your bartender was quite a hit. You make a good team." Since David was standing there at the time, she couldn't say what she wanted to, which was that he didn't seem to want her on his team. Instead, she thanked the woman politely.

David didn't even blink when she said, "And here's a little extra something from the bride's family," and tucked a one hundred dollar bill into his breast pocket.

"Thank you, ma'am," he said. "It's been our pleasure

working for you. You know what you could do for Chelsea if you really want to thank her?"

Both women stared at him in slight shock. Now what was he doing?

He smiled at them both. God, he was cute. He'd be the perfect man if only he wanted her for real. "You'd write a little reference that Chelsea could use on her Web site and her brochure. That would really help her build her business. There's nothing like a satisfied customer to bring the business in." He grinned suddenly. "And with wedding catering, it's not like you want to get repeats."

"I certainly hope not." She nodded briskly. "I'll e-mail you something in the next couple of days. If I forget, remind me. I'll also tell all my friends. You are a find."

David answered, "Thanks."

When the woman had left, Chelsea turned to him. "I can't believe you asked her for a reference. It's the night of the wedding."

"She wanted to do something nice for you. Get 'em while they're grateful, that's what I always say."

I'm grateful, she thought, *why don't you come and get me?*

DAVID WAS BACK IN THE kitchen helping her reload the van when Sarah tripped in with a slightly shaggy hottie in tow. He was one of those guys who could wear a designer suit and you'd still check to see if his feet were bare. They weren't, but his shoes were obviously built for comfort more than style.

"Great job, Chels," her friend cried, giving her a hug. "Everything was delicious."

"Thanks."

"But you'd better do something about the crappy bartender you hired." She shook her finger at her brother. "Nice one, making me show ID before you'd serve me alcohol. Everybody around gaped at me like I was seventeen."

Before sister and brother could go at each other, Sarah's date stepped forward. "I didn't get a chance to meet you. I'm Mike. I'm with Sarah." He shook hands with David. She admired the smooth way he'd prevented a family squabble, but then she remembered Sarah'd said he was a high school counselor. With David and Sarah in the same room, he was a good guy to have around.

Chelsea glanced at her best friend. She hadn't missed the way Mike had introduced himself. He hadn't said he was Sarah's date, but that he was "with" her. Interesting choice of words. Now that she took the opportunity to notice, she saw that Sarah had an unmistakably heavy-eyed look and the satisfied expression of a woman who'd spent most of the day in bed. Lucky girl.

When Mike came and shook her hand and said how much he'd enjoyed the food, she studied him, the way she studied anybody Sarah cared about, and she immediately liked what she saw. There was something honest about his eyes that appealed to her immediately.

While the guys were chatting, she grabbed Sarah's arm and pulled her outside to the van. "You actually got him into bed?"

"What? Do I have it tattooed on my forehead? I finally had sex!"

"No. You look so…relaxed. And I'm guessing it's not from yoga."

A smile older and more self-satisfied than the Mona Lisa's answered her. "I don't think I've ever been this relaxed in my whole life. That man is awesome." She dropped her voice to a whisper. "I'm sleeping over there tonight."

Chelsea might have been the only person in the world

who understood what a big deal that was for Sarah, who liked to maintain control at all times. Including doing the sleepovers at her place. If they happened, which was rare. "Did you hear the way he referred to the two of you? He said, 'I'm with Sarah.' He's totally into you."

"I know." Again with the smug, I-had-sex-and-it-was-sooo-good smile, which vanished as quickly as it dawned. "It would be perfect except for one thing."

What could possibly have gone wrong already? "What thing?"

"David can never, ever know that he brought us together."

There were a million things she could have said, about growing up, and maybe accepting that sometimes other people saw things about you that you couldn't see yourself. All she said was, "My lips are permanently sealed."

Sarah nodded. "That's why we're best friends forever."

"Yeah."

"We'd better go in before they run out of things to talk about and David asks Mike how we met."

So they went back in to find the guys discussing not romance, but baseball. Men!

It was so cozy in the kitchen and she didn't want the night to end. She said, "There's a cold bottle of champagne with our names on it."

"And a bona fide bartender to open it," David added.

So they sat around the kitchen, Sarah and Mike hiked up on the countertops and Chelsea and David standing leaning against walls. "I want to make a toast," Sarah said the minute the bubbles were poured.

They all waited expectantly while she mulled for a moment. Then she grinned. "To Chelsea's new business, may it be a huge success, to the happy couple tonight, may their marriage be long and blessed, and—" here her gaze connected with her date's "—to new beginnings."

"To new beginnings," they all dutifully echoed, and then sipped the frothy wine.

Oh, it was good after a long day on her feet, the stress and the almost-disaster of the morning and the unexpected help from a man she was pretending to be engaged to, pretending she didn't need or want, pretending she didn't love.

What a mess.

At least Sarah seemed happy with a man whom she suspected would be good for her old friend. Someone who would keep her relaxed and stand up to her when she got into one of her bullying moods.

They laughed and chatted like the old friends three of them were, and Mike seemed like he fit right in.

That relationship wasn't going to be all smooth sailing, she guessed, but there was something there. Something new and wonderful and important.

She felt David's gaze on her and glanced up to meet his eyes. She thought that he was thinking the same thoughts about his sister, and she smiled slightly, letting him know they were on the same wavelength. Then his expression changed and she saw all the longing she knew so well.

Abruptly, he put down his almost-empty glass. "I think Chelsea's tired. I need to get her home."

"Good plan," Sarah agreed almost too quickly. "I need to get to bed, too."

Mike and Sarah left arm in arm, Chelsea put the last of the glasses in the case to be returned to the rental place and she and David got into the van.

She ought to be tired. She should be dead exhausted by now, but a curious energy filled her. Part of it was the excitement of having pulled off the damn near impossible and exceeding every expectation, including her own.

Part of it, she had to acknowledge, was the man beside her. Driving with a tense concentration, as if he wanted to appear too busy handling a van he'd driven with no problem at all this morning to make conversation.

Fine. She tilted her head back and let the feelings wash over her.

When they arrived back at his town house, he parked the van. It was still and quiet this time of night, lit only by a few industrial lights. The bang of her door echoed.

The stuff didn't have to be back to the rental agency until the morning, and it should be safe there in his secure garage, but she still walked around the van to make certain they'd locked the back door.

And found David embarked on the same task. They faced each other for a split second, then, as though he had no choice, he pulled her into his arms and kissed her with so much banked hunger and passion, she knew he'd been thinking of nothing else since the last time they'd been together.

She tried to pull away. She wasn't like this, didn't let herself be used by men who didn't know what they wanted and ran like hell when they got close to what they needed.

Making a sound of protest, she started to pull away, but he only took her mouth again, more fiercely, and she was lost.

24

NEED, HUNGER, THE RELIEF of a successful first catering job and the raw excitement of being with the man she loved in spite of all his flaws was a heady combination.

She'd regret this in the morning, was almost regretting it now and nothing had happened yet, but she knew she couldn't pull away. She needed David the way an addict needed a fix.

He grabbed her hand and dragged her with him, barely letting her go for a second.

His face was more stubbly than last time they'd been together, but that was because he wasn't freshly shaven since they'd been working since morning.

Which reminded her that she wasn't at her freshest, either.

When they entered the town house, she said, "I should shower."

"Later."

Wetness flooded her at the desperate way he uttered the word. He needed her as urgently as she needed him.

He pushed open the door and pulled her inside, back into his arms. Not bothering to turn on a light, he banged into a wall, swearing softly, and then paused there to kiss her deeply.

They sprinted up the stairs and he pulled her to him again.

They bashed into the doorway of his bedroom, where he pulled up her skirt and peeled down her panties while simultaneously toeing off his shoes while she tugged his belt buckle open.

He dragged off the suit jacket and then hoisted her up, like he couldn't even manage the last two steps to his bed. She wrapped her legs around him and impaled herself on him, crying out with deep-seated pleasure as she did so. He reached so deeply into her, the head of his penis hitting the perfect spot. So she groaned, holding on and then beginning to move.

The tails of his white shirt flapped against her thighs as she thrust blindly against him. She heard a thud and realized, dimly, that she was still wearing her pumps. She was fully clothed but for her panties. Somehow, their very haste was an extra turn-on. Instead of feeling skin rubbing against skin, her breasts against his hot chest, she heard the soft hushing of two white cotton shirts getting intimate with friction. But his mouth was on hers, raw and hot and wet as they clung together. She felt the effort in his arms of holding her up, felt the stretch of her thighs as she wrapped her legs around his hips and hung on. But most of all she felt surging excitement as they took each other against the doorjamb in the dark.

All of a sudden, he moved, carrying her with him, and they fell onto the bed. "Can't hold on," he muttered, reaching for a condom.

He donned it quickly and then he was inside her, stroking, reaching, driving them both up, and up. Oh, he was good at this, she thought, wondering how many women had been pleasured by him, how many had been fooled into thinking it meant anything, when her thought process was short-circuited by the swamping waves of pleasure that drowned out thought, drowned out everything but feeling.

With a soul-deep cry, she came, hearing his own cries in the echo of her own, feeling that her heart had burst.

Oh, they were good together. Their pace perfect, their rhythm in harmony. She suspected she'd never find anyone who suited her quite so magically, wondered if he ever would and was vain enough to be certain he wouldn't.

Fool.

Well, she didn't have him for a long time, but now she was here, she was going to enjoy him to the fullest while she had this last night with him.

So, she abandoned herself to him for this one night only.

She opened.

She gave.

She accepted.

And when dawn streaked through his window, while he was sleeping, his face a shadowed pleasure to her, she kissed him softly and then rolled out of bed, gathering her clothes and tiptoeing to her own room.

The sheets were so cold, the room so empty, but then, so was her romantic future, she reminded herself. She'd indulged foolishly for one magical night. Now she had to get back to reality. A reality that sadly didn't include the man she loved.

DAVID ROLLED OVER, seeking the willing warmth of the woman sleeping beside him, and found instead a pillow, scented with her smell, and rumpled bedclothes. When he forced open heavy eyelids, he discovered he was alone in his room.

The bedside clock told him it was ten. His exhaustion told him he hadn't had much sleep.

He assumed she was in the bathroom and waited for her to return, already thinking of all the things he wanted to do to her. But when ten minutes went by and she hadn't, he got up to look for her.

He found her in her own bed, sleeping peacefully. She was so neat. She'd barely made a dent in the mattress and all the covers were as tidy as though she'd only slipped into bed and then never moved.

Unlike his bed, which bore all the evidence of a night of wild sex.

As he watched her sleeping, he felt a weird shifting feeling somewhere in his chest. Felt like all the warning symptoms of a heart attack rolled into one powerful punch.

Her dark hair was tousled, her dark lashes fanned in sleep, her breathing soft and shallow.

He wanted to crawl into bed beside her, kiss her awake, possibly never leave that bed for his whole life.

Forcing himself out of her room and backing away to the kitchen, he decided what he really needed was coffee. It was fatigue and caffeine deprivation making him feel so strange.

Had to be.

He brewed coffee and sucked back the first cup greedily, but it didn't help. If anything, the caffeine jolt only increased the strange feeling in his chest.

Deciding that action was his best bet, he scrawled a quick note for Chelsea and then headed back to the van, returned the dishes to the rental place, filled the van with gas and drove it back to his buddy.

That done, he came home to find Chelsea awake and sipping coffee. She was freshly showered, dressed in a pair of those sexy jeans she loved and a sleeveless sort of billowy top in some kind of sheer cotton that filled him with the urge to slip it off her body. The second he saw her, the tight feeling in his chest eased. "Hi."

He wasn't sure whether to cross the room and kiss her or fall back on their old routine. He took a step forward, deciding that he really needed to touch her, only to have her jump up and scamper into the kitchen, where she somehow managed to wall herself in behind the granite countertop, so she had her own personal kitchen fortress.

Her cheeks appeared a little flushed and he thought she was nervous.

"Thanks so much for returning all that stuff. You shouldn't have," she said, opening the fridge and looking into it, though he couldn't imagine what she wanted there.

"I didn't mind. I was up and you were still sleeping."

She pulled out a carton of milk. "Want some breakfast?"

What did she have in mind, a milk shake? He found her sudden shyness appealing. So he breached her fortress and came up behind her, putting his arms around her. "I had a great time last night," he said, kissing her nape.

For a moment he felt her lean back against him, a tiny murmur of agreement rumbling in her throat. Then immediately she stiffened and drew away. Turned and presented a bright face. "Me, too. This friends-with-benefits thing definitely works."

Friends with benefits? That's what they were? For some reason, the notion offended him on some deep level. He backed away. "Right. Yeah. Anytime you feel the urge."

She replaced the milk carton and shut the fridge door.

"Oh, Piers called. He left his home number. Asked you to call him back."

"Piers called me at home? On a Sunday?" It was so unusual he knew something was up. "Wow. This must be it. The official offer."

"That's great," she said. "I'm truly happy for you."

He didn't care if she did rebuff him, he walked over and hugged her. "I couldn't have got here without you."

She squeezed her arms around him and leaned in for a moment. "I guess we really have helped each other's careers. Glad it all worked out."

"Yeah, me, too."

He called his boss back and Piers asked if he could meet him that day for lunch.

"Of course." When he got off the phone, he turned to Chelsea. "Tonight let's celebrate. I got my new job, you've got a business already off the ground. How about I buy you the fanciest dinner in Philly. You pick the place."

She had this funny little line between her brows like she was in the middle of a math test and didn't know any of the answers. "I don't think so," she said. Just like that. No excuses, no reason given at all, just 'I don't think so.'

But he wasn't the subtle type. Never had been. If she was trying to send him a message he wished she'd give it to him straight. "Why not? What's up?"

"I'm happy for you, David. I really am. I'm happy we both got what we want, but I can't keep playing this game. We're not in love. We're not getting married. Let's get on with our lives and wish each other the best."

He was so stunned he could barely take it in. She was blowing him off? After last night?

But he was nothing if not cool. So he shrugged. "Sure, if that's the way you want it."

"It is."

Okay, then, he thought. *Don't be surprised if I take some other woman out to celebrate.* There were plenty who'd be only too happy to spend time in his company, he reminded himself. He didn't need a moody caterer messing with his mind.

This should be the happiest day of his life, he thought as he dressed with care for Sunday lunch with his boss.

He even wore the tie she'd picked out for him, figuring it was good luck and maybe she'd feel bad if she saw him wearing her tie even after she'd blown him off for dinner. But when he emerged from his room all ready for his big lunch, she'd left the town house.

Fine. It was all fine.

He made his way to the restaurant where he was meeting Piers and put all thoughts of Chelsea out of his mind. Mostly.

Piers was there ahead of him in his Sunday attire—he looked like a ship's captain with a navy blazer and an ascot. He rose and the men shook hands.

They made the usual chitchat until lunch was served and then Piers said, "I wanted to have a meeting with you outside of the office. It's a matter of some awkwardness."

"Absolutely, I understand," he said, even though he didn't.

"I'm going to get right to the point. Damien Macabee has decided not to retire this year after all."

"What?" He couldn't keep the shock out of his voice. After all he'd gone through to prove he was the man to be the next VP? He'd worked his ass off. He'd found a fake fiancée and pretended to be engaged! What more was he supposed to do?

"It's very surprising news. The truth is, I think as retirement grew closer he didn't know what he was going to do with himself. His wife's still working—and judges seem to go on forever—and lately he's found a renewed appetite for the business." Piers sighed, looking truly distressed. "It's rare that I make a fool of myself, David, but I feel that I have over this business. I do want you as a VP of this company, make no mistake. You've worked hard and I know you've made sacrifices."

"You have no idea."

"Yes, we don't want to lose you. And Macabee is willing to mentor you, to give you the benefit of his years of experience in the industry. I know it's disappointing not be a VP quite yet, but I think it's a great opportunity."

"How long would it be?"

"Before you had the position?"

He nodded.

"We're looking at a three-year time frame."

Three years.

His opinion of waiting three years must have shown on his face, for Piers said, "It seems like a lifetime to you now, but believe me, when you get to my age, three years is nothing. Enjoy your time with Chelsea, have a fantastic wedding and get used to married life. Your life will be hectic enough, and you're still our top salesman."

"I need to think about this." He ran one hand through his hair. "Wow." The unfairness of this whole mess began to flood him. "I get headhunted, you know?"

"Of course, I know. Any company would be lucky to have you. I can only hope, when you've had a chance to think things through, that you'll realize that you're not worse off with us. To have Damien mentor you, to have all his expertise and wisdom at your disposal, as well as the great salary you already bring in…" He let the sentence trail off. "Talk it over with Chelsea. Hasty decisions are often bad ones." He shook his head. "I made one myself. I should have waited until Macabee formally retired before speaking with you. But there, what's done is done. I truly hope we can build you to be a future leader of our company."

He wanted to throw down his napkin, maybe dash a glass of water in Piers's face and march out of the restaurant. But he managed to control himself. If lunch wasn't the outrageous success, complete with champagne toasts, that he'd anticipated, at least he managed to keep his cool.

Right now, he needed to consider his options.

A long walk in the park helped calm him and when he got home he was cooler, at least, if not exactly calm.

He walked into the town house and yelled, "Chelsea?" For some reason, it was important that she be here. He really needed to tell her about his crappy day.

"David?" She was in the living area, all dressed like she was going out, and he thought she looked a little guilty. "I didn't expect you so soon. Thought you'd be out celebrating."

He flopped onto the couch and loosened his tie. "Nothing to celebrate."

"What do you mean?"

"Macabee's not retiring after all. He wants to make a three-year plan for me to be groomed. Three frickin' years. I can't believe it."

"Oh, David. I'm so sorry." She sat beside him, put a hand on his knee, and it was the most comforting gesture he could imagine.

"Yeah. Pretty much sucks."

"What are you going to do?"

He shook his head. "I don't know. Go work for the competition maybe, take them down." But even in his own ears his threats sounded groundless. Truth was, they hadn't lied to him or done him wrong, Piers had been overeager to offer him a position he was dying to occupy. They still planned for him to be the next VP. But he was going to have to wait a little longer.

He shook himself out of his unaccustomed downer. "So, you're all dressed to go out. Hot date?" Which, after last night, would explain the look of guilt on her face.

"No. Actually, I'm moving out."

He jerked upright. "When?"

"Now. Tonight."

"But…why?"

"David, you don't need me anymore. Our deal was for me to masquerade as your fiancée until you got the VP job and for you to let me stay here and use your kitchen until my business got started. Well, you don't need a fake fiancée anymore, and I don't need a place to stay and a kitchen anymore. I have my own."

He was so outraged he didn't know what to say. He spluttered, "So, you're leaving me?"

Her smile was semisweet. "For me to leave you would imply that I ever had you. The truth is, I never did. Never could." She leaned forward and kissed him gently on the mouth. "It's better this way."

But he wasn't having any of it. "Better for who?"

She rose, picked up her bulging bag. "Me, I guess."

"But, I don't want…"

"Goodbye, David."

He thought the hollow clink of her leaving her front door key in his key dish was the saddest sound he'd ever heard.

25

CHELSEA WORKED WITH a vengeance, cleaning, organizing, ordering supplies and preparing for a busy couple of weeks. True to her word, Karen had appointed her the go-to caterer for If You Can Dream It, and so her fledgling business was already thriving. Plus, Mrs. Sloane, true to her word, had recommended Chelsea and Chelsea was catering a fiftieth wedding anniversary dinner and a business cocktail party thanks to the woman's words in the right ears.

She was scrambling to pull together a champagne breakfast for seventy in two weeks followed by an evening event for a mixed marriage. The happy couple wanted to celebrate their two cultures in food. Polish and Chinese.

"I'm thinking dim sum perogies and egg drop borscht," she joked to Karen as she tried to design a menu that made some kind of sense.

But she was having fun, more fun than she could have imagined. Her life was going exactly as it should. She was doing the work she was born to do, and woke up every day eager to leave her tiny apartment and run downstairs to her huge kitchen. The shop-front part of her operation was already profitable, thanks to Karen getting her a plug in the newspaper. So far, she was sticking to simple fare—appetizers, casserole dinners and a selection of desserts, made fresh daily that busy people could pick up on their way home from work, heat up and enjoy a gourmet feast for a fairly reasonable price.

If there was a persistent ache in her heart, she ignored it as best she could. In the daytime, it was easy. She was crazy busy and thriving on the challenges being thrown at her constantly. At night it was a lot tougher. She'd curl up in her small bed in the studio apartment and think about David. Wonder where he was, what he was doing. Was he eating properly?

Truth was, love sucked.

It was a lesson she thought she'd learned in high school but it seemed she'd needed a refresher course.

They'd even seen each other a couple of times. His parents had held the barbecue, as promised, and of course, Chelsea had gone.

If they were disappointed to find she and David distant with each other, they were too polite to mention it and besides, the obvious budding love affair between Sarah and Mike was obviously a source of huge satisfaction.

Chelsea thought he looked tired and a little gaunt, then reminded herself that he had work troubles. It had only been a couple of weeks since she'd moved out, but no doubt she was already nothing but a distant memory to him.

When was she going to get over this ridiculous unrequited love business?

A tiny voice in her head warned her that was likely to be never.

Sarah was so happy it was fun to be around her. She'd finally let herself fall and she'd fallen hard. When she heard that Mike had booked them an overnight sleepover at the zoo, and that Sarah was actually excited about the prospect, Chelsea suspected it wouldn't be long before she'd be catering her best friend's wedding. Which was going to be tough since she also planned to be the maid of honor. Oh, well, she'd cross that bridge when she came to it.

It was a busy weekday afternoon when tired workers stopped to pick up something for dinner.

Having bagged an ever popular heat-and-serve lasagna, which she sold as a package including garlic bread, Ceasar salad and her wickedly good chocolate-fudge brownies for dessert, she figured her counter staff, Giselle and Jonathan, could handle the few remaining customers on their own.

She was removing her apron so that she could retreat to her office to work on a menu plan for the masquerade ball she'd agreed to cater when a familiar figure entered the room.

She saw the tall body, the flop of black hair, the grin that went slightly crooked when he saw her, and she had to push her fingernails into her palms to stop herself running out from behind the counter and throwing herself at him.

Since the poor guy was probably here for a take-out lasagna, she doubted her tongue in his mouth would be a great substitute. So, she forced herself to speak casually.

"David, hey."

He came up to the counter, not perusing her offerings at all, but focusing all his attention on her.

"Hi. Looks like you're doing pretty well for yourself."

"So far so good."

He nodded. Gazed at her mouth so she had to put ten new dents in her palms to keep her cool. "Are you busy or do you have a few minutes to take a walk?" he asked her abruptly. She'd barely seen him for the last two weeks and now he wanted a walk?

For the first week, she'd hoped against hope that he'd come by and beg her to come back, at least that he'd call her up and maybe invite her to dinner or a movie. But nothing. It was like she'd exited his home and his memory the same day. So, she was a little surprised at his sudden invitation.

There could be only one reason he wanted to see her again. However, her days of being a fake fiancée were over. So she pulled off her apron, hung it carefully on the hook behind her door and told her staff that she'd be back in half an hour.

David held the door for her and they walked out into the evening air. It was warm, fragrant with roses and jasmine that she'd put in the windowboxes together with the fat spill of red geraniums. Maybe it was a slightly unorthodox collection of blooms, but she didn't care. She liked them all.

"It's been a while," she said after they'd walked for a few seconds in silence.

"It has."

A few more seconds of silence ticked by while she waited for him to tell her that she was needed for the company fussball tournament, or the family picnic, or some other masquerade where she'd pretend to belong to the man she wanted most in the world. Since he remained silent, she finally spoke up. "Whatever you're going to ask me, can I say right now that the answer's no?"

He turned, looked at her in stunned disbelief. "How can you possibly know what I'm going to ask you?"

"Experience." So, he was going to ask her a favor. She'd known it the second she saw him. Even as her heart plummeted, her irritation level rose. "Let me be clear. No, I don't want to be your fake date for the company golf tournament, fishing derby, or some team-building exercise involving riding a mechanical bull. No, no and no. My days of being a fake fiancée are over."

"Well, that's good. But I didn't want to ask you any of those things."

"You didn't?"

"No." He blew out a breath and stuck his hands in his pockets. "I cannot believe what an ass I was. I had no business lying to my boss and coworkers or putting you in such an awkward position." He turned to her, as sincere as she'd ever seen him. "I'm truly sorry about that."

"Thanks. Apology accepted. Then why are you here?"

"I'll get to that, but first I want to tell you about my new job."

"You have a new job?"

"Yeah. Well, no. It's sort of the same job, but after I got over myself I realized that maybe I don't know it all. I decided to try working with Macabee." He let out a low whistle. "What that guy doesn't know about insurance isn't worth knowing. And he's connected like you wouldn't believe. He's been introducing me to some of his clients. Instead of feeling like I got booted to the end of the line, I'm learning. Every day it's exciting. I think it's good for him, too. He needed a new challenge to keep it fresh."

She felt ridiculously proud of him. "That must have been a hard thing to do."

"It was at first, but now I'm glad. It was the right move. Oh, and just so you know? We all rode the mechanical bull without you." He chuckled softly. "I kept wishing you were there, though. You'd have loved it. I don't think I can adequately describe the sight of Piers riding that bronco." He shook his head, grinning in memory. "Everyone asked about you."

"What did you tell them about us?"

"That we broke up."

Even though the whole charade had been a fraud, hearing him say those words was like a kick in the stomach. "How did they take it?"

"Piers told me he was sure we'd get back together."

She snorted. "Hopefully in the next three years, before you become VP."

"Nope. That wasn't it." He turned to her and she saw an emotion in his eyes she'd never seen there before. "He said it was because he could tell we were in love with each other, and love like that always finds a way."

Oh, if only it were true. She wanted to say something slick and cool, but right now her throat seemed incapable of opening for speech.

"Piers is quite the romantic," she said, feeling incredibly foolish that her feelings had been so transparent.

"I've had some time to think about a lot of things since you left. Mostly, I needed to clear up some baggage I've been carrying around way too long. I thought I was in love once before, and I got engaged."

He'd never mentioned it to her, she owed her information to Sarah, so the fact that he was telling her now suggested he was finally able to face up to his past. "What happened?" she asked softly.

"The story I've always told myself is that she kicked me to the curb when her old boyfriend came back to town, and while that's true, the part I hadn't figured out before is that she did the right thing. Turned out she loved the guy and she didn't love me. And it took me way too long to figure out I never loved her, either."

"You didn't?"

"Nope."

A kid rode by them on a bike so she moved closer to David to let the boy by.

"Anyhow, I came by because you forgot something when you moved out of my place."

"Oh, was it my omelet skillet? I haven't been able to find that anywhere. I wondered if I'd left it at your place."

"Omelet skillet." His eyes twinkled down at her in that disturbing way. "Honey, I wouldn't know an omelet skillet from a frying pan."

"Well, technically, it is a frying pan. A smaller one, with a copper bottom. Oh, never mind. I'll come around one day and have a look for myself."

"You do that."

"So, if it wasn't my omelet skillet, what did I leave at your place?"

He plunged his hand in his pocket and pulled out something sparkly that caught in the evening light and flashed. "Your engagement ring."

"But we're not—"

"I always liked that ring on you. Seems a shame for it to go to waste."

"But, I can't—"

He turned her to face him, slid his hands down her arms and took her hands in his, the ring a hard spot against her skin. "Chelsea, I've been the biggest fool in the world. I only figured out that I never loved Suzanne when I realized that I love you." His eyes were intent on hers and she felt like her heart was going to burst right out of her chest. "I almost let the woman I love get away. There's no reason you should do it, but I have to ask you anyway. Will you marry me?"

She opened her mouth. Closed it again. Fought down the craziest feelings of hope. "Wouldn't they take the ring back?"

"I don't know. I didn't ask them. Thing is, when we started this, I thought you would only be a temporary part of my life. Turns out I was wrong. I can't stop thinking about you, I miss seeing you every day and being part of your life, and even though we never slept a whole night in the same bed, I wake up in the middle of the night reaching for you." He stopped, swallowed. "Is that crazy?"

"Probably. But I do it, too, so we must both be crazy."

He laughed, a little shakily. "So, will you?"

"Marry you?" She regarded the ring he was holding out to her. "To help you sleep through the night? That's a pretty feeble reason."

"How about because I love you. And I've never loved anyone before, so I'm pretty sure this is forever."

When she looked into his eyes she saw the truth.

"Oh, David, I've been in love with you since I was fourteen years old."

"Seriously?"

"Yes."

He took her left hand in his, kissed her fingers before he slid the ring onto her finger, and she did nothing to stop him. "I think you're right. It works better when I put the ring on your finger." And then he kissed her mouth, long and deep.

She put her arms around him and kissed him back.

When they came back down to earth, he said, "You've been in love with me for, like, fifteen years?"

"Stop gloating."

"Am I a slow learner or what?"

"Definitely slow," she agreed. Then she relented and threw her arms around him. "But worth waiting for."

* * * * *

A *VERY* EXCLUSIVE ENGAGEMENT

BY
ANDREA LAURENCE

Andrea Laurence has been a lover of reading and writing stories since she learned her Abcs. She always dreamed of seeing her work in print and is thrilled to finally be able to share her books with the world. A dedicated West Coast girl transplanted to the Deep South, she's working on her own "happily ever after" with her boyfriend and their collection of animals that shed like nobody's business. You can contact Andrea at her website, www.andrealaurence.com.

To my series mates—
Barbara, Michelle, Robyn, Rachel and Jennifer

It was a pleasure working with each of you.
Thanks for welcoming a newbie to the club.

And our editor, Charles
Sei fantastico. È stato bello lavorare con voi.
Grazie per il cioccolato le sardine.

One

Figlio di un allevatore di maiali.

Liam Crowe didn't speak Italian. The new owner of the American News Service network could barely order Italian food, and he was pretty sure his Executive Vice President of Community Outreach knew it.

Francesca Orr had muttered the words under her breath during today's emergency board meeting. He'd written down what she'd said—or at least a close enough approximation–in his notebook so he could look it up later. The words had fallen from her dark red lips in such a seductive way. Italian was a powerful language. You could order cheese and it would sound like a sincere declaration of love. Especially when spoken by the dark, exotic beauty who'd sat across the table from him.

And yet, he had the distinct impression that he wasn't going to like what she'd said to him.

He hadn't expected taking over the company from

Graham Boyle to be a cakewalk. The former owner and several employees were in jail following a phone-hacking scandal that had targeted the president of the United States. The first item on the agenda for the board meeting had been to suspend ANS reporter Angelica Pierce for suspicion of misconduct. Hayden Black was continuing his congressional investigation into the role Angelica may have played in the affair. Right now, they had enough cause for the suspension. When Black completed his investigation—and hopefully uncovered some hard evidence—Liam and his Board of Directors would determine what additional action to take.

He was walking into a corporate and political maelstrom, but that was the only reason he had been able to afford to buy controlling stock in the company in the first place. ANS was the crown jewel of broadcast media. The prize he'd always had his eye on. The backlash of the hacking scandal had brought the network and its owner, Graham Boyle, to their knees. Even with Graham behind bars and the network coming in last in the ratings for most time slots, Liam knew he couldn't pass up the opportunity to buy ANS.

So, they had a major scandal to overcome. A reputation to rebuild. Nothing in life was easy, and Liam liked a challenge. But he'd certainly hoped that the employees of ANS, and especially his own Board of Directors, would be supportive. From the night janitor to the CFO, jobs were on the line. Most of the people he spoke to were excited about him coming aboard and hopeful they could put the hacking scandal behind them to rebuild the network.

But not Francesca. It didn't make any sense. Sure, she had a rich and famous movie producer father to support her if she lost her position with ANS, but charity was her *job*. Surely she cared about the employees of the company as much as she cared about starving orphans and cancer patients.

It didn't seem like it, though. Francesca had sat at the conference room table in her formfitting flame-red suit and lit into him like she was the devil incarnate. Liam had been warned that she was a passionate and stubborn woman—that it wouldn't be personal if they bumped heads—but he wasn't prepared for this. The mere mention of streamlining the corporate budget to help absorb the losses had sent her on a tirade. But they simply couldn't throw millions at charitable causes when they were in such a tight financial position.

Suffice it to say, she disagreed.

With a sigh, Liam closed the lid on his briefcase and headed out of the executive conference room to find some lunch on his own. He'd planned to take some of the board members out, but everyone had scattered after the awkward meeting came to an end. He didn't blame them. Liam had managed to keep control of it, making sure they covered everything on the agenda, but it was a painful process.

Oddly enough, the only thing that had made it remotely tolerable for him was watching Francesca herself. In a room filled with older businesswomen and men in gray, black and navy suits, Francesca was the pop of color and life. Even when she wasn't speaking, his gaze kept straying back to her.

Her hair was ebony, flowing over her shoulders and curling down her back. Her almond-shaped eyes were dark brown with thick, black lashes. They were intriguing, even when narrowed at him in irritation. When she argued with him, color rushed to her face, giving her flawless tan skin a rosy undertone that seemed all the brighter for her fire-engine red suit and lipstick.

Liam typically had a thing for fiery, exotic women. He'd had his share of blond-haired, blue-eyed debutantes in private school but when he'd gone off to college, he found he had a taste for women a little bit spicier. Francesca, if she hadn't been trying to ruin his day and potentially his year, would've been just the kind of woman he'd ask out. But complicating this scenario with a fling gone wrong was something he didn't need.

Right now, what he *did* need was a stiff drink and some red meat from his favorite restaurant. He was glad ANS's corporate headquarters were in New York. While he loved his place in D.C., he liked coming back to his hometown. The best restaurants in the world, luxury box seats for his favorite baseball team…the vibe of Manhattan was just so different.

He'd be up here from time to time on business. Really, he wished it was all the time, but if he wanted to be in the thick of politics, which was ANS's focus, Washington was where he had to be. So he'd set up his main office in the D.C. newsroom, as Boyle had, keeping both his apartment in New York and the town house in Georgetown that he'd bought while he went to college there. It was the best of both worlds as far as he was concerned.

Liam went to his office before he left for lunch. He put his suitcase on the table and copied Francesca's words from his notebook onto a sticky note. He carried it with him, stopping at his assistant's desk on his way out.

"Jessica, it's finally over. Mrs. Banks will be bringing

you the paperwork to process Ms. Pierce's suspension. Human Resources needs to get that handled right way. Now that that mess is behind me, I think I'm going to find some lunch." He handed her the note with the Italian phrase written on it. "Could you get this translated for me while I'm gone? It's Italian."

Jessica smiled and nodded as though it wasn't an unusual request. She'd apparently done this in the past as Graham Boyle's assistant. "I'll take care of it, sir. I have the website bookmarked." Glancing down at the yellow paper she shook her head. "I see Ms. Orr has given you a special welcome to the company. This is one I haven't seen before."

"Should I feel honored?"

"I don't know yet, sir. I'll tell you once I look it up."

Liam chuckled, turning to leave, then stopping. "Out of curiosity," he asked, "what did she call Graham?"

"Her favorite was *stronzo*."

"What's that mean?"

"It has several translations, none of which I'm really comfortable saying out loud." Instead, she wrote them on the back of the note he'd handed her.

"Wow," he said, reading as she wrote. "Certainly not a pet name, then. I'm going to have to deal with Ms. Orr before this gets out of control."

A blur of red blew past him and he looked up to see Francesca heading for the elevators in a rush. "Here's my chance."

"Good luck, sir," he heard Jessica call to him as he trotted to the bank of elevators.

One of the doors had just opened and he watched Francesca step inside and turn to face him. She could see him coming. Their eyes met for a moment and then she reached to the panel to hit the button. To close the doors faster.

Nice.

He thrust his arm between the silver sliding panels and they reopened to allow him to join her. Francesca seemed less than pleased with the invasion. She eyeballed him for a moment under her dark lashes and then wrinkled her delicate nose as though he smelled of rotten fish. As the doors began to close again, she scooted into the far corner of the elevator even though they were alone in the car.

"We need to talk," Liam said as the car started moving down.

Francesca's eyes widened and her red lips tightened into a straight, hard line. "About what?" she asked innocently.

"About your attitude. I understand you're passionate about your work. But whether you like it or not, I'm in control of this company and I'm going to do whatever I have to do to save it from the mess that's been made of it. I'll not have you making a fool out of me in front of—"

Liam's words were cut off as the elevator lurched to a stop and the lights went out, blanketing them in total darkness.

This couldn't really be happening. She was not trapped in a broken elevator with Liam Crowe. Stubborn and ridiculously handsome Liam Crowe. But she should've known something bad was going to happen. There had been thirteen people sitting at the table during the board meeting. That was an omen of bad luck.

Nervously, she clutched at the gold Italian horn pendant around her neck and muttered a silent plea for good fortune. "What just happened?" she asked, her voice sounding smaller than she'd like, considering the blackout had interrupted a tongue lashing from her new boss.

"I don't know." They stood in the dark for a moment before the emergency lighting system kicked on and bathed them in red light. Liam walked over to the control panel and pulled out the phone that connected to the engineering room. Without saying anything, he hung it back up. Next, he hit the emergency button, but nothing happened; the entire panel was dark and unresponsive.

"Well?" Francesca asked.

"I think the power has gone out. The emergency phone is dead." He pulled his cell phone out and eyed the screen. "Do you have service on your phone? I don't."

She fished in her purse and retrieved her phone, shaking her head as she looked at the screen. There were no bars or internet connectivity. She never got good service in elevators, anyway. "Nothing."

"Damn it," Liam swore, putting his phone away. "I can't believe this."

"So what do we do now?"

Liam flopped back against the wall with a dull thud. "We wait. If the power outage is widespread, there's nothing anyone can do."

"So we just sit here?"

"Do you have a better suggestion? You were full of them this morning."

Francesca ignored his pointed words, crossed her arms defensively and turned away from him. She eyed the escape hatch in the ceiling. They could try to crawl out through there, but how high were they? They had started on the fifty-second floor and hadn't gone very far when the elevator stopped. They might be in between floors. Or the power could come back on while they were in the elevator shaft and they might get hurt. It probably was a better idea to sit it out.

The power would come back on at any moment. Hopefully.

"It's better to wait," she agreed reluctantly.

"I didn't think it was possible for us to agree on anything after the board meeting and that fit you threw."

Francesca turned on her heel to face him. "I did not throw a fit. I just wasn't docile enough to sit back like the others and let you make bad choices for the company. They're too scared to rock the boat."

"They're scared that the company can't bounce back from the scandal. And they didn't say anything because they know I'm right. We have to be fiscally responsible if we're going to—"

"Fiscally responsible? What about socially responsible? ANS has sponsored the Youth in Crisis charity gala for the past seven years. We can't just decide not to do it this year. It's only two weeks away. They count on that money to provide programs for at-risk teens. Those activities keep kids off the streets and involved in sports and create educational opportunities they wouldn't get without our money."

Liam frowned at her. She could see the firm set of his jaw even bathed in the dim red light. "You think I don't care about disadvantaged children?"

Francesca shrugged. "I don't know you well enough to say."

"Well, I do care," he snapped. "I personally attended the ball for the past two years and wrote a big fat check at both of them. But that's not the point. The point is we need to cut back on expenses to keep the company afloat until we can rebuild our image."

"No. You've got it backward," she insisted. "You need the charity events to rebuild your image so the company can stay afloat. What looks better in the midst of scandal than a company doing good deeds? It says to the public that some bad people did some bad things here, but the rest of us are committed to making things right. The advertisers will come flocking back."

Liam watched her for a moment, and she imagined the wheels turning in his head as he thought through her logic. "Your argument would've been a lot more effective if you hadn't shrieked and called me names in Italian."

Francesca frowned. She hadn't meant to lose her cool, but she couldn't help it. She had her mother's quick Italian tongue and her father's short fuse. It made for an explosive combination. "I have a bit of a temper," she said. "I get it from my father."

Anyone who had worked on the set of a Victor Orr film knew what could happen when things weren't going right. The large Irishman had a head of thick, black hair and a temper just as dark. He'd blow at a moment's notice and nothing short of her mother's soothing hand could calm him down. Francesca was just the same.

"Does he curse in Italian, too?"

"No, he doesn't speak a word of it and my mother likes it that way. My mother grew up in Sicily and met my father there when he was shooting a film. My mother's Italian heritage was always very important to her, so when I got older I spent summers there with my *nonna*."

"Nonna?"

"My maternal grandmother. I picked up a lot of Italian while I was there, including some key phrases I probably shouldn't know. I realized as a teenager that I could curse in Italian and my father wouldn't know what I was saying because he's Irish. From there it became a bad habit of mine. I'm sorry I yelled," she added. "I just care too much. I always have."

Francesca might take after her mother in most things, but her father had made his mark, as well. Victor Orr had come from poor beginnings and raised his two daughters not only to be grateful for what they had, but also to give to the less fortunate. All through high school, Francesca had volunteered at a soup kitchen on Saturdays. She'd organized charity canned food collections and blood drives at school. After college, her father helped her get an entry level job at ANS, where he was the largest minority stockholder. It hadn't taken long for her to work her way up to the head of community outreach. And she'd been good at it. Graham had never had room to complain about her doing anything less than a stellar job.

But it always came down to money. When things got tight, her budget was always the first to get cut. Why not eliminate some of the cushy corporate perks? Maybe slash the travel budget and force people to hold more teleconferences? Or cut back on the half gallon of hair gel the head anchor used each night for the evening news broadcast?

"I don't want to hack up your department," Liam said. "What you do is important for ANS and for the community. But I need a little give and take here. Everyone needs to tighten their belts. Not just you. But I need you to play along, too. It's hard enough to come into the leadership position of a company that's doing well, much less one like ANS. I'm going to do everything I can to get this network back on top, but I need everyone's support."

Francesca could hear the sincerity in his words. He did care about the company and its employees. They just didn't see eye to eye quite yet on what to do about it. She could convince him to see things her way eventually. She just had to take a page from her mother's playbook. It would take time and perhaps a softer hand than she had used with Graham. At least Liam seemed reasonable about it. That won him some points in her book. "Okay."

Liam looked at her for a moment, surveying her face as though he almost didn't believe his ears. Then he nodded. They stood silently in the elevator for a moment before Liam started shrugging out of his black suit coat. He tossed the expensive jacket to the ground and followed it with his silk tie. He unbuttoned his collar and took a deep breath, as if he had been unable to do it until then. "I'm glad we've called a truce because it's gotten too warm in here for me to fight anymore. Of course this had to happen on one of the hottest days of the year."

He was right. The air conditioning was off and it was in the high nineties today, which was unheard of in early May. The longer they sat in the elevator without air, the higher the temperature climbed.

Following his example, Francesca slipped out of her blazer, leaving her in a black silk and lace camisole and pencil skirt. Thank goodness she'd opted out of stockings today.

Kicking off her heels, she spread out her coat on the floor and sat down on it. She couldn't stand there in those pointy-toed stilettos any longer, and she'd given up hope for any immediate rescue. If they were going to be trapped in here for a while, she was going to be comfortable.

"I wish this had happened after lunch. Those bagels in the conference room burned off a long time ago."

Francesca knew exactly what he meant. She hadn't eaten since this morning. She'd had a cappuccino and a sweet *cornetto* before she'd left her hotel room, neither of which lasted very long. She typically ate a late lunch, so luckily she carried a few snacks in her purse.

Using the light of her phone, she started digging around in her bag. She found a granola bar, a pack of *Gocciole* Italian breakfast cookies and a bottle of water. "I have a few snacks with me. The question is whether we eat them now and hope we get let out soon, or whether we save them. It could be hours if it's a major blackout."

Liam slipped down to the floor across from her. "Now. Definitely now."

"You wouldn't last ten minutes on one of those survival reality shows."

"That's why I produce them and don't star in them. My idea of roughing it is having to eat in Times Square with the tourists. What do you have?"

"A peanut butter granola bar and some little Italian cookies. We can share the water."

"Which is your favorite?"

"I like the cookies. They're the kind my grandmother would feed me for breakfast when I stayed with her. They don't eat eggs or meat for breakfast like Americans do. It was one of the best parts of visiting her— cake and cookies for breakfast."

Liam grinned, and Francesca realized it was the first time she'd seen him smile. It was a shame. He had a beautiful smile that lit up his whole face. It seemed more natural than the serious expression he'd worn all day, as though he were normally a more carefree and relaxed kind of guy. The pressure of buying ANS must have been getting to him. He'd been all business this morning and her behavior certainly didn't help.

Now he was stressed out, hungry and irritated about being trapped in the elevator. She was glad she could make him smile, even if just for a moment. It made up for her behavior this morning. Maybe. She made a mental note to try to be more cordial in the future. He was being reasonable and there was no point in making things harder than they had to be.

"Cake for breakfast sounds awesome. As do summers in Italy. After high school I got to spend a week in Rome, but that's it. I didn't get around to seeing much more than the big sites like the Colosseum and the Parthenon." He looked down at the two packages in her hand. "I'll take the granola bar since you prefer the cookies. Thank you for sharing."

Francesca shrugged. "It's better than listening to your stomach growl for an hour." She tossed him the granola bar and opened the bottle of water to take a conservative sip.

Liam ripped into the packaging. His snack was gone before Francesca had even gotten the first cookie in her mouth. She chuckled as she ate a few, noting him eyeing her like a hungry tiger. Popping another into her mouth, she gently slung the open bag to him. "Here," she said. "I can't take you watching me like that."

"Are you sure?" he said, eyeing the cookies that were now in his hand.

"Yes. But when we get out of this elevator, you owe me."

"Agreed," he said, shoveling the first of several cookies into his mouth.

Francesca imagined it took a lot of food to keep a man Liam's size satisfied. He was big like her *nonno* had been. Her grandfather had died when she was only a few years old, but her *nonna* had told her about how much she had to cook for him after he worked a long shift. Like *Nonno,* Liam was more than six feet tall, solidly built but on the leaner side, as though he were a runner. A lot of people jogged around the National Mall in D.C. Or so she'd heard. She could imagine him down there with the others. Jogging shorts. No shirt. Sweat running down the hard muscles of his chest. It made her think maybe she should go down there every now and then, if just for the view.

She, however, didn't like to sweat. Running during the humid summers in Virginia was out of the question. As was running during the frigid, icy winters. So she just didn't. She watched what she ate, indulged when she really wanted to and walked as much as her heels would allow. That kept her at a trim but curvy weight that pleased her.

Speaking of sweating…she could feel the beads of sweat in her hairline, ready and waiting to start racing down the back of her neck. She already felt sticky, but there wasn't much else to take off unless she planned to get far closer to Liam than she ever intended.

Although that wouldn't be all bad.

It had been a while since Francesca had dated anyone. Her career had kept her busy, but she always kept her eyes open to the possibilities. Nothing of substance had popped up in a long time. But recently all of her friends seemed to be settling down. One by one, and she worried she might be the last.

Not that Liam Crowe was settling-down material. He was just sexy, fling material. She typically didn't indulge in pleasure without potential. But seeing those broad shoulders pulling against the confines of his shirt, she realized that he might be just what she needed. Something to release the pressure and give her the strength to hold out for "the one."

Francesca reached into her bag and pulled out a hair clip. She gathered up the thick, dark strands of her hair and twisted them up, securing them with the claw. It helped but only for a moment. Her tight-fitting pencil skirt was like a heavy, wet blanket thrown over her legs. And her camisole, while seemingly flimsy, was starting to get damp and cling to her skin.

If they didn't get out of this elevator soon, something had to come off. Taking another sip of water, she leaned her head back against the wall and counted herself lucky that if nothing else, she'd worn pretty, matching underwear today. She had the feeling that Liam would appreciate that.

Two

"Sweet mercy, it's hot!" Liam exclaimed, standing up. He felt as if he was being smothered by his crisp, starched dress shirt. He unfastened the buttons down the front and whipped it off with a sigh of relief. "I'm sorry if this makes you uncomfortable, but I've got to do it."

Francesca was sitting quietly in the corner and barely acknowledged him, although he did catch her opening her eyes slightly to catch a glimpse of him without his shirt on. She looked away a moment later, but it was enough to let him know she was curious. That was interesting.

He'd gotten a different insight into his feisty executive vice president of Community Outreach in the past two hours. He had a better understanding of her and what was important to her. Hopefully once they got out of this elevator they could work together without the animosity. And maybe they could be a little more than friendly. Once she had stopped yelling, he liked her. More than he probably should, considering that she worked for him.

"Francesca, take off some of your clothes. I know you're dying over there."

She shook her head adamantly, although he could see the beads of sweat running down her chest and into the valley between her breasts. "No, I'm fine."

"The hell you are. You're just as miserable as I am. That tank you're wearing looks like it will cover up enough to protect your honor. The skirt looks terribly clingy. Take it off. Really. I'm about ten minutes from losing these pants, so you might as well give up on any modesty left between us."

Francesca looked up at him with wide eyes. "Your pants?" she said, swallowing hard. Her gaze drifted down his bare chest to his belt and then lower.

"Yes. It's gotta be ninety-five degrees and climbing in this oven they call an elevator. You don't have to look at me, but I've got to do it. You might as well do it, too."

With a sigh of resignation, Francesca got up from the floor and started fussing with the latch on the back of her skirt. "I can't get the clasp. It snags sometimes."

"Let me help," Liam offered. She turned her back to him and he crouched down behind her to get a better look at the clasp in the dim red light. This close to her, he could smell the scent of her warm skin mixed with the soft fragrance of roses. It wasn't overpowering—more like strolling through a rose garden on a summer day. He inhaled it into his lungs and held it there for a moment. It was intoxicating.

He grasped the two sides of the clasp, ignoring the buzz of awareness that shot through his fingertips as he brushed her bare skin beneath it. With a couple of firm twists and pulls, it came apart. He gripped the zipper tab and pulled it down a few inches, revealing the back of the red satin panties she wore.

"Got it," he said with clenched teeth, standing back up and moving away before he did something stupid like touch her any more than was necessary. It was one thing to sit in the elevator in his underwear. It was another thing entirely to do it when he had a raging erection. That would be a little hard to disguise.

"Thank you," she said softly, her eyes warily watching him as she returned to her corner of the elevator.

As she started to shimmy the skirt down her hips, Liam turned away, although it took every ounce of power he had to do so. She was everything he liked in a woman. Feisty. Exotic. Voluptuous. And underneath it all, a caring soul. She wasn't one of those rich women that got involved in charity work because they had nothing better to do with their time. She really cared. And he appreciated that, even if it would cost him a few headaches in the future.

"Grazie, signore," she said with a sigh. "That does feel better."

Out of the corner of his eye, he saw her settle back down on the floor. "Is it safe?" he asked.

"As safe as it's going to get. Thank you for asking."

Liam looked over at her. She had tugged down her camisole to cover most everything to the tops of her thighs, although now a hint of her red bra was peeking out from the top. There was only so much fabric to go around, and with her luscious curves, keeping them all covered would be a challenge.

"You might as well just take those pants off now."

Liam chuckled and shook his head. Not after thinking about her satin-covered breasts. He didn't even have to touch her to make that an impossibility. "That's probably not the best idea at the moment."

Her brow wrinkled in confusion. "Why—" she started, then stopped. "Oh."

Liam closed his eyes and tried to wish his arousal away, but all that did was bring images of those silky red panties to his mind. "That's the challenge of being trapped in a small space with a beautiful, half-naked woman."

"You think I'm beautiful?" her hesitant voice came after a long moment of silence between them.

He planted his hands on his hips. "I do."

"I didn't expect that."

Liam turned to look at her. "Why on earth not? I think a man would have to be without a pulse to not find you desirable."

"I grew up in Beverly Hills," she said with a dismissive shrug. "I'm not saying I never dated in school—I did—but there was certainly a higher premium placed on the Malibu Barbie dolls."

"The what?"

"You know, the blond, beach-tanned girls with belly button piercings and figures like twelve-year-old boys? At least until they turn eighteen and get enough money to buy a nice pair of breasts."

"People in Hollywood are nuts," he said. "There was nothing remotely erotic about me as a twelve-year-old. You, on the other hand…" Liam shook his head, the thoughts of her soft curves pressing against the palms of his hands making his skin tingle with anticipation. He forced them into tight fists and willed the feeling away.

"It takes everything I've got not to touch you when I see you sitting there like that."

There was a long silence, and then her voice again. "Why don't you?"

Liam's jaw was flexed tight, and his whole body tensed as he tried to hold back the desire that was building inside for her. "I didn't think it was a good idea. I'm your boss. We have to work together. Things would get weird. Wouldn't they?"

Please let her say no. Please let her say no.

"I don't think so," she said, slowly climbing to her knees. "We're both adults. We know what this is and what it means." She crawled leisurely across the elevator floor, stopping in front of him. Her hands went to his belt buckle as she looked up at him through her thick, coal-black lashes. "What happens in the elevator, stays in the elevator, right?"

Liam didn't know what to say. He could barely form words as her hands undid his belt buckle, then the fly of his pants. But he didn't stop her. Oh, no. He wanted her too badly to let good sense interfere. Besides, they had time to kill, right? Who knew how long they'd be trapped in here.

His suit pants slid to the floor and he quickly kicked out of them and his shoes. Crouching down until they were at the same level, he reached for the hem of her camisole and pulled it up over her head. Francesca undid the clip holding her hair and the heavy, ebony stands fell down around her shoulders like a sheet of black silk.

The sight of her body in nothing but her red undergarments was like a punch to his guts. She was one of the sexiest women he'd ever seen—and she was mostly naked, and on her knees, in front of him.

How the hell had he gotten this lucky today?

Unable to hold back any longer, he leaned in to kiss her. They collided, their lips and bare skin slamming into one another. Francesca wrapped her arms around his neck and pulled her body against him. Her breasts pressed urgently against the hard wall of his chest. Her belly arched into the aching heat of his desire for her.

The contact was electric, the powerful sensations running through his nervous system like rockets, exploding at the base of his spine. He wanted to devour her, his tongue invading her mouth and demanding everything she could give him. She met his every thrust, running her own silken tongue along his and digging her nails frantically into his back.

Liam slipped his arm behind her back and slowly eased her down onto the floor. He quickly found his place between her thighs and dipped down to give attention to the breasts nearly spilling from her bra. It didn't take much to slip the straps from her shoulders and tug the bra down to her waist. The palms of his hands quickly moved in to take its place. He teased her nipples into firm peaks before capturing one in his mouth.

Francesca groaned and arched into him, her fingertips weaving into his thick, wavy brown hair. She tugged him back up to her mouth and kissed him again. There were no more thoughts of heat or sweat or broken elevators as he lost himself in the pleasurable exploration of her body.

And when he felt her fingers slide down his stomach, slip beneath the waistband of his underwear and wrap around the pulsating length of his erection, for a moment he almost forgot where he was, entirely.

Thank heavens for power outages.

* * *

Francesca wasn't quite sure what had come over her, but she was enjoying every minute of this naughty indulgence. Perhaps being trapped in this hot jail cell was playing with her brain, but she didn't care. There was just something about Liam. Sure, he was handsome and rich, but she'd seen her share of that kind of man in Washington, D.C. There was something about his intensity, the way he was handling the company and even how he handled her. She'd been fighting the attraction to him since she first laid eyes on him, and then his shirt came off to reveal a wide chest, chiseled abs and a sprinkle of chest hair, and she lost all her reasons to resist.

When he told her that she was beautiful, a part of her deep inside urged her to jump on the unexpected opportunity. To give in to the attraction, however inappropriate, and make a sexy memory out of this crazy afternoon.

She still wanted a solid, lasting relationship like her parents had. They'd been happily married for thirty years in a town where the typical wedding reception lasted longer than the vows. But having a fun fling in an elevator was in a totally different category. Liam would never be the serious kind of relationship, and she knew it, so it didn't hurt. This was a release. An amusing way to pass the time until the power was restored.

Francesca tightened her grip on Liam until he groaned her name into her ear.

"I want you so badly," he whispered. He moved his hand along the curve of her waist, gliding down to her hip, where he grasped her wrist and pulled her hand away. "You keep doing that and I won't have the chance to do everything I want to do to you."

A wicked idea crossed her mind. Francesca reached out with her other hand for the half-empty bottle of water beside them. "Let me cool you off then," she said, dumping the remains over the top of his head. The cool water soaked his hair and rushed down his face and neck to rain onto her bare skin. It was refreshing and playful, the cool water drawing goose bumps along her bare flesh.

"Man, that felt good," Liam said, running one hand through his wet hair as he propped himself up with the other. "I don't want to waste it, though." He dipped down to lick the droplets of water off her chest, flicking his tongue over her nipples again. He traveled down her stomach to where some of the water had pooled in her navel. He lapped it up with enthusiasm, making her squirm beneath him as her core tightened and throbbed in anticipation.

His fingertips sought out the satin edge of her panties and slipped beneath them. Sliding over her neatly cropped curls, one finger parted her most sensitive spot and stroked her gently. She couldn't contain the moan of pleasure he coaxed out of her. When he dipped farther to slip the finger deep inside her body, she almost came undone right then. The muscles tightened around him, the sensations of each stroke building a tidal wave that she couldn't hold back for much longer.

"Liam," she whispered, but he didn't stop. His fingers moved more frantically over her, delving inside and pushing her over the edge.

Francesca cried out, her moans of pleasure bouncing off the walls of the small elevator and doubling in volume and intensity. Her hips bucked against his hand, her whole body shuddering with the feeling running through her.

She had barely caught her breath when suddenly there was a jarring rattle. The silence was broken by the roar of engines and air units firing up, and the lights came back on in the elevator.

"You have got to be kidding me," he groaned.

And then, with Liam still between her thighs and their clothes scattered around the elevator, the car started moving downward. Francesca threw a quick glance to the screen on the wall. They were on the thirty-third floor and falling. "Oh, no," she said, pushing frantically at his chest until he eased back.

She climbed to her feet, tugging on her skirt and yanking her bra back into place. She didn't bother tucking in her camisole, but shrugged into her jacket. Liam followed suit, pulling on his pants and shirt. He shoved his tie into his pants pocket and threw his coat over his arm.

"You have my lipstick all over you," she said, noting less than ten floors to go. Liam ran his hand through his still wet hair and casually rubbed at his face, seeming to be less concerned than she was with how he looked when they walked out.

By the time the elevator came to the first floor and the doors opened, Francesca and Liam were both fully dressed. A bit sloppy, with misaligned buttons and rumpled jackets, but dressed.

They stepped out into the grand foyer where the building engineers and security guards were waiting for them. "Are you two—" one of the men started to speak, pausing when he saw their tousled condition "—okay?"

Liam looked at Francesca, and she could feel her cheeks lighting up crimson with embarrassment. He still had some of her Sizzling Hot Red lipstick on his face, but he didn't seem to care. "We're fine," he said. "Just hot, hungry and glad to finally be out of there. What happened?"

"I'm not sure, sir. The whole island lost power. Wouldn't you know it would be on such a hot day. Might've been everyone turning on their air conditioners for the first time today. Are you guys sure we can't get you anything? Three hours in there had to be miserable."

"I'm fine," Francesca insisted. The engineer's expression had been a wake-up call from the passionate haze she'd lost herself in. She'd very nearly slept with her boss. Her new boss. On his first day after they'd spent the morning fighting like cats and dogs. The heat must've made her delirious to have thought that was a good idea.

At least they'd been interrupted before it went too far. Now she just wanted to get a cab back to her hotel. Then she could change out of these clothes, shower and wash the scent of Liam off her skin. "Just have someone hail me a taxi to my hotel, would you?"

The engineer waved to one of the doormen. "Sure thing. It might take a minute because the traffic lights have been out and there's been gridlock for hours."

Without looking at Liam, Francesca started for the door, stepping outside to wait on the sidewalk for her car.

"Talk about bad timing," Liam said over her shoulder after following her outside.

"Fate has a funny way of keeping you from doing things you shouldn't do."

Liam came up beside her, but she wouldn't turn to look at him. She couldn't. She'd just get weak in the knees and her resolve to leave would soften.

"I'd like to think of it more as a brief interruption. To build some anticipation for later. Where are you headed?"

"To where I was going before my whole day got sidetracked—back to my hotel. To shower and get some work done. Alone," she added if that wasn't clear enough.

"Do you have plans for dinner tonight?"

"Yes, I do." She didn't. But going out to dinner with Liam would put her right back in the same tempting situation, although hopefully without power outages. She'd given in to temptation once and she'd been rescued from her bad decision. She wasn't about to do it again.

Liam watched her for a minute. Francesca could feel his eyes scrutinizing her, but she kept her gaze focused on the passing cars. "You said things wouldn't get weird. That we both knew what this was and what happened in the elevator stayed in the elevator."

Francesca finally turned to him. She tried not to look into the sapphire-blue eyes that were watching her or the damp curls of his hair that would remind her of what they'd nearly done. "That's right. And that's where it will stay. That's why I don't want to go to dinner with you. Or to drinks. Or back to your place to pick up where we left off. We've left the elevator behind us and the opportunity has come and gone. Appreciate the moment for what it was."

"What it was is unfinished," he insisted. "I'd like to change that."

"Not every project gets completed." Francesca watched a taxi pull up to the curb. It was empty, thank goodness.

"Come on, Francesca. Let me take you to dinner tonight. Even if just to say thank-you for the granola bar. As friends. I owe you, remember?"

Francesca didn't believe a word of that friend nonsense. They'd have a nice dinner with expensive wine someplace fancy and she'd be naked again before she knew it. As much as she liked Liam, she needed to stay objective where he was concerned. He was the new owner of ANS and she couldn't let her head get clouded with unproductive thoughts about him. They'd come to a truce, but they hadn't fully resolved their issues regarding her budget and the way forward for the network. She wouldn't put it past an attractive, charming guy like Liam to use whatever tools he had in his arsenal to get his way.

She stepped to the curb as the doorman opened the back door of the taxi for her.

"Wait," Liam called out, coming to her side again. "If you're going to leave me high and dry, you can at least tell me what you called me today in the board meeting."

Francesca smiled. If that didn't send him packing, nothing else would. "Okay, fine," she relented. She got into the cab and rolled down the window before Liam shut it. "I called you *figlio di un allevatore di maiali.* That means 'the son of a pig farmer.' It doesn't quite pack the same punch in English."

Liam frowned and stepped back from the window. The distance bothered her even though it was her own words that had driven him away. "I'd say it packs enough of a punch."

She ignored the slightly offended tone of his voice. He wasn't about to make her feel guilty. He'd deserved the title at the time. "Have a good evening, Mr. Crowe," she said before the cab pulled away and she disappeared into traffic.

Three

Liam had just stepped from his shower when he heard his cell phone ringing. The tune, "God Save the Queen," made him cringe. Had he told his great aunt Beatrice he was in Manhattan? She must've found out somehow.

He wrapped his towel around his waist and dashed into his bedroom where the phone was lying on the comforter. The words "Queen Bee" flashed on the screen with the photo of a tiara. His aunt Beatrice would not be amused if she knew what the rest of the family called her.

With a sigh, he picked up the phone and hit the answer key. "Hello?"

"Liam," his aunt replied with her haughty Upper East Side accent. "Are you all right? I was told you were trapped in an elevator all afternoon."

"I'm fine. Just hungry, but I'm about to—"

"Excellent," she interrupted. "Then you'll join me

for dinner. There's an important matter I need to discuss with you."

Liam bit back a groan. He hated eating at Aunt Beatrice's house. Mostly because of having to listen to her go on and on about the family and how irresponsible they all were. But even then, she liked them all more than Liam because they kissed her derrière. And that was smart. She was worth two billion dollars with no children of her own to inherit. Everyone was jockeying for their cut.

Everyone but Liam. He was polite and distant. He didn't need her money. Or at least he hadn't until the ANS deal came up and he didn't have enough liquid assets to buy a majority stake quickly. Other people also were interested in the company, including leeches like Ron Wheeler, who specialized in hacking businesses to bits for profit. To move fast, Liam had had to swallow his pride and ask his aunt to invest in the remaining shares of ANS that he couldn't afford. Together, they had controlling interest of the company, and by designating her voting powers to him, Aunt Beatrice had put Liam in charge.

Liam had every intention of slowly buying her out over time, but he wouldn't be able to do so for quite a while. So now, at long last, Aunt Beatrice had something to hold over his head. And when she snapped, for the first time in his life, he had to jump.

"Dinner is at six," she said, either oblivious or unconcerned about his unhappy silence on the end of the line.

"Yes, Aunt Beatrice. I'll see you at six."

After he hung up the phone, he eyed the clock and realized he didn't have long to get over to her Upper

East Side mansion in rush hour traffic. He'd do better to walk, so he needed to get out the door soon.

It was just as well that Francesca had turned down his dinner date so he didn't have to cancel. That would've pained him terribly, even after knowing what she'd called him.

"Son of a pig farmer," he muttered to himself as he got dressed.

He opted for a gray suit with a pale purple dress shirt and no tie. He hated ties and only wore them when absolutely necessary. Today, he'd felt like he needed to look important and in control at the board meeting. He didn't want the ANS directors to think they were in the hands of a laid-back dreamer. But as soon as he had a strong foothold in the company, the ties would be gone.

Tonight, he left it off simply because he knew to do so would aggravate Aunt Beatrice. She liked formal dress for dinner but had given up long ago on the family going to that much trouble. She did, however, still expect a jacket and tie for the men and a dress and hosiery for the ladies. It was only proper. Leaving off the tie would be a small but noted rebellion on his part. He didn't want her to think she had him completely under her thumb.

It wasn't until he rang the doorbell that he remembered her mentioning something about an important issue she wanted to discuss. He couldn't imagine what it could be, but he sincerely hoped it didn't involve him dating someone's daughter. Aunt Beatrice was single-minded in her pursuit of marriage and family for Liam. He couldn't fathom why she cared.

"Good evening, Mr. Crowe," her ancient butler Henry said as he opened the door.

Henry had worked for his aunt Liam's entire life and a good number of years before that. The man was in his seventies now but as spry and chipper as ever.

"Good evening, Henry. How is she tonight?" he asked, leaning in to the elderly man and lowering his voice.

"She's had a bee in her bonnet about something all afternoon, sir. She made quite a few calls once the power was restored."

Liam frowned. "Any idea what it's about?"

"I don't. But I would assume it involves you because you were the only one invited to dinner this evening."

That was odd. Usually Aunt Beatrice invited at least two family members to dinner. She enjoyed watching them try to one-up each other all night and get in her good favor. It really was a ridiculous exercise, but it was amazing what the family would do just because she asked. His grandfather, Aunt Beatrice's brother, had never had much to do with her, so neither did that branch of the family. It was only after all the others of the generation had died that she took over as matriarch. Then, even Liam's part of the family was drawn back into the fold.

Liam held his tongue as Henry led him through the parlor and into the formal dining room. When a larger group was expected, Aunt Beatrice would greet her guests in the parlor and then adjourn to the dining room when everyone had arrived. Apparently because it was just him they bypassed the formalities and went straight to dinner.

Aunt Beatrice was there in her seat at the head of the long, oak table, looking regal as always. Her gray hair was curled perfectly, her rose chiffon dress nicely accented by the pink sapphire necklace and earrings she paired with it. She didn't smile as he entered. Instead, she evaluated him from top to bottom, her lips tightening into a frown when she noted his lack of tie.

"Good evening, Aunt Beatrice," he said with a wide smile to counter her grimace. He came around the table and placed a kiss on her cheek before sitting down at the place setting to her right.

"Liam," she said, acknowledging him without any real warmth. That's why he'd always thought of her as royalty. Stiff, formal, proper. He couldn't imagine what she would have been like if she had married and had children. Children would require laughter and dirt—two things unthinkable in this household.

Henry poured them each a glass of wine and disappeared into the kitchen to retrieve their first course. Liam hated to see the old man wait on him. He should be in a recliner, watching television and enjoying his retirement, not serving meals to privileged people capable of doing it themselves. The man had never even married. He had no life of his own outside of this mansion.

"When are you going to let Henry retire?" he asked. "The poor man deserves some time off before he drops dead in your foyer."

Aunt Beatrice bristled at the suggestion. "He loves it here. He wouldn't think of leaving me. And besides, Henry would never die in the foyer. He knows how expensive that Oriental rug is."

Liam sighed and let the subject drop. Henry placed bowls of soup in front of them both and disappeared again. "So, what have you summoned me here to discuss tonight?" He might as well just get it over with.

There was no sense waiting for the chocolate soufflé or the cheese course.

"I received a phone call today from a man named Ron Wheeler."

Liam stiffened in his seat and stopped his spoon of soup in midair. Ron Wheeler was in the business of buying struggling companies and "streamlining" them. That usually involved laying off at least half the employees and hacking up the benefits packages of the ones who were left. Then he'd break the company up into smaller pieces and sell them off for more than the price of the whole. No one liked to hear the mention of his name. "And what did he have to say?"

"He heard I'd bought a large portion of Graham Boyle's ANS stock. He's made me an extremely generous offer to buy it."

At that, Liam dropped his spoon, sending splatters of butternut squash all across the pristine white tablecloth. Henry arrived in an instant to clean up the mess and bring him a new spoon, but Liam didn't want it. He couldn't stomach the idea of food at this point.

"Aunt Beatrice, your holding is larger than mine. If you sell him your stock, he'll gain majority control of the company. The whole network will be at risk."

She nodded, setting down her own spoon. "I realize that. And I know how important the company is to you. But I also want you to know how important this family is to me. I won't be around forever, Liam. This family needs someone strong and smart to run it. You don't need me to tell you that most of our relatives are idiots. My two sisters never had any sense and neither did their children. My father knew it, too, which is why he left most of the family money to me and your grandfather. He knew they'd all be broke and homeless without someone sensible in charge."

Liam didn't want to know where this conversation was going. It couldn't be good. "Why are you telling me this? What does it have to do with Ron Wheeler?"

"Because I think you're the right person to lead the family after I'm gone."

"Don't talk like that," he insisted. They both knew she was too mean to die. "You have plenty of years ahead of you."

Her sharp blue gaze focused on him, an unexpected hint of emotion flashing in them for a fleeting second before she waved away his statement. "Everyone dies, Liam. It's better to be prepared for the eventuality. I want you to take my place and be family patriarch. As such, you would inherit everything of mine and serve as executor of the family trusts."

The blood drained from Liam's face. He didn't want that kind of responsibility. Two billion dollars and a family full of greedy suck-ups chasing him around? "I don't want your money, Aunt Beatrice. You know that."

"Exactly. But I know what you do want. You want ANS. And as long as I have my shares, you won't truly have it. I could sell at any time to Ron Wheeler or anyone else who gives me a good offer."

Liam took a big swallow of wine to calm his nerves. Aunt Beatrice had never held anything over him. She couldn't because until now he hadn't needed her or her money and she knew it. But he'd made a critical error. He never should've agreed to this stock arrangement with her. He'd given her the leverage to twist him any way she wanted to. "Why would you do that? I told you

I would buy that stock from you at what you paid or the going rate, if it goes higher."

"Because I want you to settle down. I can't have you leading this family while you play newsman and chase skirts around D.C. I want you married. Stable. Ready to lead the Crowe family."

"I'm only twenty-eight."

"The perfect age. Your father married when he was twenty-eight, as did your grandfather. You're out of school, well established. You'll be a prize to whatever lucky woman you choose."

"Aunt Beatrice, I'm not ready to——"

"You will marry within the year," she said, her serious tone like a royal decree he didn't dare contradict. "On your one-year wedding anniversary, as a gift I will give you my shares of ANS stock and name you my sole beneficiary. Then you can truly breathe easy knowing your network is secure, and I can know this family will be cared for when I'm gone."

She couldn't be serious. "You can't force me to marry."

"You're right. You're a grown man and you make your own decisions. So the choice is entirely yours. Either you marry and get the company you want and more money than most people dream of…or you don't and I sell my shares to Ron Wheeler. Tough choice, I understand." At that, she returned to her soup as though they'd been discussing the weather.

Liam didn't know what to say. He wasn't used to anyone else calling the shots in his life. But he'd given himself a vulnerability she had been waiting to exploit. She'd probably planned this from the very moment he'd come to her about buying ANS. Liam leaned his head into his hand and closed his eyes.

"If you don't know any suitable ladies, I can make a few recommendations."

He was sure she'd just love that, too. Thankfully she'd stopped short of deciding who he should marry. "I think I can handle that part, thank you. I've been seeing someone," he said quickly, hoping she didn't ask for more details about the fictional woman.

Aunt Beatrice shrugged off the bitter tone in his voice. "Then it's time the two of you got more serious. Just remember, you have a year from today to marry. But if I were you, I wouldn't dawdle. The sooner you get married, the sooner ANS will be yours."

Francesca had deliberately avoided Liam since they'd returned to D.C., but she couldn't put off speaking to him any longer. She needed to know if they were going to be sponsoring the Youth in Crisis gala or not. It was a week and a half away. It was already too late to pull out, really, but if he was going to insist they couldn't do it, she needed to know now.

She waved as she passed his assistant's desk. "Afternoon, Jessica."

The woman looked up at her with a wary expression. "You don't want to go in there."

Francesca frowned. Did she mean her specifically, or anyone? Liam couldn't still be mad about the whole elevator thing. Could he? "Why?"

"He's been in a foul mood since we left New York. I'm not sure what happened. Something with his family, I think."

"Is everyone okay?"

Jessica nodded her head. "He hasn't had me send flowers to anyone, so I would assume so. But he's not taking calls. He's been sitting at his desk all morning flipping through his address book and muttering to himself."

Interesting. "Well, I hate to do it, but I have to speak with him."

"As you wish." Jessica pressed the intercom button that linked to Liam's phone. "Mr. Crowe, Ms. Orr is here to see you."

"Not now," his voice barked over the line. Then, after a brief pause, he said, "Never mind. Send her in."

Jessica shrugged. "I don't know what that's all about, but go on in."

Francesca gripped the handle to his office door and took a deep breath before going inside. She'd dressed in her most impressive power suit today and felt confident she would leave his office with what she wanted. The emerald-green pantsuit was striking and well-tailored. Her black hair was twisted up into a bun, and she had a silk scarf tied around her neck. Not only did she feel good in the outfit, she felt well-covered. Liam had already seen too much of her body. She intended to keep every inch out of his sight from now on.

As she opened the door, she saw Liam sitting at his desk just as Jessica had described. He was flipping through an address book, making notes on his desk blotter. As she came in he looked up and then slammed the book shut.

"Good morning, Ms. Orr." His voice was a great deal more formal and polite than it was the last time they'd spoken. Of course, then they'd been recently naked together.

"Mr. Crowe. I wanted to speak to you about the Youth in Crisis gala. We don't have much time to—"

"Have a seat, Francesca."

She stopped short, surprised at his interruption. Unsure of what else to do, she moved to take a seat in the guest chair across from his desk. Before she could sit, he leaped up and pointed to the less formal sitting area on the other side of his office.

"Over here, please. I don't like talking to people across the desk. It feels weird."

Francesca corrected her course to sit in the plush gray leather chair he'd indicated. She watched him warily as he went to the small refrigerator built into the cabinets beside his desk.

"Would you like something to drink?"

"I don't drink at work."

Liam turned to her with a frown and a bottle of root beer in his hand. "At all? I have bottled water, root beer—my personal favorite—and some lemon-lime soda. I don't drink at work, either, despite the fact that if anyone wanted to be in a drunken stupor right now, it would be me." He pulled a bottle of water out of the fridge and handed it to her. "To replace the one we... *used up* in the elevator."

Francesca started to reach for the bottle, then froze at the memory of water pouring over his head and onto her own bare chest. Damn, he'd said that on purpose to throw her off her game. Pulling herself together, she took the bottle and set it on the coffee table unopened.

Liam joined her, sitting on the nearby sofa with his bottle of root beer. "I have a proposition for you."

She didn't like the sound of that. "I told you that I wasn't interested in dinner."

Liam watched her intently with his jewel-blue eyes as he sipped his drink. "I'm not asking you to dinner. I'm asking you to marry me."

Francesca was glad she hadn't opted to drink that water or she would've spit it across the room. She sat bolt upright in her seat and glared at him. "Marry you? Are you crazy?"

"Shhh…" he said, placing his drink on the table. "I don't want anyone to hear our discussion. This is very important. And I'm dead serious. I want you to be my fiancée. At least for a few months."

"Why me? What is going on?"

Liam sighed. "I've put myself in a vulnerable position with the company. I couldn't afford all of Graham Boyle's stock, so my aunt owns the largest share of ANS, not me. She's threatening to sell it to Ron Wheeler if I don't get married within a year."

Ron Wheeler. That was a name that could send chunks of ice running through her veins. Charity didn't help the bottom line in his eyes. Francesca, her staff and the entire department would be out the door before the ink was dry on the sale. And they would just be the first, not the last to go if he were in charge. "Why would she do that?"

"She wants me married and settled down. She wants me to be the strong family patriarch when she's gone and doesn't believe my playboy ways are appropriate. I think she's bluffing, really. I'm hoping that if I get engaged, that will be enough to soothe her. In the meantime, I'm going to work with my accountant and financial advisor to see if I can arrange for a line of credit large enough to buy her out. I have no expectation that we'll actually have to get married."

"I should hope not," she snapped. Francesca had some very strong ideas about what a good marriage was made of and blackmail was not the ideal start. "Don't you have anyone else you can ask? You've known me less than a week."

Liam looked over to the book on his desk and shook his head. "I've gone through every woman's name in my address book and there's not a single suitable candidate. All those women would look at this as a romantic opportunity, not a business arrangement. That's why you're my ideal choice."

A business arrangement? That's just what a girl wanted to hear. "So if this is just a business arrangement, that means you have no intention of trying to get me into bed, right?"

Liam leaned closer to her and a wicked grin spread across his face. "I didn't say *that,* but really, that's not my first priority here. I'm asking you for several reasons. First, I like you. Spending time with you shouldn't be a hardship. My aunt will expect the relationship to appear authentic and she'll sniff out the truth if she thinks we're faking it. After our time in the elevator, I think you and I have enough chemistry to make it realistic. And second, I know I can count on you because you want something from me."

Francesca opened her mouth to argue with him and then stopped. She knew exactly where this was going. Tit for tat. "The Youth in Crisis gala?"

He nodded. "If Ron Wheeler gets a hold of this company, everything you've worked for will be destroyed. The only thing I can do to protect this company and its employees is to get engaged as soon as I can. For your assistance, I'm offering the full financial support of ANS for the Youth in Crisis charity ball. I'll even pledge to top the highest private donation with my own money. I look at it as an investment in the future of the network. And all you have to do is wear a beautiful diamond ring and tolerate my company until my aunt backs down."

It felt like a deal with the devil and there had to be a catch. "You said it had to appear authentic. Define *authentic*."

Liam sat back in his seat and crossed his leg over his knee. "No one is going to follow us into the bedroom, Francesca, and I won't make you do anything that you don't want to do. But everything we can do to convince people we are a couple in love would be helpful."

She shook her head and looked down at her lap. This was all so sudden. The idea of being Liam's fiancée, even if just temporarily, wasn't so bad. She'd be lying to herself if she said she hadn't thought about their time in the elevator as she lay alone in bed each night. But his fiancée? Publicly? What would she tell her family? She couldn't tell them the truth. And her friends? She would have to lie to everyone she knew.

But the alternative was unthinkable. She cared too much about ANS and its employees to let the company fall into Ron Wheeler's hands. Going along with Liam's plan would protect the company and earn her the charity gala she wanted so badly. When the arrangement was no longer necessary, her friends and family would just have to believe that things had soured between them and they broke it off. She could live with that. It wasn't as though they were actually going to get married.

She looked up in time to see Liam slide off the couch to his knees and crawl across the floor until he was kneeling at her feet. He looked so handsome in his navy suit, his dark, beautiful blue eyes gazing into her own. He took her hands into his, his thumb gently stroking her skin. With him touching her like that, she'd probably agree to anything.

"Francesca Orr," he said with a bright, charming smile. "I know I'm just the humble son of a pig farmer, but would you do me the honor of being my temporary fiancée?"

Four

Liam watched Francesca's terrified expression, waiting for her answer. He could see the battle raging in her head. He understood. He was having to make sacrifices for the company and what he wanted, too. He felt guilty for dragging her into his mess, but she really was the perfect choice. If she could walk away from that elevator like nothing happened, she could do the same with this engagement. In the end, they could go their separate ways, both having gotten what they wanted.

Her dark brown eyes focused on him for a moment, then strayed off to his shoulder. Her expression of worry softened then, her jaw dropping with surprise.

Confused, Liam turned to look at his shoulder. Perched there on the navy fabric was a lone ladybug. He'd opened the window of his office this morning when he was suffocating from the pressure and needed some fresh air. The tiny insect must've been a stowaway.

Francesca untangled her hands from his and reached out to scoop the ladybug from his shoulder. She got up from her seat and walked over to the window. Opening it wide, she held her palm out to the sun and watched the bug fly out into the garden outside the network offices.

She stood looking out the window for several minutes. Liam was still on his knees, wondering what the hell had just happened, when he heard her speak.

"Yes, I will be your temporary fiancée."

He leaped to his feet and closed the gap between them in three long strides. "Really?"

She turned to him, her face calm and resolute. She looked really beautiful in that moment. Serene. The dark green of her suit looked almost jewel-like against the tan of her skin. It made him want to reach out and remove the pins from her hair until it fell loose around her shoulders. He liked it better that way.

"Yes," she said. "It's the right answer for everyone."

Liam was elated by her response yet confused about what had changed. There had been a moment when he had been absolutely certain she was going to tell him no. He'd already been mentally putting together a contingency plan. He was going to offer her obscene amounts of cash. And if that didn't work, he was going to find out if Jessica, his secretary, was married. "What helped you decide?"

"The ladybug. They're an omen of good luck. Having one land on you means you are a blessed soul. It was a sign that I should accept your proposal."

Liam knew better than to question her superstitions as long as they ruled in his favor. "Well, remind me to thank the next ladybug I come across."

Francesca chuckled. "I think you owe the entomology department at Georgetown a nice check."

"And I will get right on that. After I take my fiancée to lunch and let her pick out her engagement ring."

Her head snapped up to look at him. "So soon?"

"Yes," he insisted. "The sooner my aunt hears about this, the better. That means ring shopping, an announcement in the paper here and in New York and public sightings of the happy new couple. I intend to update my relationship status on Facebook before the day is out."

Her eyes widened with every item on his list. She wasn't sold on this arrangement, ladybug or no. "Before it hits the papers, I need to make a few calls. I don't want my family to find out from someone else. This is going to come out of the blue."

Liam nodded. That was understandable. He had a few calls of his own to make. First, to his mother and younger sister, both living in Manhattan.

His family was miserable at keeping in touch, but this was big enough news to reach out to them. They had always been like ships passing in the night, waving to one another as they went along their merry way. His parents were very outgoing and traveled quite a bit his whole life. But that changed after his father died three years ago when his car hit black ice on the highway coming home from a late business meeting. Since then, his mother had kept to her place in Manhattan, nearly becoming a recluse. He just assumed she was bad about calling until she stopped altogether—then he knew something was really wrong. His sister had moved in with her to keep an eye on the situation, but it hadn't helped much.

When he spoke with them, it was because he was

the one to reach out. Maybe the news of the engagement would be exciting for her. He felt bad lying to his mother about something like that, but if it got her up and out of the apartment, he didn't care.

Liam had often wondered, even more so in the past week, how things would be different if his father hadn't been in that accident. Where would everyone be now? Perhaps Aunt Beatrice would've wanted to hand the family to him instead, and Liam wouldn't be in this mess.

That was a pointless fantasy, but it reminded him of his next call. Once he was done with his mother, he had to inform Aunt Beatrice of the "happy" news. He didn't have many people to tell, but he could see by the expression on Francesca's face that she had the opposite problem. She must have a large, close family. An out-of-the-blue engagement would send up a hue and cry of mass proportions.

"I know this is a big deal. And not at all what you were expecting when you walked in here today. But it's all going to work out." He moved closer to her and put his arms gently around her waist. She reluctantly eased into his embrace, placing her hands on his lapels and looking up into his eyes. "I promise."

The dark eyes watching him were not so certain. He needed to reassure her. To make her feel more at ease with their new situation and prove they were compatible enough to pull this off. He only knew of one way to comfort a woman. He slowly lowered his lips to hers, giving her time to pull away if she needed to. She didn't. She met his lips with her own, her body leaning into his.

The kiss wasn't like the one in the elevator. They had come together then in a passionate and desperate rush. Two people in a stressful situation looking for any way to deal with their nervous tension. This kiss was soft, gentle and reassuring. They were feeling their way around each other. Her lips were silky against his, the taste of her like cinnamon and coffee. She made a soft sound of pleasure that sent a warm heat running through his veins. It reminded him of the cries she'd made beneath him that first day. It beckoned him to explore further, but he didn't dare push this moment too far. At this point, she could change her mind and no one would know the difference.

He couldn't risk running her off. They both needed this fake engagement to work. And if it did, he would eventually have his chance to touch her again. The thought gave him the strength to pull away.

Francesca rocked back onto her heels, her cheeks flushed and her eyes a little misty. She took a deep breath to collect herself and took a full step back from him. "Well," she said with a nervous laugh, "that authenticity thing shouldn't be an issue."

Liam smiled. "Not at all. Are you hungry?"

She straightened her suit coat and shrugged. "A little."

"Okay. You're not starving, so let's go ring shopping first. Then if we run into anyone at lunch, we'll have it and can share the news like a happy couple would."

"I need to get my purse from my office before we leave. I'll meet you at…" Her voice trailed off.

"The elevator?" he said with a grin.

She blushed. "Yes, I'll meet you at the elevator."

They strolled out of Pampillonia Fine Jewelry two hours later and, frankly, Francesca was exhausted. Who knew jewelry shopping could be so tiring? She almost wished that Liam had just popped the question with ring in hand like most men would and saved her the trouble of choosing.

Instead, they had spent the past couple of hours quibbling. She was worried that Liam was spending too much, especially considering it was a fake engagement. Liam insisted that Francesca needed to choose a ring large enough for people to see from a distance. Fake or not, the engagement needed to be splashy so people like his aunt would take notice.

They finally came to a compromise when she got tired of arguing and just let herself choose the ring she'd want if this were a real relationship and she had to wear the ring every day for the rest of her life. By the time they left, she was certain there was no doubt in the jeweler's mind that they were a real couple getting a head start on a lifetime of fussing at one another.

When it was all over, Francesca was the proud owner of a two-carat emerald-cut diamond solitaire framed with micro-pavé set diamonds in a platinum split band with diamond scrollwork. It was a stunning ring, and as they walked to the restaurant where they had lunch reservations, she almost couldn't believe it was on her hand. The weight of it pulling on her finger kept prompting her to lift her hand to look at it.

Francesca had dreamed her whole life of the day a man would give her a ring like this. The ring was right. But everything else was so wrong. Her life had taken a truly surreal turn since she had woken up this morning.

"Are you hungry now?" he asked as they approached the bistro with outdoor seating. It was perfect for an early May lunch; luckily, the Manhattan heat wave had not affected the D.C. area. It was pleasant and sunny in the high seventies with a breeze.

She still wasn't really hungry. Her stomach hadn't come to terms with the day's events. But she needed to eat or her blood sugar would get low and she'd spend the afternoon eating cookies out of the network vending machines. "I could eat. I think."

They followed the hostess, who took them to a shaded table for two on the patio. As nice as it was outside, she'd secretly hoped to get a table indoors. The street was so busy with foot traffic that she was certain to see someone she knew. Of course, she could just as easily run into someone inside. Between her and Liam, they knew a lot of people in this town. Francesca wasn't sure she was ready to play the gushing new fiancée for them yet.

Liam pulled her chair out for her and saw that she was comfortably seated before taking his own seat.

"I'm starving," he said, picking up the menu.

Francesca had to admit she wasn't surprised. Liam seemed to be constantly hungry when she was around him. "No breakfast?"

He shook his head. "I really haven't eaten much since I had dinner at my aunt's house. Killed my appetite, you know?"

"I do," she agreed. Nothing on the menu looked appealing, so she settled on a spinach salad with chicken. At the very least she was eating something figure-friendly.

She had a wedding dress to fit into, after all.

The thought crept into her brain, startling her upright in her seat. Where had that come from?

"Are you okay?" Liam asked.

"Yes," she said dismissively. "I just remembered something I need to do when we get back to the office."

Liam nodded and looked back at the menu. Francesca shook her head and closed her eyes. There would be no wedding and no wedding dress. It didn't matter how real their kisses seemed or how quickly her whole body responded to Liam's touch. It didn't matter that she had a luxury condo's worth of diamonds on her hand. Because she wasn't really engaged. She was Liam's fake fiancée. It was a business arrangement, nothing more, despite what she had to tell her friends and family.

The waiter took their orders and left with their menus. Feeling awkward, Francesca sipped her water and eyeballed her ring. She didn't know what to say to her new fiancé.

"Now that all the engagement stuff is arranged, I wanted to talk to you about something else, too."

She looked up at him with a sense of dread pooling in her stomach. She couldn't take any more surprises today. "No, Liam, I will not have your baby to make your aunt happy."

He laughed, shaking his head. "No babies, I promise. This is strictly work-related. I've been kicking around this idea for a few days, but the nonsense with my aunt sidetracked me. I wanted to ask…you're friends with Ariella Winthrop, aren't you?"

Francesca sighed. Her friend Ariella had been the media equivalent of the Holy Grail since the inaugural ball in January where it was revealed that the successful events planner was the newly elected president's long-lost daughter. How many journalists and garden-variety busybodies had asked Francesca about her friend since the scandal hit? More than she could count. Yes, they were friends. They had been for several years. That didn't mean she had anything useful to share with the press, even if she would tell—and she wouldn't. Ariella was adopted. She hadn't even known who her birth father was for sure until the DNA test results came back a little more than a month ago.

"I am," she said, her tone cautious.

"I was wondering if you could talk to her for me. I've got an idea that I think she might be interested in, but I wanted to run it by you first. I know ANS reporters and old management were responsible for the whole mess with President Morrow and her. I was hoping we could make a sort of goodwill gesture to them both."

"A fruit basket?" she suggested.

"A televised reunion show with Ariella and the president."

Francesca groaned aloud. That was a horrible idea. "Go with the fruit basket. Really."

Liam held up his hand. "Hear me out. I know lots of rumors and misinformation are swirling around on the other networks, especially because everyone involved isn't talking to the press. ANS obviously has stayed out of the story after everything that happened. I want to offer them the opportunity to publically set the record straight. Give them a chance to meet and clear the air without any spin or dramatic angles."

"That has 'exploitive' written all over it."

"And that is why I would give you total control over the show. You're her friend and she trusts you. You could work directly with the White House press secretary and see to it that no one is even remotely uncomfortable. No other network will offer them an opportunity like this, I guarantee it."

Francesca couldn't hold back her frown. She didn't like the sound of this at all. If it went badly and ANS ended up with mud on its face, there would be no coming back from it and Ariella might never forgive her. "I don't know, Liam."

"This is a win-win for everyone involved. Ariella and the president get to tell their story, their way. ANS will get the exclusive on their interview and it will help us make amends for the hacking scandal. It can't go wrong. You'll see to it that it doesn't turn into a circus. It's perfect."

Perfect for ratings. But Francesca wasn't so sure television was the right environment for her friend to be reunited with her famous birth father. That was an important moment for them both. A private moment. Ariella hadn't spoken much to her about the situation, but Francesca knew it was hard for her friend.

"Just promise me you'll ask her. If she doesn't want to do it, I'll let the whole idea drop."

The waiter came with their lunches, placing them on the table and briefly interrupting their conversation.

"I'll talk to her," Francesca agreed after he left. "But I can't promise anything. She made one short statement to the press, but aside from that, she's turned down every interview request she's received."

"That's all I ask. Thank you."

Francesca speared a piece of chicken and spinach with her fork. "At last, the dirty truth comes out. You're just marrying me for my political connections."

"A completely unfounded accusation," he said with a wicked grin. "I'm marrying you for that slammin' body."

Francesca met his gaze, expecting to see the light of humor there, but instead she found a heat of appreciation for what he saw. It was the same way he'd looked at her in that elevator when she'd had only a camisole to cover her. Today, she was deliberately covered head to toe, but it didn't matter. Liam apparently had an excellent memory.

A warmth washed over her, making her squirm uncomfortably in her seat with her own memories of that day. She had wanted him so badly in that moment, and if she was honest with herself, she still did. Things were just so complicated. Would giving into her desire for him be better or worse now that they were "engaged"?

She wished she hadn't opted for the silk scarf around her neck. It was strangling her now. Her left hand flew to her throat and started nervously tugging at the fabric. "I…well, I uh…"

A voice called to them from the sidewalk, interrupting her incoherent response. "Francesca, what is that I see on your hand?"

So much for not running into anyone she knew. On the other side of the wrought-iron railing that separated the bistro seating from the sidewalk was her friend Scarlet Anders. The willowy redhead owned a party planning company with Ariella that specialized in weddings and receptions. She could smell a new diamond from a mile away.

"Scarlet!" she said, pasting a smile on her face and hoping Scarlet didn't see through it. "How are you feeling?" she asked to distract her from the ring. Her friend had suffered a head injury earlier in the year and had temporarily lost her memory. It was a reasonable question that might buy Francesca a few minutes to get their engagement story straight.

Scarlet wrinkled her nose. "I'm fine, really. The doctors say there's not a single, lingering side effect from my accident. Now stop fussing over me, you staller, and let me see that hand."

Reluctantly, Francesca held out her left hand, letting the flawless diamond sparkle in the sunlight. Scarlet looked at the ring, then at Liam and back at her. "You are engaged to Liam Crowe. *Liam Crowe.* You know, when Daniel proposed to me, I told you and Ariella almost the moment it happened."

That was true, Francesca thought guiltily. And under any other circumstances, she would've done the same thing. This just didn't feel like a real engagement. Because it wasn't. "It just happened," she insisted, grinning widely with feigned excitement at her groom to be. "We just picked out the ring before lunch."

Scarlet smiled. "It's beautiful. You two are so sneaky. I didn't even know you guys were dating. How did this happen?"

"We, uh…" Francesca realized she had no clue what to say. They hadn't really gotten around to deciding what they're relationship history was. Certainly the truth wouldn't do, or people would think they were crazy. "Actually, um…"

"We started seeing each other a while back when I first started looking to buy ANS," Liam interjected. "With everything going on, we wanted to keep it quiet for a while. But after being trapped in that elevator with Francesca, I knew I had to spend the rest of my life with her."

Francesca swallowed her snort of contempt as Scarlet sighed with romantic glee. "That is so sweet. I can't believe you didn't tell *me,* of all people, but you two are just adorable together. So when is your engagement party? You have to let Ariella and I do it for you."

"No," Francesca insisted. "You've been so busy with Cara and Max's wedding and now, planning your own big day." The former newscaster and the public relations specialist for the White House press secretary had married at the end of March. Scarlet's beau, Daniel, had proposed to her at the wedding reception. "Don't worry about us. We're probably not going to—"

"Nonsense," Scarlet said. "I insist. I'm on my way back to the office right now. I'll tell Ariella the good news and we'll get right to work on it. When would you like to have it?"

"Soon," Liam interjected, cutting off another of Francesca's protests. "This weekend, if at all possible. We can't wait to share our excitement with all our friends and family."

Scarlet's eyes widened, but she quickly recovered with a pert nod. She was used to dealing with the unreasonable demands of powerful D.C. couples. "I'm sure we can make that happen. Short notice makes it harder to find a venue, but I've got a couple of people who owe me some favors. For you, I'm thinking an afternoon garden party. Something outdoors. Light nibbles, champagne punch. Maybe a gelato bar. How does that sound?"

Francesca choked down a sip of her water. "That sounds beautiful." And it did. It was just what she would've chosen for her engagement party. Her friend knew her well. She just wished they weren't wasting their efforts on an engagement that wouldn't lead to a loving marriage.

Scarlet was bursting with excitement. Francesca could see the lists being made in her head. Flowers, caterers, maybe even a string quartet to serenade the guests. Scarlet did everything with a stylish flair that was famous in elite D.C. society. "I will give you a call tomorrow and work out some details."

"Just tell me where to send the check." Liam smiled.

"Absolutely," Scarlet said. "Talk to you soon." She swung her bag over her shoulder and disappeared down the sidewalk with an excited pep in her step. She really did live for this stuff.

Francesca wished she could work up as much enthusiasm. And she needed to if they were going to pull this off. Because this was really happening. Really, *really* happening.

What on earth had she done?

Five

Liam hadn't planned on their having dinner that night, but seeing Francesca with Scarlet had made it absolutely necessary. They really knew nothing about each other. They had no relationship backstory. Once the news of their engagement got out, people would start asking questions and they needed to get their stories straight.

Usually this kind of discussion happened before the engagement, but they were working on a steep learning curve, here. After the waiter took their orders, Liam settled back into his seat and looked at his fiancée. He knew she was beautiful, feisty, caring and exciting. He knew that he desired her more than any other woman he'd ever known. And yet, he knew almost nothing about who she was and where she'd come from. That was a problem.

"So, Francesca, tell me all about yourself. I need to know everything to play this part properly and convince everyone we're really together."

"I feel like I'm trying to get a green card or something." She took a sip of wine as she tried to determine where best to start. "I grew up in Beverly Hills. My father is a Hollywood movie producer, as you know. He met my mother on a film set in Sicily and they eloped within a month of meeting."

"So they have no room to complain about our quick engagement?"

"Not at all." She smiled. "Although that didn't stop my father from giving me an earful on the phone this afternoon. I had to assure him that we would have an extended engagement to keep him from hopping a jet over here and having a chat with you."

"The longest engagement in history," Liam quipped.

"My parents are my model for what a marriage should be. It's what I've always hoped to have one day when I get married."

Liam took note. Francesca wanted the real deal for herself, just like her parents. This was probably not what she thought her engagement would be like. He felt bad about that. But she still had her chance to have the fairy tale with the next guy. This was just a temporary arrangement.

"I have a younger sister, Therése," she continued, "who lives in San Francisco. She's a fashion photographer. I moved to D.C. after graduation to go to Georgetown."

"I went to Georgetown, too. Maybe we were there at the same time." Francesca recited the years and, thankfully, they partially overlapped with his own. He'd graduated two years before she had. "That's excellent," he said. "I think if we tell people that we dated back in college and then met up again this year, it will make the speed of this relationship more palatable. What did you study?"

"I got a degree in communications with a minor in political science. I'd originally intended to become a political news commentator."

"It's a shame you didn't. I would've loved to have you on my big screen every night. It's funny we didn't meet until now. I had a minor in communications. I'm surprised we didn't have a class together."

Francesca shrugged. "Maybe we did. A lot of those classes were pretty large."

Liam shook his head. There was no way he could've been in the same room with Francesca and not have seen her. Even in one of those freshman courses they held in the huge auditoriums. His cocky, frat boy self would've picked up on those curves and asked her out in a heartbeat. "I would've noticed you. I'm certain of that."

Francesca blushed and started fidgeting with the gold pendant around her neck that looked like some kind of horn. For dinner, she'd changed into a burgundy wrap dress with a low V-cut neckline and an abundance of cleavage. He'd noticed the necklace earlier, but every time he thought to ask about it, he'd been mentally sidetracked by the sight of her breasts.

"So what's that necklace about? You seem to have it on whenever I've seen you."

She looked down at it before holding it out a little for him to see it better. "It's a *corno portafortuna*. My *nonna* gave it to me. It's Italian tradition to wear one to ward off the evil eye. You never know when someone might curse you, especially in this town. I wear it for good luck."

The way the horn rested right in the valley of her

breasts was certainly lucky for him. It gave him an excuse to look at the firm globes of flesh he could still feel in his hands and pretend he was admiring her jewelry. "In the elevator you mentioned spending summers in Italy with your grandmother."

"Yes, I spent every summer in Sicily from when I was about five until I graduated from high school. My mother would travel with me when I was younger, but once I reached junior high, I got to fly alone. My mother said it was important for me to keep in touch with my culture. My *nonna* would teach me authentic Italian recipes and tell me stories about our family. My sister and I both learned a good bit of Italian over the years. I don't remember as much as I should now."

"You know all the dirty words," Liam noted.

"Of course." She laughed. "You always remember the words and phrases that you shouldn't know."

"You picked up all your superstitions there too?"

"Yes. Italians are a very superstitious people. My *nonna* told me she only taught me a few of them. It's amazing. My mother never really cared for all that, but it was something special I shared with *Nonna*. She died last year, but the superstitions keep her alive in my mind."

"Thank goodness she told you the one about ladybugs or I might be in big trouble right now. Any bad luck omens I should keep an eye out for?"

"Hmm…" Francesca said thoughtfully. "There are the ones most people know about—broken mirrors and such. Never leave your hat on the bed. Never set a loaf of bread upside down on the table. Birds or feathers in the home are bad luck. If you spill salt, you have to toss some over your shoulder. The most unlucky number is seventeen. Never marry on a Friday. There are a million of these."

"Wow," Liam said. "I'm probably doomed. I've been running around for years, cursed, and never knew it."

Francesca smiled, easing back in her seat to let the waiter place their food on the table. "I think you've done pretty well for yourself without it."

That was true. He'd taken the seed money from his father and built quite a name for himself in broadcast media. He was only twenty-eight. Who knew what else he could accomplish with most of his career still ahead of him? Closing the deal with his aunt and taking full control of ANS could be the launching pad to bigger, better things. Especially if the two-billion-dollar inheritance came through.

His brain couldn't even comprehend having that much money. He tried not to even think about it. He could only focus on one thing at a time and right now, it was pulling off this engagement and buying ANS outright. He'd put his financial manager on the task before he even sat down to look for a bride. Hopefully, it would all work out. But even his worries were hard to concentrate on with such a beautiful woman sitting across the table from him.

"How about some more random trivia about you? Likes and dislikes," Liam said.

"My favorite color is red. I adore dark chocolate. I'm allergic to cats. I can cook, but I don't. I hate carrots and yellow squash. My middle name is Irish and impossible to spell or pronounce properly."

Liam had to ask. "Wait, what is it?"

"My middle name? It's pronounced *kwee-vuh,* which is Gaelic for *beautiful.* Unfortunately, in English it's pronounced absolutely nothing like it's written. *C-A-O-I-M-H-E*." She spelled out the name for him and then said it again. "Try explaining that to the woman at the DMV."

Liam laughed, not trusting himself to repeat the name without slaughtering it. "My middle name is Douglas. Not very exciting or hard to spell."

"I envy you."

"What about your dad's side of the family? You haven't mentioned much about them."

"My dad isn't that close with his family, which is silly considering they live in Malibu, only about thirty miles from Beverly Hills. I only ever saw my grandparents on holidays and birthdays. I'm much closer with my mother's side of the family."

"Sounds more like my family. I almost never see them. Tell me something else about you."

"What else? I never exercise—I hate to sweat. And I enjoy luxurious bubble baths and long walks on the beach." She finished with a laugh. "This is turning into a lame personal ad."

"It's not lame. If I ran across it, I'd be messaging your in-box in an instant."

"Thanks. But enough about me. What about you?" Francesca asked. "Your turn to tell me all about Liam Crowe."

Dinner had been very nice. The conversation flowed easily and Francesca had to admit she had a good time. She enjoyed spending time with Liam. Honestly, she liked him. He was handsome, smart, funny and easy to talk to. It was nice to hear him talk about his family and his work. He was so passionate about his career; it made her understand just how important the success of ANS was to him. A part of her wished she had met him in college. Who knows what would've happened then?

Well, that wasn't true. She knew what would've happened. They would've dated, she would've fallen for him and he would've broken it off at some point, breaking her heart. Liam wasn't much of a long-term guy. They were only engaged now because his aunt had recognized that in him and twisted his arm.

Despite that, he seemed to be taking the whole thing pretty well. She wasn't exactly sure how Liam felt about their forced proximity, but he didn't let it show if he wanted to be someplace else. Actually, he'd been quite complimentary of her, listening to her when she spoke and watching her over his wineglass with appreciative eyes.

Liam pulled up his gray Lexus convertible outside her town house and killed the engine. He turned in his seat to face her, a shy smile curling his lips. He watched her collect her purse and sweater, not speaking but also not making a move to let her out of the car, either.

Their plotting dinner suddenly felt like a date and it made her a little nervous. It was silly considering he'd not only seen her naked, but they were engaged. Technically.

"I had a good time tonight," she said, feeling stupid the moment the words left her lips.

"Me, too. I, uh, wanted to say thank-you again for doing this for me. And, you know, for the company. I feel like I've hijacked your entire life today."

Francesca tried to think about what she was supposed to have done today. She certainly had plans of some kind, but Liam had wiped her memory clean along with her calendar. "I'm sure I didn't have anything important planned and if I did, it will still be around for me to do tomorrow."

"Do you have time on your schedule to have some engagement portraits taken? I wanted a picture to put with the newspaper announcement."

"I think so. Just have Jessica look at my calendar in the morning. Do I need to wear anything in particular or do something special with my hair or makeup?"

Liam watched her, shaking his head. "You're perfect just as you are. I couldn't ask for a more beautiful fiancée."

Francesca blushed. She couldn't help it. To hear him talk, she was the most beautiful woman in the world. It was ridiculous. She was a pretty enough woman but nothing special. He had a knack for making her feel special, though. "You're just sucking up so I don't change my mind."

"Absolutely," he admitted. "But it's easy when it's true. You don't know how much I've thought about you since that afternoon we spent together. And now, spending all day with you, I've been struggling with myself. I've spent the past three hours trying not to kiss you. I'm not sure I can hold out much longer."

Francesca couldn't help the soft gasp of surprise when he spoke so honestly about his desire for her. Before she could think of something intelligent to say, he leaned across her seat and brought his lips to hers.

It wasn't their first kiss. Or even their second, but somehow it felt like it. It lacked the raw heat of their time in the elevator and the reassuring comfort of this morning's kiss. This one felt like the kiss of a blossoming romance. His hand went to the nape of her neck, pulling her closer to him and gently massaging her with his fingertips.

His mouth was demanding but not greedy, coaxing her to open to him and give in to the pleasure he promised. She felt herself being swept up in his touch. It was so easy, just like letting herself flow with the current of a river. It felt natural to let her tongue glide along his, to let her fingers roam through the thick strands of his wavy hair.

His lips left hers, traveling along the line of her jaw to nibble the side of her neck. The sensation of it sent a wave of desire through her whole body. When his hand cupped her breast through the thin microfiber of her dress, she leaned into his touch, moaning softly in his ear.

It wasn't until her eyes peeked open and she saw the giant diamond on her hand that she came to her senses. This relationship was supposed to be for show. One that appeared authentic to friends and family. But as Liam had said, no one would follow them into the bedroom. Somehow, Francesca knew that if she crossed that line, it would be hard for her to keep this relationship in perspective.

Liam was her fiancé, but he would never be her husband. He wasn't in love with her, nor was she in love with him. Sex would just blur the lines.

Francesca gently pushed at Liam's shoulders. He pulled away, watching her with eyes hooded with desire. His breath was ragged. That was one hell of a kiss. And it was begging for one hell of a night together. She could tell that he intended to come inside. A nice dinner, a bottle of wine, good conversation, a dynamic kiss... now she was supposed to invite him in for coffee and take off her dress. That was all too much too soon, no matter how badly she might want him.

Francesca reached for the door handle. "Good night, Liam."

"Wait," he said with a frown as he reached out to her. "Good night?"

She nodded, clutching her purse to her chest as a sub-par barrier between them. "It's been a long day filled with a lot of excitement. You went from my boss to my fiancé just a few short hours ago. I think adding 'lover' to the list tonight is a bad idea."

Liam sighed but didn't try to argue with her. Instead, he opened his car door and came around to help her out. He escorted her to her doorstep.

Francesca paused, clutching her keys in her hand. Right or wrong, she couldn't help leaning into him and placing a quick but firm kiss on his lips.

"I'll see you tomorrow at the office."

"Yes, I'm engaged." Liam sat back in his office chair and looked at the newly framed photograph of Francesca and himself that sat on the corner of his desk. They'd had it taken for the newspaper announcement, and Liam couldn't help sending a copy to the Queen Bee herself. When the phone rang the next afternoon, he wasn't surprised.

"Congratulations to you both. I didn't expect you to move so quickly on my offer," she noted, her tone pointed. She obviously thought that Liam was trying to pull one over on her somehow. She missed nothing. "I did give you a year, not a week, to get engaged."

"Well," Liam began, "I told you I had been seeing someone. You helped me realize that I needed to move forward in my relationship. Francesca and I are perfect for each other—I was just hesitant to take that last step. Thank you for the encouragement." He hoped he'd managed to work out the bitterness from his voice after practicing this speech several times before her call.

"That is wonderful, Liam. The picture of the two of you is lovely. I've sent Henry to have it framed for the mantle. She's quite the striking young lady. Where did you meet her?"

She was fishing for details. Thank goodness they'd worked all this out at dinner. "We met the first time in college through mutual friends and dated for a while." He recalled their fabricated past, linking it together with what he'd told Scarlet at lunch. "When I started looking into buying ANS, we ran into each other at a media event. She works there doing community outreach programs and we started seeing each other again."

Liam had no doubt that his aunt was taking notes and would have someone look into the fact that they had both attended Georgetown at the same time. "What a lovely coincidence that you two would find each other again. It must be meant to be."

"I think so."

"I hope both of you will be very happy together. I can't wait to meet her. In fact, I'm coming to D.C. later this month to speak to Congress. I'd love for the three of us to have dinner and celebrate while I'm there."

Liam frowned at the phone, glad for the miles between them and the lagging technology of camera phones that prevented her from seeing his pinched expression. He'd never known his aunt to have any political involvement before beyond writing checks. If she was coming to D.C., it was to check on him. She didn't trust

Liam a bit and rightfully so. They would have to perfect their lovey-dovey act before she arrived. Frankly, Francesca had been miserable at it when they ran into Scarlet.

It wasn't just the details of their relationship that had tripped her up. Her smile of engaged bliss had looked a little pained. She'd lacked the excited glow. She had had to be asked to show the engagement ring, whereas any other woman would thrust it out at anyone that would look.

Despite her hesitation to embark on a physical relationship the other night after dinner, something had to be done. She needed some real romantic inspiration to draw on because she couldn't fake it. Liam was all too happy to provide it.

He may have told Francesca that he didn't choose her with the intention of seducing her, and that was true. If they did become lovers, it would simply be a pleasant bonus to a potentially unpleasant scenario.

Heaven knew, he wanted Francesca. Every time he closed his eyes he saw her in the elevator. Red panties. Flushed cheeks. Soft, passionate cries of pleasure echoing in the small space. Yes, he didn't need a romantic entanglement complicating this arrangement, but he'd be lying if he said he didn't want to pick up where they'd left off.

Sex wouldn't be a problem as long as they both knew that's all it was. Given the way Francesca had writhed beneath him and walked away like nothing happened, she knew how to play that game. He just had to coax her into taking another spin at the wheel.

Gripping the phone, Liam struggled to remember what his aunt had just said. The mere thought of Francesca's red panties had completely derailed his train of thought. *Dinner.* Aunt Beatrice was coming to town and wanted to have dinner. "Absolutely," he said. "Francesca is very excited to meet you."

"I'm sure she is. I hope you two have a lovely engagement party tonight. I'm going to let you go. I need to call Ron Wheeler and let him know I'm turning down his proposal. For now," she added, making it clear they weren't out of the woods quite yet.

"It was good to speak with you," he said between gritted teeth. "I'll see you soon."

Hanging up the phone, he spun in his chair to look back at the photo of Francesca and him. His aunt made him absolutely crazy, but if this scheme landed that voluptuous, feminine form back in his arms, he just might have to send the Queen Bee a thank-you card.

Six

Francesca was fastening on her last earring when the doorbell rang. Giving herself one final look in the mirror, she was pretty pleased with how her outfit turned out. She'd purchased something new for the engagement party—a pale turquoise dress that was strapless and hit just below the knee. Around the waist was a cream-colored sash with a fuchsia flower for a pop of color. It came with a crocheted cream shrug to keep her shoulders warm when the sun went down.

She'd opted to wear her hair half up, with the front pulled back into a stylish bump and the rest loose in long waves down her back. Wearing her hair back highlighted her face and the sparkling aquamarine jewelry she was wearing at her ears and throat. And, of course, she was wearing the most important piece of her ensemble—her engagement ring.

Satisfied, she went down the stairs to the front door.

She watched Liam waiting patiently through the peep-hole. He was looking very handsome in a light gray suit, ivory dress shirt and turquoise tie to coordinate with her outfit.

Even though he'd dropped her off the other night after dinner, he hadn't been inside her town house yet. They'd decided he should pick her up and get familiar with her home just in case someone asked questions.

So far, no one had, and it was likely no one would. None of their friends in D.C. were remotely suspicious about their quick engagement. Romance seemed to be in the air this spring. So many of her friends had gotten married or engaged, so they were on trend. It was only Liam's crafty aunt they had to please.

"Hello," she said as she opened the door and gestured for him to come inside. "Come on in. This is my place."

"Very nice," he said, strolling into the living room and admiring his surroundings.

Francesca had always liked her home. She'd bought the small, red-brick town house near the university while she was a student. It was only two bedrooms, but the floor plan was open and the walled courtyard off the living room was the perfect oasis from the world. When she'd first bought it, nearly every room in it was white. She'd painted each room a warm, inviting color and filled them with lush fabrics and comfortable fixtures. That was her biggest update over the years. She loved her place.

She led him into the two-story living room so he could see out into her little garden and to the nicely remodeled kitchen she rarely used. "It's not very big, but it suits me. I love the location—right across from the park."

"You've done a lot with the place," he said. "It looks comfortably lived in. Very much what I'd expect for you. My town house still looks like a showroom model. I never got around to hiring a decorator. Who did yours?"

"I did," Francesca said, her nose wrinkling. "I couldn't let someone else decorate my house. That's too personal."

Liam shrugged. "You've got the eye for it. Maybe while we're engaged, I'll let you decorate mine."

She turned away from him without answering and went in search of her clutch instead. She didn't like the sound of that at all. It wasn't as though she would be moving into his house one day. She didn't need to put her own personal stamp on his space or leave anything behind of her once all this was over. That made things seem more permanent than they were. But she wasn't going to make much of it. They had a long night to get through without her adding more worries to the pile.

"Are you ready?" she asked.

"Absolutely."

Liam followed her out and then escorted her to the curb, where his convertible was waiting for them. Once he merged into traffic, they didn't have far to go. Scarlet and Ariella had secured a location at one of the large historical mansions in Georgetown. The two-hundred-year-old estate had acres of gardens with fountains and an overabundance of spring flowers this time of year. It was the perfect location for a sunny, happy engagement party.

As they pulled onto the property, the valet opened the doors, pointed them to the garden entrance and took the car around back to park it with the others.

Standing on the lawn, facing her engagement celebration, Francesca was more nervous than she cared to admit. Her knees were nearly shaking. She'd done okay enduring the excited hugs and fielding questions from her friends and coworkers, one by one. But this was almost everyone she knew at one time. It made her wonder if she could pull this off. An engagement party. *Her* engagement party.

Liam sensed her hesitation and approached her. Putting his hands on the back of her upper arms, he stroked her gently, reassuringly. "Everything will be fine. You look beautiful. I'm sure Scarlet and Ariella did a great job with all the arrangements. There's no need to be nervous."

"I know," she said with a shake of her head. She looked down toward the grass, but Liam's finger caught her chin and turned her face up to him.

"You can do this. I know it. But I have to say you are missing something."

Her eyes widened in panic. What had she forgotten? Ring? Check. Lipstick? Check. Overwhelming sense of paranoia? Check. "What did I forget?"

"You don't have the rosy blush of a young woman in love. But I do believe I can fix that." Liam leaned in and pressed his lips to hers.

As much as she had tried to deny her attraction to Liam, her body always gave her away. The heat of his touch immediately moved through her veins and she could feel the tingling of the kiss from the top of her head to the tips of her toes. She suddenly felt flush under her dainty sweater. Her knees were still shaking, although for different reasons than before. She gripped at his lapels to keep steady and pull him closer to her.

Liam's kisses were dangerous. She should've learned

that the very first day. A girl could get lost in one if she wasn't careful. And right now, it seemed like the perfect escape from everything else. Couldn't they just stay in each other's arms here on the front lawn? That seemed like the kind of thing a new couple might do, right?

When Liam finally pulled away, he held her close to keep her from swaying. She felt a definite heat in her cheeks as she looked up at him. "No lipstick on you this time," she noted.

"I was being more cautious today. But it worked— you officially have the bridal glow. Let's get in there before it wears off."

He looped her arm through his and escorted her down the stone pathway that led into the garden reception.

At first the party was a blur. There were easily a hundred and fifty people there, which was impressive on such short notice. Someone announced their arrival, and a rush of people came over to hug and congratulate them. There were pictures and toasts to the happy new couple. Francesca worried it would be hard to keep up the act, but after a little practice and a little champagne, showing people her ring and gushing about how beautiful the party was became easier and easier.

It wasn't long before Francesca was able to slip away from Liam and the crowds to get herself a drink and admire her friends' party-planning handiwork. Scarlet and Ariella really did an excellent job. The garden itself was beautiful, but she could spot the touches they'd added, like white paper lanterns in the trees and a gauzy fabric and flower arch behind the string quartet. The layout of the food and seating areas generated the perfect traffic pattern through the space. It was those details that made what her friends did special. Hassle-free events were their forte.

She picked up a glass and filled it at the four-foot-high silver punch fountain. Just as the lifted the frothy pink drink to her lips, she heard a woman's voice from behind her.

"That's got champagne in it, you know."

Francesca turned to find Ariella with a silver tray of pastel petit fours in her hands. "Am I not allowed to have champagne at my own engagement party?"

Her friend smiled and passed the tray off to one of the catering staff. "That depends on why you and Liam Crowe are in such a rush to get married."

"I am not pregnant," Francesca said with a pout. She should've known that rumor would be one of the first to start circulating. They liked nothing better than juicy gossip in these circles and they weren't above making some up if it was in short supply. She swallowed the whole glass of punch just to prove the rumor wrong.

"Good." Ariella refilled Francesca's glass and filled one of her own, then gestured over to a few chairs under a wisteria tree dripping with purple flowers. "So, just between you and me, what's going on?" she asked once they were seated.

Francesca knew her friend would grill her, although not in the same way that Aunt Beatrice probably would. She just wanted the details so she could understand and be happy for her. Or concerned, depending on if she thought she was being stupid or hasty. That's what good girlfriends did. They kept your head on straight. "It all happened so quickly, I can hardly tell you. The moment I saw him, it was like the last few years we've been apart never happened. There were fireworks." That wasn't exactly a lie. It was more like armed missiles, but there were explosions nonetheless.

Ariella looked into her eyes, searching her face for a moment. Then, satisfied, she smiled and patted Francesca on the knee. "Then I'm happy for you. I just wish you had told us what was going on."

Francesca wished she could really tell her what was going on. She could use a sounding board, but Liam had been adamant that no one know about their arrangement. No one. That was tough for her, considering how close she was with her friends and family.

"Everyone has been so busy with their own lives. I just decided to keep things quiet until there was something to tell."

"How'd your dad take the news?" Ariella asked.

"Ah." She sighed, "you know Dad. He'll adjust eventually. He's concerned that we're rushing things, and that he had no idea who my groom even was. I had to remind him that he and my mother met and eloped within a month. He didn't want to hear that."

Ariella smiled. "I imagine not."

Hoping to shift the subject, Francesca decided to use the topic of fathers to fulfill her first obligation to Liam. "Can I talk to you about something?"

"Sure," Ariella said. "Anything."

Francesca nodded. "Okay. Now I want you to tell me 'no' the moment you're uncomfortable with the idea, but I told Liam I would ask. Now is as good a time as any."

"He wants an interview?" she said wearily. Francesca could tell the last few months were really wearing on her friend.

"Not exactly. He wants to offer you and President Morrow the opportunity to meet and get your story out there. A televised reunion show. No spin, no intruding interview questions. Just you and your father, however you want to do it. Liam has even said he'd put me in charge of the show to make sure you'd be comfortable with it. I told him that I thought it was—"

"Okay."

Francesca's head shot up and she stared at Ariella. Surely she'd heard that wrong. "What?"

She shrugged. "I said okay. If the president is okay with doing the show, I think it's a great idea. We've gone too long without saying anything publicly, and I think it's starting to hurt both of us in the court of public opinion. Neither of us has done anything wrong, but the silence makes us look like we have something to hide."

"But do you think television is the right place for you to be reunited with your birth father? Won't that be hard for you?"

"Not any harder than anything else that's happened this year. Frankly, I'd be relieved to clear the air so the news networks can find some other story to sniff out. Tell Liam I'm in."

Francesca took another large sip of her champagne punch and sighed. Everyone had lost their minds—she was certain of it. "Okay, great," she said, feigning enthusiasm. "I'll let Liam know."

Liam had to admit that it was an excellent engagement party. One of the better ones he'd been forced to attend over the years. He was exhausted and well-fed, as he should be. If and when he did get married, he intended to keep D.C. Affairs Event Planners in his address book.

It was dusk now. The party was winding down, with

guests making their way out amid glowing paper lanterns and white twinkle lights.

He'd lost track of Francesca a little while earlier as he started talking politics with a few other men. Now, he picked up his champagne glass and went in search of his elusive fiancée. That sounded so odd to say, even just in his head.

He found her sitting alone at a table near one of the cherub fountains.

"Hey, there," he said as he approached. "Thought you'd run off on me."

Francesca smiled wearily and slipped off one of her heels. "I'm not running anywhere right now."

"Are you ready to go?"

"Yes. I think the party is over. And was successful, I might add. I got several people to agree to buying tickets to the Youth in Crisis gala next week."

"You're not supposed to recruit at our engagement party."

She shrugged. "Why not? It's what I do, just like you talk politics all the time with folks." She slipped her shoe back on and stood gingerly. *"Ahi, i miei piedi."*

Liam watched her hobble a few steps and decided the walk to the car would be too far for her. "Stop," he insisted, coming alongside her and sweeping her up into his arms.

"Oh!" she hollered in surprise, causing a few people left at the party to turn and look their way. They immediately smiled at his romantic gesture and waved good-night to them.

Francesca clung to his neck, but not with a death grip. "You didn't have to do this," she said as he walked the path to the front of the house.

"I don't have to do a lot of things, but I do them because I want to. Gray Lexus convertible," he said to the valet, who immediately disappeared to the car lot.

"I think I can manage from here."

"What if I'm doing this for selfish reasons? What if I just like holding you this way?" he asked. And he did. He liked the way she clung to him. The way her rose perfume tickled his nose and reminded him of their time together in the elevator. His body tightened in response to the press of her breasts against his chest and the silk of her bare legs in his arms. He didn't want to put her down until he could lay her on a plush mattress and make love to her the way he'd wanted to for days.

Francesca's only response was a sharp intake of breath as she turned to look into his eyes. She watched his face with intensity, reading his body's reactions through his expression. He saw an acknowledgment in her eyes—something that told him she was feeling the same way. She opened her mouth to say something when the car pulled up beside them.

Liam wanted to know what she was about to say, but instead, she turned away and struggled in his arms. He reluctantly set her down in the grass and went around to his side of the car and got in. The moment had passed and whatever she had to say was left unspoken.

It wasn't until the car pulled up outside her town house that they spoke again. And when they did, it was all at once in a jumble of words.

"Would you like to come in?"

"I had a great time today."

"So did I."

"Yes."

Francesca smiled at the way they'd talked over each

other. "Now that we have that all cleared up, come in and I'll make us some coffee."

Liam was thrilled to get an invitation inside tonight. He got out and opened her door, following her up the brick stairs to her entranceway. He laid a gentle hand at the small of her back as she unlocked the dead bolt and he felt her shiver beneath it, despite the warm evening. She couldn't help responding to his touch, he noted. If he had anything to say about it, they wouldn't worry too much about coffee until the morning.

They went inside and he followed her to the kitchen, where she dropped her purse on the counter and slipped out of her heels. "So much better," she said with a smile. "Now, coffee." Francesca turned to the cabinets and started pulling out what she needed to brew a pot.

While she scooped beans into the machine, Liam slipped off his coat, draped it on one of the bar stools and came up behind her. He wrapped his arms around her waist and pressed the full length of his body against her. He swept her hair over one shoulder and placed a warm kiss on the bare skin of her neck.

The metallic coffee scoop dropped to the counter with a clank as Francesca reached out to brace herself with both hands. "You don't want coffee?" she asked, her voice breathy as his mouth continued to move across her skin. She pressed into him, molding her body against his.

Liam slipped her sweater down her shoulders. "Coffee would keep me awake. I think I'd like to go to bed." He pushed the firm heat of his arousal against her back and let his hands roam over the soft fabric of her dress. "What about you?" he asked. He knew Francesca had been in a war between her body and her mind since they met. She'd practically run from him the other night, yet when he kissed her, he could tell she wanted more.

But tonight, this step had to be her decision. Playing the happy couple would be much easier the next few weeks if he wasn't battling an erection whenever they were together. Sex wasn't required in their arrangement, but damn, being engaged was a really great excuse to indulge.

"No," she said.

Her words caused Liam's hands to freeze in place. *Had she just said no?* Damn. He must've been reading her wrong. Did she really only invite him in for coffee? Maybe she was a better actress than he thought.

Before he could pull away, Francesca turned in his arms to face him and wrapped her arms around his neck. She looked up at him with her large dark eyes, a sly smirk curling her pink lips. "I don't want to go to bed," she explained. "I want you right here."

Liam was all too happy to grant her wish. With a slide of his arm, he knocked her bag to the floor and cleared the countertop bar. He encircled her waist with his hands and lifted her up to sit at the rounded edge of the granite slab. His hands slid up the smooth length of her legs, pushing the hem of her turquoise dress high enough to spread her thighs and allow him to settle between them.

"How's this?" he asked, gripping her rear end and tugging her tight to him.

Francesca smiled and wrapped her legs around his waist. *"Perfetto."*

She leaned in to kiss him, and the floodgates opened. The moment their lips met, everything they'd held back for the past week came rushing forward. Their hands moved frantically over each other, pulling at zippers and buttons until they uncovered skin. Their tongues glided along one another, tasting, tempting and drinking it all in.

Liam couldn't get enough of her. The feel of her skin, the soft groans against his mouth as he touched her. He tried to be gentle as he unzipped her dress and pushed the hem up to her waist, but his patience was coming to its end. Especially when Francesca pulled the dress up over her head and he caught a glimpse of the hot pink lace panties and strapless bra she was wearing.

He took a step back to appreciate the view of her body and give himself a moment to recover. As badly as he wanted her, he wasn't going to rush this. Francesca delicately arched her back, reaching behind her to unfasten the bra and toss it aside. The sight of her full, round breasts was his undoing. His palms ached to cover them.

"Touch me," Francesca whispered, noting his hesitation. "I want you to."

"Are you sure? The other night…"

"That was then. Now I'm ready and I don't want to wait any longer."

He was ready too, but first things first. With his eyes focused on hers, he slipped off his unknotted tie and shrugged out of his shirt. The belt, pants and everything else followed until the only stitch of clothing on the two of them were those pink panties. Stepping back between her thighs, he put a condom on the counter and let his hands glide up her outer thighs to her lace-covered hip. "Are these your favorite pair?" he asked.

Francesca shook her head. He was glad. He was at the point of not caring if they were. He'd order ten pair to replace them tomorrow. His fingers grasped the fabric and gave it a hard tug. There was a loud rip, and the panties gave way as scraps in his hands.

At last. Her beautiful nude body was on full display in front of him. This time there was no power restoration to interrupt them, no reason for them to hold back.

Liam placed one forearm across the small of her back and used the other to press down on her chest until she was lying across the breakfast bar. He leaned over her and his lips joined both hands as they made their way over her breasts and down her stomach. His mouth left a searing trail down her belly, pausing at her hip bone as one hand sought out the moist heat between her thighs.

Francesca gasped and squirmed against him. Her back arched off the counter, her hands clawing futilely at the cold stone beneath her. She was ready for him, and as much as he wanted to take his time, he had to have her now. They had all night to savor one another.

Slipping on the condom, Liam gripped her hips and entered her in one, quick movement. Sinking into her hot, welcoming body was a pleasure he'd rarely experienced before. A bolt of sensation, like lightning, shot down his spine and exploded down his arms and legs, making his fingertips tingle where he touched her. He gritted his teeth, balancing on the edge of control as he eased out, then buried deep inside her again.

Francesca pushed herself up, wrapping her legs around his waist and her arms around his neck. Pressing her bare breasts against his chest, she whispered, "Take me," into his ear, flicking the lobe with her tongue.

Gripping at her back and pulling her so close to the edge she might fall without his hold, he did as he was told. He filled her again and again, losing himself in her until she cried out with pleasure and his legs began to shake. It was only then that he let go. Moving quickly, he gave in to the sensation of her body wrapped around his own and flowed into her with a deep growl of long-awaited satisfaction.

Seven

Francesca rolled over and snuggled into her blanket, opening her eyes only when a weight kept the covers from moving the way she wanted. The sunlight was streaming in through her bedroom window, illuminating the wide, bare back of Liam beside her.

What had she done?

She'd had a night of fantastic, passionate sex with her fake fiancé—that's what she'd done. Giving up on the blanket, she moved slowly onto her back, hoping not to wake him. She wasn't quite ready to face the morning after with the man she wasn't going to marry.

She glanced under the sheet at her nude body and cursed that she didn't think to slip into *something* once it was over. Bringing her hand up to her head, she swallowed a groan. This situation was complicated enough. Feigning an engagement wasn't for the faint of heart. Had she really added sex to the mix? On her kitchen counter, of all places? It was a good thing she didn't cook.

Now things were going to go from complicated to downright tricky. Liam was her boss. Her pretend fiancé. She had no business sleeping with either, much less both. And yet she was undeniably attracted to him. She couldn't help it.

He was handsome, wealthy, powerful…. He had a wicked sense of humor and a boyish smile that made her heart melt a little when he looked at her. And most important, he cared about his employees. They'd gotten off on the wrong foot over the budget, but that issue aside, she respected him for what he was doing. She respected him even more for the lengths he was willing to go to protect the network.

Liam was just the kind of man she could fall for—and hard. The only problem was that he wasn't the kind of man that would feel the same about her.

Francesca took relationships seriously. She wasn't one for flings, despite losing her sense in the elevator, and she certainly didn't make a habit of sleeping with men when she didn't see any relationship potential.

She wanted a marriage like her parents had. Victor and Donatella Orr had been married thirty years. When she was growing up, they'd set a good example of what a relationship should be. They argued, but they compromised and never held grudges. They were affectionate and understanding. They allowed each other their space, yet were always certain to spend quality time together as a family and as a couple.

At twenty-seven, Francesca had yet to run across a man she could have that kind of relationship with. Some were too clingy; others were too self-absorbed. Some were quick-tempered or arrogant. Then there were the kind like Liam—work-focused dreamers who looked at marriage as something they'd do later. They indulged in a variety of women, never taking anything but their jobs seriously. They were the kind of men who would wake up at fifty and realize they had missed out on their chance for a family unless they could find a willing younger woman with a fondness for expensive gifts.

Despite being engaged to Liam, he was the last man on Earth she would marry. And that's why she knew sleeping with him was a mistake. As a passionate woman, she put her heart in everything she did. But she couldn't put her heart into this. She couldn't look at her engagement ring and their portrait together and imagine it was anything more than a well-crafted fantasy.

Francesca turned to look at Liam as he grumbled in his sleep and rolled onto his back. The blankets fell across his torso, his hard, muscular chest exposed to the early-morning sunlight. She wanted to run her fingertip along the ridges of his muscles and bury her hands in the patch of dark hair across his chest. She wanted to reach under the covers and wake him up in the most pleasant way possible.

This sure didn't feel like a business arrangement.

Turning away, she spied her robe hanging on the knob of her closet door. Easing silently out of bed, she snatched the silk wrap off the handle and slid into it. She gave another glance to Liam, still sleeping, and slipped out of the room.

Downstairs, she found she could breathe a little easier. At least until she saw the scraps of her pink underwear on the kitchen floor. She snatched them off the tile and dumped them in the trash, and then went around gathering other bits of their clothing. She tossed the pile onto her sofa and went to the front door to pick up the paper. Laying it onto the kitchen table, she decided to make coffee. The caffeine would help her think so she could sort all this out.

The last few drops were falling into the pot when she heard Liam's shuffling footsteps across her hardwood floors. A moment later, he appeared in the kitchen wearing nothing but the suit pants she'd just gathered up.

"Morning," she said, pouring a cup for both of them.

"You snuck out on me," Liam complained, his voice still a touch low and rough with sleep. He ran his fingers through his messy hair and frowned at her with displeasure.

"I promised you coffee last night," she explained. "I had to come down here and make it so it was ready when you woke up." That sounded much better than saying she'd gotten weirded out and had to leave. "How do you take it?"

"One cream, one sugar," he said, sitting at the small round table in her breakfast nook. He unfolded the paper and started scanning the articles, oblivious to the nerves that had driven her to the kitchen.

Francesca busied herself making their coffee and grabbed a box of pastries from the counter. She set the two mugs and the carton on the table and plucked two napkins from the container in the center of the table. "Breakfast is served."

"Thank you," he said, looking up from the paper. "Our party made the society pages in the Sunday edition." Liam slid the section with their photo across the table to her. "I should clip it out and send it to the Queen Bee."

"I'm sure she hated missing it. My friends throw parties even she couldn't find fault with. Oh—" Francesca said, pausing to take a sip of her hot drink. That had reminded her of the important information she hadn't shared with Liam yet. "I forgot to tell you that Ariella said yes."

Liam looked up from the paper. "Ariella said yes to what?"

"I got a chance to talk to her at the party about the televised reunion show. I can't fathom why, but she's agreed to do it if the president is willing."

Liam's eyes grew wide, and he folded the paper back up as he grinned. "That's excellent. Wow. How could you forget to tell me something like that? We've been together since the party."

Francesca looked at him over her cup with an arched eyebrow. "Yes. We were together *all* night. And highly occupied, if you recall."

Liam grinned. "Indeed, we were. It's just as well because there was nothing I could do about it last night." He picked a pastry out of the box and set it on his napkin, sucking some icing from his thumb. "Well, now you'll need to contact the White House press secretary to see if President Morrow will participate."

"Me?"

"Yes. I told you that you would be in charge of the event. That means the ball is in your court."

"The Youth in Crisis gala is Saturday night. I've got my hands full with that."

"I have every confidence," he said with a meaningful gaze, "that you can handle everything I'm giving you and more. It's likely the ball won't really get rolling on the show until after the gala, and you just need to get White House buy-in. By the time everything is in place, the show will probably air in June."

Francesca could handle June. "I'll call over there Monday morning," she agreed. Part of her hoped the president and his staff would see what a bad idea this was. She knew it would mean good ratings, and maybe a boost in public opinion for ANS, but it felt wrong. If she had been adopted, she didn't think she'd want those first reunion moments captured for the world to see.

"Sounds great." Liam set aside the folded paper and reached his hand across the table to rest on hers. "Thank you for asking her. I know you felt uncomfortable about it."

"It's Ariella's decision to make, not mine. If she thinks it's the right choice, far be it for me to tell her no. It's her life."

"I think you'll do a great job running the show. I know it isn't something you've handled at the network before, but you'll do a bang-up job. Everything has been so crazy since I started at ANS, but I really believe that we can bring this network back. If all goes well, I'll get absolute control of the stock and we can end the fake engagement. The exclusive with the president and his daughter will earn us Brownie points and market share for our time slot. I know I can rebuild this network—with your help. So thank you for everything you've done so far."

"Don't thank me yet," she said, fidgeting with her coffee mug. A lot of pieces had to click together for these miracle scenarios to work out. And deep in her heart, Francesca worried that eventually, things would start to go awry.

* * *

Monday morning, Francesca breezed into Liam's office without Jessica's usual announcement. He looked up from his computer as she entered and a wide grin broke out across his face. He *should* be smiling after the weekend they'd spent together. "I see you're enjoying the new privileges of being the owner's bride-to-be."

"Exclusive access, anytime," she said with a grin.

Liam was glad to see her relaxed and happy. At first, he wasn't sure they could pull this off. Liam would never admit to that out loud; this had to work or he'd lose the network. And he knew Francesca had her own worries. She wore every emotion on her face. But after their time together this weekend, he was certain they both had sunnier outlooks on the arrangement. The lines of doubt were no longer wrinkling her brow, replaced with a contented smile that suited her much better.

Francesca set a to-go cup of coffee and a bag of Italian breakfast cookies in front of him. She was going to get him addicted to those things and he'd never be able to find them without her help.

"Grande drip with one cream, one sugar," she announced.

"Just how I like it," he said, turning in his chair to give her a hello kiss.

Francesca leaned into him but pulled away before his hands roamed too far. As much as it annoyed him to not be able to touch her when and where he wanted, he understood. Their relationship might be for the sake of the company, but public displays of affection at the office were a little much. She sat down in the guest chair with her own cup.

"Have you called the White House yet?" he asked.

"It's nine in the morning and I just handed you a hot, fresh coffee from the bakery. No. I haven't been to my office yet."

"Okay, sorry," he said, taking a sip. "You know I'm excited to move this plan forward."

"I know. I'll call once I get to my desk. Hopefully it won't take very long. I have a million things to wrap up this week before the gala on Saturday."

Liam nodded, but the details of the event didn't really interest him. The gala was really just a blip on his radar. And they were only doing it because she had agreed to be his fiancée. He couldn't have justified the expense given the state of the network. As it was, every mention of centerpieces and orchestras made dollar signs run through his mind.

"Now about the gala," she continued. "I've got most everything in place. Ticket sales have gone well and our sponsorship will see to it that it's the best year we've had yet. You'll need to make sure your tuxedo goes to the cleaners."

Liam made a note on his blotter so he wouldn't forget to ask Jessica about that later. "Check."

"And write a speech."

"What's that?" Liam looked up, his brow furrowed. He didn't like public speaking. As a matter of fact, he hated it. Avoided it at all costs and had since prep school debate class. Not even his aunt's declaration of mandatory matrimony made his stomach turn the way approaching a crowd of people with a microphone could do. There was a reason he preferred to be behind the camera instead of in front of it.

"As the major event sponsor, it's your job to give the

evening's welcome speech and encourage everyone to donate well and often."

"I don't remember Graham ever doing that." He tried to remember the times he'd gone. Maybe Graham did speak, but Liam was far too interested in his date for the evening to pay much attention. "Shouldn't that be the responsibility of the Youth in Crisis people?"

Francesca's red lips turned up with a touch of amusement. He must look like a damn deer in the headlights. "They do speak but not for long. Graham did it every year. And without bellyaching, I might add."

Liam grumbled under his breath and made another note to write a speech. This wasn't in their original agreement, but he could make concessions. Sleeping with him wasn't in their agreement either, but that had worked out splendidly. He would get something out of this. "Fine. I'll write a speech. But you'll have to go out to dinner with me tonight then."

"Why?"

Liam leaned across the desk, his most seductive gaze focused on her. "Because I'm going to ply you with sushi and expensive sake, and once you're drunk, I'm going to…talk you into letting me off the hook or writing the speech for me."

Francesca laughed. "I'm no speechwriter. But you do have several in your employ. I suggest you bribe them instead."

That wasn't a bad idea. Being a media mogul had its perks. If only he could get one of his news anchors to deliver the speech, too. He made another note on his blotter. "Does that mean you don't want to have sushi with me tonight?"

"I do. And I will. But first I have a president to cajole

and a charity ball to throw." She got up from her chair and leaned down to give him a goodbye kiss.

This time, because they were alone, Liam wasn't about to let her get away with just a peck. When she leaned down to him, he quickly reached for her and tugged her waist to him. She stumbled in her heels and fell into his lap. He clamped his arms around her so she couldn't get away.

Before she could complain, his lips found hers. He really enjoyed kissing her. He enjoyed kissing women in general, but there was something about Francesca's lips that beckoned him to return to them as soon as he could. Maybe it was the way she clung to him. Or the soft sighs and moans against his mouth. Maybe it was the taste of her—like a sweet, creamy sip of coffee. But he couldn't get enough of her.

Francesca indulged him for as long as she could, then pulled away. "I've got to get to work," she insisted, un-tangling herself from his arms. She straightened her skirt and rubbed her fingers along the edge of her lips to check for smeared lipstick.

"You look beautiful," he assured her. And she did. Dressed up, not dressed at all, perfectly styled or fresh from bed. He liked it all.

Liam wanted to tug her into his lap again and maybe make better use of his desk than he had since he'd moved into this office. But Francesca wouldn't hear of it—he could tell. As it was, that kiss guaranteed she would be on his mind all day. He probably wouldn't be able to focus on anything until after dinner, when he could get his hands on her again. But it had been worth it.

"You can flatter me all you want, but you're not getting out of this speech, Liam." She pulled away and sauntered out of his office, closing his door behind her.

Liam sat in his chair for a moment after she left. If he breathed deeply, the scent of her rose perfume still lingered in his office. Was there anything about this woman he didn't like?

He thought for a moment, then shook his head. Not yet. He'd been physically attracted to her the moment he laid eyes on her, but getting to know her had made the attraction that much stronger. She was beautiful. And smart. And thoughtful.

He picked up the coffee she'd brought him and took another sip. Her flaring temper could be a handful to deal with, but there were two sides to that passionate coin and he was certainly enjoying the other half at the moment.

The situation Aunt Beatrice had forced him into was unfortunate. But he couldn't regret asking Francesca to be his fiancée. Drawing her into this circus wasn't fair, but she was the right woman for the job. He couldn't imagine it going nearly as well with any of the women in his address book.

He liked being around Francesca. Working with her last week had been nice. Liam had gotten very comfortable having Francesca around, and that was saying a lot. He'd dated his share of women, never for more than a few months at a time. But he had boundaries. He very rarely had them over to his house and if he did, it wasn't overnight. They didn't meet any of his family or at least hadn't gotten to a point in the relationship where he thought it would be appropriate.

And he absolutely never brought them into his workplace. His romantic life and his work were two wires that never crossed. He usually didn't date at work, Francesca being a notable exception. He even tried to date outside the business. It took a bit of effort when you lived in D.C. not to date someone in media or politics—his usual circles—but he liked it that way. Usually.

Francesca was changing everything. This fake engagement was growing into something else with every passing moment. He didn't just want Francesca to come to his house; he also wanted her to help him decorate it. He liked starting his mornings chatting with her over coffee in his office or at her kitchen table. She may not have met his family yet, but if Aunt Beatrice had anything to say about it, she would—and soon. If the engagement went on for long, maybe he could convince his mother and sister to come to D.C. for a visit. He actually liked the idea of introducing them. He was certain his sister would really like Francesca.

All his rules were being broken. Stomped on with a red stiletto was more like it.

Normally, that would make Liam cringe. This woman he'd lassoed and pulled into his life was blurring all his boundaries. And he liked it.

A gentle rap at the door made him look up from their engagement photo. "Yes?"

Jessica came in, a couple of files stacked in her arms. "Good morning, sir."

"Good morning, Jessica."

She smiled as she approached his desk. "You're looking quite chipper this morning. Love looks good on you, sir. As does Ms. Orr's lipstick."

Liam grinned sheepishly and got up to look in the mirror over the minibar. He spotted a touch of reddish-pink lipstick, which he quickly wiped off. "Thanks, Jessica. She would've let me walk around like this all day, I bet."

"Of course. I've got those things you asked for this morning." Jessica set the stack of paperwork on his desk. "Last month's ratings numbers for the 5:00 to 7:00 p.m. weekday time slots, the budget breakout for the gala this weekend and the copy of *Italian for Idiots* you asked me to order came in from Amazon."

"Excellent. Thank you, Jessica. I've got a meeting with the CFO today, right?"

"At four."

Liam nodded. "Would you call and make reservations for Francesca and me at that nice sushi place in Dupont Circle? At six? I should be done with my meeting by then."

"I'll take care of it. Anything else?"

"That should do it for now."

When Jessica turned to leave, Liam thought of something. "Wait, one more thing. I'd like to send something to Francesca. An unexpected gift. Any suggestions?"

His secretary thought for a moment. "Well, for most men, I would suggest flowers or candy."

"Am I not most men?"

"Not at all, sir."

At least she was honest. "Then what would you recommend for the smaller minority of men?"

"Perhaps something for the gala this weekend? Do you know what dress she's wearing? Maybe something sparkly to go with it?"

Liam seemed to remember her saying something about that yesterday. That she had to go find a dress, but she didn't know when she would have the time. Perhaps he could help with that. Aunt Beatrice had the personal shoppers from Saks Fifth Avenue and Neiman Marcus come to her when she was choosing an outfit for an event. His aunt rarely left her mansion anymore.

"Check Ms. Orr's calendar for tomorrow afternoon and move anything she has to another time. Then call Neiman Marcus and have them send over a personal shopper."

"They'll need her size, colors and any other preferences."

Liam wrote down a few things on a Post-it note and handed it to her. "This is a fairly solid guess on her size, although tell them to bring a few things larger and smaller in case I'm wrong. I want the whole outfit, so shoes too. She wears an eight." He'd seen the label on her shoe as he'd carried her from the engagement party.

"Anything else, sir?"

"Yes. I want her to be the most stunning woman there. She is gorgeous on her own, but I'd like her to have a dress almost as beautiful as she is. And as such, let them know there's no price limit."

Eight

Liam had wanted to escort Francesca to the gala, but she'd insisted she had to go early and that she would just meet him there. He anticipated that she would be running around for most of the evening. That meant loitering on his own. Normally that wouldn't bother him, but lately being separated from Francesca brought on an awkward tightness in his chest. The only thing that would cure it was holding her in his arms.

As he walked through the front doors of the hotel's grand ballroom, he was greeted by the sound of a ten-piece orchestra accompanied by the dull roar of several hundred people mingling. The light was dim, but his eyes quickly became accustomed to it. He searched around the room for Francesca, but he began to think it was a lost cause. She was a needle in a haystack.

Despite the fact that he'd paid for the outfit she had chosen for tonight, he had no idea what she would be wearing. She had been exceedingly pleased with the gift and had thanked him in several ways over the past week, but the only details she would share was that it was a Marchesa and "*molto bellisima.*"

Then the crowds parted near the bar and he saw her. There was no mistaking this needle in any size haystack. The personal shopper from the department store had certainly taken Liam's requests into consideration. Francesca was the most stunning woman in the room tonight. He didn't even have to look around to check. He knew it in his gut.

The gown was black and gray with a swirling design. It was off the shoulder and clung to each curve all the way to the knee, where it fanned out into a delicate cascade of black marabou feathers. Her breasts were tastefully showcased by the neckline of the gown, which was trimmed with more feathers—there wasn't so much showing as to make him jealous of other men looking at her, but it was enough to make *him* notice. Her hair was swept up, making her neck look impossibly long and ready for his kisses. Her only jewelry was a pair of sparkling diamond dangles at her ears and a bracelet on one wrist.

When she turned to speak to someone, he noticed the feathers continued into a short train that draped behind her. It was grand, elegant and extremely sexy. And the best part was that *his* fiancée was wearing it.

He'd tried not to think too much of her that way. It implied more than there was between them, but he felt a surge of territoriality rush through him when she started talking to another man. He had the urge to rush to her, kiss her senseless and stake his claim before anyone got any ideas.

Then she held up her hand to show off her engagement ring. Even across the room, he could see the massive gem sparkle as her hand turned and she smiled. At long last, she radiated joy like a future bride should. The man said a few things, then they parted ways and she started walking in his direction.

The second her eyes met his, she stopped in her tracks. With a seductive grin curling her ruby lips, she held out her arms to showcase the gown and did a little turn for him. Lord, he thought, curling his hands into fists at his side. It was even more incredible from the back, where it dipped low to showcase her flawless, tanned skin.

Liam closed the gap between them as fast as he could without running across the ballroom. Up close, the dress sparkled as the lights hit little crystals sprinkled across the fabric, but it didn't shine as radiantly as she did.

"What do you think? Did I spend your money wisely?"

Not caring if he ruined the look she'd so carefully crafted, he leaned down and kissed her. He couldn't help it.

When he pulled away, Francesca smiled. "I guess so."

"Incredible," he said.

"Thank you for buying it for me. Having the woman from the department store just show up with gowns was perfect. I felt like I was an Oscar nominee with designers fighting for me to wear their looks on the red carpet."

"Hollywood is all the poorer for you not being on the big screen."

"Oh, stop," she said, smacking him lightly on the arm. "There's no one around to hear us, so you don't have to lay it on so thick."

Liam shook his head. "I mean every word. It wouldn't matter if we were all alone. I'd say the same thing. Of course, I'd be saying it as I unzipped you from the gown."

Francesca smiled and slipped her arm through his. "Let me show you where we're sitting. People are still milling around the silent auction tables, but the event should be starting shortly. You'll give your speech after the video plays about the youth facilities."

The speech. He'd almost forgotten about that weight dragging him down when he saw her looking so stunning. "Hooray," he said flatly.

"Did you bring it?"

He patted his lapel. "Got it right here. And I wrote it myself, I might add. No bribery was involved."

"I'm looking forward to hearing it."

They approached a round banquet table front and center, just beside the steps that led up to the stage. He helped her into her seat and took his own just as the orchestra music increased in intensity and the lights on the stage shifted to indicate the program was about to start.

Salads were brought to every place setting as the director of Youth in Crisis welcomed everyone and introduced the short video about their program.

Liam could only pick at his salad. With every minute of the video that went by, he felt more and more nauseated by the idea of speaking to three hundred people.

When the credits started rolling, Francesca sought out his hand and squeezed it gently. "It's time," she said, looking over to him. "You'll do great."

Liam took a large sip of wine and got up from the table. He made his way to the stairs and up onto the stage, where he was bathed in blinding white lights. He reached in his pocket for his speech, adjusted the microphone and tried to keep the frantic beating of his heart from being audible to the crowd. It was now or never.

"Thank you and welcome, everyone, to the eighth annual Youth in Crisis charity gala. As some of you may know, I recently bought the ANS network, which has a longstanding commitment to this organization. It's a partnership I'm proud of, and there are many people who work hard to make it possible."

He looked down in front of the podium, where he could see Francesca's dim silhouette. Her excited expression fueled his courage to continue. His heart seemed to slow and the subtle shaking of his hands subsided. He just might make it through the speech with her sitting there, silently cheering him on.

"First, I would like to thank ANS's Executive Vice President of Community Outreach and organizer of tonight's grand event, my beautiful fiancée, Francesca Orr. For those of you that don't know Francesca, she cares so deeply about this cause. With everything that has happened with our network in the past few months, there was some uncertainty about whether or not we could sponsor this event like we have for the past seven years.

"Well," he corrected, "I should say everyone *but* Francesca had some uncertainty. Come hell or high water, this gala would go on as far as she was concerned. The woman would give back her own salary to fund this event if she had to. I hope everyone rewards her determination by writing a big, fat check. I have agreed to match the largest private donation tonight as an engagement present for my bride, so feel free to stick it to me for a good cause."

The crowd laughed and Liam felt his confidence

boost. He shuffled to the next index card, gave Francesca a wink and continued in his bid to get the attendees to part with their money.

Francesca loved her dress. She really did. But after a long night, she was just as happy to change into a breezy slip dress and zip the gown into the garment bag she'd brought with her to the hotel. She couldn't stuff all those feathers into her little BMW and drive around. With that done, she stepped into the comfortable black flats she'd stashed away with her change of clothes and sighed in relief. Not only did her feet feel better, but the gala was a roaring success and—more important—it was over.

The ballroom was nearly empty by the time Liam found her gathering up the last of her things. "That was a very painful check to write," he said. "Remind me to kick Scarlet's fiancé for donating that much the next time I see him."

She smiled, standing and turning to look at him. His bow tie was undone, his collar unbuttoned. He managed to look casually sexy yet elegantly refined at the same time. "Daniel knows that it's for a good cause, as should you. And an excellent tax deduction," she added.

"It was worth it to see the look on your face when they announced how much money we raised."

"I can't believe it, really. We blew last year's donations out of the water. Everyone was buzzing about ANS tonight—and for a good reason." Francesca slipped her bag over her shoulder and took Liam's arm.

"It's about time," he said, leading them back to the front of the hotel where the party had been held. He approached the valet and handed him his ticket.

"I parked over there," she said, pointing to an area she didn't really want to walk to.

"We'll get your car in the morning," he said. "I want you to come home with me tonight."

That was an interesting development. Liam had yet to have her over to his place. She figured that it was a personal retreat for him. They'd always gone to her town house instead. And tonight, she really wished they were sticking with that arrangement. She had no change of clothes. She had what she had worn to the hotel and her dress. The designer gown, while fabulous, would look ridiculous in the morning.

"I don't have any clothes for tomorrow," she said.

"You won't need any," he replied with a wicked grin as the valet brought the car out.

Francesca gave up the fight. She was too exhausted after a long day to argue. They loaded her things into his convertible and she sat back in her seat, going with the flow. It wasn't until they reached his place that she perked up.

Liam had described where he lived as a town house, just a little bigger than hers, but he'd lied. As they pulled up the circular brick driveway, she found herself outside what looked like a two-story home. It was detached with a courtyard out front. Two stories of red brick with an elegantly arched front doorway and dormer windows on the roof.

"I thought you said you lived in a town house."

Liam shrugged and pulled the car into the attached garage. "It's close."

He came around the car and opened the door for her, escorting her toward a few steps leading up into the house. They entered through the kitchen. The cabinets were a stark white with glass fronts, set against stainless appliances and gray granite countertops. There wasn't a single dish in the sink and not a piece of mail sitting on the counter.

Liam took her garment bag and led her through to the front entryway, where he hung it in the closet. She set her bag containing the other items she'd needed tonight on the floor beside the door and wandered into the living room.

"It's a beautiful place," she said, walking over to the staircase and running her hand along the wood railing. The space had so much potential. It was a stunning home, but as he'd said before, it was probably just as it was when he'd moved in. White walls, hardwood floors, minimal furniture. There wasn't a single piece of art on the walls or personal item on a shelf. It looked like a model home or one stripped to sell. "But it does need a woman's touch," Francesca admitted.

"I told you I needed you to help me decorate."

"I didn't realize it would be such a large task."

Liam shrugged out of his tuxedo jacket and laid it across the arm of the couch. "Not what you were picturing?"

"I guess I was anticipating this place as more of a reflection of you. You seemed to guard it so fiercely that I thought coming into your home would give me some insight into who you are as a person."

"You don't see me in this place?"

Francesca glanced around one last time. "Not really. But I see what I should've expected to see. A house owned by someone too wrapped up in his work to make it a home. That speaks volumes about you, I think."

Liam's eyes narrowed at her. "My work is more important to me than the color of the walls."

"My work is important to me. But I make time for other things, too. I want to get married and have a family someday soon. When I do, I want not only a successful man, but also one that can take a step back from his job to enjoy family life. You'll burn out without that."

As Francesca said the words aloud, she realized she may have made a grave tactical error with Liam. He might not read much into what she'd just said, but it struck a painful chord with her. When she'd said the words, when she'd mentally envisioned getting married and having a family, she'd seen Liam in her mind. She had pictured this place filled with color and life and toddlers who looked like him.

She had let her heart slip away, piece by piece. It had happened so slowly over the past few weeks that she'd barely noticed the change until it was too late. Liam didn't know it, but Francesca had given her heart to him.

The man she could never really have.

It was unexpected, really. She was passionate about everything she did, but she knew from the beginning that this was business. There was no future for her with a man like Liam.

And yet she could see more now. Their future together was as crystal clear as the illuminated swimming pool she caught sight of from his living-room window.

"There's plenty of time for all that," he insisted.

This man, this workaholic, had so many layers to him she was anxious to explore. She knew there was more to him than he showed the world. The way he cared about his employees. The way he was handling the interview with Ariella. He had an attention to detail that went beyond just doing quality work. He was just as passionate about what he did as she was.

How could she not love that about him?

Love. Francesca swallowed hard and turned away from him to look out the window at his darkened yard and glowing turquoise pool. She couldn't look him in the eye with these kinds of thoughts in her mind. He'd know. And he could never know. Because it would never work between them.

Despite the future she could envision, there was a critical piece missing between them. He didn't love her. He wouldn't even be with her right now if it wasn't for his aunt and her demands. That was a bitter dose of reality to swallow, but the sooner she reminded herself of that, the better off she'd be when this "arrangement" came to an end.

"Would you like to see the upstairs?"

Pulling herself together, Francesca turned and nodded with a smile. Liam led the way up the stairs, showing her his home office, the guest room and finally, his bedroom.

Knowing they'd reached their final destination, she slipped out of her shoes and stepped onto the plush carpeting. She ran her hand over the soft, blue fabric of his duvet as she made her way to the window. She watched the glow of the city lighting the black night above the tree line, hiding any stars from her view of the sky. On a night like this, she really needed a sign to help her. Something to tell her she was making the right choices with Liam.

She reached for the *corno portafortuna* necklace she always wore and realized she'd taken it off tonight. It was in a pouch in her purse. She suddenly felt exposed without it, as though something could get through her protective armor without it. Looking down, she saw a rabbit sitting on Liam's front lawn. Before she could move, something startled it and the bunny shot across the yard, crossing her path.

A sign of disappointment to come.

Francesca took a deep breath and accepted the inevitable. She was in love with a man she couldn't have. She didn't need a rabbit to tell her disappointment was on the horizon.

The heat of Liam's body against her back was a bittersweet sensation. Just as her mind began to fight against it, her body leaned back into him. His bare chest met her back, his fingertips sliding beneath the thin straps of her dress to slide them off her shoulders.

The flimsy sundress slid down her body, leaving her completely naked with it gone. Liam's hands roamed across her exposed skin, hesitating at her hip.

"No panties?" he asked.

She hadn't worn any undergarments tonight. The dress was almost sheer and wouldn't allow for them. Besides, she knew how the night would end. "I can't have you ripping up all my nice lingerie," she said.

"That's very practical of you. I find that sexy. Everything about you just lures me in. I don't know that I'll ever be able to get away."

Francesca closed her eyes, glad her back was still to him. She wished he wouldn't talk that way sometimes. It was nice to hear, but it hurt to know it wasn't really true. The minute his aunt let him off the hook, this whole charade would end. At least now she wouldn't have to worry about faking the heartbreak when their engagement was called off. The tears she would shed on Ariella's shoulder would be authentic.

"Look at me," Liam whispered into her ear.

She turned in his arms, wishing away the start of tears in her eyes that had come too early. They weren't done just yet. She needed to make the most of her time with him.

When her gaze met his dark blue eyes, she felt herself fall into them. She wrapped her arms around his neck and stood on her toes to get closer. His lips found hers and she gave in completely. The feel of his hands on her body, his skin against hers, was an undeniable pleasure. She had to give in to it, even if it put her heart even more at risk.

They moved together, still clinging to one another as they slow-danced across the room to the bed. Her bare back hit the silky softness of the duvet a moment later. Liam wasted no time covering her body with his own.

As his lips and hands caressed her, Francesca noted a difference in his touch. The frenzied fire of their first encounters was gone, replaced with a leisurely, slow-burning passion. He seemed to be savoring every inch of her. At first, she wondered if maybe she'd had too much champagne tonight. That perhaps she was reading more into his pensive movements.

But when he filled her, every inch of his body was in contact with hers. He moved slowly over her, burying his face in her neck. She could feel his hot breath on her skin, the tension of each muscle in his body as it flexed against hers. When he groaned her name into her ear, it sent a shiver through her whole body.

Francesca wrapped her arms around his back and pulled him closer. She liked having him so near to her like this. It was a far cry from their wild, passionate encounter in her kitchen. Nothing like the times they'd come together over the past week. Something had changed, but she didn't know what it was. It felt like…

It felt like they were making love for the first time.

The thought made Francesca's heart stop for a hundredth of a second, but she couldn't dwell on it. Liam's lips found the sensitive flesh of her neck just as the movement of his hips against hers started building a delicious heat through her whole body. She clung to him, cradling his hips between her thighs as they rocked closer and closer to the edge.

When she reached her breaking point, she didn't cry out. There was only a gasp and a desperate, panting whisper of his name as her cheek pressed against his. His release was a growl against her throat, the intense thrashing of his body held to almost stillness by their tight grip on one another.

Instead of rolling away, he stayed just as he was. His body relaxed and his head came to rest at her breast. She brushed a damp strand of hair away from his forehead and pressed a kiss to his flushed skin.

As they drifted to sleep together, one of Francesca's last thoughts was that she was totally and completely lost in this man.

Nine

"Aunt Beatrice," Liam said, trying to sound upbeat.

After the maître d' had led Francesca and him to the table where the older woman was seated, she looked up at him and frowned. "Liam, do you ever wear a tie?"

He smiled, pleased he'd finally pushed her far enough to mention it. And now he got the joy of ignoring her question. He turned to his left and smiled. "This is my fiancée, Francesca Orr. Francesca, this is my great aunt, Beatrice Crowe."

Francesca let go of his hand long enough to reach out and gently shake hands with the Queen Bee. "It's lovely to meet you," she said.

Aunt Beatrice just nodded, looking over his fiancée with her critical eye. Liam was about to interrupt the inspection when she turned to him with as close to a smile on her face as she could manage. "She's more lovely in person than she is in her pictures, Liam."

He breathed a sigh of relief and pulled out Francesca's chair for her to sit. He hadn't been looking forward to this dinner. In fact, he'd deliberately not told Francesca about it until after the gala was wrapped up. She would just worry, and there wasn't any sense in it. His aunt would think and do as she pleased.

"I can't agree more," he said.

The first few courses of the meal were filled with polite, stiff pleasantries. His aunt delicately grilled Francesca about her family and where she came from. She was subtle, but Liam knew she was on a fishing expedition.

Francesca must've realized it also. "So what brings you to D.C.?" she asked, deflecting the conversation away from herself.

Liam swallowed his answer—that she was here to check up on him and their agreement.

"I'm speaking before a congressional committee tomorrow," Aunt Beatrice said, allowing the waiter to take away her plate.

She had mentioned that before, but Liam thought it had just been an excuse she'd made up. "What for?" he asked.

His aunt's lips twisted for a minute as she seemed to consider her words. "I'm speaking to a panel on federal funding for cancer treatment research."

Liam couldn't hide his frown. He also wasn't quite sure how to respond.

"Have you lost someone to cancer?" Francesca asked. Better that she ask the question because she had no real knowledge of her family history, as Liam should.

"Not yet," Beatrice said. "But the doctors give me

about three to six months. Just enough time to get my affairs in order before I take to my bed permanently."

Liam's glass of wine was suspended midair for a few moments before he set it back down. "What?" He couldn't have heard her correctly.

"I'm dying, Liam. I have stage four brain cancer and there's nothing they can do. Some of the treatments have shrunk the tumor and bought me a little more time, but a little more is all I'm going to get."

Unable to meet her eyes, his gaze strayed to her perfectly curled gray hair and he realized, for the first time, that it was a wig. How long had this been going on? "When did this happen? Why haven't you told anyone?"

At that, his aunt laughed. "Please, Liam. The sharks have been circling me for years. Do you really think I'm going to let them know it's close to feeding time?"

That was a true enough statement. The vultures had been lurking outside her mansion his whole life. This must be why she was so insistent on Liam marrying and taking over as head of the family. She knew the shoes needed to be filled quickly. She'd given him a year knowing she'd never live to see it come to fruition.

She'd been silently dealing with this for who knew how long. Worrying about her estate planning and altering her will even as she went for treatments and reeled from the aftereffects. "How can you go through this on your own? You need someone with you."

"I have someone with me. Henry has been by my side for more than forty years. He's held my hand through every treatment. Sat by me as I cried."

Henry. He'd never understood why her butler stayed around, even at his advanced age. Now perhaps he comprehended the truth. Neither of them had ever married.

They'd grown up in a time where they could never be together due to the wide social chasm between them, yet they were in love. Secretly, quietly making their lives together without anyone ever knowing it.

And now Henry was going to lose her. It made Liam's chest ache for the silent, patient man he'd known all his life.

"I don't know what to say, Aunt Beatrice. I'm so sorry."

"Is there anything we can do?" Francesca asked. Her hand sought out his under the table and squeezed gently for reassurance. He appreciated the support. Like her mere presence at his speech, knowing she was there made him feel stronger. As if he could handle anything.

"Actually, yes. I'd like the two of you to get married this weekend while I'm in town."

Anything but that.

"What?" Liam said, his tone sharper than he would've liked after everything they'd just discussed.

"I know our original agreement gave you a year, but I've taken a turn for the worse and I'm forced to move up the deadline. I want to ensure that you go through with it so I have enough time to have all the appropriate paperwork drawn up. I also want to see you married before I'm too much of an invalid to enjoy myself at the reception."

Francesca's hand tightened on his. It was never meant to go this far. He never expected something like this. "This weekend? It's Monday night. That's impossible."

"Nothing is impossible when you have enough money to make things happen. I'm staying at the Four Seasons while I'm here. I spoke to the manager this morning and he said they could accommodate a wedding and reception there this Friday evening. They have a lovely terrace for the ceremony and the Corcoran Ballroom is available for the reception."

Liam felt a lump in his throat form that no amount of water or swallowing would budge. He turned to look at Francesca. Her gaze was focused on her plate, her expression unreadable. She looked a little paler than usual, despite her olive complexion. Obviously, she was as pleased with this development as he was.

"I see no reason for you to wait any longer than necessary," his aunt continued, filling the silence at the table. "After all, you've found a lovely woman. By all accounts you two seem to be very much in love."

Her pointed tone left no doubt. His aunt had nailed them. He thought they had put on a good show. That it would be enough to pacify her until he could find the funding to buy her out. But he'd already heard from his accountant. The amount of money he needed was nearly impossible to secure, especially with the network in such a vulnerable place. They were looking at some other alternatives, but it would take time. Certainly longer that the few days they'd been given with her new deadline. That would take a miracle.

The Queen Bee was calling their bluff and he had too much riding on this hand to fold.

The waiter arrived then, setting their dessert selections in front of them. His aunt had never been much for sweets, but he noted a glimmer of pleasure in her eye as she looked down at the confection before her. He supposed that once you know you're going to die, there was no sense holding back on the things doctors told you were bad for you. What was the point?

Aunt Beatrice lifted a spoon of creamy chocolate

mousse and cheesecake to her mouth and closed her eyes from pleasure. Liam couldn't find the desire to touch his dessert. He'd lost his appetite.

"Don't make my mistakes, Liam. Life is too short to wait when you've found the person you want to spend your life with, I assure you."

At that, Francesca pulled her hand from his. He suddenly felt very alone in the moment without her touch to steady him. "We'll have to discuss it, Aunt Beatrice. Francesca's family is from California. There's a lot more to pull together than just booking a reception hall. But we'll be in touch."

Liam pushed away from the table to stand and Francesca followed suit.

"Aren't you going to finish your dessert?" his aunt asked, watching them get up.

"We've got a lot to sort out. I'm sorry, but we have to go."

His aunt took another bite, not terribly concerned by their hasty exit. "That's fine. I'll take it back to the hotel with me. Henry will enjoy it."

Liam's car pulled up outside Francesca's town house, but neither of them got out. It had been a silent drive from the restaurant. They must've both been in some kind of shock, although Francesca was certain they had different reasons for being struck mute.

When his aunt first started this, Liam had asked Francesca to be his fake fiancée. There was never even a mention that they would actually get married. He assured her it would never go that far. It seemed safe enough, even as she could feel herself slowly falling for him. Nothing would come of it, no matter how she felt. She wanted the kind of marriage Liam couldn't offer, but they only had an engagement.

Marrying Liam was a completely different matter.

Not just because it would never work out between them. But because a part of her wanted to marry him. She loved him. She wanted to be his bride. But not like this. She wanted to marry a man who loved her. Not because he had a metaphorical shotgun pointed at him.

When Liam killed the engine, she finally found the courage to speak. "What are we going to do?"

When he turned to her, Francesca could see the pain etched into his face. He was facing the loss of everything he'd worked for, and he wasn't the only one. She might not agree with Aunt Beatrice's methods, but she understood where the woman was coming from. Desperation made people do crazy things. This was an ugly situation for everyone involved.

"She called my bluff. I'm just going to have to call hers. Tomorrow I'm going to tell her that the engagement was a setup and that we're not getting married. I don't think she'll sell her stock to Wheeler. It's not what she wants. She's a woman accustomed to getting her way, but she's not vindictive." He ran his hand through his hair. "At least I don't think she is."

Francesca frowned. She didn't like the sound of that plan. She didn't exactly get a warm maternal feeling from the Crowe family matriarch. His aunt had nothing to lose. If she was willing to go so far as to force him into marriage, she had no doubt she'd follow through with her threat. "You can't risk it, Liam."

"What choice do I have? I can't ask you to really marry me. That wasn't a part of the deal. I never intended for it to go this far."

Neither did she, but life didn't always turn out the way you planned. "When would you get the balance of the stock?"

Liam sighed. "It doesn't matter. I'm not doing it. She's taken this way too far."

"Come on, Liam. Tell me."

"I have to be married for a year. The ANS stock would be an anniversary gift, she said."

A year. In the scheme of things it wasn't that long. But she'd managed to fall in love with Liam in only a few weeks. A year from now, how bad off would she be? That said, the damage was done. Maybe a year of matrimony would cure her of her romantic affliction. It might give her time to uncover all his flaws. It was possible she wouldn't be able to stand the sight of him by May of next year.

And even if she loved him even more…what choice did they have? Their network would be destroyed. They were both too invested in the company and the employees to let that happen. Her heart would heal eventually. It was a high price to pay but for a great reward.

"We have to get married," she said.

Liam's eyes widened. "No. Absolutely not."

She couldn't help the pout of her lower lip when he spoke so forcefully. She knew what he meant, but a part of her was instantly offended by his adamancy. "Is being married to me so terrible that you'd rather risk losing the network?"

Liam leaned in and took her face in both his hands. He tenderly kissed her before he spoke. "Not at all. I would be a very lucky man to marry you. For a year or twenty. But I'm not going to do that to you."

"*To* me?"

"Yes. I know you're a true believer. You want a marriage like your parents. I've seen your face light up when you talk about them and their relationship. I know that's not what I'm offering, so I won't ask you to compromise what you want, even for a year."

She couldn't tell him that *he* was what she wanted. If he thought for a moment that their arrangement had turned into anything more than a business deal, he would never agree to the marriage. He'd chosen her because he thought she could keep all of this in perspective. Knowing the truth would cost ANS everything.

Francesca clasped Liam's hands and drew them down into her lap. "I'm a big girl, Liam. I know what I'm doing."

"I can't ask you to." His brow furrowed with stress as he visibly fought to find another answer. They both knew there wasn't one.

"You are the right person to run ANS. No one else can get the network back on top the way you can. Ron Wheeler might as well carve up the company if you're not running it because the doors will be closed in a few months' time." She looked into his weary blue eyes so he would know how sincere she was. "It's just a year. Once you get your stock, we can go our separate ways."

"But what about your friends and family? It's one thing to lie about an engagement that gets broken off. But to actually get married? Can you look your father in the eye and tell him you love me before he walks you down the aisle?"

Francesca swallowed the lump in her throat. She was very close to both her parents. They could read her like a book, and even as a teenager she couldn't lie to them without getting caught. This would be hard, but she could do it because it was true. Just as long as they didn't ask if *he* loved *her*…

"Yes, I can."

"What about your town house? You'll have to move in with me."

That would sting. Francesca loved her town house. She could hardly imagine living anywhere else. But she saw the potential in Liam's place. She could make that place her own for a while. "I'll rent out my town house."

"You don't have to do that. It's only fair I cover your expenses to keep it up even while you're not living there."

"Don't you think your aunt would find it odd if the place was left vacant?"

"This is going to sound a little harsh, but if what she says is true, she won't be around long enough to know what we're doing. She will probably write the marriage stipulation into the stock agreement, but she can't dictate what you do with your real estate holdings."

Francesca wouldn't put it past her. She didn't seem like the kind of woman who missed anything. "I suppose we can worry about the details later." She waited a moment as she tried to process everything they'd talked about. "So…is it decided then? We're getting married this weekend?"

Liam sat back in his seat. He was silent for several long, awkward minutes. Francesca could only sit there and wait to see what he said. "I guess so."

"You're going to have to work on your enthusiasm pretty quickly," she noted. "We'll have to tell our families tonight so they have enough time to make travel arrangements."

He nodded, his hands gripping the steering wheel as

though someone might rip it away from him. "I'll have Jessica call Neiman's again and get you a bridal appointment. Can you call Ariella and Scarlet tomorrow? They did a good job on the engagement party. Maybe they can pull off a miracle of a wedding in three days."

"I can. They'll think we've lost our minds."

Liam chuckled bitterly. "We have. Let's go inside," he said.

They went into her town house, and Francesca went straight into the kitchen. She needed something to take the edge off and she had a nice merlot that would do the trick. "Wine?" she asked.

"Yes, thank you."

Liam followed her into the kitchen as she poured two large goblets of wine. When she handed him his glass, he looked curiously at her hand for a moment before he accepted it. "Can I see your ring for a minute?"

Francesca frowned, looking at it before slipping it off. "Is something wrong with it?" She hadn't noticed any missing stones or scratches. She'd tried really hard to take good care of the ring so she could return it to him in good shape when it was over.

"Not exactly." Liam looked at it for a moment before getting down on one knee on the tile floor.

Francesca's eyes widened as she watched him drop down. "What are you doing?"

"I asked you to be my fake fiancée. I never asked you to marry me. I thought I should."

"Liam, that isn't neces—"

"Francesca," he interrupted, reaching out to take her hand in his own. "You are a beautiful, caring and passionate woman. I know this isn't how either of us expected things to turn out. I also know this isn't what you've dreamed about since you were a little girl. But if you will be my bride for the next year, I promise to be the best husband I know how to be. Francesca Orr, will you marry me?"

She underestimated the impact that Liam's proposal would have on her. It wasn't real. It lacked all those critical promises of love and devotion for her whole life, but she couldn't help the rush of tears that came to her eyes. It felt real. She wanted it to be real.

All the emotions that had been building up inside her bubbled out at that moment. Embarrassed, she brought her hand up to cover her mouth and shook her head dismissively. "I'm sorry," she said. "Just ignore me. It's been a rough couple of weeks and I think it's catching up with me."

"That wasn't the reaction I was hoping for," he said with a reassuring smile.

Francesca took a deep breath and fanned her eyes. "I'm sorry. Yes, I will marry you."

Liam took the ring and slipped it back onto her finger. He rose to his feet, still holding her hand in his. His thumb gently brushed over her fingers as he brought her hand up to his lips and kissed it. "Thank you."

Francesca was surprised to see the faint shimmer of tears in his eyes as he thanked her. It wasn't love, but it was emotion. There was so much riding on this marriage. She had no doubt that he meant what he said. He would be as good a husband as he could be. At least, as good as he could be without actually being in love with his wife.

Liam pulled Francesca into his arms and hugged her fiercely against him. She tucked her head under his chin and gave in to the embrace. It felt good to just be held by the man she loved. As she'd said before, this had been an emotionally exhausting couple of weeks. The next year might prove to be just as big a challenge. But somehow, having Liam hold her made her feel like it just might work out okay.

It felt like he held her forever. When he finally pulled away, they both had their emotions in check and were ready to face whatever the next week might hold for them.

"It's official then," he said with a confident smile. "Let's call your parents."

Ten

Francesca's precious retreat was a mess. Her beautiful townhome was in a state of disarray with moving boxes and bubble wrap all over the place.

Liam was maintaining the payments on her town house, so the bigger pieces of furniture she didn't need could stay, but everything else was going to his place. She'd probably need these things over the next year. This wasn't some overnight trip or long weekend she was packing for. She was getting ready to move in with the man who would be her husband in a few days' time.

Her parents had taken it well. At least they'd seemed to. Who knew how long her father had ranted after they hung up the phone. Either way, they were making arrangements to fly to Washington on Thursday afternoon. Liam's mother was thrilled. She didn't hesitate to say how excited she was to come and meet Francesca. Liam's mother and sister were coming Friday morning.

Their story was that they were so in love they didn't want to wait another minute to be husband and wife. Incredibly romantic or unbelievably stupid, depending on how you looked at it. But no parent wanted their child to elope and miss their big day, no matter what they might think about the situation.

Things were coming together, although it didn't look like it from where she was sitting.

The doorbell rang and Francesca disentangled herself from a pile of her things to answer the door. She'd asked Ariella to come over for lunch, hoping she and Scarlet could pull off the wedding hat trick of the year.

When she pulled open the door, she found her friend on the doorstep, but Ariella didn't have the bright smile Francesca was expecting. Her brow was furrowed with concern, her teeth wearing at her bottom lip. She had faint gray circles under her eyes as though she hadn't slept. And, most uncharacteristic of all, her hair was pulled back into a sloppy ponytail. That wasn't the Ariella she knew at all.

"Are you okay?"

Ariella's weary green gaze met hers as she shook her head almost imperceptibly.

Alarmed, Francesca reached for her friend's hand and pulled her inside. She sat Ariella down on one of the overstuffed living-room chairs that wasn't buried in packing tape and cardboard. "I'll make tea," she said, turning to the kitchen.

"Is it too early for wine?" Ariella called out.

Probably, but if her friend needed wine, she'd serve it with breakfast. "Not at all. Red or white?"

"Yes," she responded with a chuckle.

At least she was able to laugh. That was a step in the

right direction. Francesca quickly poured two glasses of chardonnay, which seemed more of a brunch-appropriate wine, and carried them into the living room with a package of cookies under her arm.

It took several minutes and several sips before Ariella finally opened up. She set the glass on the coffee table and reached into her purse. Pulling out an ivory envelope, she handed it over to Francesca to read the contents.

Francesca quickly scanned over the letter, not quite sure if what she was reading could possibly be true.

"It's from my birth mother, Eleanor Albert," Ariella said after a moment, confirming the unbelievable thoughts Francesca was already having.

The letter didn't give many details. It was short and sweet, basically asking if Ariella would be willing to write her back and possibly meet when she was ready. There was nothing about the circumstances of the adoption, the president or where Eleanor had been the past twenty-five years. Nothing about the letter screamed authenticity aside from a curious address in Ireland where she was to write back.

"When did you get this?"

"It came yesterday afternoon. To my home address, which is private and almost no one knows. Most of my mail goes to the office. I must've read it a million times last night. I couldn't sleep." Despite her weary expression, there was a touch of excitement in Ariella's voice. She'd waited so long to find out about her birth mother. Yet she seemed hesitant about uncovering the truth.

Francesca understood. The truth wasn't always pretty. People didn't always live up to the fantasy you built up in your mind. Right now, Ariella's mother was like

Schrödinger's cat. Until she opened that box, Eleanor would remain both the fantasy mother Ariella had always imagined and the selfish, uncaring woman she'd feared. Was it better to fantasize or to know for certain?

Francesca looked at the envelope and shook her head. After everything that had happened in the past few months, she'd grown very suspicious and protective where Ariella was concerned. It wouldn't surprise her at all if a journalist was posing as her mother to get details for a story. But she hesitated to say it out loud. She didn't want to be the one to burst the small, tentative bubble building inside her friend.

"Go ahead and say it," Ariella urged.

Francesca frowned and handed the letter back over to her. "I'm excited for you. I know that not knowing about your birth parents has been like a missing puzzle piece in your life, even before the news about the president hit. This could be a step in the right direction for you. I hope it is. Just be careful about what you say until you're certain she's really your mother. And even then, you can't be sure she won't go to the press with her story if someone offers her money."

Ariella nodded, tucking the letter back in her purse. "I thought the same thing. I'm going to respond, but I'm definitely going to proceed with caution. I don't want to be the victim of a ruthless journalist."

"I'm sure the letter is real, but it can't hurt to be careful."

Ariella reached for her wineglass and then paused to look around the living room. "What's going on here?"

"I'm packing."

Ariella's nose wrinkled as she eyed the boxes stacked around. Her mind must've been too wrapped up in the letter to notice the mess before. "You're moving in with Liam? So soon?" she added.

"Yes."

"Wow," she said with a shake of her head. "You two certainly don't move slowly. Next thing you'll be telling me you're getting married next weekend."

Francesca bit her lip, not quite sure what to say to that.

Ariella's head snapped toward Francesca, her green eyes wide. "Tell me you're not getting married in a week and a half. Francesca?"

"We're not," she assured her. "We're getting married Friday."

Ariella swallowed a large sip of wine before she could spit it out. "It's Tuesday."

"I know."

"What is the rush with you two? Does one of you have an incurable disease?"

"Liam and I are both perfectly healthy." Francesca wasn't about to mention his aunt's incurable disease. That would lead to more questions than she wanted to answer. "We've just decided there is no sense in waiting. We're in love and we want to get married as soon as possible."

With a sigh, Ariella flopped back into her chair. "Scarlet is going to have a fit. Putting together a wedding in three days will be a nightmare."

"We have a venue," Francesca offered. She loved how she didn't even need to ask her friend if she would do the wedding. It was a foregone conclusion. Francesca wouldn't dare ask someone else. "The Four Seasons. We've reserved the terrace for the ceremony and the ballroom for the reception."

Ariella nodded, but Francesca knew she was deep in planning mode. "Good. That's the hardest part with a quick turnaround. We'll have to use the hotel caterer, so I'll need to get with them soon about the menu for the reception. Did you guys have anything in mind?"

Francesca was ashamed to admit she didn't. As a child, she'd always fantasized more about her marriage than her actual wedding. And even if she had dreamed of a princess dress and ten thousand pink roses for the ceremony, none of that seemed appropriate for this. She wanted to save those ideas for her real marriage. One that would last longer than a year.

"We will be happy with whatever you two can pull together on short notice. We don't have room to be picky."

Ariella reached into her purse and pulled out her planner. She used her phone for most things, but she'd told Francesca that weddings required paper and pen so she could see all the plans laid out. "Color or flower preferences?"

"Not really. Whatever is in season and readily available. I'm not a big fan of orange, but I could live with it."

Her friend looked up from her notebook and frowned. "Live with it? Honey, your wedding isn't supposed to be something you *live with* no matter how short the notice. Tell me what you want and I'll make it happen for you."

She could tell Ariella wasn't going to let her off the hook. She would give her friend her dream wedding no matter how much Francesca resisted. She put aside her reservations and closed her eyes. Fake or no, what did she envision for her wedding day with Liam? "Soft and romantic," she said. "Maybe white or pale-pink roses. Candlelight. Lace. A touch of sparkle."

Ariella wrote frantically in her book. "Do you like

gardenias? They're in season and smell wonderful. They'd go nicely with the roses. And maybe some hydrangeas and peonies."

"Okay," she said, quickly correcting herself when Ariella looked at her with another sharp gaze. "That all sounds beautiful. Thank you."

"What does your dress look like? It helps sometimes with the cake design."

Francesca swallowed hard. "My appointment is tomorrow morning."

"You don't have a dress," she said, her tone flat.

She'd been engaged less than two weeks. Why would she have a dress already? "I don't have anything but a groom and a ballroom, Ariella. That's why I need you. I will make sure that Liam and I show up appropriately attired. The rest of the details are up to you."

"Please give me something to work with here. I know you trust me, but I want you to get what you want, too."

"I've got to buy off the rack with no alterations, so I'm not going in with a certain thing in mind because it might not be possible. I'm hoping to find a strapless white gown with lace details. Maybe a little silver or crystal shimmer. I don't know how that would help with the cake. It doesn't have to be very complicated in design. I prefer white butter cream to fondant. Maybe a couple flowers. I just want it to taste good."

"Any preference in flavor?"

"Maybe a white or chocolate chip cake with pastry cream filling, like a cannoli. My mom would love that."

"I can do that," Ariella said, a smile finally lighting her face.

"And speaking of food, I did invite you over here for lunch. Are you hungry?"

Ariella shoved her notebook into her purse and stood up. "No time to eat, darling. I've got a wedding to put together."

Francesca followed her to the door and gave Ariella a huge hug. "Thank you for all your help with this. I know I haven't made anything easy on you two."

"Do you know how many bridezillas we usually have to work with? You're easy. Anyway, that's what friends do—pull off the impossible when necessary. It's only fair considering you just talked me off the proverbial ledge over this stuff with my birth mother. And taking on a huge job like this will take my mind off everything, especially that upcoming reunion show."

The president had agreed to Liam's show proposal right before the gala. Francesca had jumped from one event to the next, getting everything in place for the televised reunion. "You don't have to do it, you know. You can change your mind."

"No, I can't." Ariella smiled and stepped through the doorway. "I'll email you our preliminary plans and menus to look over tomorrow afternoon."

Francesca nodded and watched her friend walk to her car. It all seemed so surreal. She would be married in three days. Married. To a man she'd known less than a month. To a man she'd grown to love, but who she knew didn't feel the same way about her.

A deep ache of unease settled in her stomach. She'd first felt the sensation when the shock wore off and she realized they were getting married on a Friday. That was considered to be very bad luck. Italians never married on a Friday. Unfortunately, the hotel wasn't available any other day.

Francesca hadn't seen a single good omen since that

ladybug landed on Liam's shoulder. Marrying Liam was looking more and more like a bad idea. But there was nothing she could do about it now.

Liam clutched a thick envelope of paperwork and a sack of Thai takeout as he went up the stairs to Francesca's town house. He'd met with his lawyer today to go over some details for the marriage. Now he planned to help Francesca with some packing.

"Hello," he yelled as he came through the door.

"I'm upstairs," Francesca answered.

He shut the door behind him and surveyed the neat stacks of labeled and sealed boxes in the foyer. "I have dinner."

"I'll be right there."

Francesca came down the stairs a few minutes later. Her hair was in a ponytail. She was wearing a nicely fitted tank top and capris with sneakers. It was a very casual look for her and he liked it. He especially liked the flush that her hard work brought to her cheeks and the faint glisten of sweat across her chest. It reminded him of the day they met.

God, that felt like ages ago. Could it really have been only a few weeks? Now here he was, helping her pack and clutching a draft of their prenuptial agreement in his hands.

"I see you've been hard at work today."

She nodded and self-consciously ran her hands over her hair to smooth it. "I probably look horrible."

"Impossible," he said, leaning in to give her a quick kiss. "I picked up some Thai food on the way from the lawyer's office."

"Lawyer's office?" Francesca started for the kitchen and he followed behind her.

"Yes. I got a draft of the prenup ready for you to look over."

Francesca stopped dead in her tracks, plates from the cabinet in each hand. Her skin paled beneath her olive complexion. There was a sudden and unexpected hurt in her eyes, as though he'd slapped her without warning. She set down the plates and quickly turned to the refrigerator.

"Are you okay?" Liam frowned. Certainly she knew that with the size of both their estates they needed to put in some protective measures now that they were making their relationship legally binding.

"Yes, I'm fine," she said, but she didn't look at him. Instead, she opened the refrigerator door and searched for something. "What do you want to drink?"

"I don't care," he said. Liam put the food and paperwork on the counter and walked over to her. "You're upset about this. Why?"

"I'm not," she insisted with a dismissive shake of her head, but he could tell she was lying. "It just surprised me. We hadn't talked about it. But, of course, it makes sense. This is a business arrangement, not a love match."

The sharpness in her tone when she said "love match" sent up a red flag in Liam's mind. He wished he could have seen her expression when she said it, but she was digging through the refrigerator. Then again, maybe he didn't want to see it. He might find more than he planned for.

He'd chosen Francesca for this partly because he thought she could detach emotionally from things. After she walked away from the elevator, he thought she could handle this like a champ. Maybe he was wrong. They'd spent a lot of time together recently. They'd had dinner, talked for hours, made love…. It had felt very much like a real relationship. Perhaps she was having real feelings.

Francesca thrust a soda can at him and he took it from her. She spun on her heel and started digging in the take-out bag. "So what are the high points?" she asked, popping open a carton of noodles.

She would barely look at him. She was avoiding something. Maybe the truth of the situation was in her eyes, so she was shielding him from it. If she was feeling something for him, she didn't want him to know about it. So he decided not to press her on the subject right now and opted just to answer her question. "Everything that is yours stays yours. Everything that is mine stays mine."

She nodded, dumping some chicken onto her plate. "That sounds fairly sensible. Anything else?"

"My lawyer insisted on an elevator clause for you. I couldn't tell him it wasn't necessary since we only plan to be married for a year. He said he likes to put them in all his prenups, so I figured it was better for it to be more authentic anyway."

"What is an elevator clause?"

"In our case, it entitles you to a lump sum of money on our first anniversary and an additional sum every year of our marriage after that. The money goes in trust to you in lieu of an alimony agreement. The longer we stay married, the more you're given."

Francesca turned to him, her brow furrowed. "I don't want your money, Liam. That wasn't part of our agreement."

"I know, but I want you to have it. You've gone far

beyond what we originally discussed and you deserve it. I'm totally uprooting your life."

"How much?"

"Five million for the first year. Another million every year after that. Milestone anniversaries—tenth, twentieth, etc., earn another five million."

"Five million dollars for one year of marriage? That's ridiculous. I don't want anything to do with that."

"If we pull this off, I'm inheriting my aunt's entire estate and all her ANS stock. That's somewhere in the ballpark of two billion dollars. I'd gladly give you ten million if you wanted it. Why not take it?"

"Because it makes me look like a gold digger, Liam. It's bad enough that we're getting married knowing it's just for show to make your aunt happy. If people find out I walked away after a year with five million bucks in my pocket...I just..." She picked up her plate and dumped rice onto it with an angry thump of the spoon. "It makes me feel like some kind of a call girl."

"Whoa," Liam said, putting his hands up defensively. "Now back up here. If we were getting married because we were in love, we'd probably have the same prenuptial agreement. Why would that be any different?"

Francesca shook her head. "I don't know. It just feels wrong."

Liam took the plate from her hand and set it on the counter. He wrapped his arms around Francesca's waist and tugged her against him. When she continued to avoid his gaze, he hooked her chin with his finger and forced her face to turn up to him. He wanted her to hear every word he had to say. "No one is going to think you're a gold digger. You will have earned every penny of that money over the next year. And not," he clarified, "on your back. As my wife, you're like an on-call employee twenty-four hours a day for a year."

He could tell his explanation both helped and hurt his cause. It justified the money but reduced her to staff as opposed to a wife. And that wasn't true. She was more than that to him. But if she was having confusing feelings about their relationship, would telling her make it worse?

"This isn't just some business arrangement anymore, Francesca. We're getting married. It may not be for the reasons that other people get married, but the end result is the same. You didn't have to agree to do this for me or for the network, but you chose to anyway. You're... *important* to me. So I'm choosing to share some of the benefits with you. Not just because you've earned them or because you deserve them. And you do. But because I want to give the money to you. You can donate every dime to charity, if you'd like. But I want you to have it regardless."

That got through. Francesca's expression softened and she nodded in acceptance before burying her face in his chest. Liam clutched her tightly and pressed a kiss into the dark strands of her hair.

It wasn't until that moment that he realized what a large price they were both paying to save the network and protect his dream. The reward would be huge, but the emotional toll would be high.

Five million didn't seem like nearly enough to cover it.

Eleven

Liam stood at the entrance to the terrace where the ceremony would take place. As instructed, he was wearing a black tuxedo with a white dress shirt and white silk tie and vest. A few minutes earlier, Ariella had pinned a white gardenia to his lapel. He looked every bit the proper groom, even if he didn't feel quite like one.

Beyond the doors was possibly the greatest wedding ever assembled on such short notice. Rows of white chairs lined an aisle strewn with swirls of white and pink rose petals. Clusters of flowers and light pink tulle draping connected the rows. A small platform was constructed at the front to allow everyone a better view of the ceremony. A large archway of white roses and hydrangeas served as a backdrop and were the only thing blocking the view of the city and the sunset that would be lighting the sky precisely as they said their vows.

About an hour ago, Ariella had given him a sneak

peek of the ballroom where the reception would be. It seemed as if an army of people was working in there, getting everything set up. The walls were draped in white fabric with up-lighting that changed the colors of the room from white, to pink, to gray. Tables were covered with white and delicate pink linens with embroidered overlays. Centerpieces alternated between tall, silver candelabras dripping with flowers and strings of crystals and low, tightly packed clusters of flowers and thick, white candles in hurricane vases. In the corner was a six-tiered wedding cake. Each round tier was wrapped at the base with a band of Swarovski crystals. The cake was topped with a white and pink crystal-studded *C*.

It was beautiful. Elegant. And completely wasted on their wedding, he thought with a pang of guilt.

Nervous, and without a herd of groomsmen to buy him shots in the hotel bar, he'd opted to greet guests as they came through the door. The wedding party itself was small with no attendants, but there were nearly a hundred guests. It had been a lightning-quick turnaround with electronic RSVPs, but nearly everyone invited had said yes, even if just out of morbid curiosity. So far, no one had asked any tacky questions at the door, like when the baby was due, but he was certain talk was swirling around the crowd inside.

"Ten minutes," Scarlet reminded him as she brushed by him in her headset, a clipboard clutched to her chest.

Ten minutes. Liam swallowed hard and pasted the wedding-day smile back on his face. In less than a half hour, he would be legally bonded to Francesca with all his friends and family as witnesses. A month ago, he'd been celebrating his purchase of ANS and looking forward to the excitement of fulfilling his dream of running a major network. Now he was about to marry a virtual stranger to keep the dream from crumbling into a nightmare.

"Liam," a proper female voice called to him.

He looked up to see Aunt Beatrice rolling toward him in a wheelchair pushed by Henry. He knew she was sick, but seeing her in a wheelchair was startling. Surely she could still walk? He thought back to every time he'd seen her in the past month. She had already been seated whenever he arrived. On their last few visits, she hadn't so much as stood up or walked over to get something from her bag. Now he realized it was because she couldn't. She'd done well hiding it until now.

"Aunt Beatrice," he said with a smile, leaning down to plant a kiss on her cheek. "And Henry," he added, shaking the butler's hand. He had a new appreciation for the quiet, older man who had served and loved his aunt all these years. "Seats have been reserved for you both in the first row on the right."

Aunt Beatrice nodded, and Henry rolled them into the room. There wasn't a "congratulations" or a "last chance to back out" from her. She hadn't even bothered to question him about his and Francesca's relationship any longer. He supposed that even if they were faking it, as long as it was legally binding, she was getting her way. She probably figured that within a year, they'd fall for each other for real. Or she'd be dead and wouldn't care any longer.

"Liam," Ariella said, approaching him quietly from the side. "We have a problem."

He wasn't surprised. As quickly as this had come together, things were bound to go awry. "What is it?"

"Security has spotted an uninvited guest in the lobby heading this way."

Liam frowned. "Who? A reporter?"

"Sort of. Angelica Pierce. How would you like us to handle this?"

Oh. That was certainly cause for a bit of excitement, especially where Ariella was concerned because Angelica had been suspended for her possible involvement in the hacking scandal that had revealed Ariella as the president's secret daughter. "Don't do anything. She's liable to make a scene if we have her escorted out. Better just to let her come and act like it's not a big deal."

Ariella nodded. "Agreed." She turned away and muttered into her headset. "Five minutes," she added, before disappearing toward the room serving as a bridal suite.

Liam busied himself greeting other guests and tried not to worry about Angelica. He'd only met the woman in person once, and he got the distinct impression that she was a suck-up who would do anything to keep her job. Right now, she was suspended pending the results of Hayden Black's investigation, so he wasn't surprised she'd shown up today. She was here to make an appearance and kiss up to her boss and his new bride.

He hoped that was all she was up to. He knew for a fact that Hayden and his fiancée, Lucy Royall, were already inside. Lucy was Graham Boyle's stepdaughter and there was some bad blood between her and Angelica. With any luck, they would sit far apart and not cross paths the whole evening. But he wasn't feeling very lucky today.

That's when he saw her. "Angelica," he said with a smile, accepting the hug she offered. "So good to see you." He wanted to keep this evening together, so he wasn't about to let on that she was an unwelcome party crasher.

Angelica seemed very pleased by the warm welcome. She'd certainly dressed up for the occasion, looking radiant even, if not a touch heavier than she had been a few weeks ago. Her face was rounder and her purple dress was a bit snug. The stress of Hayden's investigation must have been catching up with her.

"I wouldn't miss this for the world. I just love weddings. And my boss's wedding is an especially important event. I wish you both great happiness together."

Liam smiled and thanked her, turning to the next guests approaching. It was his rival network's former star, Max Gray and his new bride, Cara. They'd been married in March and had just come back from their extended honeymoon in Australia. The two of them were practically beaming with love for each other, and Cara's dress showed the gentle swell of her pregnancy. She had started doing public relations for D.C. Affairs since leaving the White House, but he could tell that motherhood was her true calling. She was just glowing.

As they approached the door, they both stopped to watch Angelica go inside. Max's jaw dropped, his eyes widening. His field research had helped uncover the hacking scandal back in January. "What is she doing here?" he asked.

Liam shrugged. "Trying to make friends, I suppose. Did you two have a nice trip?"

"Amazing," Cara said. "We slept in late, ate great food, did some sightseeing. It was wonderful. Where are you and Francesca going on your honeymoon?"

That was a good question. "We don't have anything planned yet. Things moved so fast and work has been so busy, we haven't had a chance. We're hoping things will slow down soon and we'll have the opportunity to get away. Sounds like a trip to Australia is a great choice. I'll have to talk to you two about it more later."

Max and Cara went to their seats and the last few arriving guests followed them. Liam straightened his tie and took a deep breath as he saw Scarlet and another man in a suit heading toward him with determination and purpose.

"Okay, showtime. This is your officiant, Reverend Templeton. He will go down the aisle first, then you. We'll seat the parents, and then the bride will come down the aisle with her father. Are you ready, Liam?"

That was another good question. He was ready as he was ever going to be for a corporate, shotgun marriage of convenience. The only thing that made him feel better was that he'd get to spend the next year with a sexy spitfire who made his blood boil with passion and excitement.

"I am."

Francesca sat still as stone at her dressing table, letting her mother pin the large, white gardenia in her hair. Looking at herself in the mirror, she was the perfect image of a beautiful bride on her big day. Her shiny, black hair was twisted up into an intricate updo, the gardenia pinned just to the side. Her makeup was airbrushed and flawless. She'd found the perfect gown in her size without much trouble. Even with such a time crunch, everything had worked out just as it should. It was as though this wedding was meant to be.

Only it wasn't.

Her persistent stomachache had kept her from eating

too much at breakfast or lunch. She had a plate of fruit and crackers beside her that she would pick at from time to time, but it just made the feeling worse.

Not even a saltine cracker could cure the ache of impending doom. This wedding was a mistake. She knew it. But the part of her that loved Liam and cared for ANS and its employees was overpowering her common sense.

She took one last look at herself in the mirror and inhaled a deep breath to pull herself together. Now was not the time to fall apart. Not while her parents' concerned eyes were watching her.

Since her father had come in, he'd been sitting in the corner, scowling in his tuxedo. Honestly, he'd had the same look on his face since she had met them at the hotel the day before. There had been a moment when he first saw her in her gown that his expression had softened and tears came to his eyes, but it hadn't lasted long.

Francesca was pretty sure her own wary appearance hadn't helped. But there was nothing she could do about it. She had to save her smiles and energy for the wedding and reception.

"Are you okay, *bella?*" her mother asked. She was a tinier version of Francesca, with the same dark eyes and warm brown skin. Her thick, brown hair was pulled back into a bun, with elegant streaks of gray running through it like professionally added highlights. She was wearing a shimmering gray dress with a jacket. Ariella had pinned a pink and white rose corsage to her lapel earlier. Her father had one very similar on his tuxedo.

Francesca nodded and stood, straightening her gown. She'd hoped for and found a white, strapless gown; there had been many to choose from because that style was in fashion. This one had a lace overlay that went to the floor and was delicately embroidered in a pattern with silver beads, crystals and pearls down to the chapel train. What she liked best about it was the silver sash around her waist with a crystal embellishment in the center. It accented her hourglass figure and gave the dress a little something special.

"Why do you ask?" Francesca asked innocently.

"You just don't look as happy as I was expecting. Where is my beautiful, blushing bride?" Her mother reached up to gently caress her face.

She stopped fidgeting with the dress and smiled, gripping her mother's hand reassuringly. "Yes, Mama, I am fine. I'm just a little nervous."

"You should be, marrying a man you hardly know," her father snarled from the corner.

"Victor!" her mother scolded over her shoulder. "We discussed this. We did the same thing, didn't we? And aren't you happy thirty years later?"

He shrugged and slumped into his chair. This was one argument he would lose, and he knew it. But he didn't have to like it. Francesca could easily see where she got her own stubborn streak and fiery temper.

"Mama, could you give me that small hand mirror so I can see the back?"

Donatella handed her the silver mirror and Francesca held it so she could make sure everything looked okay. Satisfied, she laid it on the edge of the dresser, but it tipped with the heavy weight of the handle and fell to the floor with a crash.

"Oh, no," Francesca lamented, crouching down to pick up the shattered hand mirror. There were only a few slivers of the reflective surface left, the rest scattered on the floor. Slumping into her chair, she looked at the broken glass and shook her head. "Seven years bad luck," she said. "As though I needed another sign."

"Nonsense," her mother chided. "Your *nonna* filled your head with silliness when you were a child. This means nothing aside from having to sweep up and buy a new mirror. Your marriage will be whatever you make it. And if you believe in your heart that it is doomed before it starts, you'll be right. You must fill your heart and soul with joy, not fear, as you walk down that aisle, *bella*."

Francesca hoped her mother was right. She should ignore the signs and try to make the most of her year with Liam. It was all she was going to get so she shouldn't spend the precious time she had moping about losing him.

A gentle rap sounded at the door and Ariella stuck her head in. "Mrs. Orr, it's time for you to be seated. I'll be back for the bride and her father in just a moment." She gave Francesca a quick wink of encouragement as they slipped out of the room.

Now was the moment Francesca was dreading the most. Five minutes alone with her father without her mother to be the buffer. Hopefully she could distract him with idle conversation until Ariella returned.

"How do I look, Daddy?"

The large Irishman crossed his arms over his chest and admired her for a moment before he spoke. "Like the saddest, most beautiful bride I have ever seen."

Francesca frowned at him. How could he see into her so well? "I'm smiling. Why do you think I'm sad?"

"There's something in your eyes. Something isn't quite right about all this—I can tell."

"Don't be silly, Daddy."

Victor stood up and walked over to her. He helped

Francesca up from her seat and held her hand tightly. "Look me in the eye and tell me that you love him."

Francesca fixed her gaze on her father. If she really wanted to back out of this wedding, this was her chance. All she had to do was say the word and he would have her on a plane to California before Aunt Beatrice knew what hit her. But she couldn't do that. Wouldn't.

She had to answer him honestly, or he would know. He sensed a problem, but he was barking up the wrong tree. If he wanted the truth of the matter, he should be asking Liam these questions. Without blinking, she spoke sincere words to him. "Yes, I love Liam. Very much."

"And you want to marry him?"

She did. It was fast, but she had fallen hard for her fiancé. Her trepidation was in knowing that no matter how she felt about him, their marriage would be over this time next year. How could she walk down the aisle knowing their wedding was a pointless exercise? Yes, it would save ANS and make a dying woman happy, but Francesca herself would be crushed in the process.

"Yes, Daddy. I want to marry Liam."

His gaze moved over her face, looking for a thread to pull at to unravel the truth, but there was nothing to find.

Another knock at the door came and Ariella stepped in holding Francesca's bouquet.

"It's beautiful," Francesca said as she took the flowers and admired them. There were pink and white roses, white hydrangeas and tiny white stephanotis. She'd given Ariella very little direction on this wedding, but with the bouquet, at least, she'd hit the nail on the head. Everything else would likely be just as perfect.

"Did you expect anything less?" she said with a smile. "It's time."

Francesca's father took her by the arm and led them down the hallway to the terrace. When she got the cue, Ariella opened the doors. They stepped onto the balcony to the sound of music from a string quartet. A hundred people stood up from their seats and turned to look Francesca's way as they kicked through rose petals down the aisle.

She was almost halfway down the aisle when she finally got the nerve to look at Liam.

Francesca had avoided it because she didn't want to see the truth in his eyes. He would likely look nervous. Maybe even fearful for what he'd gotten himself into. There would be no tears of love and joy. He would not be beaming with pride after seeing the woman he adored looking more beautiful than ever before. She knew she would be disappointed. But she looked anyway.

When her gaze met his, she felt her stomach do a flip. He looked so incredibly handsome. She'd seen him in a tuxedo before, but there was something different about the way he looked tonight. It was the expression on his face. There wasn't love there, but she did see admiration. Unmasked attraction. Deep respect. He knew how big a sacrifice she was making for him and he appreciated it. He just didn't love her for it. Not the way she loved him.

Francesca had to remind herself to smile and not get lost in her thoughts as they took the last few steps to the ceremony platform.

The minister began the ceremony, and her father leaned in to kiss her before handing her over to Liam for good. She couldn't meet his eyes then. If he saw the panic and fear there, he'd drag her down the aisle while everyone watched in horror. Instead, she closed her eyes and leaned in to his kiss.

"I love you, Daddy."

"I love you, too."

At that, he put her hand in Liam's and they stepped up together to be married.

Francesca thought she would be okay until she had to take that first step and her knees turned soft. It was only Liam's firm, reassuring grasp that kept her upright. He guided her to the minister, her hand clasped tightly in his.

"I won't let you fall. We can do this," he whispered with a smile and a wink.

She nodded and squeezed his hand.

The ceremony began, but it was a blur to her. The minister spoke, she repeated her vows, they exchanged rings and the next thing she knew, she was kissing her husband in front of a hundred people.

The roar of applause and the cheers were like a slap in the face, snapping her back into reality. The minister presented them as Mr. and Mrs. Liam Crowe as they turned to the audience. She clung to Liam's arm as they walked back down the aisle together as husband and wife.

When they rounded the corner to exit the terrace, Ariella was waiting for them. She escorted them back to the bridal room to wait for pictures while the guests made their way to the ballroom for cocktails.

Francesca rested her bouquet on the dressing table beside the broken mirror and slumped into her chair.

It was done. They were married.

They still had to sign the official paperwork for the license, but that would arrive any second now.

She almost couldn't believe it. She felt numb, like she was walking through a dream wedding instead of one in real life. It had been a beautiful ceremony, but it wasn't how she imagined her wedding day would be. No matter how many different ways she had pictured her big day, there was always a common element.

She looked over at Liam. He eyed the champagne glasses for a moment before crossing the room to pick them up. He handed one to her and held out his own for a toast.

"One day of marriage done. Three hundred and sixty-four to go."

With a sigh, she took a deep draw from her champagne flute and closed her eyes before the tears threatened to spill over.

One critical thing was missing from her fantasy wedding: a man who loved and adored her more than anything else on earth. And that was the one thing Scarlet and Ariella hadn't been able to provide.

Twelve

Liam was worried about Francesca. As she'd walked down the aisle toward him, she was literally the most beautiful bride he'd ever seen. The white gown was quite flattering against the warm color of her skin and it fit her curves like a glove.

For a moment, it had all become a little too real. His breath had caught in his throat. His mouth had gone bone-dry. His heart had raced a thousand miles an hour in his chest. Francesca was about to be his wife. And in that instant, he'd wanted her to be in every sense of the word.

It was a strange feeling. One he hadn't experienced before. He'd been fond of a lot of women over the years. He genuinely liked and respected Francesca. That was probably as close to "love" as he'd ever gotten. Marriage hadn't crossed his mind yet. He assumed he would get to that point in his life eventually. The Queen Bee had just accelerated his schedule.

Liam wasn't sure if it was the flowers or the music. The way she looked in that dress or the happy tears of his mother. But he was committed to the moment. He was excited to marry Francesca. Maybe this year wouldn't be so bad. Maybe…maybe there could be more than just a business arrangement between them. A real relationship.

He was snapped back to reality by the stony expression on Francesca's face. There was no happy, bridal glow. No tears of joy. No smile of excitement. She didn't look outright unhappy; she was covering it well, but Liam knew she was on the edge. The reality of lying to all their friends and family must be weighing heavily on her. He understood. That was why he'd given her the option not to go through with the marriage. But she'd insisted. She wasn't the type of woman to go back on her word. She would choke it down and do what had to be done.

Since they'd left the bridal suite, she'd become like a robot. She smiled, she went through the motions, but her dark eyes were dead. He wasn't sure what would happen when she couldn't hold in her emotions any longer. But he knew it wouldn't be pretty.

Fortunately, they were able to lose themselves in the smiles, handshakes and hugs of the receiving line. After that, the reception should be fairly short. With little notice, Scarlet and Ariella had only been able to arrange a catered hors d'oeuvres and cocktail reception. No band or dancing, no five-course sit-down dinner. Just an hour or so of mingling and cake, and then everyone would be on their way. It should be fairly simple to get through it without drama.

The last few guests came through the line and Liam and Francesca were able to leave their stations. He put his arm around her waist and leaned into her. "Are you okay?" he whispered.

Her wary eyes looked to him and she nodded. "I'm just a little overwhelmed."

"Do you want me to get you a drink?"

"Yes," she said with emphasis. "Please."

Liam left her side to get them both something from the bar. He was returning with a glass in both hands when he caught an unwelcome sight out of the corner of his eye. Hayden Black and Angelica Pierce were chatting. No, that wasn't the right word. They were having a discussion that verged on heated, if Angelica's stiff posture and tight mouth were any indication. What was she thinking, having a conversation with the investigator out to prove she was guilty? This couldn't be good.

As far as Liam knew, Angelica hadn't been called to testify before the congressional committee about the hacking scandal. He assumed it was because Hayden hadn't been able to piece together the details of her involvement. Or at least, to prove it. The suspicion of her guilt was nothing Liam could act on. He needed hard evidence to fire her, and if Angelica was involved, she had been very, very careful. She wasn't stupid. She was a ruthless, cunning reporter willing to do nearly anything to get the big story. He appreciated her ambition. But not her moral code.

Secretly, he hoped Hayden would find what he needed. Liam was nervous running ANS with Angelica still in his employ. He needed a reason to cut her loose permanently.

Their discussion was getting a little more animated. Liam searched the room for Ariella and Scarlet, but he didn't see them or the security they'd hired. He might have to intervene on this situation himself. Francesca's drink would have to wait.

As Liam got closer to them, he could hear what they were saying a little better. They were trying to speak quietly, but their passions were getting the best of them. At least, Angelica's were. Hayden was always very calm and collected.

"I find it laughable that people seem to think you were behind this whole thing," Hayden said. "As though the peroxide-bleached brain cells you have left could plan something more intricate than what kind of shoes to wear with what outfit."

A flush of anger rose to Angelica's cheeks. Her eyes narrowed at Hayden. She didn't notice Liam approaching them because she was so focused on their argument. "You think you're so smart, Hayden, but I'm not going to fall for your tricks. Is calling me a dumb blonde the best you've got? I expected better of you. All men see is what women want them to see. The hair and the makeup and the clothes blind you to the truth. But don't let appearances fool you. We may have the same hair color, but I'm not sweet and pliable like your precious Lucy. I earned my place at the company. It wasn't because my stepfather owned the network."

Liam expected Hayden to take offense at the insults Angelica was levying at his fiancée, but it didn't seem to faze him. "Yes," he agreed, "but Lucy has something you'll never have no matter how hard you work or how many people you trample."

Angelica nearly snorted with contempt. "And what's that? The love of a man like you?"

"Nope. Her daddy's undying affection. She's the beautiful little girl he always wanted. The one he raised as his own. He bought her ponies and went to her ballet recitals. He got her a convertible on her sixteenth birthday. I bet it breaks his heart that he'll be in jail and can't walk Lucy down the aisle when we get married."

Angelica stiffened beside him, but she brushed off his words with a shrug of indifference. "So what? Her stepfather spoiled her. Am I supposed to be jealous of her for that?"

"No. But you might be jealous because he didn't have to bribe people to keep *Lucy* a secret. He wasn't embarrassed of her."

"I don't know what you're insinuating," she said slowly, although the tone of her voice said otherwise. It was cold and flat, issuing a silent warning to Hayden.

It made Liam wonder what they were really talking about. He'd heard that Lucy and Angelica hadn't gotten along, but Lucy had left ANS to work with Hayden before he took over. He certainly didn't know anything about Angelica's past or her family. Why did Lucy's relationship with Graham make Angelica so angry?

Hayden really seemed to know how to push her buttons. Was he rattling her cage for amusement or was he trying to get her to make a mistake? Liam turned to his left and spied the wedding videographer, a field cameraman from ANS. Perfect. He waived the man over.

"I want you to very quietly, subtly, record their conversation. She can't know you're taping them."

The camera man worked on ANS investigations and undercover stings, so he was likely more comfortable doing this than taping greetings for the bride and groom. He eased into the crowd, coming up from behind Angelica, partially hidden by the towering wedding cake beside them.

Liam watched Hayden's gaze fall on the video camera for an instant, then back to Angelica. They both knew this was their chance to catch her at something when she didn't expect it.

"Admit it, Angelica. All this hacking business had nothing to do with presidential scandals or career-launching headlines. It was just a high-profile distraction to get what you were really after. The truth is that you were trying to ruin him. Getting your revenge, at last."

Liam held his breath, waiting to see where this conversation might go when she thought no one else was watching.

"That's a ridiculous, unfounded accusation. Graham was a lousy boss with questionable ethics, but he was hardly a blip on my radar. I've got better things to do with my time than try to ruin someone like him. In time, they always ruin themselves."

"It's interesting you would say that. But I've got a stack of pictures that say otherwise. Pictures of you modified to remove your fancy hairdo and contact lenses. It made me think of something Rowena Tate told me. She mentioned that you reminded her of a troubled, unstable girl at her private school. The girl had always gloated about her rich father, but he never showed up for parent weekends. He just mailed a check."

"I didn't go to private school," Angelica said, her jaw clenched tighter with every word he said.

"I did a little research and found old school records showing her tuition was paid for by Graham Boyle. Isn't that odd? He's always told people he didn't have any children of his own. It must've been hard growing up knowing your father didn't want anything to do with you. That you were just a mistake that could be fixed with enough money. If it were me, I'd want revenge, too."

"Shut up, Hayden."

"He didn't even recognize you when you came to work at ANS, did he? Sure, you looked different, but a father should be able to recognize his own daughter, right? Then you had to sit back and watch him fawn over Lucy, a child that wasn't even his."

"I don't have to listen to your wild stories. You're obviously grasping at straws." She shook her head, turning to walk away from their discussion.

"The sad thing is that you went to all this trouble, ruined so many lives, and in the end, you failed."

Angelica stopped dead in her tracks. She swung back to him, her eyes wide and furious. "Oh, really? What makes you think this isn't exactly the way I planned it? Those fools they arrested, Brandon and Troy, will take the fall for the wiretaps. All the evidence shows that Marnie Salloway orchestrated it. Graham Boyle is going to rot in prison and his precious network will be destroyed before too long. It sounds pretty perfect to me. My only regret is that in the end, I couldn't find a way to get Lucy's hands dirty enough to send her to jail with dear old dad."

"But he didn't go to jail because he loved you and wanted to protect you. It was pure guilt."

"I don't need his love," she snapped. "I've gotten this far in life without it. What I did need was to see that bastard brought to his knees. And I got that."

Hayden smiled wide and turned toward the cameraman. "You get that, Tom?"

The videographer pulled away from his lens and nodded. "Every single word."

Angelica's jaw dropped open, her skin flushing crimson in anger. "You bastard!" she shrieked. "You deliberately set me up. If you think I'm going to let you ruin my career with no physical proof of my involvement with the hacking, you've got another think coming. Even with that tape, no one will believe you."

Hayden just shook his head. "I didn't have to ruin your career. Like you said, in time, people always ruin themselves. I just happened to get that moment on film. I'm pretty sure ANS will terminate you when I show them that tape. And the FBI and congressional committee will find it very interesting. Soon, people will start rolling on you to cut a better deal for themselves. There's no loyalty among criminals. You'll be wearing matching orange jumpsuits with your daddy in no time."

Graham Boyle was Angelica's father? Liam frowned in confusion but was jerked away from his thoughts when Angelica reared back and slapped Hayden. He barely reacted to the assault, simply shaking his head and looking at her with pity in his eyes. "It's a shame you wasted your whole life on this. I feel sorry for you."

By now, a large crowd of the wedding guests had gathered around the argument. More witnesses. The more people that gathered, the higher Angelica's blood pressure seemed to climb. "I don't want your pity," she spat.

Liam watched her fingertips curl and uncurl as she tried to keep control, but she was unraveling quickly. At last, she reached out, and before anyone could stop her, she grabbed a large fistful of wedding cake. Less than a second later, she flung it at Hayden, silencing him with a wet slap.

"What are you looking at?" she screamed at the crowd. She grabbed more cake in each hand and started launching it at the crowd. Buttercream icing flew through the air, pelting the wedding guests. They screamed and scattered. Liam checked to ensure Francesca, Aunt Beatrice and his mother were out of the line of fire, but Henry wasn't so lucky. He took a large piece of cake to the front of his suit. But he only laughed, scraping it off his shirt and taking it in stride. After forty years with Beatrice, flying cake was probably nothing.

Before Liam could turn to get help, two burly security officers rushed past him. Angelica's eyes went wild when she saw them. She started kicking and screaming when they tried to restrain her.

"Don't you touch me!" she howled. "Let me go!"

Liam could only watch in amazement as she wrenched herself from the men's grasp, only to stumble backward into the cake table. It turned over, taking Angelica and the cake with it. Angelica landed smack-dab in the middle of the towering confection, coating her from hair to rear in buttercream. She roared in anger, flailing as she tried to get up and couldn't. When she did stand again, it was only with the help of the guards gripping her upper arms.

On her feet, she was a dripping mess. Her perfectly curled blond hair was flat and greasy with white clumps of frosting. Icing was smeared across her face and all over her purple dress. She huffed and struggled in her captors' arms, but there was no use. They had her this time. At last, Angelica had gotten herself into a situation she couldn't weasel out of.

"You know," Hayden said, "looking like that, I'm surprised people didn't see the resemblance before."

Angelica immediately stilled and her face went as pale as the frosting. "I don't look anything like *her*."

"Oh, come on, *Madeline*. There's no sense lying anymore about who you really are."

The calm in her immediately vanished. "Never call me that name. Do you hear me? Never! Madeline Burch is dead. *Dead*. I am Angelica Pierce, you understand? Angelica Pierce!" she repeated, as though that might make it true.

Several people gasped in the crowd. Cara stood stock-still a few feet away with Max protectively at her side. "Rowena and I went to Woodlawn Academy with Madeline," she said before turning to Angelica. "We were right. It *is* you."

"You shut up," Angelica spat. "You don't know anything about me."

"You're right. I don't," Cara answered.

The guards then escorted a wildly thrashing Angelica—or *Madeline*—out of the ballroom. By now, the local police were likely on their way to take her into custody. First, for disorderly conduct and assault. Then, maybe, for her involvement in the hacking scandal. Either way, a scene like that was enough cause for Liam to terminate her from ANS for good.

"I'm sorry about the mess," Hayden said, wiping some cake from his face. "I never expected her to come talk to me. She was so confident that she had me beaten. I couldn't pass up the chance to put a crack in her facade, but I didn't realize she'd go nuclear. It ruined your reception. Just look at the cake."

Liam shrugged. Somehow knowing it wasn't his real

wedding made it easier to stomach. "Nailing Angelica is important. You have to take every opportunity you can get."

He walked with Hayden out of the ballroom to where a few police officers were waiting outside. They answered their questions and gave out their contact information. Hayden opted to go with them to the station, but Liam knew he needed to get back inside and salvage what was left of his wedding reception.

When Liam returned, people seemed to be milling around, at a loss for what to do with themselves. "Sorry about that, folks," he said, raising his hands to get everyone's attention. "Please stick around and enjoy the reception. I'm sad to say there won't be any cake, though." A few people chuckled and most awkwardly returned to nibbling and drinking as they had before the fight broke out.

Liam noticed the drinks he'd fetched from the bar still untouched on the table. He'd gotten wrapped up in the scene and had forgotten to take Francesca her champagne. He picked them back up and turned, looking for her. After all that, they'd need another round pretty quickly.

But she was nowhere to be found.

Frowning, he searched the ballroom, finally turning to a frazzled Ariella for help. "Have you seen the bride?" he asked.

"Not since I put her in a cab."

"A cab?" Liam frowned. "You mean she's left her own reception? Without me?"

Ariella bit her lip and nodded. "About ten minutes ago. Right about the time Angelica started bathing in wedding cake. She needed to get out of here."

Liam glanced around the mess of a ballroom. Scarlet was frantically informing staff of their cleanup duties. The guests were still standing around, but despite his assurances, they seemed unsure of whether they should stay. It was a wedding disaster.

He didn't blame Francesca one bit for leaving.

Francesca couldn't get out of her wedding dress fast enough. The corset-tight bodice made her feel like she couldn't breathe. It was all just too much.

Initially, she'd been relieved when Hayden and Angelica started making a scene. For the first time that day, every eye in the room wasn't on her. It was a blessed break. It was the first moment since she started down the aisle that she thought she might be able to let the facade of bridal bliss drop and regather herself.

And then the cake started flying.

Her *nonna* had never specifically mentioned that having her wedding cake flung across the room was bad luck, but Francesca was ready to make her own deduction about that. Their reception was a disaster. Their sham of a marriage would no doubt be a mess, too. It was just one more thing, one more blazing neon sign trying to point her in the right direction. She'd ignored all the other portents of bad luck. The fates had ensured this last one would be undeniable.

When she'd asked Ariella to get her a cab, her friend probably thought she was upset about having her reception ruined. The truth was that she just couldn't pretend anymore. If she'd had to be in that ballroom one more minute, she would have blown everything for Liam and ANS.

Now that she was back at Liam's place, in a pair of

jeans and a light sweater, she felt better and worse all at once. Boxes of her things still sat around the ground floor of his town house ready to be incorporated into her new life with him. But they might as well go back onto the moving truck.

She poured herself a glass of wine to calm her nerves and went upstairs to the master bedroom to repack. The only things of hers that had been put away were her clothes and personal effects for the bed and bath. Those could easily be rounded back up, and she intended to do it right now.

If she hurried, she would be sleeping in her own bed tonight. Not quite the wedding night everyone was expecting her to have.

She had one suitcase filled and zipped closed when she heard the front door open.

"Francesca?" Liam called.

"I'm upstairs," she answered and pulled another bag onto the bed. She was stuffing it with lingerie and pajamas when he came through the doorway of his bedroom.

Francesca tried not to think about how handsome he looked in his rumpled tuxedo. His tie was undone, his collar unbuttoned. She liked him tousled. Despite everything, she felt her body react to his presence. Her pulse started racing, and her skin tightened in anticipation of his touch. But thinking about how much she wanted Liam wouldn't help. It would make her want to stay. And she needed to go.

"What are you doing?" he asked. His voice wasn't raised. It was quiet and tired. They'd both had a long day and didn't need any more drama. But this had to happen tonight.

"I'm packing my things and moving back into my

place." Francesca shoved another few items into her bag and looked up. "Don't worry, I'll lie low until Aunt Beatrice leaves town on Monday, but then I'm calling the moving company to come get my stuff."

Liam took a few steps toward her. She could feel the magnetic pull of him grow stronger as he came closer. She wanted to bury her face in his lapel and forget about everything that was going wrong. But she couldn't.

"Why?"

Francesca put the last of her clothes into the bag and zipped it closed. She looked at the bag as she spoke to ensure she could get all the words out. "I'm sorry, Liam. I thought I could do this. But I just can't."

There was a pause before he answered, his voice a touch strained. "Do you want an annulment?"

She looked up at him and shook her head. "No. I'll remain legally married to you for the sake of the network. Hopefully that will be enough because I can't play house with you. It's too hard on…" Her voice started to falter as tears rushed to her eyes. She immediately turned from him before she gave away how she really felt. "It's too hard on my heart, Liam."

He took another step forward, but stopped short of reaching out to her. "What do you mean?"

Francesca took a deep breath. "I want more."

"More than the five million?"

At that, Francesca jerked her head up to meet his gaze. "You just don't get it, do you? I don't want your money. I never did. I have plenty of my own. I want the things that you can't give me. I want love. A real family. A marriage like my parents have. I want a man who cares for me more than anyone or anything."

She shook her head and hoisted the strap of the bag

over her shoulder. "This isn't your fault. You were right when you said I was a true believer. I am. But I've been lying to myself. First, I told myself that I could be with you and it would be fine. That I could spend the next year pretending. But I can't because I was stupid enough to fall for you. Then I kept hoping that maybe, just maybe, you would fall for me and this could become more than just a business arrangement. Silly, right?"

Liam reached out to her, but Francesca sidestepped him. "Don't," she said. "Just don't. I know you don't have feelings for me. Anything you say right now will make it worse."

She extended the handle of her suitcase and rolled it to the bedroom door.

"Francesca, wait."

She stopped and turned to him. This was the moment everything hinged on. If she was wrong and he did care for her, this was the time for him to say it. She looked into his dark blue eyes, hoping to see there the love she wanted so desperately. Etched into his pained expression was desperation and confusion. He didn't want her to go, but he didn't know how to ask her to stay.

"Liam, would you have ever considered marrying me if your aunt hadn't forced us into this situation? I mean, would you even have asked me on a date after what happened between us in the elevator? Honestly."

Liam frowned and shoved his hands into his pockets. "No, I probably wouldn't have."

At least they were both telling the truth now. Nodding, she turned away and hauled her luggage down the stairs. It was time for her to go home and pick up the pieces of her life.

Thirteen

Liam signed Angelica's termination paperwork and pushed the pages across his desk. He thought he would be happy to see this issue put to bed, but he wasn't. He was the most miserable newlywed in history.

For one thing, he hadn't seen the bride since their wedding night. It had been a long, lonely weekend without her there. He'd quickly grown accustomed to having her around. Now his town house felt cold and empty.

The office wasn't much better. Francesca didn't greet him first thing with coffee and a kiss. He wasn't even sure if she was at work today. He wanted to call her. Email her. But he knew he shouldn't. It would make it easier on her if he took a step back and let her have the space she needed. She deserved that much.

But he missed his wife.

How quickly she had become that in his mind. She was no longer his employee. She was his wife. There was no differentiation in his mind about the terms of their marriage. Their engagement may have been a ruse, but the wedding and the marriage felt real to him. Frighteningly real.

Liam had never given much thought to a wife and family, but the minute Francesca walked out the door, a hole formed in his chest. It was as though she'd ripped out his heart and taken it with her. All he was left with was the dull ache of longing for her.

That didn't feel fake to him.

Yes, he'd been pushed into the marriage to please his aunt. He had to admit that much to Francesca because it was true. But now that he was married to her, it felt right. It felt natural. He no longer cared about Aunt Beatrice's opinion on the matter. He…was in love with Francesca.

"I love my wife," he said out loud to his empty office. There was no one to hear him, but saying it had lifted a huge weight from his shoulders. Unfortunately, admitting the truth was just the first step.

How could he prove to Francesca that he really did love her? That this wasn't about the network or stock deals? There was no way for her to know for sure that he wasn't just playing nice for appearances.

The only way to convince her, the only sure path, would be to take the stock deal and the network woes off the table. If his aunt had no negotiating power over him, then he stayed married to Francesca because he wanted to, not just because he had to.

But to do that without risking the company would mean that he needed enough stock to control ANS without his aunt's shares. That seemed virtually impossible. Unless…

Liam grabbed his phone and leaped out from behind

his desk. He had to find Victor Orr before they returned to California. Francesca had mentioned they were staying on a few days to tour the Smithsonian, so if he had any luck, they were still in D.C.

It took two phone calls and a drive to their hotel in bumper-to-bumper traffic, but Liam was finally able to track down Francesca's parents. He was standing at the door, waiting for them to answer the buzzer, when he realized he didn't know exactly what he was going to say to them. He would have to admit the truth. And that would mean that a very large, angry Irishman might be beating him senseless within minutes for hurting his daughter.

Victor answered the door with a frown. Without speaking a word, he seemed to realize something was wrong. Why else would his new son-in-law show up alone just days after the wedding? He led Liam into their suite and gestured for him to sit down in one of the chairs in the living room.

He watched Liam through narrowed eyes for a few minutes before Liam gathered the nerve to speak.

"There are some things I need to tell you," Liam said.

"I'm sure there are." Victor leaned back in his chair, ready to listen.

Without knowing the best way to tell the story, Liam chose to start at the beginning. He began with the stock arrangement with his aunt, delicately skipping over the elevator debacle, and followed with Beatrice's later demand that he marry to keep control of the network.

"And my daughter agreed to go along with this phony engagement?"

"Yes, sir. She seemed hesitant at first, but apparently she saw a sign that she should do it. A ladybug."

Victor shook his head. "Her and those damned signs. She gets into more trouble that way. Married to a man she hardly knows because of a ladybug!"

"We never intended to go through with the marriage, but my aunt was adamant we do it now. She's ill and wanted to make sure we followed through. I told Francesca she didn't have to do it, but she insisted."

"She's stubborn like I am."

Liam chose not to touch that statement. "What neither of us realized was that we might actually fall for one another. On our wedding night, Francesca told me she had feelings for me that she knew weren't mutual and she couldn't go on that way."

"You just let her walk out like that?"

Liam frowned and looked down at his hands. "I didn't know what to tell her. I wasn't sure how I felt about everything. What was real between us and what was a fantasy? I didn't know."

"And now?"

"Now I know. I love your daughter, and I want to ask your permission to marry her."

"Son, you're already married."

"I know, but things are different now. I want to be married to her for real. I want to go to her and tell her how I feel, but I need your help. Francesca will never believe our marriage is anything more than a business deal as long as my aunt is holding the stock over my head. I can't afford to buy her out. But if I could get enough minority stockholder support, I might be able to get majority control without her shares."

Victor nodded. "I don't think I have enough, but I've got a good bit. So does my friend Jimmy Lang. Together, that might tip the scales. Let me make a call."

As Victor got up and headed into the bedroom, a simmer of hope started bubbling in Liam's gut. He really hoped that he could pull this off. He didn't want to go to Francesca and tell her he loved her if there were any suspicions about his motives. This was the only way.

"Good news," Victor said as he returned a few minutes later. "I spoke with Jimmy and did the math. Combined with yours, we have fifty-two percent of the company stock. Close, but we made it. Jimmy and I are both really excited about the direction you're taking the network, so we have no qualms about delegating our voting authority to you. So," he said, extending his hand to Liam, "congratulations. You're still running this network."

Liam leaped from his seat and excitedly shook his father-in-law's hand. "Thank you so much, sir."

Victor shrugged. "I didn't do it for you. I did it for my little girl. You have my consent to marry her, so get out of here and make it right between you two."

Liam's eyes widened as he nodded. There was no arguing with Victor Orr, even if he wanted to. "Thank you again," he said as he turned and bolted from their hotel suite.

As badly as he wanted to rush to find Francesca, he had one other stop to make. Fortunately, that stop was located in the same hotel.

Liam rang the doorbell at the penthouse suite and waited for Henry to answer the door. The older man arrived a few minutes later, welcoming Liam with the same smile and nod he'd always received.

"Come in, Liam. I don't believe she's expecting you this morning. We're packing to return to New York."

"I'm sorry to pop in unannounced, Henry, but I need to talk to my aunt. It's important."

Henry held out his hand to gesture toward the bedroom. Liam didn't wait for him, moving quickly across the carpet and around the corner.

Aunt Beatrice looked up as he charged in. She was sitting in her wheelchair folding her clothes. "Liam," she said. "I expected you to be off somewhere basking in wedded bliss."

"No, you didn't," he said, sitting on the edge of the bed beside her. "You and I have been playing a dangerous game that could end up doing nothing but hurting people."

She didn't bother acting offended by his insinuation. "I did what I thought was best for the family. And for you, despite what you might think."

"I know," Liam agreed. "And I came here to thank you."

That, at last, got a rise out of the Queen Bee. She sat up straight in her chair, her eyes narrowing at him in confusion. "Thank me?"

"Yes. If you hadn't forced me to get married, I might've let Francesca walk right out of my life. I love her. And I hope she stays married to me for forty years—not for the network, or because of your demands, but because I want us to grow old together. That said, I'm not going to let you control me any longer. I don't need your ANS stock or you holding it over my head. I now have enough backing to maintain control of ANS without your shares or your billions. I don't care about any inheritance."

Aunt Beatrice sat silently for a few minutes, absorbing his words. After a while, he began to wonder if she was mentally going over the new changes to her will. He didn't care. Cut him out. Cut him *loose*.

"Those," she said at last, "are the words of a man who can take charge of this family." Beatrice smiled softly to herself and placed a blouse in her suitcase. "It's what I've been waiting for. I never intended to sell my stock to Ron Wheeler. I just wanted to see you settled down, in control and happy with your place in life. Francesca is the right woman for you. I knew that just as certainly as I knew you two were pretending. In time, I figured things would work out between you. Once you both stopped fighting it. It's a shame I'll be dead before I can see you two genuinely happy together."

"You knew we were faking the relationship?"

"It takes a smart, observant person to head this family. Very little gets past me, even now. But it's okay. I'm sorry for meddling in your private life. Blackmail really isn't my forte, but I did what I thought I needed to for the good of you and the family. I'll call my stockbroker this afternoon and have the shares of ANS transferred to you."

"What? Now?" He had years and millions to pay off before he owned those shares outright.

"It's your wedding present. Most people don't give networks as gifts, but you're not the typical bride and groom."

Liam reached out and took his aunt's hand. It was something he rarely did; she wasn't very affectionate, but he was seeing the dents in her armor. Her illness was revealing the person inside that she kept hidden. "Thank you, Aunt Beatrice."

She turned her head, dismissing his sentiment with a wave of her hand, but he could see a moist shimmer in her eyes. "It will be thanks enough when you save that company and take over handling our motley crew of relatives when I'm gone."

"Do I really have to be executor of the estate?"

"Absolutely. And don't worry. Eventually, you will grow accustomed to the constant ass-kissing."

Francesca left ANS early. She'd been a self-imposed prisoner in her office all morning, afraid she'd run into Liam in the hallway. She had had a few days to sit at home alone, licking her wounds, but she wasn't ready to see him again. Especially knowing that everyone still expected them to be a happy, newly married couple.

After overhearing Jessica tell someone on the phone that Liam was out of the office, she figured this was her opportunity to escape.

She made it back to her town house without incident. Relieved, she dropped her purse on the coffee table, kicked off her shoes and went into the kitchen for a drink.

When Francesca rounded the corner and found Liam sitting at her kitchen table, she nearly leaped out of her skin. *"Oh, dio mio!"* She jumped, pressing her back against the counter and clutching her rapidly beating heart. "What the hell are you doing here, Liam? You scared me to death."

He looked a little sheepish as he stood up and came over to her. "I'm sorry. I didn't mean to scare you. I thought you'd notice my car out front. You gave me a key, so I figured I would wait around until you got home. When I called Jessica she told me you'd left."

"I gave you that key when we were going to be a happily married couple. Using it after everything that happened is a little creepy. Why are you here, anyway? We don't have anything to talk about."

Liam shook his head and came closer. She was able to catch of whiff of his cologne and her body immediately began responding to him. Apparently, it hadn't gotten the message about the breakup of their nonrelationship.

"We have a lot to talk about. Starting with how much I love you and how miserable I've been since you left."

Francesca started to argue with him and then stopped. *Did he just...* She couldn't have heard him right. "What did you say?"

Liam smiled, sending her heart fluttering at the sight. He was wearing a navy collared shirt that brought out the dark blue of his eyes as he closed in on her. She noticed a few weary lines around them. He looked a little tired and tense, but she had attributed that to the stress of running the network and the fiasco of their wedding.

Could it be that he was losing sleep over her?

He stopped just short of touching her, forcing her to look up at him. His hands closed over her upper arms, their warmth sinking deep into her bones. "I love you, Francesca. I'm in love with you."

As much as she wanted to melt into him, she couldn't let herself fall prey to him. She ignored the excited flutter of butterflies in her stomach and pulled back out of his grasp, watching him with wary eyes. "You didn't love me Friday night. You could've told me then and you didn't. You let me leave. And now you show up singing a different tune. What happened? Did your aunt find out? Trying a different tactic to keep the network?"

Liam swallowed hard, a flash of resignation in his eyes. "I thought you would say something like that.

Which is why it took me so long to come see you today. I had some important business to take care of."

Francesca crossed her arms defensively over her chest, but she didn't think it would do much good. Her armor where Liam was concerned had been permanently breached. "It's always business first with you."

"You're right. First, I had to go confess to your father."

Francesca's eyes grew wide with unexpected panic. "You told my father? Why? He's going to kill me. How could you do that without asking me?"

"Because I needed his help. And his blessing to marry you."

"It's a little late for that."

"It's never too late where an overprotective father is concerned. Not only did he give his permission, but he and his associate have pledged their stock to support me at ANS, giving me a majority share without my aunt."

Francesca tried to process what he was saying, but she kept getting hung up on what kind of conversation he'd had with her father when she wasn't there. "You don't need your aunt's stock anymore?"

"No."

That meant they didn't have to be married. "But you don't want an annulment?"

"Absolutely not." Liam crowded back into her space, closing the gap she'd put between them. "I have no intention of letting you out of my sight, or my bed, for the next forty years."

The butterflies in her gut went berserk. She brought her hand to her belly to calm them. "Wait. You love me. You want to stay married to me. And it has nothing to do with the network?"

Liam nodded. "Not a thing. I told my aunt this morning that I wasn't going to play along anymore. I didn't want you to think for a moment that I wasn't one hundred percent sincere in my love for you. This isn't about my aunt or the network or appearances. It's about you and me and the rest of our lives."

His arms snaked around her waist and this time, she didn't pull away. She molded herself against him and let out a small sigh of contentment at the feel of being in his arms again.

"I am in love with you, Francesca Crowe. I want to stay married to you until the day I die."

Her heart skipped a beat at the use of her married name. She hadn't heard anyone use it since the wedding. "I love you, too."

Liam dipped his head down to capture her lips with his own. This kiss—their first as two people in love—blew away all the others they'd shared before. Every nerve in her body lit up at his touch. She wrapped her arms around his neck to try and get closer to him, but it could never be close enough. She lost herself in the embrace, letting his strong arms keep her upright when her knees threatened to give way beneath her.

Pulling away after what felt like an eternity, he said breathlessly, "I want us to get married."

Francesca wrinkled her nose and put her palm gently against the stubble of his jaw. "*Mio caro,* we're already married."

"I know," he said with a devious smile. "But I want a do-over. With a tropical honeymoon. And this time, it will just be the two of us. No family, no pressure and especially no cake throwing."

Epilogue

Antigua, One Week Later

Francesca had no idea a vacation could be so perfect. With Ariella's televised reunion show coming up, they didn't have the luxury of taking a long honeymoon, but they did manage to sneak away for a long weekend in the Caribbean.

So far, they had sunbathed, swum in the ocean, dined on the best seafood she'd ever tasted and renewed their vows in a private white gazebo hovering over the water.

Their previous ceremony had been legally binding but tainted by his aunt's machinations and Angelica's tantrum. Their vow renewal had been just for them. A chance to say the words again and wholeheartedly mean it. Afterward, they drank champagne in their private bungalow and shared a tiny cake for two that no one could ruin.

Today they had planned a snorkeling trip in the morning, followed by marathon lovemaking and lots of luxurious naps. The snorkeling trip had been excellent. The water was crystal clear and a rainbow of fish was in abundance. They were on their way back to the bungalow when Francesca stopped and tugged at Liam's arm.

"Liam, stop. Look," Francesca said, pointing out the television mounted above the cantina bar.

It was the live coverage of Madeline Burch's arraignment. Before they left, the video of her confession had played repeatedly at every news outlet, with ANS breaking the story. The media had jumped on the tale about her involvement in the hacking scandal after both Brandon Ames and Troy Hall agreed to testify against her. The news of her double life was just the icing on the ratings cake.

For a moment, Francesca almost felt badly for Madeline. She looked awful. Orange was not her color. Going without her expensive hair coloring and extensions, she had mousy brown roots at the crown of her stringy, thin hair. Her last dose of Botox had faded away, as had her spray tan. Her colored contacts had been replaced with thick, prison-issued glasses. Several more pounds also had been added to her frame since their reception. There was no doubt that Angelica was Madeline Burch now.

"The news is out," Liam said as the news banner at the bottom changed. They couldn't hear what was being said on the television, but the words scrolling at the bottom announced the breaking news that investigator Hayden Black had testified that Madeline was Graham Boyle's secret, illegitimate daughter. Liam had told Francesca what he'd overheard during the argument at the reception, but her motivation for taking down Graham had been withheld from the press so far.

"Wow," Francesca said, shaking her head. "It's just so sad. And senseless. How many lives were ruined just so she could get back at Graham for the way he treated her?"

When she turned, Liam was pulling his phone out of his pocket. He had done well to unplug from the news world while they were on their honeymoon, but now that the news was out, all his journalistic buttons were being pushed.

He unlocked his screen and started typing something, and then he stopped. He pressed the power button and slipped the phone back into his pocket.

Francesca arched an eyebrow at him in surprise. "Really?" she asked.

"I am sure the network and my employees have this story well in hand. And even if they didn't, I am on my honeymoon. I couldn't care less about Graham Boyle's secret daughter."

He turned to face Francesca, snaked his arms around her waist and pulled her tightly against him. She melted into him, surprised to feel the firm heat of his desire pressed into her belly.

"Right now," he said with a wicked grin, "I'm more interested in making love to my wife."

* * * * *

MILLS & BOON®
By Request

RELIVE THE ROMANCE WITH THE BEST OF THE BEST

A sneak peek at next month's titles...

In stores from 16th November 2017:

- **His Best Acquisition** – Dani Collins, Rachael Thomas *and* Tara Pammi

- **Her Ex, Her Future?** – Lucy King, Louisa Heaton *and* Louisa George

In stores from 30th November 2017:

- **The Montoros Dynasty** – Janice Maynard, Katherine Garbera *and* Andrea Laurence

- **Baby's on the Way!** – Ellie Darkins, Rebecca Winters *and* Lisa Childs

Just can't wait?
Buy our books online before they hit the shops!
www.millsandboon.co.uk

Also available as eBooks.

MILLS & BOON®

Why shop at millsandboon.co.uk?

Each year, thousands of romance readers
find their perfect read at millsandboon.co.uk.
That's because we're passionate about
bringing you the very best romantic fiction.
Here are some of the advantages of
shopping at www.millsandboon.co.uk:

* **Get new books first**—you'll be able to buy
  your favourite books one month before they
  hit the shops

* **Get exclusive discounts**—you'll also be
  able to buy our specially created monthly
  collections, with up to 50% off the RRP

* **Find your favourite authors**—latest news,
  interviews and new releases for all your
  favourite authors and series on our website,
  plus ideas for what to try next

* **Join in**—once you've bought your favourite
  books, don't forget to register with us to rate,
  review and join in the discussions

Visit **www.millsandboon.co.uk**
for all this and more today!